SICILIAN TALES

by Luigi Capuana

C'era una volta

Once Upon a Time

Translated with an Introduction by

Santi V. Buscemi

Dante University Press
Boston

Library of Congress Cataloging-in-Publication Data

Capuana, Luigi, 1839-1915.
  [C'era una volta. English]
  Sicilian tales = C'era una volta = Once upon a time / by Luigi
Capuana ; translated with an introduction by Santi V. Buscemi.
    p. cm.
  ISBN 978-0-937832-51-6 (pbk. : alk. paper)
  I. Buscemi, Santi V.
  II. Title.
  III. Title: C'era una volta.
  IV. Title: Once upon a time.

  PQ4684.C8C3413 2009
  858--dc22

                                                    2008048009

Dante University Press
PO Box 812158
Wellesley MA 02482

Table of Contents

The Literature of Sicily: A Brief History

I first set foot in Sicily in 1976 during my first trip to Italy. On the night train from Naples, I was befriended by a sweet working man and his son, who were returning to Palermo after taking care of legal business in Naples. I shared their supper of spicy salami, cheese, and bread, and we bought a few small bottles of red wine from an itinerant vendor at one of our station stops. About midnight, our train was put on a ferry to cross the Straits of Messina. After the ship pulled away from the dock, we went topside, where the air was clean and sweet. As we sailed on, the older man tapped me on the shoulder and, pointing back to Reggio Calabria, informed me that this was the very journey Odysseus had made 3000 years before. "Back there's Scylla," he motioned, "and in front is Charybdis"—the sea monster and the whirlpool responsible for the death of ancient seafarers including some who served with Odysseus.

I had been born into a Sicilian household in Brooklyn, and my first language was Sicilian, but I really knew very little about my heritage. In fact, my primary purpose in going abroad was to soak up as much of the culture of Rome, Venice, and Florence as I could. Sicily was to be a short diversion, an opportunity to visit an aunt and uncle I had not seen in years and to get a glimpse of my parents' hometowns. But the seven short days I spent there changed everything.

The moment I got off the train I was greeted by Aunt Nina and Uncle Ignazio, then whisked off—via horse and carriage—to a seaside restaurant in Mondello. The next two days brought an epiphany. Palermo was not the stagnant backwater I had envisioned. It quickly revealed itself as an historical and cultural treasure. The first intimation of Sicily's rich past came when I visited the Palazzo Reale and the cathedral and cloister the Normans had built at Monreale. I had known, of course, about the their invasion of England, but I had no idea they had ruled

Sicily for nearly two centuries. "They came here first," boasted my aunt, who reminded me that my 6' 2" red-haired Sicilian grandfather resembled a Nordic warrior. And then there were signs— scant to be sure—of Sicily's Arab past. In the next few days, I was to discover the magnificent Doric temple at Segesta, the sprawling remains of a major Greek city called Selinunte, and of course Agrigento's Valley of the Temples, which has been designated a UNESCO World Heritage site. Years later, I would read that Sicily contains more Greek ruins than Greece itself.

My astonishment over Sicily's history continued when we visited Erice, high in the mountains overlooking Trapani. The city's foundations go back to the Elymni, an indigenous people. Later occupied by Phoenicians, Carthaginians, Romans, Byzantines, and Arabs, Erice offers signs, here and there, of the depth of Sicily's history and the complexity of its culture. However, the "modern" town of Erice dates from the Norman era. Walking its cobblestone streets—especially in the early morning—one is transported to the twelfth century, for most of Erice's buildings look much as they did 800 years ago. No English village from the same period can match its charm and authenticity. In Erice, one is blessed with a vision of the world created by Sicily's beloved King Roger (the Norman king who reigned between 1112-1154) and his knights.

Since my first trip to the island, I have made a point of reading Sicilian history and literature whenever possible. Today, when anyone asks me the derivation of my name, I proclaim proudly that my roots are Sicilian. I have been known even to lecture my hapless listeners about the richness of Sicilian culture, delivering a panegyric to dispel the myth that Sicilians are prone to criminality and that their island has contributed little to European culture.

6 Luigi Capuana

Several years ago, my return to teaching after a long stint as a college administrator gave me extra time to pursue an academic project I had dreamed about ever since first visiting Sicily: an anthology of Sicilian literature in translation (a work now postponed). My academic training is in literature, and I have published several collections f writing used in collegiate writing courses. I began by acquainting myself with the works of as many Sicilian authors as I could, looking first for those whose works had been translated: Lampedusa, Verga, Sciascia, Pirandello, and the like. A few months later, I came upon Luigi Capuana. I had heard the name only once before. The aunt and uncle I visited had lived on a tiny street called Via Capuana in Menfi, my father's birthplace. I had never even bothered to ask my relatives how their street had gotten its name, but at that point I decided to find out more about this author.

It turns out that Capuana was no minor figure in Italian literature. Along with Frederico De Roberto and Giovanni Verga, his fellow Sicilians, he created the most important literary movement in nineteenth-century Italy: *verismo.* He was a journalist, theater critic, playwright, poet, novelist, and writer of fairy tales. (But more about that later.) As I continued to research, I realized that little of Capuana's work has been translated into English. Initially, I found a translation of only one poem in *Arba Sicula.* So, I thought it appropriate to translate Capuana myself, and I decided to focus on the fairy tales in the current volume, originally entitled *C'era Una Volta* or *Once Upon a Time.* (Since then, I have come upon another translation by Dorothy Emmrich, published in 1929).

My research also led me to the conclusion that precious little of the Sicilian literary heritage is known in this country. What exposure there has been is the result of publications like *Arba Sicula, The Journal of Italian Translation, Italica,* and *Forum Italicum.* Thus, at the suggestion of my publisher,

Adolfo Caso of Dante University of America Press, I decided
to include a short history of Sicilian literature in this introduction in addition to a biography of Capuana and an overview of
his work.

The Greeks

The works of Archimedes, especially his discovery of the prin-
ciple of specific gravity, are well known. But few Americans
realize that this genius was Sicilian, and fewer still realize how
rich and complex was the culture that produced him. Like
mainland Greece, Sicily was an important locus of the ancient
world. It had a thriving economy, and its agricultural output
made it known as the "granary of Europe." Sicily also boasts
some of the best-preserved classical architecture, sculpture, and
pottery in the world. And like their mainland forbearers, the
Sicilian Greeks created a vibrant literature.

One of the most important writers of ancient Sicily is Diodorus Siculus, the historian who wrote the *Library of World
History*, a work in forty volumes, beginning with the rise of
Egypt and ending (it is believed) with Rome's First Triumvi-
rate. Born in Agyrium, in the present-day Province of Enna,
Diodorus traveled to numerous cities around the Mediterranean
researching the work of older historians. In fact, there is good
evidence that Diodorus visited Alexandria to do research in its
library. Thus, while his *Library of World History* draws upon
research from a variety of foreign sources, the very fact that
Diodorus took on such a monumental task gives testimony to
the state of cultural sophistication in Greek Sicily.

Only 25 of the 40 volumes of this work survive; the last
complete version was destroyed during the Turkish conquest of
Constantinople. According to Jona Lendering, Diodorus's *Library* is "the largest surviving corpus of any ancient Greek

historian.... His description of Alexander's last weeks in Baby-
lon is high-grade material," and according to several historians
of Assyria, "no other Greek author shows so much understand-
ing of Babylonian civilization and the teaching of the Chal-
daeans...." Lendering closes the discussion of Diodorus with
"no ancient historian can afford not to read the entire work."

Among the most famous Sicilians is the important pre-
Socratic philosopher Empedocles, whose theory of the four
elements (earth, water, fire, and air) was adopted by Aristotle
and influenced Western philosophy, science, and medicine
through the Middle Ages and into the Renaissance. Empedocles also advanced the theory of the transmigration of souls and
of reincarnation.

It is known that the dramatist Aeschylus visited Sicily and is
probably buried in Gela. However, ancient Sicily produced its
own dramatists including Achaeus of Syracuse, who is credited
with the writing of as many as 14 tragedies and who won at
least one drama contest in Athens. Another fourth-century tragedian from Syracuse was Antiphron. While none of his works
survive, we know that he wrote at least five plays: *Andro-
mache*, *Medea*, *Meleager*, *Jason*, and *Philoctetes*. In addition,
he is believed to have collaborated on some dramas with Dionysius I (432-367 BC), who had the playwright executed for
some remark the tyrant found offensive. Dionysius himself is
credited with five plays: *Adonis*, *Alcmena*, *The Bath of Hector*,
Leda, and *Limos*. In the third century, Syracuse produce yet
another dramatist, Sosiphanes, who is credited with writing an
estimated 73 tragedies.

Some literary historians believe that the father of rhetoric
was Corax, who lived in Syracuse in the fifth century BC.

Little is known about him, but Corax is said to have created the principles by which people could argue their own cases in-courts of law. Gorgias, another fifth-century figure, was born in Leontini. His work as rhetorician was recognized across the Greek world and, among some scholars, Leontini, his home-town, has become known as the birthplace of rhetoric. Indeed, one of his major accomplishments is that he transplanted the study of rhetoric from Sicily to the Greek mainland. Greek po-etry flourished in Sicily as evidenced by writers such as the fourth-century writer Archestratus, who wrote a long humorous poem, *Life of Luxury*, a kind of food and restaurant guide to the ancient Mediterranean. Nearly five hundred years later, Ar-chagathus of Calacte became one of the most important rheto-ricians in the history of the Roman Empire. Living during the Augustan period, Archagathus changed his name to Caecilius, in honor of his patron, after relocating to Rome. Only frag-ments of his work survive, but we know that he wrote *On the Style of the Ten Orators*, *On the Sublime*, and a *History of the Servile Wars*, a record of the slave revolt in Sicily.

The Muslims

After the fall of the Roman Empire, Sicily was invaded by both Vandals and Goths. It then came under the control of the East-ern Empire, known eventually as the Byzantine Empire. In 827, at the invitation of rebellious Greek general Eufemius, an army of nearly eleven thousand Arabs and Berbers from vari-ous parts of the Mediterranean basin attacked Mazara, on Sic-ily's western coast. Over the next seventy-five years, Muslim armies waged continual warfare, capturing Palermo (then Panormus) in 831, Messina in 843, Enna in 859 and Siracusa in 878. The last Greek holdout was Tauromenium (today, the re-sort city of Taormina), which fell in 902. The Muslins held the island until 1091, when the Normans succeeded in taking their last stronghold and assuming complete control of Sicily. Few original examples of Arab architecture survive in Sicily. The Baths of Cefala Diana and the castle of Favara (from "al Faw-wara" or gushing spring) are the most notable. However, there are several buildings, which— although constructed during the Norman era—betray a strong Arab influence.

Among the most famous are the church of San Giovanni degli Eremiti in Palermo (with its characteristic Islamic domes), the La Zisa palace, and a building known as La Cu-bula. The Norman conquerors of Sicily, who are discussed be-low, became enamored of Saracen ceremonials, dress, and de-sign; many of them supported the study of Arabic culture and of the Arabic language. In fact, much of the extant Arabic po-etry in Sicily dates from the Norman, not the Muslim, era.

The most obvious legacy of the Arabs comprises hundreds of Sicilian place and surnames. My own family name, which is also the name of a small town in the province of Siracusa, de-rives from the phrase "Qal'at abi Samah," which morphed into Buxema, Bussema, and finally Buscemi. The name of Marsala, a city on Sicily's western shore, means "harbor of God" in Arabic ("Mars Allah"). Caltanissetta, a city in central Sicily, derives its name from "Kalat an-nisa," which means "castle of women," while Caltabellotta comes from Kalat -al ballut, or "castle on the rock." Caltagirone is from "Qal'at -a ganom," or "castle of the genies," after the mythical creatures who were said to live in the nearby mountains. Girgenti is the Arabic name for Agrigento, and the names of towns such as Niscemi, Mussolmeni, and many others derive from Arabic.

Little is left of the work of Siculo-Arab writers, and most of what remains was written by those who left Sicily before or during the Norman era. Giuseppe Quatriglio in *A Thousand*

Years in Sicily estimates that, with the coming of the Normans, over 170 Arabic poets left Sicily to write nostalgically about their homeland in foreign lands. Among these were Ballanubi who, born in Agrigento, wrote about Sicily from his exile in Egypt, and Abu al-Arab, who settled in Seville (18).

The most famous of the Sicuolo-Arab writers was Ibn Hamdis (1056-1133) of Syracuse, whom Karla Mallette calls "the premier Arab poet of Sicily" (131). He left Sicily at the age of 22 and spent the rest of his life in exile. His odes, (called *qasidas* in Arabic) testify to the beauty of the island and the richness of a culture he was forced to leave behind. "Oh sea, you conceal my paradise," he writes from exile. "I recall Sicily in my soul/pain resurrects her image" (qtd. in Quatriglio 18). Ibn Hamdis also wrote love poetry in a style that almost certainly influenced writers of the later Sicilian School, a group that was to introduce the first literature in an Italian vernacular.

Al-Atrabanishi, from Trapani, a poet who remained in Sicily during Norman rule, also wrote odes, the most famous of which is a tribute to King Roger II (1095-1154); it describes the beauty of a park at the king's palace at Favara. Only a fragment remains, but it is enough to reveal how integrated Moslem and Christian cultures were becoming in the twelfth century.

Other poets who wrote panegyrics to Roger II were Al-Buthayri; Abu al-Daw, who served in Roger's government; and Abu Hafs, who wrote a tribute to him while imprisoned, hoping perhaps that his praise for the monarch would win his freedom.

According to Mallette, Abu Hafs depicts Roger "victoriously dispelling the darkness" (144). It might very well be that such works were simply attempts to gain favor with the ruler. On the other hand, what is noteworthy about their poetry is that it contains clear evidence of the advanced state of Sicilian civilization during their lifetimes. Studying the body of Siculo-Arab literature, in fact, one cannot help believe that whether exiled to a foreign shore or serving in the royal court, these writers saw Sicily and its culture as things to be envied. That does not mean that Arabs were always treated well by their Norman conquerors. Nonetheless, as already noted, the Normans enlisted many Arabs into government service, encouraged the continued use of the Arab language, and drew heavily from Arab art and learning.

Evidence of the robust culture of twelfth-century Sicily is found in the writings of al-Indrisi, specifically in a work that has come to be known as *The Geography.* In his introduction, the writer claims that the research for this lengthy work was completed by Roger II himself. The king, we are told, relied on first-hand testimony of many travelers, whom he interviewed and whose information he evaluated and had corroborated by agents he sent abroad. Al-Indrisi makes a point of claiming that Roger was able to disavow older written accounts, and, instead, relied heavily on his own empirical research, a method that predates the use of the scientific method by centuries.

One of the most important travel writers of the Middle Ages was Ibn Jubayr, who visited Sicily in 1184, during the reign of William II. According to Kate Mallette, Ibn Jubayr "catalogues the wonders of the court of William II, the 'Orientalist' Christian monarch, whom he commends for his learning and, in particular, for his admiration of Muslim culture and his promotion of Muslim men of learning at his court" (2).

Finally, it is important to mention Muhammad Ibn Zafar al Siqilli (1104-1172?), an author of 32 prose works about a variety of subjects including Judeo-Christian literature, Indian literature, Persian history, and theology and moral philosophy. His masterpiece is translated as *The Just Prince*, a book designed to give advice to monarchs, which pre-dates the work of Machiavelli by centuries. According to "Machiavelli's Arab Precursor," an article in the *British Journal of Middle Eastern Studies,* among the principles of effective rule, Ibn Zafar includes 1) trust in God, 2) forti-tude and bravery, 3) perseverance and patience, 4) submission to the will of God, and 5) humility (Dekmejian and Thabit 125).

La Scuola Siciliana

In "Syllabi of Literary Coursers by Centuries: The Duecento," Kenneth McKenzie argues that "with the Sicilian School....the real evolution of Italian literature begins" (63). During the 12th and 13th centuries, a new type of poetry was born and came of age in Sicily. Some of the members of the Sicilian School, as it has come to be known, were born in Sicily, while others emigrated from other parts of Italy and settled in Palermo and other cities in the *regno*, or kingdom, of Frederick II (1194-1250), Holy Roman Emperor and King of Sicily. Frederick was the son of Henry IV, the Swabian, (and the grandson of the legendary emperor Frederick Barbarossa) and of Constance, the posthumous child of King Roger II. In Frederick II were combined two important European bloodlines—the Hauteville and the Hohenstaufen. Pre-dating other, more famous Renaissance men by some three hundred years, Frederick had a voracious appetite for learning and an interest in a variety of arts and sciences. In addition, he was passionate about importing learning from other cultures, especially the Greek and Arabic, by inviting scholars from abroad to join his retinue and by underwriting the cost of translating many classics of ancient and medieval learning. In this connection, it is important to note that Frederick was extending a practice begun under Roger II and his son William, who supported translations of Plato, Euclid, and Ptolemy into Latin. Nonetheless, under Frederick, who wrote poetry and is himself numbered among the members of the Sicilian School, the culture of Sicily received a new burst of energy and continued the growth begun under the Normans.

Although influenced by the troubadour poetry of southern France, the Sicilian poets made a number of important breakthroughs in the history of Western literature, not the least of which was the invention of the sonnet. Moreover, members of the *Scuola Siciliana* were the first to use an Italianate vernacular as a vehicle for poetry. To this point, Arabic and Latin had been the chief languages in which Italians composed poetry and works in other genres. The language of Frederick's court—Medieval Sicilian—which had been developing ever since the Norman conquest of the island, was a romance language with an Italianate structure. Distinguished from modern Sicilian, which is more fluid and closer to contemporary Italian, it contained Norman French, Greek, Arabic, and even Longobardic elements, according to Daniela Paglia, writing in the *Best of Sicily Magazine.* With so rich a linguistic repertoire, the Sicilians exerted a major influence on later Italian poets, including Dante and his contemporaries, those who were to write in the "dolce stil nuovo."

Some literary historians believe that the Sicilians were among the last to develop a literary vernacular in the long chain of such traditions already developed on the continent, particularly in southern France. They see the Sicilians merely as translators, not the inventors of a new cultural medium. On the other hand, Mallette argues that, in the absence of established cultural forms, in the absence even of a unified linguistic traditions to serve as the basis of a literary culture, the Sicilian environment called forth an extraordinary level of activity from its men of letters. Sicilian poets responded by inventing a new literary tongue—an innovation welcomed by the poets of the Italian peninsula, who would naturalize the Sicilians' language and use it as a medium for their own poetic compositions. (71)

First and foremost, then, the Sicilians must be remembered as the inventors of a new literary language, the first in an Italianate tongue. They are also to be remembered for an number of literary inventions that influenced later cultures, well beyond Italy's.

Unlike their troubadour predecessors, the Sicilians wrote poetry to be read, not performed to the accompaniment of music. Nor were they professional entertainers. The great majority of them were intellectuals and government officials, who were occupied primarily with matters other than poetry. As a result, much of their poetry seems grounded in a realistic psychology concerning the day-to-day concerns of people like those with whom they lived and worked.

They also differed from the French in that they focused their poetry on the subject of romantic love, while their predecessors had used poetry as a tool for discussing philosophical and moral concerns as well. Because of this, the Sicilian opus might, at first glance, seem to be more limited in scope than earlier poetry, but it is important to note that the Sicilians— precisely because they were not first and foremost professional poets— departed from the romantic tradition of the Medieval troubadours. They introduced materials—images, information, and language—from a variety of disciplines, studies, and occupations, which they put in service to the poetry of love. This tendency was surely to influence the poets of later cultures. According to Mallette, both scientific discourse and philosophic meditation find their way into their love poetry, especially in the works of Giacomo Lentini and Rinaldo d'Aquino, both of whom drew from the study of thermodynamics. Lentini also made use of his knowledge of optics. In this sense, then, the Sicilians used a technique that pre-dates a tendency seen in Donne and the English Metaphysicals, who wrote 400 years later.

Their third contribution to the development of western poetry can be seen in the inclination to adopt a persona to speak their verses; sometimes this was the voice of a woman. Not only did this render their poetry more lively, sinewy, and colorful, but it added a psychological complexity never seen before in lyrical poetry.

Finally, as mentioned earlier, the Sicilian School—specifically Giacomo di Lentini—invented the sonnet. This was a monumental achievement, for, as Paul Oppenheimer points out in "The Origin of the Sonnet," "Since Giacomo, no major poets—one is tempted to say, no minor one either—in Italian, German, French, Spanish, and English has failed to write sonnets" (285). It is believed that in adding a sestet to an eight-line poem to make the sonnet, Lentini simply copied an earlier Arabic poetic form called the *zajal*. But that theory has now been discarded, and the addition is thought to have derived purely from Lentini's creative genius (285).

It may have been that Dante had a fascination with Sicily, for he mentions members of the Swabian royal family in three books of the *Commedia*. Frederick II, though admired by Dante for his interest in learning and art, is condemned to the *Inferno* for his supposed denial of the immortality of the soul. Manfred, the son of Frederick, appears in the *Purgatorio*, while Constance, Frederick's mother, and William II, his cousin, find their way into the *Paradiso,* along with the man who brought the Normans into Italy, Robert Guiscard. Whatever the case, according to Mallette, "In *De vulgari eloquentia (On Eloquence in the Vernacular),* Dante acknowledges the primacy of the Kingdom of Sicily in the field of Italian letters and places Manfred and Frederick at the center of Sicilian literary life" (67). In fact, Dante mentions several poets of the Sicilian school and explains the major role they played in transforming Italian into a literary language. It is clear then that, as J. A. Palermo points out in "The Latinity of Sicily," the Sicilian School was "held in high favor by their Tuscan successors of the *dolce stil nuovo* as was their linguistic medium by Dante himself " (77).

The Sicilian School comprises an estimated 24 poets writing over two generations: the first during the reign of Frederick, the second during the reign of Manfred. Lentini is perhaps the most highly respected of the poets of the first generation; Guittone d'Arezzo holds first place among those of the second. As noted earlier, Frederick himself was a member of the school but, while seven extant poems are thought to be his, only three can be attributed to him with certainty. The most important of these is "Dolze meo drudo" ("My Sweet Lover"), which is a dialogue between two lovers, the woman speaking first. The subject is the impending departure of the man to war, a subject with which Frederick was all too familiar.

As noted earlier, Giacomo Lentini (?- 1246) is the father of the sonnet. He was a notary at the court of Frederick II, hence his nickname "il notaro." Dante was so taken with Lentini that, in the *Purgatorio*, he called him the first of his literary ancestors. His most famous poem is "Maravigliosamente" (Wondrously"), which begins oxymoronically with "Wondrously/a love distresses me/and fills my thought every moment."* Another important work is his "Amor no vole" ("Love Does Not Wish"), in which the poet draws upon images from gemology to convince his lady of the sincerity of this love.

Lentini verges on the metaphysical conceit when, in the sonnet "Or come pote si gran donna intrare" ("Now, How Can So Large a Woman Enter"), he compares his lover to "light" and himself to "the glass within which it is placed." Something similar occurs in "A l'aire claro o vista plggia dare," which begins "I have seen a clear sky give rain/and flaying fire become ice,/and cold snow produce heat...." However, all of this, claims Lentini in the sextet, cannot compare with what he has "seen from Love." Readers of Shakespeare's sonnets cannot be but impressed with this earlier poet's deftness. Lentini uses the sestet to respond to images and sensibilities expressed in the octet, just as Shakespeare would do in numerous sonnets. The Sicilian sounds especially like Shakespeare when he claims that "the life [love] gave me was death./I burn now with the fire which extinguished me...."

One of the most important Sicilian writers mentioned by Dante is Cielo d'Alcamo, (sometimes spelled Ciullo), whose only finished work is a dialogue between a lover and the woman he desires. It is known alternately as *Contrasto Amoroso* or *Rosa fresca aulentisima* (*Lovely, Fragrant Rose*) from the opening line. Most scholars believe that the poem was

---

*From this point, translations of the poetry of the Sicilian School are from Karla Mallette's *The Kingdom of Sicily, 1100-1250: A Literary History*.

composed about 1230. Given Dante's praise of Cielo in *De vulgari eloquentia*, it is interesting to note that his language bears a striking resemblance to dialects spoken on the mainland, evidence of a linguistic and, perhaps literary sharing that casts a favorable light on the culture of Sicily at that time (Mallette 89).

Cielo's first name may be a variant of Michele (Michael), and he probably came from the town of Alcamo. Although a full-ledged member of the Sicilian School, Cielo seems unique in that the *Contrasto* may be a parody of the courtly love tradition expressed in *langue d'oc* of the troubadours. Following that tradition, Cielo places his lover in the position of servant, supplicant, or vassal who begs the attention of a cold, distant lady. The dialogue begins in the courtly love tradition with the lover pledging his undying loyalty and love to her. She, as expected, parries every advance with disdain and skepticism. Before the poem ends, however, we realize that all along this has been a parody of the early French villanelle. The lady's chilly demeanor, we learn, is only a pretense, and she eventually succumbs. Some scholars believe that Sicilian poets had been writing such parodies before Cielo. If so, this would certainly be evidence that the Sicilians were doing much more than imitating the French; they were creating a completely new form.

Pier delle Vigne (1180-1249) was born into a modest family, entered the court of Frederick II as a scribe, and quickly gained the Emperor's trust and admiration. In 1228 he was appointed notary to the Imperial court; in 1225 he was named a judge; and in 1247, he was appointed Chancellor to the Emperor, a very powerful position because the Chancellor was responsible for issuing the royal government's legal writs. However, delle Vigne was falsely accused of treason by other members of the government envious of his talents and his success. His enemies succeeded in getting the Emperor to turn against him, and he was eventually blinded and imprisoned. Unable to cope with his fall from favor and his treatment at the hands of a man he once loved, delle Vigne committed suicide. We meet him for the last time in the *Inferno's* "Wood of Suicides," where he comments upon the vicissitudes of fortune and the fleeting character of fame. Perhaps delle Vigne's most famous poem is "Amando con fin cor e con speranza" ("Loving with Gentle Heart and Hope").

Little is known of Rinaldo d'Aquino, Frederick II's "falconiere," who died in about 1280. However, we still have eleven of his splendid poems, among them a *canzone* entitled "Gia mai non mi conforto" ("Never Will I Be Comforted"). This is another one of those splendid poems in which the writer speaks in a woman's voice. In this case, the woman sees her lover sail away to fight in a Crusade. It was probably written when the poet was sent by Frederick on a military mission. Rinaldo is another poet mentioned by Dante. He is said to have come from the family of St. Thomas Aquinas; some speculate that he was Thomas's brother. This is a distinct possibility in that Frederick II and Thomas were cousins.

Mazzeo di Ricci (d. 1250?) also writes about the vicissitudes of love and the pain it causes. Like Lentini, he draws upon knowledge from many diverse disciplines to create startling metaphors that predate those of the poets of seventeenth-century Britain. In "Sei anni o travagliato" ("Six Years Have I Labored"), he compares himself to a child "who believes that he can grasp the brilliance/of a burning candle...." Later, he says that he has been a "man who has wagered/and thinks that he is gaining/and loses what he has." In calling into question his mistress's fidelity, Mazzeo remarks that "masters know well/how to counterfeit their work."

Finally, it is important to mention Guido delle Colonne, whom Dante Gabriel Rossetti says "has few equals among his contemporaries" (8). Like many others of the Sicilian School, he is mentioned in Dante's *De vulgari eloquentia.* In addition to poetry, Guido translated into Latin a history of the Trojan War (1287), which some scholars believe helped introduce the subject into Europe through subsequent translations. Guido was a judge in the court of Frederic II, where many works of Arab and Greek philosophers were translated. Some of these were scientific treatises that postulated the notion of determinism as opposed to Christian free will, posing for Guido, and probably other members of the court, an intellectual conundrum that he had difficulty addressing. Indeed, Frederick himself was excommunicated presumably on the grounds that he denied free will and the immortality of the soul.

Renaissance and Enlightenment
Fifteenth - Eighteenth Centuries

Although, the two great periods of Sicilian literature are the Medieval (12th-14th centuries) and the Modern (19th-20th centuries), Sicilians made significant contributions to the Renaissance and the Enlightenment. In fact, these periods produced a host of writers. Unfortunately, little has been written about them in English.

Among the earliest in this period is Antonio Beccadelli, (1394-1471), who was nicknamed "il Panormita," a word that derives from the Latin for Palermo, his birthplace. Highly educated and well respected, he studied canon law and the classics, and he served as a diplomat. Because of his reputation as a scholar, Beccadelli was invited to the court of King Alfonso of Naples to enhance the royal library's collection and to attract other scholars to the capital.

He wrote most of his poetry in Latin, his most famous work being *Hermaphroditus* (1425), a collection of works by a variety of poets including some who defended homosexuality. The volume was condemned by the Church, and copies of it were burned in public. In 1455, he wrote *On the Words and Deeds of King Alfonso*, a flattering biography, which contributed to the King's being referred to as "The Magnanimous" because of his presumed charity and good will to others. While in Napels, Beccadelli found the Pontaniana a famous academy named after his patron Giovanni Pontano.

A contemporary of Beccadelli, Giovanni Aurispa (1369-1419), was born in Noto. In 1413, he traveled to Constantinople where he studied Greek and became a collector of texts containing the works of ancient authors such as Sophocles, Euripides, Aeschylus, Demosthenes, Xenophon, and Plato. Aurispa continued to collect important manuscripts throughout his life, bringing over 200 of them to Italy. Many of these works had been unknown in the West. Among some of the later manuscripts he retrieved were works by the Church fathers. This contribution alone would have secured his fame in the intellectual history of Europe. However, he also wrote poetry and completed several translations from the Greek and Latin classics. After teaching Greek in Bologna and Florence, he became a cleric and took a post in the Vatican as secretary to Pope Eugene IV and, later, Nicholas V.

Constantino Lascaris (1435-1500), who made important contributions to the revival of classical learning in Europe, was not a Sicilian by birth, but he became a permanent resident of Messina. Lascaris escaped from Constantinople, his birthplace, after the Turks captured the city in 1453. He traveled throughout Italy, giving lectures on Greek culture in Milan, Florence, and Naples. Though invited to join the royal court in Naples, Lascaris accepted another invitation by the city of Messina, where he spent the rest of his life teaching Greek and Greek culture. Because of Lascaris and other scholars like him, Italy provided the impetus to revive classical scholarship, a trend that spread throughout Europe and contributed to the coming of the Renaissance.

The most important author of the sixteenth century is Antonio (Antonello) Veneziano (1543-1593), who was born in Monreale, just outside of Palermo. He is sometimes called the "father of Sicilian poetry" because of his unashamed support for Sicilian as both a literary and governmental language as opposed to Tuscan or Siculo-Tuscan, which some of his contemporaries adopted.

In 1578, while sailing from Palermo to Spain, the ship on which Veeziano was traveling was attacked by Barbary pirates, who abducted the crew and passengers and held them for ransom in an Algerian prison. While detained there, Veneziano met Miguel de Cervantes, author of *Don Quixote* (1605), who had met the same fate three years before. The men struck up a strong friendship, which lasted for years, with Cervantes showing great interest in and admiration for Veneziano's octaves (*canzuni*) collected in his *Celia*. So taken was Cervantes by the poetry of his new friend that he wrote his own poem in twelve octaves praising Veneziano. The poem appeared with a letter that Cervantes sent from prison to the Sicilian, who had already been ransomed.

Veneziano is also known as the "Sicilian Petrarch." However, as Gaetano Cipolla argues, while "Veneziano used the themes and the psychological situations in Petrarch's *Canzoniere*...it is also true that much of his repertory was derived from the Sicilian folkloric and popular tradition" (*Antonio Veneziano: Ninety Love Octaves* 19). On the other hand,

Veneziano's careful choice of words is sophisticated. He uses a Sicilian perfectly suited to the medium of poetry—it is learned, mellifluous, and smooth. "His language," adds Cipolla, "was meant as an affirmation of the validity of an illustrious Sicilian that could be put side by side with Tuscan without being considered inferior" (19).

Veneziano is known for his translation of Latin epigrams, but his reputation rests chiefly on his poetry. He wrote over 800 *canzuni*. Among the best-known of his collections are *Celia, Book II of Sicilian Love Songs, Songs of Contempt*, and *Proverbs,* all of which are contained in Cipolla's collection.

In the sixteenth century, Sicily gave the world Ortensio Scammacca (1562-1648), a tragedian and poet whose contemporaries called "Sicily's divine poet." As a young man, he left his native Lentini to study at the College of the Jesuits in Palermo, and, in time, began to teach classes in theology, philosophy, and the scriptures. Of his tragedies, 45 are extant. Nineteen of these were inspired by the works of Sophocles and Euripides, to which Scammacca applied a distinctively Christian interpretation. The remaining 26 are on sacred subjects.

Another important Enlightenment thinker was Tommaso Campailla (1668-1740), who was born in Modica, only a few houses away from where, 200 years later, the Nobel-Prize laureate Salvatore Quasimodo would be born. In 1684, Campailla went to Catania to pursue a degree in law, but the death of his father forced his return to his native city, where he began to teach himself the classics, especially the works of Aristotle. He also became interested in physics after the great earthquake that destroyed Modica and several other nearby localities in 1693.

Campailla was a student of the French philosopher Descartes. In fact, with philosopher Michelangelo Fardella (1650-1718), he is responsible for the spread of Cartesian philosophy in Sicily. His chief work is a didactic poem based on Cartesian thought: *L'Adamo, ovvero il Mondo Creato* (*Adam, or the World Created*), which he published in 1709. So widespread did his reputation become that he was sought out and visited by George Berkeley, the British empiricist. In 1738, Campailla published *L'Apocalisse di San Paolo* (*The Apocalypse of St. Paul*), in which he refutes the theories of the Spanish spiritualist Miguel Molinos, a proponent of Quietism. Quietism was a popular movement in the 15th, 16th and 17th centuries, but it was eventually declared a heresy by the Catholic Church.

The greatest poet of the Enlightenment in Sicily was Giovanni Meli (1740-1815), whom Gaetano Cipolla calls "the most accomplished poet who ever wrote in Sicilian" (*Giovanni Meli: Moral Fables and Other Poems* xiii). Born in Palermo, Meli was trained in medicine and chemistry. He was well versed in the works of French and British Enlightenment thinkers, from which he developed an appreciation for the empirical method. This produced in him a strain of skepticism that, when combined with traditional Sicilian family and cultural values, created an artistic and intellectual tension that Meli exploited. His works include lyric, elegiac, and bucolic poetry as well as satires. His language differs from that of his major predecessors, for he experimented with the idiom of the common folk in order to create realism.

In one of his first major works, *The Origin of the World*, Meli chides both the materialists and the idealists of his time, the former for denying the existence of the human soul and the latter for claiming that only that which can be conceived by the mind is real. Meli's most important work, however, is *Don Chisciotti e Sanciu Panza* (1787), a mock-heroic thought by

some to be simply a Sicilian rendering of Cervantes' masterpiece. On the contrary, Meli's work is a new conception, in
which Panza takes on a far more important role than he did in
the Spanish novel. (Recall that Cervantes does not mention
Panza in his title.) For Meli, Panza and Don Chisciotti com-
prise an archetype of opposites—the skeptic and the idealist—
with, as Cipolla has noted, the skeptic being more important
(xxvii).

This is a work, Cipolla maintains, that is truly worth studying "from a number of perspectives":

> as an historical document embodying the dynamic ideas
> of the Enlightenment and the deeply conservative ideals
> of the tradition-bound Sicilian society; as a record of
> several customs and traditions of a society that until re-
> cently has not changed appreciably; as an important
> moment in the struggle between social classes; and as a
> literary work of considerable scope and depth, which
> shares in a tradition having deep roots in the Italian
> spirit and which has produced such poets as Pulci,
> Ariosto, Tassoni, and Berni, to name a few of the best
> known." (xxv)

The Nineteenth Century

In the late nineteenth century, Sicily experienced a literary renaissance that was to last well into the next century. Indeed, it
may be argued that it continues to this day. In "Writer and Society in the New Italy," Robert Dombroksi claims that "it was
from Sicily that the narrative tradition, begun my Manzoni,
gained its greatest impetus" (463). It is not astonishing, then,
that building on this strong literary tradition, Sicily produced
two Nobel laureates in literature in the twentieth century.

Verismo, perhaps the most important literary movement to develop in Italy in the last three hundred years, was born in Sicily. The three major Sicilian *veristi*—Capuana, Verga, and De Roberto—were influenced by nineteenth-century French naturalists, especially Zola. Naturalism, which is related to realism, took root in Europe and America as a reaction to romanticism. While the romantics emphasized nature's beneficence and energy, the naturalists saw it as an uncontrollable determinant wholly indifferent to humanity. Influenced by the Darwin's theory of evolution, the naturalists sought to explain a character's behavior by examining the influence of forces outside his or her control—heredity, the natural environment, and society. Unlike Zola and his countrymen, however, the Sicilians harbored no allusions about the possibility that the future, shaped by new discoveries in science and technology, might bring about a better world. Their novels focus on the social, economic, and natural forces in the universe, which they saw as indifferent—even inimical—to human prospects, especially in Sicily. Ordinary Sicilians had been exploited politically, economically, and culturally for centuries by foreign powers and by a native baronial class. History had eliminated all hope that small landowners or shop keepers—not to mention landless peasants—could ever ameliorate their condition. Moreover, the v*eristi* were writing at a time when the promises of the Risorgimento had long been forgotten by the government of a now-unified Italy. It is no wonder, then, that such a mindset would take hold among Sicily's most talented writers.

Sicilian naturalism also dictated that characters and events be viewed dispassionately, scientifically in order to report on the human condition accurately. For Capuana, Verga, and De Roberto, the writer is a researcher looking through a microscope in order to examine the world, diagnose its illnesses, and report on their causes—but not to prescribe treatment.

Especially important in this regard is the V*eristi's* ability to delve deeply into the psychology of their characters and to portray the effects exerted upon them by the hostile—sometimes even paradoxical— natural, cultural, and economic environments in which they lived.

The youngest member of the group was Frederico De Roberto (1861-1927) who, unlike Verga and Capuana, spent almost all of his life in Sicily, particularly in Catania. For De Roberto, there were forces within the human context that were simply irresistible and that, for the most part, sealed an individual's fate. Indeed, of the three major v*eristi,* De Roberto may have been the most fatalistic.

His best-known work is *I Vicere* (*The Viceroys*) 1894. The novel focuses on a family of landed aristocrats who trace their ancestry to the Spanish viceroys, a class of bureaucrats that for centuries ruled Sicily with ineptitude and callousness. In many ways, they represent Sicily's entire ruling class. As members of the family fight to keep power against the Risorgimento and a more liberal Italy, De Roberto takes no sides. He simply reports on the odious way in which they treat others—and themselves—as they try to hold on to their patrimony. Nonetheless, the stench of their decadence, callousness, and madness is unmistakable—as is the overwhelming evidence that they represent an entire class.

Giovanni Verga (1840-1922), is the best-known v*eristi.* (The life and works of Luigi Capuana are discussed after this introduction.) Verga was born to a prosperous family in Vizzini, a small town in Catania. The Vergas owned farmland on which, as young man, Giovanni observed the difficult lives of peasants and, although his early novels concern the gentry, his masterpieces detail the lives of the poor farmers and fisherman he observed in Catania.

Always interested in writing, Verga left Sicily in 1869 for Florence and Milan, where he intended to launch a literary career. At the time, Verga's tendencies verged on the romantic, not the naturalistic, and he wrote about the sins of the noble and bourgeois classes—especially the vanities of wealthy women—sometimes betraying traces of sentimentality, self-reflection, and melancholy. In *Una peccatirce* (*A Sinner*) 1866 and *Tigre reale* (*Royal Tigress*) 1875, for example, the main characters—both young artists—fall in love with and are destroyed by wealthy women.

The first signs of Verga's naturalism emerge with the publication of *Eros* (1875), a novel that uses an objective point-of-view. From this point on, he divorced himself from romanticism. In 1879, Verga returned to Vizzini and, shortly thereafter, published a collection of short stories, *Vita dei campi* (*Life in the Fields*) 1880, of which "Cavalleria Rusticana" is one. Later, Verga was to dramatize this story, a work that became the libretto for Mascagni's opera.

Like V*ita dei campi,* the novels of the mature Verga focus on more simple folk who, day after exhausting day, must fend off starvation and danger, both physical and emotional. *I Malavoglia*, Verga's first masterpiece, was completed in 1881. Translated as *The House by the Medlar Tree*, it was the first in what would have been a series of five novels on the same theme. (However, the only other book in the series that Verga completed was *Mastro-don Gesualdo,* 1889). Il *Malavoglia* concerns a family of Sicilian fishermen who barely make a living. After a series of tragedies, they eventually lose everything they own, including their beloved home. The novel's theme is that despite hard work, ingenuity, and the support of one's family, success and happiness are only illusions. The family, whose real name is Toscano, operates a fishing boat, known ironically as "La Provvidenza." When a grandson is drafted into the Italian army, the family loses its strongest and most productive fisherman. To ameliorate the resultant economic setback, they mortgage their boat and invest in a load of lupins, the sale of which, they hope, will yield a quick profit. But nature has other ideas: the boat and its load of lupins is lost at sea during a storm in which one of the sons is drowned. The Toscanos fall into a ruinous debt, sell everything—including their house—and become outcasts in a world that, in the end, seems too cruel for words. The grandson who had been conscripted becomes more and more alienated—both from his family and from the new world of capitalism in which he seeks to make his fortune. Then, to add dishonor to the mix, the daughter, Lia, is forced to sell herself as a prostitute.

Verga's other great novel is *Mastro-don Gesualdo*. The title character is a hard-working stone mason, who is obsessed with making money and climbing the social ladder. Intelligent and resourceful, Gesualdo's only concern is his property and his net worth. But his ambition proves to be his undoing. His money-making schemes earn the enmity of the local peasantry, among whom he was born, and he turns his back on his heritage by marrying into a noble, but penniless, family. Unfortunately, this attempt to improve his social standing fails, for he enjoys no real intimacy with his wife and family. In fact, as he discovers, the daughter he thought he had sired is the child of another man. At the end of the novel, Gesualdo is completely alienated, living out his last days in the home of a daughter who hates him. Both *Il Malavoglia* and *Mastro-don Gesualdo* were translated by D.H. Lawrence, who recognized Verga's genius early.

Verga also wrote several plays, the first of which, as noted, is a dramatization of his short story "Cavalleria Rusticana." In 1885, he wrote *In portenera* (*In the Porter's Lodge*), which exposes life in the poorest quarter of Milan. In 1896, *La lupa*

(*The She Wolf*) was produced, an extremely successful play about a madwoman who sacrifices her family and even her life in an attempt to satisfy her desire for a young man. An unfaithful wife appears in *La caccia al lupo* (*The Wolf Hunt*) 1902. When the affair is discovered, she betrays her lover to a crazed husband who, gun in hand, rounds up his friends and goes after the young man.

The Twentieth Century

It seems fitting to begin this section with a novelist who, while writing in the twentieth century, is often associated with nineteenth-century Sicily: Giuseppe di Lampedusa (1896-1957). Firmly ensconced in the nobility (he was both a Duke of Parma and Prince of Lampedusa), he wrote only two novels. The more famous *Il gattopardo* (*The Leopard*) was published posthumously in 1958 and later turned into an important motion picture (1963). The novel chronicles the life of a noble family (based on Lampedusa's own) as it tries to survive the results of Garibaldi's invasion of Sicily and the island's subsequent inclusion in a unified Italy.

Lampedusa served in the Italian army in World War I, during which he was taken prisoner and sent to Hungary. At the war's end, he made his way home by walking the entire distance. Always interested in literature (he read more than a few modern and ancient language), he published several critical essays on sixteenth-century French literature and on Stendhal during the years between the wars. After the Fascists took power, Lampedusa left Italy and lived abroad for several years. Upon his return after World War II, he found that his home had been destroyed by Allied bombs.

Like many Sicilian novelists who preceded him, Lampedusa uses an omniscient point of view in *Il gatopardo* to trace the decline of a noble family from 1860-1910. (The Lampedusas had lost most of their wealth by the time Giuseppe was born.) The protagonist and family patriarch, Don Fabrizio Corbera, Prince of Salina, opposes the new order but does not have the energy to lift a finger against it. He even accepts his nephew's joining the *Garibaldini* and resigns himself to the decline of the aristocracy in Italy. As such, *Il gatopardo* becomes more than an historical novel, for Lampedusa's ability to penetrate the minds and motives of his characters make it a psychological *tour de force*. Particularly interesting is the tension between the Prince's nostalgia for the past and the pain he feels over his realization that the world must change. Lampedusa's only other novel, *Racconti* (*Tales*) was also published posthumously in 1961. His essays have been collected in two volumes, which were published in 1959 and 1971.

Americans know Lampedusa chiefly because *Il gatopardo's* having been turned into a classic film starring Burt Lancaster. However, the best-known Sicilian writer remains Luigi Pirandello (1867-1936), who won the Nobel Prize for literature in 1934. He was born near Agrigento in the town of Caos, and Pirandello enjoyed calling himself a "child of chaos." This becomes more significant, however, when one realizes that his writing reflects a profound skepticism about our ability to control the world around us and, in fact, to distinguish the real from the illusory. In an essay entitled "Pirandello," Felicity Firth puts it well when she says that Sicily's "volcanic, earthquake-ridden landscape…provided him with a constantly recurring image of life as a seething luminous flow…. This substratum of turbulence, which erupts in violence and disaster, he found echoed in Sicilian society" (481).

An even more important cause of the disillusionment and sense of isolation that pervades his work can be traced to his personal life. In 1894, he married Antonietta Portulano, whose father was the elder Pirandello's business associate. After the Pirandello family sustained severe financial losses in a flood, Antonietta experienced a severe emotional breakdown, which sometimes caused her to become violent and to engage in other aberrant behavior. She should have been hospitalized, but Pirandello could not afford the cost of a private sanitarium, so she was kept at home. During that time—a period of seventeen years—she frequently hurled profanities and invectives at her family, making their lives impossible. It is no wonder that, in several of his works, Pirandello explores subjects such as insanity and the inability to distinguish illusion from reality.

Pirandello is especially famous for his plays, the most celebrated of which is *Sei personaggi in cerca d'autore* (*Six Characters in Search of an Author*), which was first produced in Rome in 1921. His other plays include *Better Think Twice About It!; Liol*à; *It is So!, If You Think So; and Henry IV.* In fact, he ranks with Ibsen, Shaw, and Chekhov as a master of modern drama. However, he also wrote several works of fiction. Among his early novels are *L'esclusa* (*The Outcast*) 1893 and, his most widely read novel, *Il fu Mattia Pascal* (*The Late Mattia Pascal*) 1904. In the latter, he explores the problem of maintaining self-identity in world that lacks certitude and order, a theme that has become a hallmark of twentieth-century literature. It is the story of a man who is given the chance to leave home and assume a completely new identity. Casting off the past, however, leaves Mattia an empty shell, a man who eventually loses the knowledge of self that would have helped him navigate in an unpredictable world. Though a work of genius in itself, the novel is also important because it prepares us for several of the themes Pirandello develops in his plays. Moreover, it also reflects his explicit rejection of the rationalism that had infused eighteenth- and nineteenth-century literature. For Pirandello, the search for knowledge is fraught with illusion, making the truth—even about ourselves—virtually unattainable.

Pirandello's short stories, even more than his plays, show us world devoid of rational design. Indeed, he was an avowed atheist. Nonetheless, his style offers a paradox that makes his tragic and futile view of life even more profound. A sense of the ironic—even the comical—emerges as he observes an absurd world, smiling sardonically at the notion that all human action, whether benign, malignant, or meaningless, leads to oblivion.

Another native of the Province of Agrigento, Leonardo Sciascia (1921-1989) was born in the small town of Racalmuto. As a child, he loved reading, especially history and literature. In 1935, after moving to Caltanisetta, he began studying with Vitaliano Brancati (1907-1951), a satirist of bourgeois values, whose impact on the young Sciascia was profound. While at school, he was also introduced to American literature. Both of these influences inform Sciascia's novels, many of which feature a detective whose frustration over his inability to discover the truth behind a crime derives in no small measure from the ineptitude and corruption of the bureaucracy to which he reports.

Like Pirandello, he believes that, ultimately, the search for truth is futile. What accounts for this in Sciascia, however, is a social and political structure that intentionally distorts the light. In the preface to an early autobiographical novel, *Le parrocchie di Regalpetra* (*The Parishes of Regalpetra*), Sciascia declares that he believes "in human reason," a conviction that, though weakening over time, remained in his philosophy. On the other hand, Sciascia had a profound distrust of government, a trait not unusual in Sicilians, whose history gives them every right to be distrustful. Sciascia himself held public office as a member of both the Italian and European parliaments. He was even a member of the Italian Chamber of Deputies that investigated the Red Brigades' kidnapping and murder of Aldo Moro, a prominent politician and former prime minister, in March 1978. For Sciascia, the investigation marked a nadir in government ineptitude, apathy, and callousness. By the end of that year, Sciascia published *L'affare Moro* (*The Moro Affair*), a scathing denunciation of way the government and police had handled the case. In some ways, his mindset mirrors what we see in Shakespeare's *King Lear,* where the death of Cordelia proclaims forcefully that there is no justice and no hope of deliverance.

Among Sciascia's other well-known works are *Il giorno della civetta* (*The Day of the Owl*) 1961; *Il consiglio d' Egitto* (*The Council of Egypt*) 1963; *A ciascuno il suo (To Each His Own*) 1966; *Il mare color del vino* (*The Wine-Dark Sea*), a collection of short stories, 1973; *Todo modo* (*One Way or Another*) 1974; and *Il cavaliere e la morte* (*The Knight and Death*) 1988.

Another great twentieth-century novelist is Elio Vittorini (1908-1966), who was born in Syracuse. In his youth, Vittorini had been a Fascist, but he was denounced and forced out of the party because he backed the Republicans during the Spanish Civil War. His first novel, *Conversazione in Sicilia* (1939), earned him a cell in a Fascist jail because of its criticism of the regime. Later, as a member of the Communist Party, he joined in the fight against Mussolini, an experience on which his 1945 novel *Uomini e no (Men and not Men)* is based. Other novels include *Il garofano rosso* (*The Red Carnation*) 1936 and *Le donne di Messina* (translated as *Women on the Road*) 1949.

Italo Calvino compared Vittorini to Picasso, calling *Conversazione in Sicilia* his *Guernica*. Perhaps his most widely read novel is the unfinished *Erica e suoi fratelli* (*Erica and her Sisters*) 1951.

Two other contemporary Sicilian novelists worth our attention are Vincenzo Consolo (b.1933) and Gesualdo Bufalino (1920-1996). Consolo's *Il sorriso dell'ignoto marinaio* (*The Smile of the Unknown Sailor*), published in 1976, concerns the impact of the Risorgimento on Sicilan life. He is also author of *Nottetempo, casa per casa* (*Night Time: House by House*) 1992, a novel set in the picturesque seaside city of Cefalu during the 1920s. Bufalino is the author of over thirty books of poetry and fiction. Among them are *Diceria dell'untore* (*The Plague Sower*) 1981 and *Le menzogne della notte*. (*Night's Lies*) 1988, for which Bufalino was given the Strega Prize, Italy's greatest literary award.

Among Sicily's greatest poets is Salvatore Quasimodo (1901-1968), who won the Nobel Prize for literature in 1959. Born in Modica, he moved to Messina when his father went to help victims of the 1908 earthquake. In 1919, he worked in Rome as a graphic artist and studied the classics in his spare time. In 1929, he moved to Reggio Calabria, where in that year he wrote *Acque e terre* (*Waters and Earth*). In 1934, he went to Milan, where he wrote for *Letteratura*, a journal devoted to the Hermetic school of poetry, which had developed in Italy. The name derives from *Hermes Trismegistu,* a figure who is purported to have been a holy man and philosopher in Hellenistic Egypt. Often using sophisticated—sometimes obscure—language, the Hermetics believed in the mystical power of words. Rich with metaphorical language, especially analogies, Hermetic poetry often takes isolation, alienation and the evils of life as its themes.

While still being influenced by the Hermetics, Quasimodo took a another path in 1942 with the publication of *Nuove Poesie* (*New Poems*), a volume clearly influenced by his studies of the classics. Writing during and after the Second World War, Quasimodo argued that the poet should take on the role of social activist, using his or her talents for the betterment of society, a stance very much unlike those of earlier Sicilian writers. Two important works published during this period are *Giorno dopo giorno* (*Day after Day*) 1946 and *La vita non e sogno* (*Life Is Not a Dream*) 1949. Toward the end of his life, Quasimodo became even more optimistic, as seen in *La terra impareggiabile* (*The Incomparable Earth*) 1958, a volume that posits a world of hope despite its unpredictability and danger.

Quasimodo is perhaps the only twentieth-century Sicilian poet American readers will recognize. But Sicilian poetry has experienced a virtual renaissance. While an extended discussion of the subject is impossible here, at least three modern poets must be mentioned.

Nino Martoglio (1870-1921) was born in Belpasso, Catania. A journalist, poet, theatrical producer, and movie director, Matrtoglio wrote much of his poetry in Sicilian because he wanted to capture the nuances of a language spoken every day by ordinary people. In 1889, he founded *D'Artagnan*, a magazine written wholly in Sicilian, which was published until 1904. Martoglio's most important contribution was helping to make modern Sicilian recognized as a literary language. *Centona*, a collection of poems published in 1899, is his most significant work.

Ignazio Buttitta (1899-1997), born in Palermo, was both a businessman and a poet. In the Second World War, Buttitta joined the partisans against Mussolini's Fascists. Experiencing an economic setback on this return to Sicily after the war, he moved to Milan, where he met Salvatore Quasimodo and other poets. Buttitta is clearly a populist who, as Lucio Zinna tells us "stigmatizes the immense tragedy of war, exalting socialism and Christian solidarity." Like Martoglio, he wrote in Sicilian. Among his best-known works are *Lu pani si chiama pani* (*Bread is Bread*) 1954, *Lamentu pi Turriddu Carnivali* (*Lament for Turridu Carnivali*) 1956, and *La paglia bruciata* (*Burnt Straw*)1968.

Santo Cali (1918-1972), who was born in Linguaglossa in eastern Sicily, used the idiom of his region. According to Zinna, his poems contain "jargon, current and obsolete expressions, digging deep to bring back to light linguistic vestiges of Sicilian history." Cali was a also a prolific essayist and literary critic. Among his poetic words are *Canti Siciliani* (*Sicilian Songs*) 1966 and *Josephine* 1969. These and others are collected in *La notti longa* (*The Long Night*) 1968.

Works Cited

Cipolla, Gaetano, ed. *Antonio Veneziano, Ninety Love Octaves.* Mineola [NY]: Legas, 2006

---. *Giovanni Meli. Moral Fables and Other Poems.* Brooklyn: Legas, 1995.

Dekmejian, Hrair, and Adel F. Thabit. "Machiavelli's Arab Precursor: Ibn Zafar al- Siqilli." *British Journal of Middle Eastern Studies* 27.2 (2000): 125-137.

Dumbroski, Robert "Writer and Society in the New Italy." *The Cambridge History of Italian Literature.* Eds. Peter Brand and Lino Pertile. Cambridge: Cambridge U, 1999. 459-479.

Firth, Felicity. "Pirandello." *The Cambridge History of Italian Literature.* Eds. Peter Brand and Lino Pertile. Cambridge: Cambridge U. Press, 1999. 480-490.

Lendering, Jona. "Diodorus of Sicily." *Livius: Articles on Ancient History.* 1 May 2008 www.livius.org/di-dn/diodorus/ siculus.html.

McKenzie, Kenneth. "Syllabi of Literary Courses by Centuries: The Duecento." *Italica* 10:3 (1933): 61-66.

Mallette, Karla. *The Kingdom of Sicily, 1100-1250: A Literary History.* Philadelphia: U of Pennsylvania, 2005.

Paglia, Daniela "Ciullo d'Alcamo." *Best of Sicily Magazine.* Best of Sicily (2006). 5 May 2008 <http:www.bestofsicily.com/ mag/art191.htm>.

Oppenheimer, Paul. "The Origins of the Sonnet." *Comparative Literature* 34.4 (1982): 289-304.

Palermo, J.A. "The Latinity of Sicily." *Italica* 30.2 (1953): 65-80.

Quatriglio, Giuseppe. *A Thousand Years in Sicily*. Trans. Justin Vitiello. 2nd ed. Brooklyn: Legas, 1997.

Rossetti, Dante Gabriel. *The Early Italian Poets: Ciullo D'Alcamo to Dante Alighieri: 1100-1300*. London: George Newnes. Ltd., 1904.

Zinna, Lucio. "Iganzio Buttitta." *Italian Dialect Poetry*. Ed. Luigi Bonaffini. 29 May 2008 http://userhome.brooklyn. cuny. edu/ bonaffini/DP/index.html.

---. "Santo Cali." *Italian Dialect Poetry*. Ed. Luigi Bonaffini. 29 May 2008 http://userhome.brooklyn.cuny. edu/ bonaffini/DP/index.html.

Luigi Capuana: Father of *Verismo*

Luigi Capuana (1839-1915) helped to found *verismo,* the most important literary movement in nineteenth-century Italy. Along with his friend and fellow Sicilian, Giovanni Verga (1840-1922), Capuana created a narrative technique that viewed the human personality with detachment, allowing for no sentimentality or moral posturing. For the *veristi,* fiction was a way to apply scientific analysis to human motives and behavior, thereby providing the reader with an unvarnished view of the pains and passions of human life, no matter how disturbing. Influenced heavily by the French naturalists, especially Emile Zola, the *veristi*—later to include Federico De Roberto (1861-1927), among others—placed their characters in natural and social environments that were capricious and often inimical. They were intent on exposing the futility and desperation of life, especially as manifested in nineteenth-century Sicily.

Unlike the French naturalists, however, they did not believe that the human condition—especially in their homeland—could ever be improved. According to Robert Dombroski, writing in *the Cambridge History of Italian Literature*, "from the works of the Sicilian *veristi*, an entirely new literary landscape emerged: one devastated by nature and dominated by the blind passions and voracious instincts of characters for whom economic survival is the one and only motive force of existence" (463).

Luigi Capuana was born in Mineo, (Catania) Sicily, the son of landed gentry. While attending school at the Royal College at Bronte, Capuana first tried his hand at writing, composing poems in honor of the Madonna as well as a satire about his school's faculty. At 18, he began studying law at the University of Catania. However his attention soon turned elsewhere, and he began reading the classics, especially Dante, Virgil, and Ariosto. He also became fascinated with Sicilian folklore and started collecting songs indigenous to his native province.

In 1859, Capuana returned home to support Garibaldi's Thousand. Two years later he wrote *Garibadi*, a verse drama and, in that year, moved to Florence, where he frequented literary salons and met important French and Italian writers, including Giovanni Verga. Soon making a name for himself as an intellectual, he became the theater critic for the newspaper *La nazione* and, after having read Balzac and Flaubert, he decided to try writing fiction.

In 1868, Capuana returned to Sicily for reasons of ill health. His father died in 1869, and a succession of bad harvests on the family estates created severe economic difficulties for the Capuanas. As a result, Luigi took a job as a school inspector. Shortly thereafter, he was elected to the Mineo city council and was even elected mayor. At this time, he also began a love affair with Giuseppina Sansone, an illiterate family servant. The couple had several children, but social pressures made marriage impossible, and the children were placed in an orphanage. In 1892, with Capuana's consent, Giuseppina married another man. Reflections of this affair and its effects on the author's psyche are seen in his masterpiece *Il marchese di Roccaverdina* (*The Marquis of Roccaverdina*), a novel in which a nobleman gives his mistress in marriage to another so as to avoid the risk of damaging his family name.

In 1877, Capuana published *Profili di donne (Profiles of Women),* his first book of short stories. In the same year, he moved to Milan and became theater critic at the important newspaper *Corriere della sera.* In 1879, he published the novel *Giacinta*, the first clear example of his *verismo,* which received critical acclaim, despite the public outcry against its treatment of rape, adultery, and suicide. The novel was a milestone in his career, and he continued to write untiringly from that point.

In 1882, he became editor of a literary journal in Rome and taught Italian literature at the Institute of Higher Learning. In that year *C'era Una Volta* (*Once Upon a Time*— here entitled *Sicilian Tales*) appeared, followed by *Il regno delle fate* (*The Kingdom of the Fairies*) in 1883. After a brief return to Mineo, he departed again for Rome in 1888, where he met the French novelist Emil Zola and the young Luigi Pirandello, the latter acknowledging Capuana as a mentor. The next 13 years were prolific: he published six short story collections, including *Le paesane* (*The Neighbors*) in 1894; three novels, including *Il marchese di Roccaverdina* in 1901; and another collection of fairy tales, *Raccontafiabe (Teller of Tales)* 1894, the sequel to *C'era Una Volta*. Capuana is also remembered as the theorist of *verismo*, and, during this period, he wrote a body of criticism that made him the most important literary thinker in Italy.

In Rome, he met Adelaide Bernardini, a woman with emotional problems whom Capuana helped to recover. After returning to Catania to teach at the University, he married Adelaide in 1908. Retiring from the University in 1914, he spent his last year in Mineo reading Italian literature and studying Hegel and the positivists. He died at age 75.

In the preface to *C'era una volta*, Capuana suggests that he has departed from the naturalism found in his other works in order to create "that marvelous world of fairies, magicians, kings, queens, monsters and spells that make up the artistic landscape of a young mind." He claims that his tales are "an art form so spontaneous, so primitive and, therefore, so contrary to the nature of modern art." Clearly, this book, like every other collection of fairy tales, must be judged, ultimately, by children like the "sweet little devils" for whom Capuana wrote it.

Nonetheless, the author encourages us "to judge it not only as a book written for children, but also as a work of art." It derives from the same creative imagination as the world of his plays and novels. For Capuana and the other *veristi*, literature—whatever the intended audience—is a tool by which to comment on human experience, not to ameliorate it. In works aimed at his adult readers, he pictures a world in which forces present in our natural and social environments can, intentionally or not, bring on misery and suffering. Viewing the *fiabe* (fairy tales) through adult eyes, we realize that, to a great extent, Capuana has held to this credo even in them. Take "Ranocchino," for example, a tale in which a poor father is faced with the horrible choice of seeing his children starve to death or of killing them with his own hands.

Many of the tales take on a decidedly anti-monarchial tone. Royalty, in fact, is often depicted as egotistical, greedy, spoiled, and morally myopic. Take the greedy king in "L'arance d'oro" ("The Golden Oranges"); the queen in "Testa di rospo" ("Toad Head"), who would kill her own child; or the prince in "Spera di sole" ("Ray of Sunshine"), who spits at and kicks a poor, unwashed bakery girl. Then there is "Tì, tìriti, tì," in which an envious king twice destroys a peasant's small but bountiful garden simply because the man will not sell it to him. Of course, some of the tales portray a more sympathetic image of nobility. Consider the portrayal of the queen who risks her life to rescue her daughter from a werewolf in "Il lupo mannaro" ("The Werewolf").

While the *fiabe* often betray a dislike for the well-connected, Capuana's view of peasants and laborers is balanced. He depicts most common folk as hard-working and virtuous—even in the face of terrible suffering. But he is no Pollyanna. In "Spera di sole," for example, Tizzonchino's spiteful neighbors delight in her every misfortune. Common folk are portrayed no better in "Il soldo bucato" ("The Penny with a Hole in It") in which a woman who asks a neighbor to watch her child returns to find that the neighbor has sold him to a peddler for a penny. Indeed, heroes and villains abound among all social classes and in both the natural and supernatural worlds of the *fiabe*. For every werewolf and ogre, there is a fairy godmother or a beneficent witch!

Overall, the *fiabe* reflect the kind of objective vision seen in Capuana's other works, with the author's refusing to moralize. He remains, even in these stories written for children, the naturalist who views the world of fairies, werewolves, and princesses as objectively as such a world can be viewed. The only exception is "I tre anelli" (The Three Rings"), a Cinderella story in which the speaker condemns the avarice of the two older sisters while rewarding the humility and compassion of their younger sibling.

Nonetheless, what lies behind these *fiabe* is a disturbing irony that Capuana hides behind the tales' plots and characters as masterfully as he does behind those of his novels and plays. Viewing "I tre anelli" a second time, we notice that, behind his outright condemnation of envy and avarice, there lurks a subtler and even darker message. The intervention of visitors from the supernatural—the old woman who dispenses the rings and the Sun King—shows that, even when gifted with wealth and power, human beings can become more spiteful, envious, and stupid than they were before. In fact, the two older sisters remain so hateful and jealous that, from their graves, they refuse the offer of the Sun King (perhaps a Christ symbol) to restore them to life.

Just as disturbing and ironic are tales such as "Cecina," "Spera di sole," and "La fontana della bellezza" ("The Fountain of Beauty") in which stupid, selfish and sometimes violent royals get to marry beautiful, virtuous, and gifted heroines whom they have earlier insulted and abused. Such tales end happily, but the reader cannot help but wonder: If the spoiled neurotic prince in "La fontana della bellezza" gets to marry a beautiful girl with magical powers, what does *she* get for a husband? And what entitles the gluttonous snob of a king in "Cecina" to marry the young beauty who turns out to be the princess of Spain?

Then there is the story of Topolino, the little mouse. At the end of the tale, the king and his ministers are burned to death. When the princess begs Topolino—now a handsome prince— to restore her father, he acquiesces, they get married, and they live happily ever after. However, in the last two lines, Capuana makes a point of reminding us that no one cares about the ministers, who are left in their graves.

There are several other important themes in this work, which adult readers can discover for themselves. Returning to Capuana's preface, however, we recall that these tales were written primarily for Capuana's *nipotini*, the children whom he treasured and who waited eagerly at his study door as he finished the next story. Yet, no author abandons his voice or his craft simply because he decides to create a new reality or address a different audience. Therefore, as we read about Serpentina or about the king who suffers twenty-one years in sun and rain to earn the hand of a beautiful lady, the image of Capuana's *nipotini* clearly emerges. Such an image can emerge, however, precisely because this is a work of art—the product of the creative genius who infused it with the same passion, vision, and care he put into all of his writing.

Santi Buscemi
Skillman, NJ
July 2008

A Note on Translation

I have tried to retain as much of the sinewy and sometimes startling character of Capuana's prose as much as possible. In cases where literal translation was impossible or inappropriate, I tried to capture the author's intent and the energy of his language in way that would appeal to readers familiar with fairy tales popular in the English-speaking world. In a few cases, I relied on contemporary figures of speech to capture what appeared to be the author's clear intent.

Capuana indicates in his preface that he uses the terms *Reuccio* and *Reginotta,* not as royal *prince* and *princess* but according to their meaning in Sicilian and to their common usage in fairy tales, i.e., "king or queen of a small realm." However, since this phrase seemed cumbersome, I translated *Reuccio* and *Reginotta* simply as *prince* and *princess,* which carry both meanings in English

I am very indebted to my good friend Nino Russo for his help in translating a number of particularly difficult idiomatic expressions and for all of his encouragement on this project. A gentle, kind, and generous man, Nino is a true patriot of both Sicily and America.

Prefazione

Ai miei cari nipotini
Queste fiabe son nate così.
Dopo averne scritta una per un caro bimbo che voleva da
me, ad ogni costo, una bella fiaba, mi venne, un giorno, l'idea
di scriverne qualche altra pei miei nipotini.

In quel tempo ero triste ed anche un po' ammalato, con
un'inerzia intellettuale che mi faceva rabbia, e i lettori non
immagineranno facilmente la gioia da me provata nel vedermi,
a un tratto, fiorire nella fantasia quel mondo meraviglioso di
fate, di maghi, di re, di regine, di orchi, di incantesimi, che è
stato il primo pascolo artistico delle nostre piccole menti.

Vissi più settimane soltanto con essi, ingenuamente, come non
credevo potesse mai accadere a chi è già convinto che la realtà sia
il vero regno dell'arte. Se un importuno fosse allora venuto a
parlarmi di cose serie e gravi, gli avrei risposto, senza dubbio, che
avevo ben altre e più serie faccende pel capo; avevo Serpentina in
pericolo, o la Reginotta che mi moriva di languore per Ranocchino
o il Re che faceva la terza prova di star sette anni alla pioggia e al
sole per guadagnarsi la mano di un'adorata fanciulla.

Avevo anche la non meno seria preoccupazione del giudizio di
quel pubblico piccino che irrompeva rumorosamente, due, tre volte
al giorno, nel mio studio, per sapere quando la nuova fiaba
sarebbe finita.

Quei cari diavoletti, che poi mi si sedevano attorno
impazienti, che diventavano muti e tutti occhi ed orecchi
appena
incominciavo: C'era una volta..., mi davano una gran
suggezione. Pochi autori, aspettando dietro le quinte la
sentenza del pubblico, credo abbiano tremato al pari di me nel
vedermi davanti quelle vispe e intelligenti testoline che
pendevano dalle mie labbra, mentre io tentavo di balbettare
per loro il linguaggio così semplice, così efficace, così
drammatico, che è l'eccellenza naturale della forma artistica
delle fiabe.

Preface

Dear nieces and nephews:

Listen to how these tales were born.

After having written one for a dear child who desperately wanted a beautiful tale from me, it occurred to me one day to write some others for my grandchildren.

At that time, I was sad and also a little ill with an intellectual inertia that made me angry. Readers will not easily imagine the joy I experienced from this work as I found myself, all of a sudden, creating in my imagination that marvelous world of fairies, magicians, kings, queens, monsters, and spells that make up the artistic landscape of a young mind.

I lived many weeks alone with them, never before believing, naively, that this could happen to one who is convinced that reality is the true kingdom of art. Therefore, if some pest were to come and talk to me about serious matters, I would have responded, without a doubt, that I had better and more serious and grave matters on my mind. I was thinking about Serpetina in danger, or the princess who was pining over Ranocchino, or the king who was trying, for the third time, to remain exposed to the elements for seven years just to earn the hand of the girl he adored.

I was also seriously worried about the judgment of my young public who, two or three times a day, noisily barged into my studio to find out when the next tale would be finished.

These dear little devils, who, one after the other, sat impatiently around me, became silent, all eyes and ears as I began: "Once Upon a Time...." They made a great impression upon me. I believe that few authors, waiting in the wings for the reaction of the public, have trembled like me as I saw myself before these bright and intelligent little heads who hung on every word of mine, while I attempted to babble for them in a language so simple, so effective, and so dramatic—a language that is the natural greatness of the fairy tale's artistic form.

Non mi è parso superfluo dir questo al benigno lettore, pel caso che il presente volume trovasse qualcuno che volesse giudicarlo non soltanto come un libro destinato ai bambini, ma anche come opera d'arte.

Il mio tentativo ha una scusa: le circostanze che lo han prodotto. Senza dubbio non mi sarebbe passato mai pel capo di mettere audacemente le mani sopra una forma di arte così spontanea, così primitiva e perciò tanto contraria al carattere dell'arte moderna.

Rivedendo le bozze di stampa ho sentito un po' di rimorso. Non commettevo forse un'indegnità chiamando il pubblico a parte di quella mia deliziosa allucinazione che io non posso mai rammentare senza commozione e senza rimpianto?

Allora ben mi stia, se le Fate che vennero ad aleggiare tra le bianche pareti del mio studio mentre il sole di gennaio lo scaldava col tepore dei suoi raggi, mentre i passeri picchiavano famigliarmente col becco all'imposta chiusa della finestra e i miei cari diavoletti non osavan rifiatare avvertendo la presenza delle Dee; ben mi stia, se le Fate, per dispetto, abbandoneranno ora il mio libro alla severa giustizia della critica!

Roma, 22 giugno 1882
I
Luigi Capuana

Avvertenza. *Ho usato i vocaboli Reuccio e Reginotta secondo il significato che essi hanno nel dialetto siciliano e unicamente nel linguaggio delle fiabe, cioè invece di principe reale e di principessa reale. Reuccio trovasi nelle lettere del Sassetti per Re di piccola potenza.*

It does not seem to me superfluous to tell the kind reader all of this, in case the present volume finds someone who wants to judge it, not only as a book written for children but also as a work of art.

My attempt has a reason: the circumstances that have produced it. Without a doubt, it never crossed my mind to put my hands so audaciously on an art form so spontaneous, so primitive and, therefore, so contrary to the nature of modern art.

Reviewing the proofs, I felt a little remorse. Perhaps, I would not commit an indignity by asking the public to be part of my delicious hallucination, which I can never remember without emotion and without regret?

Therefore, it would serve me right if the Fairies, out of spite, now abandoned my book to the severe justice of the critics—the Fairies who came hovering down the white walls of my study while the January sun heated them up with the warmth of its rays, while the sparrows pecked familiarly with their beaks at the window's closed shutter, and while my sweet little devils, feeling the presence of those goddesses, did not even dare to breathe!

Rome, June 22, 1882

Luigi Capuana

NOTE: I have used the terms *Reuccio* and *Reginotta* according to their meaning in the Sicilian dialect and uniquely in the language of the fairy tales, that is instead of *royal prince* and *royal princess. Reuccio* can be found in the letters of Sassetti as the "king of a small realm."

Spera di sole

C'era una volta una una fornaia, che aveva una figliuola nera come un tizzone e brutta più del peccato mortale. Campavan la vita infornando il pane della gente, e Tizzoncino, come la chiamavano, era attorno da mattina a sera:

- Ehi, scaldate l'acqua! Ehi, impastate! - Poi, coll'asse sotto il braccio e la ciambellina sul capo, andava di qua e di là a prender le pagnotte e le stiacciate da infornare; poi, colla cesta sulle spalle, di nuovo di qua e di là per consegnar le pagnotte e le stiacciate bell'e cotte. Insomma non riposava un momento.

- Tizzoncino era sempre di buon umore. Un mucchio di filiggine; i capelli apelli arruffati, i piedi scalzi e intrisi di mota, in dosso due cenci che gli cascavano a pezzi; ma le sue risate risonavano da un capo all'altro della via.

- Tizzoncino fa l'uovo - dicevan le vicine.

All'Avemaria le fornaie si chiudevano in casa e non affacciavano più nemmeno la punta del naso. D'inverno, passava... Ma d'estate, quando tutto il vicinato si godeva il fresco e il lume di luna? O che eran matte, mamma e figliuola, a starsene tappate in casa con quel po' di caldo?... Le vicine si stillavano il cervello.

- O fornaie, venite fuori al fresco, venite!

- Si sta più fresche in casa.

Ray of Sunshine

Once upon a time, there was a woman who was a baker. She had a daughter who was as black as an ember and uglier than mortal sin. They spent their lives baking people's bread, and Tizzoncino, the "little ember" as they called her, was out and about morning and night.

"Hey, boil the water! Hey, knead the dough," her mother would tell her. Then, with a board under her arm and a bread basket on her head, she went here and there to collect the bread and rolls that needed baking. Next, with the basket on her shoulders, she once again went here and there to deliver the freshly baked loaves and rolls. In short, she never rested.

Tizzoncino was always in a good mood. But she looked like a pile of soot: her hair was disheveled, her bare feet were covered with dirt, and she was dressed in rags that fell around her in pieces. Nonetheless, her laugh resounded from one end of the street to another.

"Tizzoncino is laying an egg," the neighbors liked to say.

When the Angelus was recited, the two baker women shut themselves up in their homes and didn't as much as stick out their noses. This was fine in winter. However, in summer, when the entire neighborhood enjoyed the fresh air and the moonlight, the neighbors asked whether both mother and daughter were mad for staying trapped indoors in a stuffy house. They wracked their brains trying to figure this out.

"Oh, bakers, come out into the fresh air, come out!"

"The air is fresher in the house," they answered.

-O fornaie, guardate che bel lume di luna, guardate!
- C'è più bel lume in casa
Eh, la cosa non era liscia! Le vicine si misero a spiare e a origliare dietro l'uscio. Dalle fessure si vedeva uno splendore che abbagliava, e di tanto in tanto si sentiva la mamma:
- Spera di sole, spera di sole, sarai Regina se Dio vuole!
E Tizzoncino che faceva l'uovo.
Se lo dicevano che erano ammattite!
Ogni notte così, fino alla mezzanotte: - Spera di sole, spera di sole, sarai Regina se Dio vuole!
La cosa giunse all'orecchio del Re. Il Re montò sulle furie e mandò a chiamare le fornaie.
-Vecchia strega, se seguiti, ti faccio buttare in fondo a un carcere, te e il tuo Tizzoncino!
- Maestà, non è vero nulla. Le vicine sono bugiarde.
Tizzoncino rideva anche al cospetto del Re.
- Ah!... Tu ridi?
E le fece mettere in prigione tutte e due, mamma e figliuola.
Ma la notte, dalle fessure dell'uscio il custode vedeva in quella stanzaccia un grande splendore, uno splendore che abbagliava, e, di tanto in tanto, sentiva la vecchia:
- Spera di sole, spera di sole, sarai Regina se Dio vuole!
E Tizzoncino faceva l'uovo. Le sue risate risonavano per tutta la prigione. Il custode andò dal Re e gli riferì ogni casa.
-Il Re montò sulle furie peggio di prima.
- La intendono in tal modo? Sian messe nel carcere criminale, quello sottoterra.
Era una stanzaccia senz'aria, senza luce, coll'umido che si aggrumava in ogni parte; non ci si viveva. Ma la notte, anche nel carcere criminale, ecco uno splendore che abbagliava, e la vecchia:
- Spera di sole, spera di sole, sarai Regina se Dio vuole!

"Oh, bakers, look at the beauty of the moonlight."

"There is better light in our house," they responded.

But the neighbors didn't understand. And they began to spy at the door. Through cracks in the door, they saw a dazzling radiance, and, from time to time, heard the mother say:

"Ray of Sunshine, Ray of Sunshine. You will be queen if God's will be done!"

And Tizzoncino laughed and laughed.

It was said that they were mad!

Every night it was the same, until midnight. "Ray of Sunshine, Ray of Sunshine. You will be queen if God's will be done!"

Learning this, the king became angry and called for the bakers.

"Old witch," he said, "if you continue in this way, I will have you thrown into prison, you and your Tizzoncino!"

Majesty," answered the baker, "none of what they say is true. The neighbors are liars."

Tizzoncino laughed even in the presence of the king.

"Ah ha, and you laugh?" exclaimed the king. And he had both mother and daughter thrown into prison.

At night, from the cracks in the door of their cell, the guard saw a great light, a dazzling radiance, and from time to time, he heard the old woman say:

"Ray of Sunshine, Ray of Sunshine, you shall be queen if God's will be done."

And Tizzoncino laughed and laughed. Her laughter echoed through the prison. The guard reported all that occurred.

The king got angrier than before: "So this is how they respond?" He ordered that they be placed in a dungeon for criminals. It was a cell without air and light, and it was filled with a thick dampness. Nothing could be seen within. However, at night, even in this prison for criminals, a dazzling radiances was seen, and the old woman said: "Ray of Sunshine, Ray of Sunshine, you shall be queen if God's will be done."

Il custode tornò dal Re, e gli riferì ogni cosa Il Re, questa volta, rimase stupito. Radunò il Consiglio della Corona: e i consiglieri chi voleva che alle fornaie si tagliasse la testa, chi enava che fosser matte e bisognasse metterle in libertà.

-Infine, che cosa diceva quella donna? Se Dio vuole. O che male c'era? Se Dio avesse voluto, neppure Sua Maestà sarebbe stato buono d'impedirlo.

- Già! Era proprio così.

Il Re ordinò di scarcerarle.

Le fornaie ripresero il loro mestiere. Non avevan le pari nel cuocere il pane appuntino, e le vecchie avventore tornarono subito. Perfin la Regina volle infornare il pane da loro; il Tizzoncino così saliva spesso le scale del palazzo reale, coi piedi scalzi e intrisi di mota. La Regina le domandava:

-Tizzoncino, perché non ti lavi la faccia?

-Maestà, ho la pelle fina e l'acqua me la sciuperebbe.

-Tizzoncino, perché non ti pettini?

-Maestà, ho i capelli sottili, e il pettine me li strapperebbe.

-Tizzoncino, perché non ti compri un paio di scarpe?

-Maestà, ho i piedini delicati; mi farebbero i calli.

-Tizzoncino, perché la tua mamma ti chiama Spera di sole?

- Sarò Regina, se Dio vuole!

La Regina ci si divertiva; e Tizzoncino, andando via colla sua asse sulla testa e le pagnotte e le stiacciate di casa reale, rideva, rideva. Le vicine che la sentivan passare:

- Tizzoncino fa l'uovo!

Intanto ogni notte quella storia. Le vicine, dalla curiosità, si rodevano il fegato. E appena vedevano quello splendore che abbagliava e sentivano il ritornello della vecchia, via, tutte dietro l'uscio: non sapevano che inventare.

The guard returned to the king and told him everything.

This time the king was stupefied. He called together his royal council; some of the ministers said the bakers should be beheaded, but others believed they were simply mad and should be set free.

"What was the woman actually saying? 'If God's will be done.' And what harm was there in that?" asked one of the ministers. "If this be the will of God, not even his majesty would be able to prevent it."

"Yes, it was just so!" and the King ordered their release.

The bakers resumed their work. No sooner had they begun to bake the bread than their customers returned. Even the queen wanted them to bake her bread. So, Tizzoncino frequently climbed up the stairs of the royal palace barefoot and covered with mud:

"Tizzoncino, why don't you wash your face?" the queen asked.

"Majesty, my skin is delicate, and water will damage it."

"Tizzoncino, why don't you comb your hair?"

"Majesty, my hair is fine, and the comb will tear it."

"Tizzoncino, why don't you buy a pair of shoes?"

"Majesty, my feet are delicate, and shoes will cause calluses."

"Tizzoncino, why does your mother call you Ray of Sunshine?"

"I will be queen someday, if God wishes."

The queen was amused by her; and Tizzoncino laughed and laughed as she went along with the board on her head carrying the royal palace's loaves and rolls. The neighbors, who heard her pass, remarked:

"Tizzoncino is laying an egg."

And every night, it was the same story. The neighbors consumed themselves with curiosity. And after a while they saw that dazzling radiance, and they heard the old woman's refrain, all from behind the door. They did not know what to think.

- *Fornaie, fatemi la gentilezza di prestarmi lo staccio; nel mio c'è uno strappo.*
Tizzoncino apriva l'uscio e porgeva lo staccio.
-*Come! Siete allo scuro? Mentre picchiavo, c'era lume.*
- *Uh! Vi sarà parso.*
La cosa era arrivata anche alle orecchie del Reuccio, che aveva già sedici anni. Il Reuccio era un gran superbo. Quando incontrava per le scale Tizzoncino, coll'asse sulla testa o colla cesta sulle spalle, si voltava in là per non vederla. Gli faceva schifo. E una volta le sputò addosso. Tizzoncino quel giorno tornò a casa piangendo.
-*Che cosa è stato, figliuola mia?*
-*Il Reuccio mi ha sputato addosso.*
-*Sia fatta la volontà di Dio! Il Reuccio è padrone.*
Le vicine gongolavano:
- *Il Reuccio gli aveva sputato addosso; le stava bene a Spera di sole!*
Un altro giorno il Reuccio la incontrò sul pianerottolo. Gli parve che Tizzoncino lo avesse un po' urtato con l'asse, e lui, stizzito, le tirò un calcio. Tizzoncino ruzzolò le scale.
Quelle pagnotte e stiacciate, tutte intrise di polvere, tutte sformate, chi avrebbe avuto il coraggio di riportarle alla Regina? Tizzoncino tornò a casa piangendo e rammaricandosi.
-*Che cosa è stato, figliuola mia?*
- *Il Reuccio mi ha tirato un calcio e mi ha rovesciato ogni cosa.*
- *Sia fatta la volontà di Dio: il Reuccio è padrone.*
Le vicine non capivano nella pelle dall'allegrezza.
- *Il Reuccio gli aveva menato un calcio: le stava bene a Spera di sole!*
Il Reuccio pochi anni dopo pensò di prender moglie e mandò a domandare la figliuola del Re di Spagna. Ma l'ambasciatore arrivò troppo tardi: la figliuola del Re di Spagna s'era maritata il giorno avanti. Il Reuccio volea impiccato l'ambasciatore.

"Bakers, do me the courtesy of lending me a rag, for mine is torn," asked one neighbor.

Tizzoncino opened the door and handed her the rag.

"What! Are you in the dark? While I was knocking at the door, I saw light coming through a crack."

"Oh, it only seemed that way."

News of this strange thing had even reached the ears of the prince, who was now sixteen. The prince was a great snob. When he met Tizzoncino on the stairs, with the board on her head and the basket on her shoulders, he turned away, for she disgusted him. Once he even spit on her. That day, Tizzoncino went home crying.

"What has happened, my child?"

"The prince spit on me."

"The will of God be done. The prince is the master."

The neighbors were delighted.

"The prince spit on her; it serves her right, Ray of Sunshine!"

Another day, the prince happened to meet her on the landing. It appeared to him that Tizzoncino had bumped into him with the board. Irritated, he kicked her, and Tizzoncino tumbled down the stairs.

The loaves and rolls were squashed and covered with dust. Who would have had the courage to take them back to the queen? Tizzoncino went home crying and depressed.

"What has happened, my child?"

"The prince kicked me, and he ruined everything."

"The will of God be done. The prince is the master."

The neighbors went out of their minds with joy.

"The prince kicked her. Serves her right, that Ray of Sunshine!"

A few years later, the prince thought about taking a wife. He sent out a messenger to ask for the hand of the daughter of the king of Spain. However, the ambassador arrived too late; the king of Spain's daughter had gotten married the day before.

Ma questi gli provò che avea spesa nel viaggio mezza giornata di meno degli altri. Allora il Reuccio lo mandò a domandare la figliuola del Re di Francia. Ma l'ambasciatore arrivò troppo tardi: la figliuola del Re di Francia s'era maritata il giorno avanti.

Il Reuccio volea ad ogni costo impiccato quel traditore che non arrivava mai in tempo: ma questi gli provò che avea spesa nel viaggio una giornata di meno degli altri. Allora il Reuccio lo mandava dal Gran Turco per la sua figliuola. Ma l'ambasciatore arrivò troppo tardi: la figliuola del Gran Turco s'era maritata il giorno avanti. Il Reuccio non sapea darsi pace; piangeva. Il Re, la Regina, tutti i ministri gli stavano attorno:

-Mancavano principesse? c'era la figliuola del Re *d'Inghilterra: si mandasse per lei.*

Il povero ambasciatore partì come una saetta, camminando giorno e notte finché non arrivò in Inghilterra. Era una fatalità! Anche la figlia del Re d'Inghilterra s'era maritata il giorno avanti. Figuriamoci il Reuccio!

Un giorno, per distrarsi, se n'andò a caccia. Smarritosi in un bosco, lontano dai compagni, errò tutta la giornata senza poter trovare la via. Finalmente, verso sera, scoprì un casolare in mezzo agli alberi. Dall'uscio aperto, vide dentro un vecchione, con una gran barba bianca, che, acceso un bel fuoco, si preparava la cena.

-Brav'uomo, sapreste indicarmi la via per uscire dal bosco?

- Ah, finalmente sei arrivato!

A quella voce grossa grossa, il Reuccio sentì accapponarsi la pelle.

-Brav'uomo, non vi conosco; io sono il Reuccio.

- Reuccio o non Reuccio, prendi quella scure e spaccami un po' di legna.

Il Reuccio, per timore di peggio, gli spaccava la legna.

-   Reuccio o non Reuccio, vai per l'acqua alla fontana.

The prince wanted to hang the ambassador. But the man proved that he had taken half a day less than the others to travel to the court. The prince sent him to ask for the hand of the daughter of the king of France. But he arrived too late; the king of France's daughter had been married the day before.

The prince wanted to hang this "traitor," who never arrived on time, in the worst way. However, the man proved that he had taken half a day less than the others in traveling to the court. So, the prince sent him to the Grand Turk to ask for his daughter's hand. However, the ambassador arrived too late; the daughter of the Grand Turk had gotten married a day earlier. The prince did not know what to do, and he began to weep. But the king, the queen, and all of the ministers reassured him:

"Is there any lack of princesses? There's the daughter of the king of England; send for her."

The poor ambassador took off like an arrow, traveling day and night until he finally arrived in England. But it was fate! Even the daughter of the king of England had gotten married the day before. Imagine the prince's reaction!

One day, to take his mind off his troubles, the prince went hunting. But he got lost in the forest, a long way from his friends, and he was unable to find his way even though he searched all day. Finally, around evening time, he found a cottage among the trees. Through the open door, inside he spotted an old man with a long white beard, who, by the light of a bright fire, was preparing his dinner.

"Good fellow, can you show me the way out of this forest?"

"Oh, you have finally arrived!" said the old man.

Upon hearing his deep voice, the prince got goose bumps.

"Good fellow, I don't know you. I am the prince."

"Prince or no prince, take this ax and split a few logs for me."

Fearing the worst, the prince split the wood.

"Prince or no prince, get me some water from the fountain."

Il Reuccio, per timore di peggio, prendeva l'orcio sulle spalle e andava alla fontana.
- Reuccio o non Reuccio, servimi a tavola.
E il Reuccio, per timore di peggio, lo servì a tavola.
All'ultimo il vecchio gli diè quel che era avanzato.
- Buttati lì; è il tuo posto.
Il povero Reuccio si accovacciò su quel po' di strame in un canto, ma non poté dormire.
Quel vecchio era il Mago, padrone del bosco. Quando andava via, stendeva attorno alla casa una rete incantata, e il Reuccio rimaneva in tal modo suo prigioniero e suo schiavo.
Intanto il Re e la Regina lo piangevano per morto e portavano il lutto. Ma un giorno, non si sa come, arrivò la notizia che il Reuccio era schiavo del Mago. Il Re spedì subito i suoi corrieri:
-Tutte le ricchezze del regno, se gli rilasciava il figliuolo!
- Sono più ricco di lui!
A questa risposta del Mago, la costernazione del Re fu grande. Spedì daccapo i corrieri:
-Che voleva? Parlasse: il Re avrebbe dato anche il sangue delle sue vene.
-Una pagnotta e una stiacciata, impastate, infornate di mano della Regina, e il Reuccio sarà libero.
- Oh, questo era nulla!
La Regina stacciò la farina, la impastò, fece la pagnotta e la stiacciata, scaldò il forno di sua mano e le infornò. Ma non era pratica; pagnotta e stiacciata furono abbruciacchiate.
Quando il Mago le vide, arricciò il naso:
- Buone pei cani.
E le buttò al suo mastino. La Regina stacciò di nuovo la farina, la impastò e ne fece un'altra pagnotta e un'altra stiacciata. Poi scaldò il forno di sua mano e le infornò. Ma non era pratica. La pagnotta e la stiacciata riuscirono mal cotte.
Quando il Mago le vide, arricciò il naso:

Fearing the worst, the prince went to the fountain.

"Prince or no prince, wait on me at the table."

And fearing the worst, he waited on him. Finally, the old man told him what else was to be."

"Lie down here; it is your place."

The poor prince lay down in a corner on a little pile of straw, but he could not sleep.

The old man was a wizard, the lord of the forest. When he went out, he stretched a magic net around the house, and because of this the prince remained his prisoner and his slave.

Meanwhile, the king and the queen grieved, believing that their son had died; they went into mourning. But one day, no one knows how, news came that the prince had been enslaved by the wizard. Immediately, the king sent out his messengers.

"All the riches of the kingdom will be yours if you release the boy!" they told the wizard.

"I am richer than the king."

Hearing the wizard's response, the king became greatly dismayed. However, he sent out the messengers once again.

"What do you want? Tell us; the king would give you even the blood from his own veins."

"Give me a loaf of bread and a roll mixed and baked by the hands of the queen, and the prince will be set free."

"Oh, that's nothing!"

The queen sifted the flour, kneaded the dough, made a loaf and a roll, heated the oven with her own hands, and baked them. But, she wasn't very skillful, and she burned the loaf of bread and the roll. When the wizard saw them, he curled up his nose.

"Fit for dogs," he said.

And he threw them to the mastiff. So, the queen sifted the flour again, kneaded the dough, and made another loaf of bread and another roll. She heated up the oven with her own hands. However, she was not skillful, and the bread and roll were undercooked. When the wizard saw them, he curled up his nose.

- Buone pei cani.   E le buttò al mastino.
La Regina provò, riprovò; ma il suo pane riusciva sempre o troppo o poco cotto; e intanto il povero Reuccio restava schiavo del Mago.
Il Re adunò il Consiglio di Ministri.
-Sacra Maestà - disse uno dei Ministri - proviamo se il Mago è indovino. La Regina staccerà la farina, la impasterà, farà la pagnotta e la stiacciata; per scaldare il forno ed infornare chiameremo Tizzoncino!
- Bene! Benissimo!
E così fecero. Ma il Mago arricciò il naso:
-Pagnottaccia, stiacciataccia. Via, lavatevi la faccia!
E le buttò al cane. Aveva subito capito che ci avea messo le mani Tizzoncino.
-Allora - disse il ministro - non c'è che un rimedio.
-Quale? - domandò il Re.
- Sposare il Reuccio con Tizzoncino. Così il Mago avrà il pane stacciato, impastato, infornato dalle mani della Regina, e il Reuccio sarà liberato.
- È proprio la volontà di Dio - disse il Re.
- Spera di sole, spera di sole, sarai regina se Dio vuole!
E fece il decreto reale, che dichiarava il Reuccio e Tizzoncino marito e moglie. Il Mago ebbe la pagnotta e la stiacciata, stacciate, impastate e infornate dalle mani della Regina, e il Reuccio fu messo in libertà.
Veniamo intanto a lui, che di Tizzoncino non vuol saperne affatto:
-Quel mucchio di filiggine sua moglie? Quella bruttona di fornaia regina?
- Ma c'è un decreto reale.
- Sì? Il Re lo ha fatto, e il Re può disfarlo!
Tizzoncino, diventata Reginotta, era andata ad abitare nel palazzo reale. Ma non s'era voluta lavare, né pettinare, né mutarsi il vestito, né mettersi un paio di scarpe:

"Fit for dogs," he said. And he threw them to the mastiff.

The queen tried and tried, but her bread always came out overcooked or undercooked. Meanwhile, the poor prince remained the wizard's slave.

The king called together his royal council.

"Holy Majesty," said one of the ministers. "Let's try to fool the wizard. The queen will sift the flour, knead the dough, and form the bread and roll. But Tizzoncino will bake them."

"Excellent!" said the king.

So they did this. However, the wizard curled up his nose: "This bread and roll are not right. Get out of my sight!"

And he tossed them to the dog. He knew immediately that Tizzoncino had a hand in baking them.

"Therefore," said the minister, "there is but one solution."

"What?" asked the king.

Marry the prince to Tizzoncino. That way, the wizard will have bread that is prepared and baked by the hands of the queen, and the prince will be free.

"This is certainly the will of God," said the king.

"Ray of Sunshine, Ray of Sunshine, you will be queen if God's will be done."

He issued a royal decree declaring the prince and Tizzoncino husband and wife. The wizard had a loaf of bread and a roll sifted, kneaded, and baked by the hands of the new princess, and the prince was set free.

Meanwhile, the prince wanted nothing to do with Tizzoncino.

Was that pile of soot to be his wife? That eyesore of a bakery girl to be queen?

"But a royal decree has been issued," he was reminded.

"Yes?" he said. "The king has made it; he can rescind it."

Having become princess, Tizzoncino had gone to live in the royal palace. But she did not wish to bathe herself, nor comb her hair, nor change her clothing, nor put on a pair of shoes.

-*Quando verrà il Reuccio, allora mi ripulirò.*

Era possibile? E aspettava, chiusa nella sua camera, che il Reuccio andasse a trovarla. Ma non c'era verso di persuaderlo.

- *Quella fornaia mi fa schifo! Meglio morto che sposar lei!*

Tizzoncino, quando le riferivano queste parole, si metteva a ridere:

-*Verrà, non dubitate; verrà.*

- *Verrò? Guarda come verrò!*

Il Reuccio, perduto il lume degli occhi e colla sciabola in pugno, correva verso la camera di Tizzoncino: volea tagliarle la testa. L'uscio era chiuso. Il Reuccio guardò dal buco della serratura e la sciabola gli cadde di mano. Lì dentro c'era una bellezza non mai vista, una vera Spera di sole!

- *Aprite, Reginotta mia! Aprite!*

E Tizzoncino, dietro l'uscio, canzonandolo:

-*Mucchio di filiggine!*

- *Apri, Reginotta dell'anima mia!*

E Tizzoncino ridendo:

- *Bruttona di fornaia!*

- *Apri, Tizzoncino mio!*

Allora l'uscio s'aperse, e i due sposini s'abbracciarono.

Quella sera si fecero gli sponsali, e il Reuccio e Tizzoncino vissero a lungo, felici e contenti...E a noi ci s'allegano i denti.

"When the prince arrives, I will clean myself up."

Was it possible? And she waited, shut up in her room, for the prince to come and find her. But there was no way to persuade him to come.

"That bakery girl disgusts me! I would rather die than marry her!"

When his words were repeated to Tizzoncino, she began to laugh.

"He will come, to be sure; he will come."

"Really?" asked the prince. "We'll see if I come!"

Abandoning all reason and with a sword in his hand, he ran to Tizzoncino's room. He wanted to cut her head off. The door was closed. When the prince looked through the key hole, however, he dropped his sword. Within was a beauty the likes of which had never been seen. Truly she was a "Ray of Sunshine."

"Open, my princess, open the door!"

But, behind the door, Tizzoncino mocked him:

"Pile of soot, eh?"

"Open the door, princess of my soul!"

But Tizzoncino laughed:

"Eyesore of a bakery girl, eh?"

"Open, my Tizzoncino!"

Finally, the door opened, and the couple embraced.

That night they got married, and the prince and Tizzoncino lived happily and long.

And so here ends our tale, right or wrong.

Le arance d'oro

Si racconta che c'era una volta un Re, il quale avea dietro il palazzo reale un magnifico giardino. Non vi mancava albero di sorta; ma il più raro e il più pregiato, era quello che produceva le arance d'oro.

Quando arrivava la stagione delle arance, il Re vi metteva a guardia una sentinella notte e giorno; e tutte le mattine scendeva lui stesso a osservare coi suoi occhi se mai mancasse una foglia.

Una mattina va in giardino, e trova la sentinella addormentata. Guarda l'albero... Le arance d'oro non c'eran più!

- Sentinella sciagurata, pagherai colla tua testa.

- Maestà, non ci ho colpa. È venuto un cardellino, si è posato sopra un ramo e si è messo a cantare. Canta, canta, canta, mi si aggravavano gli occhi. Lo scacciai da quel ramo, ma andò a posarsi sopra un altro. Canta, canta, canta, non mi reggevo dal sonno. Lo scacciai anche di lì, e appena cessava di cantare, il mio sonno svaniva. Ma si posò in cima all'albero, e canta, canta, canta..., ho dormito finora!

Il Re non gli fece nulla.

Alla nuova stagione, incaricò della guardia il Reuccio in persona.

Una mattina va in giardino e trova il Reuccio addormentato. Guarda l'albero...; le arance d'oro non c'eran più! Figuriamoci la sua collera!

- Come? Ti sei addormentato anche tu?

- Maestà, non ci ho colpa. È venuto un cardellino, si è posato sopra un ramo e si è messo a cantare. Canta, canta, canta, mi s'aggravavano gli occhi. Gli dissi: cardellino traditore, col Reuccio non ti giova! Ed esso a canzonarmi: il Reuccio dorme! il Reuccio dorme! Cardellino traditore, col Reuccio non ti giova! Ed esso a canzonarmi: il Reuccio fa la nanna! il

The Golden Oranges

It is said that there was a king, who had a magnificent garden
behind his royal palace. Every type of tree could be found
there, but the rarest and most valued bore golden oranges.

When the season for the oranges arrived, the king ordered a
sentry to guard it night and day. And every morning he came
down himself to inspect the oranges with his own eyes to make
sure that not even one leaf was missing.

One morning, he went into the garden and found the sentry
asleep. He looked at the tree...The golden oranges were gone!

"Oh, wretched sentry, you will pay with your head."

"Majesty, it is not my fault. A goldfinch landed on a branch
and began to sig. He sang, and sang, and sang so much that my
eyes became heavy. I drove him from that branch, but he then
flew to another. He sang and sang so much that I could not
fight off sleep. I drove him from that branch too, and as soon as
he stopped singing, my sleepiness disappeared. However, he
then perched on the top of the tree and he sang, and sang, and
sang. I have been sleeping until this very moment!"

The king did not hurt the man.

The next season, he placed the prince himself in charge of
guarding the tree.

One morning he went into the garden and found the prince
asleep. He looked at the tree...the golden oranges were gone!
Imagine his anger!

"What? Even you fell asleep?"

"Majesty, it is not my fault," said the prince. "A goldfinch
landed on a branch and began to sing. He sang, and sang, and
sang so much that my eyes became heavy. I told him, 'Traitorous goldfinch, don't fool with the prince!' But he simply
mocked me: 'The prince is falling asleep! The prince is falling
asleep.' 'Traitorous goldfinch,' I said, 'don't fool with the
prince! But he simply mocked me. 'The prince is falling

Reuccio fa la nanna! E canta, canta, canta..., ho dormito finora!

Il Re volle provarsi lui stesso; e arrivata la stagione si mise a far la guardia. Quando le arance furon mature, ecco il cardellino che si posa sopra un ramo, e comincia a cantare. Il Re avrebbe voluto tirargli, ma faceva buio come in una gola. Intanto aveva una gran voglia di dormire!

- Cardellino traditore, questa volta non ti giova! - Ma durava fatica a tener aperti gli occhi.

Il cardellino cominciò a canzonarlo:

- Pss! Pss! Il Re dorme! Pss! Pss! Il Re dorme!

E canta, canta, canta, il Re s'addormentava peggio d'un ghiro anche lui.

La mattina apriva gli occhi: le arance d'oro non ci eran più!

Allora fece un bando per tutti i suoi Stati:

- Chi gli portasse, vivo o morto, quel cardellino, riceverebbe per mancia una mula carica d'oro.

Passarono sei mesi, e non si vide nessuno.

Finalmente un giorno si presenta un contadinotto molto male in arnese:

- Maestà, lo volete davvero quel cardellino? Promettetemi la mano della Reginotta, e in men di tre giorni l'avrete.

Il Re lo prese per le spalle, e lo messe fuor dell'uscio.

Il giorno appresso quegli tornò:

- Maestà, lo volete davvero quel cardellino? Promettetemi la mano della Reginotta, e in men di tre giorni l'avrete.

Il Re lo prese per le spalle, gli diè una pedata e lo messe fuor dell'uscio.

asleep!' And he sang, and sang, and sang...I have been sleeping until this very moment!"

The king wanted to try guarding the tree himself. And when the oranges ripened, the goldfinch perched on a branch and began to sing. The king wanted to pull him down, but the garden was covered in darkness, and the king felt very sleepy.

"Traitorous goldfinch, this time you will not succeed, but he had a hard time keeping his eyes open."

The goldfinch began to serenade him: "Hush! Hush! The king is sleeping! Hush! Hush! The king is sleeping!"

As he sang and sang, the king himself fell into a deep sleep.

In the morning, he opened his eyes; the golden oranges were gone!

Therefore, he proclaimed throughout his realm:

"Whoever brings me this goldfinch, dead or alive, will receive a mule loaded with gold as a reward."

However, six months later, no one had come forward.

Finally, one day there came a crusty, old peasant, who was shabbily dressed:

"Majesty, do you truly want that goldfinch? Promise me the hand of the princess, and in fewer than three days you shall have him."

The king grabbed him by the shoulders and threw him out.

The next day, he returned.

"Majesty, do you truly want that goldfinch? Promise me the hand of the princess, and in fewer than three days you shall have him."

The king grabbed him by the shoulders, gave him a strong kick, and put him out the door.

Ma il giorno appresso, quello, cocciuto, ritornava:

- Maestà, lo volete davvero il cardellino? Promettetemi la mano della Reginotta, e in men di tre giorni l'avrete.

Il Re, stizzito, chiamò una guardia e lo fece condurre in prigione.

Intanto ordinava si facesse attorno all'albero una rete di ferro; con quelle sbarre grosse, non c'era più bisogno di sentinella. Ma quando le arance furon mature, una mattina va in giardino...; l'arance d'oro non c'eran più.

Figuriamoci la sua collera! Dovette, per forza, mettersi d'accordo con quel contadinotto.

- Portami vivo il cardellino e la Reginotta sarà tua.

- Maestà, fra tre giorni.

E prima che i tre giorni passassero era già di ritorno.

- Maestà, eccolo qui. La Reginotta ora è mia.

Il Re si fece scuro. Doveva dare la Reginotta a quello zoticone?

- Vuoi delle gioie? Vuoi dell'oro? Ne avrai finché vorrai.

Ma quanto alla Reginotta, nettati la bocca.

- Maestà, il patto fu questo.

- Vuoi delle gioie? Vuoi dell'oro?

- Tenetevi ogni cosa. Sarà quel che sarà!

E andò via.

Il Re disse al cardellino:

- Ora che ti ho tra le mani, ti vo' martoriare.

Il cardellino strillava, sentendosi strappare le penne ad una ad una.

- Dove son riposte le arance d'oro?

However, the peasant was stubborn and the next day returned.

"Majesty, do you truly want that goldfinch? Promise me the hand of the princess, and in less than three days you shall have him."

Annoyed, the king called for a guard and had the peasant thrown into prison.

Meanwhile, he ordered that an iron net be built around the tree; such a barrier eliminated the need for a guard. When the oranges had ripened, the king went into the garden one morning…and the golden oranges were gone.

Imagine his anger! Now he was obliged to come to terms with the crusty, old peasant.

"Bring me the goldfinch alive, and the princess is yours."

"Majesty, within three days."

And before three days had passed, he returned.

"Majesty, here he is. Now the princess is mine."

A dark look came over the king's face. "Must I give the princess to this lout?" he thought.

"Do you want jewels? Do you want gold? You can have as much as you want. But as for the princess, say no more."

"But, Majesty, that was our agreement," said the peasant.

"Do you want jewels? Do you want gold?"

"Keep all you have," answered the peasant. "Whatever happens, happens!"

And he went on his way.

The king turned to the goldfinch.

"Now that I have you in my hands, I am going to torture you."

The goldfinch shrieked as he felt his feathers being pulled out one by one.

"Where are the golden oranges hidden?"

- Se non mi farete più nulla, Maestà, ve lo dirò.

- Non ti farò più nulla.

- Le arance d'oro sono riposte dentro la Grotta delle sette porte. Ma c'è il mercante, col berrettino rosso, che fa la guardia. Bisogna sapere il motto; e lo sanno due soli: il mercante e quel contadino che mi ha preso.

Il Re mandò a chiamare il contadino.

- Facciamo un altro patto. Vorrei entrare nella Grotta delle sette porte, e non so il motto. Se me lo sveli, la Reginotta sarà tua.

- Parola di Re?

- Parola di Re!

- Maestà, il motto è questo:

"Secca risecca! Apriti, Cecca."

- Va bene.

Il Re andò, disse il motto, e la Grotta s'aperse. Il contadino rimase fuori ad attenderlo.

In quella grotta i diamanti, a mucchi per terra, abbagliavano. Vistosi solo, sua Maestà si chinava e se ne riempiva le tasche. Ma nella stanza appresso, i diamanti, sempre a mucchi, eran più grossi e più belli. Il Re si vuotava le tasche, e tornava a riempirsele di questi. Così fino all'ultima stanza, dove, in un angolo, si vedevano ammonticchiate le arance d'oro del giardino reale.

C'era lì una bisaccia, e il Re la colmò. Or che sapeva il motto, vi sarebbe ritornato più volte.

Uscito fuor della Grotta, colla bisaccia in collo, trovò il contadino che lo attendeva.

- Maestà, la Reginotta ora è mia.

Il Re si fece scuro. Dovea dare la Reginotta a quello zoticone?

"I will tell you, Majesty, if you stop torturing me."

"I will stop," said the king.

"The golden oranges are hidden in the grotto of the seven doors. However, guarding them is a merchant wearing a red cap. You need to know the magic words, and only two people know them: the merchant and the peasant who captured me."

The king called for the peasant.

"Let's make another agreement. I want to enter the grotto of the seven doors, but I don't know the secret words. If you tell me them, the princess is yours."

"Your word as king?"

"My word as king!"

"Majesty, the magic words are these:
Dry, dry, very dry! Open up, open up, say I."

"Very well."

When the king said the magic words, the entrance to the grotto opened. The peasant waited outside for him.

In the grotto on the ground was a pile of diamonds shining brilliantly. Seeing that he was alone, the king stooped down and filled his pockets. But in the next room, the diamonds, also in a pile, were bigger and more beautiful. The king emptied his pockets, and he refilled them with these. Thus it was until he came to the last room, where he saw the golden oranges of the royal palace piled up in a corner.

Nearby, there happened to be a knapsack, and the king filled it. Now that he knew the magic words, he would return over and over again.

As he left the grotto with the knapsack on his back, he found the peasant waiting for him.

"Majesty, now the princess is mine."

A dark look came over the king's face. "Must I give the princess to this lout?" he thought.

- *Domanda qualunque grazia e ti verrà concessa. Ma per la Reginotta nettati la bocca.*
- *Maestà, e la vostra parola?*
- *Le parole se le porta il vento.*
- *Quando sarete al palazzo ve ne accorgerete.*
Arrivato al palazzo, il Re mette giù la bisaccia e fa di vuotarla. Ma invece di arance d'oro, trova arance marce.
Si mette le mani nelle tasche, i diamanti son diventati tanti gusci di lumache!
Ah! quel pezzo di contadinaccio gliel'avea fatta!
Ma il cardellino la pagava.
E tornò a martoriarlo.
- *Dove sono le mie arance d'oro?*
- *Se non mi farete più nulla, Maestà, ve lo dirò.*
- *Non ti farò più nulla.*
- *Son lì dove le avete viste; ma per riaverle bisogna conoscere un altro motto, e lo sanno due soli: il mercante e quel contadino che mi ha preso.*
Il Re lo mandò a chiamare:
- *Facciamo un altro patto. Dimmi il motto per riprendere le arance e la Reginotta sarà tua.*
- *Parola di Re?*
- *Parola di Re!*
- *Maestà il motto è questo:*
"Ti sto addosso:
 Dammi l'osso."
-*Va bene.*
Il Re andava e ritornava più volte colla bisaccia colma, e riportava a palazzo tutte le arance d'oro.
Allora si presentò il contadino:
- *Maestà, la Reginotta ora è mia.*
Il Re si fece scuro. Dovea dare la Reginotta a quello zoticone?

"Ask for whatever reward you want, and I will grant it to you," said the king. "But as for the princess, say no more."
"But you gave your word, Majesty."

"My word is gone with the wind."

"When you return to the palace, you will realize what you have done."

Back at the palace, the king put down the knapsack and emptied it. But instead of golden oranges, he found rotten oranges.

He put his hands in his pockets, and he found that the diamonds had turned to snail shells.

This was the work of that crusty, old peasant! But the goldfinch would pay for it.

And he decided to torture the bird.

"Where are my golden oranges?"

"I will tell you, Majesty, if you stop torturing me."

"I will stop," said the king.

"They are where you saw them; however, to get them back, you will need to know other magic words, and only two people know them: the merchant and the peasant who captured me."

The king sent for the peasant.

"Let's make another agreement. Tell me the magic words to get back the oranges and the princess will be yours."

"Your word as king?"

"My word as king!"

"Majesty, here are the magic words:
I am coming after you; give me your bones."

"Very well."

The king came and went many times with a full knapsack, and returned all of the golden oranges to the royal palace.

Therefore, the peasant returned:

"Majesty, now the princess is mine."

A dark look came over the king's face. "Must I give the princess to this lout?" he thought.

- *Quello è il tesoro reale: prendi quello che ti piace. Quanto alla Reginotta, nettati la bocca.*
- *Non se ne parli più.*

E andò via.

Da che il cardellino era in gabbia, le arance d'oro restavano attaccate all'albero da un anno all'altro.

Un giorno la Reginotta disse al Re:
- *Maestà, quel cardellino vorrei tenerlo nella mia camera.*
- *Figliuola mia, prendilo pure; ma bada che non ti scappi.*

Il cardellino nella camera della Reginotta non cantava più.
- *Cardellino, perché non canti più?*
- *Ho il mio padrone che piange.*
- *E perché piange?*
- *Perché non ha quel che vorrebbe.*
- *Che cosa vorrebbe?*
- *Vorrebbe la Reginotta. Dice:*
  "Ho lavorato tanto,
    E le fatiche mie son sparse al vento."
- *Chi è il tuo padrone? Quello zotico?*
- *Quello zotico, Reginotta, è più Re di Sua Maestà.*
- *Se fosse vero, lo sposerei. Va' a dirglielo, e torna subito.*
- *Lo giurate?*
- *Lo giuro.*

E gli aperse la gabbia. Ma il cardellino non tornò.

Una volta il Re domandò alla Reginotta:
- *O il cardellino non canta più? È un bel pezzo che non lo sento.*
- *Maestà, è un po' malato.*

E il Re s'acchetò.

Intanto la povera Reginotta viveva in ambascia:
- *Cardellino traditore, te e il tuo padrone!*

"Here is the royal treasure: take what you like. But as for the princess, say on more."

"There is nothing more to say," responded the peasant, and he went away.

Because the goldfinch was in a cage, the golden oranges stayed on the tree from one year to the next.

One day, the princess said to the king:

"Majesty, I want to keep the goldfinch in my room."

"My child, please take him, but be careful not to let him escape."

Once in the princess's room, the goldfinch no longer sang.

"Goldfinch, why don't you sing anymore," asked the princess.

"Because my master is crying."

"And why is he crying?"

"Because he lacks what he desires."

"What does he want?"

"He wants the princess. He says: 'I have worked so hard, but all of my efforts have been scattered by the wind.'"

"Who is your master? That lout?"

"Yes, princess, but he is more of a king than his Majesty."

"If this is true, I will marry him. Tell him that and return right away."

"Do you swear it?"

"I swear it."

And, so, she opened the cage. But the goldfinch did not return.

One day, the king asked the princess:

"Why doesn't the goldfinch sing anymore? I have not heard him for quite a while."

"Majesty, he is a little ill." The king accepted this excuse.

Meanwhile, the poor princess lived in anguish.

"Traitorous goldfinch, you and your master!"

E come s'avvicinava la stagione delle arance, pel timore del babbo, il cuore le diventava piccino piccino.

Intanto venne un ambasciatore del Re di Francia che la chiedeva per moglie. Il padre ne fu lieto oltremodo, e rispose subito di sì. Ma la Reginotta:

- Maestà, non voglio: vo' rimanere ragazza.

Quello montò sulle furie:

- Come? Diceva di no, ora che avea impegnato la sua parola e non potea più ritirarla?

- Maestà, le parole se le porta il vento.

Il Re non lo potevan trattenere: schizzava fuoco dagli occhi. Ma quella, ostinata:

- Non lo voglio! Non lo voglio! Vo' rimanere ragazza.

Il peggio fu quando il Re di Francia mandò a dire che fra otto giorni arrivava.

Come rimediare con quella figliolaccia caparbia?

Dallo sdegno, le legò le mani e i piedi e la calò in un pozzo:

- Di' di sì, o ti faccio affogare!

E la Reginotta zitta. Il Re la calò fino a metà.

- Di' di sì, o ti faccio affogare!

E la Reginotta zitta. Il Re la calava più giù, dentro l'acqua; le restava fuori soltanto la testa:

- Di' di sì, o ti faccio affogare!

E la Reginotta zitta.

- Dovea affogarla davvero?

E la tirò su; ma la rinchiuse in una stanza, a pane ed acqua. La Reginotta piangeva:

- Cardellino traditore, te e il tuo padrone! Per mantenere la parola ora patisco tanti guai!

Il Re di Francia arrivò con un gran seguito, e prese alloggio nel palazzo reale.

- E la Reginotta? Non vuol farsi vedere?

And as the season of the oranges grew near, the princess got more and more depressed fearing what her father might say.

Meanwhile, there arrived an ambassador from the king of France, who wanted to marry the princess. Her father was extremely happy, and he quickly gave his consent. However, the princess refused:

"Majesty, I don't want to marry. I want to remain a maid."

The king became furious.

"What? Are you saying 'no' now that I have given my word and can no longer take it back?"

"Majesty, words are blown away by the wind."

The king was beside himself; fire was coming out of his eyes. But she was obstinate: "I don't want him. I don't want him. I want to remain a maid."

It got even worse when the king of France sent word that he would arrive within eight days.

How was the king to deal with his stubborn daughter?

He became so angry that he tied her hands and feet, and he lowered her into a well:

"Say, yes, or I will let you drown!"

But the princess remained silent. The king then lowered her half way down.

"Say yes, or I will let you drown!"

But the princess remained silent. The king then lowered her even further into the water with only her head above it.

"Say yes, or I will let you drown!"

But the princess remained silent.

"Must I truly drown her?" asked the king.

He pulled her up and locked her in a room, giving her only bread and water. The princess cried: "Traitorous goldfinch, you and your master! I must suffer just so I can keep my word."

The king of France arrived with a great retinue, and he took lodgings in the royal palace.

"And the princess? Won't you let me see her?"

- *Maestà, è un po' indisposta.*
Il Re non sapeva che rispondere, imbarazzato.
- *Portatele questo regalo.*
*Era uno scatolino tutto d'oro e di brillanti. Ma la Reginotta
lo posò lì, senza neppur curarsi d'aprirlo. E piangeva.*
- *Cardellino traditore, te e il tuo padrone!*
- *Non siamo traditori, né io, né il mio padrone.*
*Sentendosi rispondere dallo scatolino, la Reginotta lo
aperse.*
- *Ah, cardellino mio! Quante lagrime ho sparse.*
- *La tua sorte volea così. Ora il destino è compito.*
*Sua Maestà, conosciuto chi era quel contadino, le diè in do*te
*l'albero che produceva le arance d'oro, e il giorno appresso la
Reginotta sposò il Re di Francia.*

E noi restiamo a grattarci la pancia.

"Majesty, she is a little ill."

The king didn't know how to respond, for he was embarrassed.

"Take this gift to her," said the king of France.

It was a small box made of gold and diamonds.

However, the princess put it aside without desiring to open it. And she cried: "Traitorous goldfinch, you and your master!"

"We are not traitors, neither I nor my master."

Hearing this response from within the box, the princess opened it.

"Oh, my goldfinch! I have shed so many tears."

"That was your fate, princess. Now your destiny is fulfilled."

His majesty, realizing who the peasant was, gave him as a dowry the tree that produced the golden oranges,

The next day, the king of France and the princess were wed.
And about these two, that's all that can be said.

Ranocchino

*Questa è la bella storia di Ranocchino porgi il ditino, e
sentirete qui appresso perché si dica così.*

*Si racconta dunque che c'era una volta un povero diavolo, il
quale aveva sette figliuoli, che se lo rodevano vivo. Il maggiore
contava dieci anni, e l'ultimo appena due.*

Una sera il babbo se li fece venire tutti dinanzi.

*- Figliuoli - disse - son due giorni che non gustiamo neppure
un gocciolo d'acqua, ed io, dalla disperazione, non so più dove
dar di capo. Sapete che ho pensato? Domani mi farò prestar
l'asino dal nostro vicino, gli porrò le ceste e vi porterò attorno
per vendervi. Se avete un po' di fortuna, si vedrà.*

*I bimbi si misero a strillare; non volevano esser venduti, no!
Solo l'ultimo, quello di due anni, non strillava.*

*- E tu, Ranocchino? - gli domandò il babbo, che gli avea
messo quel nomignolo perché era piccino quanto un ranocchio.*

- Io son contento - rispose.

*E la mattina quel povero diavolo se lo prese in collo, e
cominciò a girare per la città.*

- Chi mi compra Ranocchino! Chi mi compra Ranocchino!

Ma nessuno lo voleva, un cosino a quella maniera!

S'affacciò alla finestra la figlia del Re.

- Che cosa vendete, quell'uomo?

- Vendo questo bimbo, chi lo vuol comprare.

*La Reginotta lo guardò, fece una smorfia e gli sbatacchiò le
imposte sul viso.*

*- Bella grazia! - disse quel povero diavolo. E riprese ad
urlare:*

- Chi mi compra Ranocchino! Chi mi compra Ranocchino!

Ma nessuno lo voleva, un cosino a quella maniera!

The Little Frog

This is the charming tale of Ranocchino, the little frog who stuck out his finger. Now listen carefully; it goes like this.

Once upon a timethere was a poor chap with seven children, whom he could not feed. The oldest was ten years old, the youngest barely two.

One evening, the father called them all together. "Children," he said. "In two days, we have enjoyed not even a drop of water, and, out of desperation, I no longer know where to turn."

"Do you know what I think? Tomorrow, I will borrow our neighbor's donkey, and I will place each of you in the basket and take you one by one to be sold. If you have a little luck, you will be sold."

The children began to scream; no, they did not want to be sold. Only the youngest, who was two years old, remained quiet.

"And you, Ranocchino?" asked the father, who had given him this nickname because he was as small as a frog.

"I am content," he responded.

And in the morning, the poor chap put him on his shoulder and began to travel around the city.

"Who will buy my Ranocchino? Who will buy my Ranocchino?"

But no one wanted him, a tiny thing like that!

The daughter of the king came to the window.

"What is that man selling?"

"I am selling this little child; who wants him?"

The princess looked him over, grimaced, and slammed the shutters in his face.

"Thank you very much!" said the poor man. And he continued to shout: "Who will buy my Ranocchino? Who will buy my Ranocchino?"

But no one wanted him, a tiny thing like that!

Quel povero diavolo non avea coraggio di tornare a casa, dove gli altri figliuoli lo aspettavano come tant'anime del purgatorio, morti di fame.

Ranocchino intanto gli s'era addormentato addosso.

Allora lui pensò ch'era meglio ammazzarlo, piuttosto che vederlo patire: gli avrebbe ammazzati tutti, quei figliuoli, ad uno ad uno; e cominciava da questo!

Era già sera: e, uscito fuor di città, si ridusse in una grotta, dove non poteva esser veduto da nessuno. Adagiò per terra il bimbo che dormiva tranquillamente, e prima d'ammazzarlo si mise a piangerlo:

- Ah, coricino mio!

-E debbo ammazzarti con queste mani, debbo ammazzarti!

-Ah, Ranocchino mio!

- E non ti vedrò più per la casa, non ti vedrò!

- Ah, coricino mio!

- E chi fu la strega che te lo cantò in culla, chi fu?

- Ah, Ranocchino mio!

- E debbo ammazzarti con queste mani, debbo ammazzarti!

Spezzava il cuore perfino ai sassi.

- Che cosa è stato, che piangi così?

Il povero diavolo si voltò e vide una vecchia seduta a traverso la bocca della grotta, con un bastoncello in mano.

- Che cosa è stato! Ho sette figliuoli piccini e moriamo tutti di fame. Per non vederli più patire, ho deliberato d'ammazzarli; e comincio da questo.

- Come si chiama?

- Si chiama Beppe; ma noi gli diciamo Ranocchino.

- E Ranocchino sia!

La vecchia toccava appena il bimbo col bastoncello, che quegli era già diventato un ranocchio e saltellava qua e là.

The poor man did not have the courage to return home, where the other children waited for him like souls in Purgatory, dying of hunger.

Meanwhile, Ranocchino fell asleep in his arms.

Therefore, he thought it was better to kill the child rather than to see him suffer. He would kill all of his children, one by one, and he would start with this one!

Evening had already fallen, and after leaving the city, he ended up in a cave, where he could not be seen by anyone. He slowly lowered the peacefully sleeping child to the ground, and before killing him, he began to cry.

"Oh, sweet little heart of mine!"

"Must I kill you with these very hands, must I kill you?"

"Oh, my Ranocchino!" Will I never see you again around the house? Never again?"

"Oh sweet little heart of mine!"

"Who was the witch who cast a spell on you in the cradle?"

"Who was it? Ah, my Ranocchino!"

"Must I kill you with these very hands, must I kill you?"

Even a heart of stone would have broken.

"What has happened, why do you weep so?"

The poor man turned around and saw an old woman sitting in front of the mouth of the cave with a small club in her hand.

"'What has happened,' you ask? I have seven small children, and they are all dying of hunger. Not to see them suffer any longer, I have decided to kill them; I will begin with this one."

"What is his name?"

"His name is Beppe, but we call him Ranocchino (little frog)."

"And a little frog he is."

The old woman only lightly touched the child with the little club, and he actually became a little frog, jumping here and there.

Il povero padre rimase spaventato.
- Fatti coraggio! - gli disse la vecchia.
- Fruga in quel canto; c'è del pane e del formaggio:
mangerete per questa sera. Domani a mezzogiorno, aspettami
sotto le finestre del palazzo reale: sarà la tua fortuna.
Quando i figliuoli lo videro tornare senza il fratellino, si
misero a strillare.
- Zitti! Ecco del pane e del formaggio.
- Ma Ranocchino dov'è?
- È morto!
Disse così per non esser seccato.
E il giorno appresso, prima dell'ora fissata, andava ad
appostarsi sotto le finestre del palazzo reale. Aspetta, aspetta,
la vecchia non compariva. La figlia del Re era a una finestra,
che si pettinava. Lo riconobbe e gli domandò, per canzonatura:
- O quell'uomo, e Ranocchino ve l'han comprato?
Ma prima che quello rispondesse, ecco la vecchia con una
coda di gente dietro. La gente fece crocchio e la vecchia, nel
mezzo, diceva:
- Ranocchino, porgi il ditino!
E Ranocchino stendeva la zampina e porgeva il ditino alla
vecchia. Gli altri avevano un bel dirgli:
- Ranocchino, porgi il ditino -; non se ne dava per inteso.
Una meraviglia non mai vista. E tutti pagavano un soldo.
La Reginotta fece chiamar la vecchia sotto la finestra;
voleva veder anche lei.
- Ranocchino, porgi il ditino!
Rimase ammaliata. E corse subito dal Re.
- Babbo, se mi vuoi bene, devi comprarmi quel Ranocchino.
- Che vorresti tu farne?
- Allevarlo nelle mie stanze: mi divertirò.

The poor father became frightened.

"Courage!" said the old woman. "Search in that corner; there you will find bread and cheese that you can eat this evening. Tomorrow at noon, wait for me under the windows of the royal palace, and good luck will be yours."

When the children saw him return without their brother, they began to scream.

"Quiet! Here is some bread and cheese."

"But where is Ranocchino?" asked the children.

"He is dead."

He said this only so that they would not trouble him.

The next day, before the appointed hour, he stationed himself under the windows of the royal palace. He waited and waited, but the old woman did not appear. The daughter of the king was at one of the windows, combing her hair. She recognized him and asked sarcastically:

"You there, has anyone bought Ranocchino?"

But before he answered, the old woman appeared with a line of people behind her. The people gathered around, and the old woman, in the middle, said:

"Ranocchino, point!"

And Ranocchino stretched out his hand and pointed at the old woman. The others could say what they liked, but when they asked him to stick out his finger, he paid no attention. It was a wonder to see, for which each of the spectators paid a penny.

The princess had the old woman summoned under the window; she too wanted to see.

"Ranocchino, point!"

The princess was fascinated and immediately ran to the king.

"Father, if you love me, you will buy me that Ranocchino."

"What do you want to do with him?"

"I want to raise him in my room; I will enjoy it."

Il Re acconsentì.

- Buona donna, quanto volete di quel Ranocchino?

- Maestà, lo vendo a peso d'oro. È quel che vale.

- Voi canzonate, vecchia mia.

- Dico davvero. Domani varrà il doppio.

- Ranocchino, porgi il ditino!

E Ranocchino stendeva la zampina e porgeva il ditino alla vecchia. Gli altri avevano un bel dirgli:

- Ranocchino, porgi il ditino -; non se ne dava per inteso.

- Vedi?- disse il Re alla Reginotta.

- Occorre anche la vecchia.

La Reginotta non s'era provata.

- Ranocchino, porgi il ditino!

Ranocchino spiccò un salto, le fece una bella riverenza e le porse il ditino.

Allora bisognò comprarlo: se no, la Reginotta non si chetava.

Posero Ranocchino in un piatto della bilancia e un pezzettino 'oro nell'altro, ma la bilancia non lo levava. Possibile che quel Ranocchino pesasse tanto? Colmarono d'oro il piatto ma la bilancia non lo levava. La Reginotta e la Regina si tolsero gli orecchini, gli anelli, i braccialetti e li buttarono lì. Nulla! Il Re si tolse la cintura, ch'era d'oro massiccio, e la buttò lì. Nulla!

- Anche la corona! Vorrei ora vedere!...

Allora la bilancia levò esatta; non mancava un pelo.

La vecchia si rovesciò quel mucchio d'oro nel grembiule e andò via.

Quel povero diavolo l'attendeva all'uscita.

- Tieni!

E gli riempì le tasche.

- Però bada! Spendi tutto a tuo piacere; ma la corona reale, se tu la vendi o la perdi, guai a te!

The king agreed.

"Good woman, how much do you want for that little frog?"

"Majesty, I'll sell him for his weight in gold."

"You're joking, my dear old lady."

"I'm telling the truth. Tomorrow, he will be worth double."

"Ranocchino, stick out your finger!"

And Ranocchino stretched out his hand and pointed at the old woman. The others could say what they liked, but when they asked him to stick out his finger, he paid no attention.

"Do you see?" said the king to the princess. "It is necessary to have the old woman as well."

But the princess was not satisfied.

"Ranocchino, stick out your finger!"

Ranocchino leaped into the air, bowed to the princess, and pointed his finger at her.

Therefore, the king had to buy Ranocchino; otherwise the princess would not quiet down.

They placed Ranocchino on one side of the scale and a small piece of gold on the other, but the scale did not move. Was it possible that Ranocchino weighed so much? Even when it was loaded with gold, the scale did not move. The princess and the queen took off their ear rings, rings, and bracelets, and they put them on the scale too. Nothing! The king took off his belt of solid gold, and he placed it on the scale. Nothing!

"Now I would also like to see the crown," said the old woman.

And so the scale balanced exactly, not a hair less.

The old woman slid the stack of gold into her apron and left.

That poor old man was waiting for her at the exit.

"Take this!"

And she filled his pockets.

"However, beware! Spend what you like, but don't sell or lose the royal crown, or woe to you!"

La Reginotta si spassava, tutto il giorno, con Ranocchino.

- Ranocchino, porgi il ditino!

Era una bellezza. Lo teneva sempre in mano, lo portava seco dovunque. A tavola, Ranocchino dovea mangiare nel piatto di lei.

- Una cosa sconcia! - diceva la Regina.

Ma quella era figlia unica, e le perdonavano tutti i capricci.

Arrivò il tempo che la Reginotta dovea andare a marito. L'avea chiesta il Reuccio del Portogallo, e il Re e la Regina n'eran contentissimi. Lei disse di no:

Voleva sposare Ranocchino!

Poteva darsi? Intanto non c'era verso di persuaderla.

- O Ranocchino, o nessuno!

- Te lo do io Ranocchino!

E il Re, afferratolo per una gambetta, stava per sbatacchiarlo sul pavimento; ma entrò un'aquila dalla finestra che glielo strappò di mano e sparì.

La Reginotta piangeva giorno e notte. Povera figliuola, faceva pena! E tutta la corte stava in lutto.

Intanto in casa di Ranocchino pareva tutti i giorni carnovale. Spendi e spandi; mezzo vicinato banchettava lì e i danari andavano via a fiumi. Finalmente non ci fu più il becco d'un quattrino.

- Babbo, vendiamo la corona reale.

- La corona reale non si tocca!

- Si dee crepar di fame? Vendiamola!

- La corona reale non si tocca.

Quel povero diavolo tornò nella grotta in cerca della vecchia, e si mise a piangere.

- Che cosa è stato?

- Mammina mia, i quattrini son finiti e quei figliuoli vorrebbero vendere la corona reale; ma io non l'ho permesso.

The princess enjoyed herself all day long with Ranocchino.
"Ranocchino, stick out your finger."

It was a wonder. She held him in her hand at all times wherever she went. At table, Ranocchino had to eat from her plate.

"This is indecent!" said the queen.

However, the princess was an only child, and they forgave
all her whims.

There came the time when the princess would have to take a
husband. The prince of Portugal had asked for her hand, but the
king and queen were not very happy, for she said no. She
wanted to marry Ranocchino!

How could she marry him? But there was no way to persuade her otherwise.

"Either Ranocchino, or no one!"

"I'll give you Ranocchino!" exclaimed the king.

And grabbing him by one leg, he was about to smash him on
the ground; however, an eagle suddenly appeared at the window, ripped him from the king's hand, and flew away.

The princess cried day and night. Poor girl; it was heart-
breaking. And the entire court was in mourning.

Meanwhile, at Ranocchino's home, each day seemed like a
carnival. Half the neighborhood feasted there, and the money
flowed like a river. At the end, not even a penny was left.

"Father, let's sell the royal crown."

"The crown cannot be touched!"

"Should we die of hunger, then? Let's sell it!"

The father's answer was the same: "The crown cannot be
touched."

The poor man then returned to the cave in search of the old
woman, and he began to cry.

"What has happened?" she asked.

"Oh my, all the money is gone, and my children want to sell
the royal crown; however, I won't permit it."

*- Fruga in quel canto. C'è del pane e del formaggio;
mangerete per questa sera. Domani a mezzogiorno, aspettami
sotto le finestre del palazzo reale: sarà la tua fortuna.*

*Tornò a casa, e trovò una tragedia! Cinque figliuoli erano
stesi morti per terra in un lago di sangue; uno respirava
appena:*

*- Ah, babbo mio! È venuta un'aquila forte e picchiò alla
finestra. "Ragazzi, fatemi vedere la corona reale." "Il babbo la
tiene sotto chiave." "E dove l'ha riposta?" "In questa cassa."
Allora, a colpi di becco, cominciò a scassinarla; e siccome noi
ci si opponeva, ci ha tutti ammazzati.*

Detto questo, spirò.

*Quel povero diavolo si sentì rizzare i capelli. I figliuoli morti
e la corona sparita!*

*Il giorno dopo, quando vide la vecchia, le raccontò ogni
cosa.*

- Lascia fare a me! - rispose quella.

*La Reginotta stava malissimo. I medici non sapevano più
quali rimedi adoprare.*

*- Maestà, - dissero, all'ultimo - qui ci vuol Ranocchino, o la
Reginotta è spacciata.*

Il Re si disperava:

*- Dove prenderlo quel maledetto Ranocchino? L'aquila lo
aveva già digerito da un pezzo.*

Si presentò la vecchia:

*- Maestà, Ranocchino ve lo farei trovare io; ma ci vuole un
gran coraggio.*

- Mi lascerei anche fare a pezzi, rispose il Re.

*- Prendete un coltello di diamante, il più bel bue della
mandria, una corda lunga un miglio, e venite con me.*

*Il Re prese il coltello di diamante, il più bel bue della
mandria, una corda lunga un miglio, e partì insieme colla
vecchia. Nessuno dovea seguirli.*

"Search in that corner. There you will find bread and cheese; eat it this evening. Tomorrow at noon, wait for me under the window of the royal palace; good luck will be yours."

He returned home, and found a tragedy! Five of his children were lying dead on the ground in a pool of blood; one was just breathing:

"Oh, father! A large eagle came and tapped at the window. 'Children, let me see the royal crown,' he demanded. 'Our father has it locked up,' we answered. 'And where has he put it?' 'In this chest,' we told him. So, he began to break it open with his beak, but because we tried to stop him, he killed us all."

Having said that, the child died.

The poor man was beside himself with grief. His children dead and the crown gone!

The next day, when he saw the old woman, he told her everything.

"Leave everything to me!" she answered.

The princess was not well. The doctors didn't know what remedies to use.

"Majesty," they said at last, "you need to find Ranocchino, or the princess is done for!"

The king despaired.

"How can I get this cursed Ranocchino?" The eagle had swallowed him in one piece.

The old woman appeared and said:

"Majesty, I will help you find Ranocchino, but you need to have great courage."

"Let me tear him to shreds," responded the king.

"Take a diamond knife, the best ox of your herd, and a rope a mile long, and come with me."

The king took a diamond knife, the best ox of his herd, a rope a mile long, and he went with the old woman. No one was to follow them.

Camminarono due giorni, e al terzo, verso il tramonto, giunsero in una pianura. Lì c'era la torre incantata, senza porte e senza finestre, alta un miglio.

- Ranocchino è qui! - disse la vecchia. - Quegli uccellacci che aliano attorno alla cima, sono i suoi carcerieri. Bisogna montare lassù.

- O come?

- Maestà, ammazzate il bue e vedrete.

Il Re ammazzò il bue.

- Maestà, scorticatelo e lasciate molta carne attaccata al cuoio.

Il Re lo scorticò e lasciò molta carne attorno al cuoio.

- Ora rivolteremo questo cuoio - disse la vecchia.- Io vi ci cucirò dentro. Scenderanno gli uccellacci e vi porteranno lassù. La notte, spaccherete il cuoio col coltello di diamante; e la mattina quando l'aquila e gli uccellacci saranno andati via per la caccia, attaccherete la corda alla cima, prenderete Ranocchino e la corona reale, metterete il coltello fra i denti e vi lascerete andar giù.

Il Re esitava.

- E se la corda si spezzasse?

- Tenendo il coltello fra i denti non si spezzerà.

Il Re, per amor della figliuola, si lasciò cucire dentro il cuoio. E, subito, ecco gli uccellacci di preda che lo afferrano cogli arti gli e se lo portano lassù.

La notte, spaccò il cuoio col coltello di diamante e andò a nascondersi in fondo a uno stanzino. Quando fu giorno, aspettò che l'aquila e gli uccellacci di preda andassero a caccia, attaccò la corda alla cima della torre, prese Ranocchino e la corona reale, e si lasciò andar giù.

E il coltello? L'aveva dimenticato.

Allora la corda cominciò a nicchiare:

- Ahi, ahi! Mi spezzo! Dammi da bere.

They walked for two days; on the third, around sunset, they came upon a plane on which was an enchanted tower, without doors or windows, which was a mile tall.

"Ranocchino is here," said the old woman. "Those large birds that are gliding around the peak are his guards. You must climb up there."

"And how?"

"Majesty, kill the ox, and you will see."

The king killed the ox.

"Majesty, skin the animal, but leave a great deal of meat attached to the hide."

The king skinned the ox and left a great deal of meat attached to the hide.

"Now, let's turn the hide over," said the old woman. "I will sew you into it. The birds will fly down and carry you up. At night, cut open the hide with the diamond knife; and in the morning when the eagle and the other birds are out hunting, tie the rope to the peak, grab Ranocchiono and the royal crown, place the knife between your teeth, and let yourself down."

The king hesitated.

"And what if the rope breaks?"

"If you hold the knife in your teeth, the rope will not break."

Because he loved his daughter so much, he let himself be sown into the hide. And immediately, the birds of prey grabbed him securely and brought him up.

At night, he cut open the hide with the diamond knife and hid himself in the back of a closet. The next day, he waited for the eagle and the birds to leave for the hunt, tied the rope to the peak of the tower, grabbed Ranocchino and the royal crown, and let himself down.

However, he had forgotten the knife.

Suddenly the rope itself became afraid and cried:

"Oh, oh! I am breaking. Give me something to drink."

Come rimediare? Il Re si morse una vena del braccio e ne fece schizzar il sangue. Intanto scivolava giù.

Ma poco dopo la corda da capo:

- Ahi, ahi! Mi spezzo! Dammi da bere.

Il Re si morse la vena dell'altro braccio e ne fece schizzar il sangue. Intanto scivolava giù.

Ma la corda da capo:

- Ahi, ahi! Mi spezzo! Dammi da bere.

Il Re, visto che ci voleva pochino a toccar terra:

- E spezzati! - rispose.

Infatti si spezzò; ma lui, per sua fortuna, se la cavò con qualche ammaccatura. Per le vene ferite delle braccia la vecchia cercò un'erba, e gliele medicò con essa, e gli sanarono a un tratto.

Appena visto Ranocchino, la Reginotta cominciò a riaversi.

- Ranocchino, porgi il ditino!

E Ranocchino porgeva il ditino, e a lei soltanto.

Il Re, per finirla, voleva far subito le nozze. Ma la vecchia gli disse:

- Bisogna aspettare ancora un mese. Intanto fate preparare una caldaia d'olio bollente.

- A che farne?

- Lo saprete poi.

Quando fu il giorno, l'olio bolliva nella caldaia. Venne la vecchia e dietro a lei quel povero diavolo con un carro, su cui erano distesi i cadaveri dei sei figliuoli.

- Reginotta, - disse la vecchia - volete sposare Ranocchino? Bisogna prenderlo per un piede e tuffarlo tre volte in quell'olio.

La Reginotta esitava.

- Tuffami, tuffami! - le disse Ranocchino.

Allora lei lo tuffò. Uno, due! Ma la terza volta le scappa di mano e casca in fondo alla caldaia. La Reginotta si svenne.

What could the king do? He bit a vein in his arm and let blood spurt onto the rope. Meanwhile, he slid down.

But a little later, the rope said again.

"Oh, oh! I am breaking. Give me something to drink." The king bit a vein in his other arm and let blood spurt onto the rope. Meanwhile, he slid down.

But the rope said again.

"Oh, oh! I am breaking. Give me something to drink."

Seeing that he was close to the ground, the king responded: "So break!"

Sure enough, it broke; however, as luck would have it, the king escaped with only a bruise. The old woman treated the wounds in his arms with an herb she found, and in a little while he was healed.

As soon as the princess saw Ranocchino, she began to recover.

"Ranocchino, stick out your finger!"

And Ranocchino pointed, but to her alone.

To end the matter once and for all, the king wanted them to get married quickly. However, the old woman said:

"You need to wait another month. Meanwhile, have your servants prepare a cauldron of boiling oil."

"For what purpose?" asked the king.

"You will find out later."

On the day of the wedding, the oil was boiling in the cauldron. The old woman arrived with the poor father close behind with a cart in which were stretched out his dead children.

"Princess," said the old woman, "do you want to marry Ranocchino? You need to take him by one of his feet and dip him three times into this oil."

The princess hesitated.

"Dip me, dip me!" Ranocchino told her. Therefore, she dipped him into the oil! One, two! However, the third time he slipped from her hand and fell to the bottom of the cauldron.

Il Re voleva far ammazzare la vecchia; ma questa, afferrati in fretta in fretta quei morticini e buttatili nell'olio bollente, cominciò a rimestare col suo bastone, e intanto cantava:
 - Oh, il bel ranno! Oh, il bel ranno!
 Presto fuori salteranno.
 Infatti ecco il figlio maggiore che salta fuori vivo, il primo.
 - Oh, il bel ranno! Oh, il bel ranno!
 Presto fuori salteranno.
 E rimestava. Ed ecco saltar fuori il secondo. Così tutti e sei i fratellini.
 - Oh, il bel ranno! Oh, il bel ranno!
 Presto fuori salteranno.
 E rimestava. Ma Ranocchino venne soltanto a galla e non saltò.
 La Reginotta, appena lo scorse, tentò d'afferrarlo; la vecchia la trattenne.
 - Voleva scottarsi? Doveva fare come al solito.
 - Ranocchino, porgi il ditino!
 Ranocchino porse il ditino alla Reginotta..., e chi uscì fuori? Un bel giovane che pareva un Sole. La Reginotta lo riconobbe pel bimbo che quel povero diavolo volea vendere, e gli domandò scusa d'avergli sbatacchiato le impòste sul viso. Ranocchino, si capisce, le aveva già perdonato.
 Si fecer le nozze con magnifiche feste, e Ranocchino, a suo tempo, ebbe la corona reale.

Chi la vuol cruda, chi la vuol cotta;
Chi non gli piace, me la riporti.

The princess fainted.

The king wanted to have the old woman killed; however, she quickly took hold of the corpses, threw them into the boiling oil, began stirring with her club, and meanwhile began to sing:

"Oh beautiful frog! Beautiful frog! Jump out quickly."

Sure enough, it was the oldest son who jumped out alive, the first born.

"Oh beautiful frog! Beautiful frog! Jump out quickly."

And she continued to stir the cauldron. Then the second child jumped out, and all of the other children followed.

"Oh beautiful frog! Beautiful frog! Jump out quickly!"

And she continued to stir the cauldron. However, Ranocchino only floated to the top and did not jump out.

As soon as she saw him, the princess tried to grab him, but the old woman stopped her.

"Do you want to burn yourself? Do as you did before." And she did:

"Ranocchino, stick out your finger!"

Ranocchino pointed his finger at the princess….But who came out? A handsome young man who looked like the sun. The princess recognized him as the child whom the poor chap had wanted to sell, and she asked him to forgive her for slamming the shutters in his face. But it was clear that Ranocchino had already forgiven her.

They celebrated their wedding with a magnificent feast, and Ranocchino, in time, became king.

Some like their food cooked, some straight from the tree.
If you don't like this story, return it to me.

Senza orecchie

C'era una volta un Re che avea una bimba.

La Regina era morta di parto, e il Re avea preso una balia che gli allattasse la piccina.

Un giorno la balia scese, insieme colla bimba, nel giardino reale. La bimba avea tre anni, e si divertiva a fare chiasso sull'erba, all'ombra dei grandi alberi. Sull'ora di mezzogiorno la balia s'addormentava; ma quando si svegliò, non trovò più la Reginotta. Cerca, chiama per tutto il giardino; nulla! La bimba era scomparsa.

Come presentarsi al Re, che andava matto per quella figliuola?

La povera balia si picchiava il petto, si strappava i capelli:

- Dio! Dio! Sua Maestà l'avrebbe fatta impiccare!

Agli urli della balia erano accorse le guardie.

Fruga e rifruga, tutto fu inutile.

Venne l'ora del pranzo.

- E la Reginotta? - domandò il Re.

I ministri si guardarono in faccia, più bianchi di un panno lavato.

- La Reginotta dov'è?

- Maestà, - disse un ministro - è accaduta una disgrazia!

Il Re pareva fuori di sé dal gran dolore. Fece subito un bando:

- Chi riporta la Reginotta, gli si concede qualunque grazia.

Ma eran già passati sei mesi, e al palazzo reale non s'era visto nessuno.

I banditori andavano di regno in regno:

- Sia cristiano, sia infedele, chi riporta la Reginotta, gli vien concessa qualunque grazia.

Ma passò un anno, e al palazzo reale non si presentò nessuno.

No Ears

Once upon a time there was a king who had a little daughter.

The queen had died in childbirth, and the king had gotten a wet nurse to feed the baby.

One day, the nurse came down to the royal garden with the baby. The child was three years old, and she enjoyed herself by playing on the grass in the shadow of the large trees. At about noon, the nurse fell asleep; however, when she woke up, the princess was gone. She searched and called for her all over the garden, but she did not find her. The child had disappeared.

How was she to tell the king, who was mad about his daughter?

The poor nurse beat her breast and pulled out her hair.

"Lord! Lord!" His majesty would have her hanged!

Upon hearing the nurse's screams, the guards rushed in. They searched and searched, but to no avail.

At lunchtime, the king asked: "Where is the princess?"

The ministers looked at each other, their faces whiter than a sheet.

"Where is the princess?"

"Majesty," said one minister, "a tragedy has occurred."

The king seemed to be beside himself with pain. Quickly, he issued a proclamation.

"Whoever brings back the princess will be granted whatever he wishes."

However, after six months, there was no news of the princess.

A proclamation was brought from realm to realm:

"Whether Christian or infidel, whoever brings back the princess will be granted whatever he wishes."

But a year passed and still no one came to the royal palace.

Il Re era inconsolabile: piangeva giorno e notte.

Nel giardino reale c'era un pozzo. La Reginotta, mentre la balia dormiva, s'era accostata all'orlo e vi si era affacciata.

Vedendo, laggiù, nello specchio dell'acqua, un'altra bimba sua pari, l'avea chiamata: - Ehi! Ehi!-accennando colle manine. Allora era sorto dal fondo del pozzo un braccio lungo lungo, peloso peloso, che l'afferrò e la tirò giù. E così, da parecchi anni, lei viveva in fondo a quel pozzo, col Lupo Mannaro che l'aveva tirata giù.

In fondo al pozzo c'era una grotta grande dieci volte più del palazzo reale. Stanze tutte oro e diamanti, una più bella e più ricca dell'altra. È vero che non ci penetrava mai sole, ma ci si vedeva lo stesso. La bimba veniva servita da quella Reginotta che era. Una cameriera per spogliarla, una per vestirla, una per lavarla, una per pettinarla, una per recarle la colazione, una per servirla a pranzo, una per metterla a letto. S'era già abituata e non ci viveva di cattivo umore.

Il Lupo Mannaro russava tutto il santo giorno e la notte andava via. Siccome la bimba, quando lo vedeva, strillava dalla paura, si facea veder di rado: non volea spaventarla.

Intanto la Reginotta s'era fatta una bella ragazza.

Una sera, entrata in letto, non poteva dormire. Sentito che il Lupo Mannaro si preparava ad andar via, tese meglio l'orecchio. Il LupoMannaro con quella sua vociaccia ròca, urlava:

- Chiamatemi il cuoco.

Il cuoco venne.

- Credo che siamo in punto, - gli disse - mi pare una quaglia.

- Bisogna vedere - rispose il cuoco.

La Reginotta sentì che giravano adagino il pomo della serratura:

Ahimè! Dunque si trattava di lei? Il Lupo Mannaro voleva mangiarsela.

The king was inconsolable; he cried day and night.

In the royal garden, there was a well. While the nurse was asleep, the princess had come near the edge and looked into it.

She saw down there, in the water's reflection, what appeared to be another little girl, and she called to her, "Hey! Hey!" as she waved to her with her little hands. Now, from the bottom of the well there arose a very long, very hairy arm that grabbed her and pulled her down. And in this way, for quite a few years, she lived in the bottom of that well, with the werewolf who had pulled her down.

At the bottom of the well, there was a cave ten times larger than the royal palace, with rooms made of gold and diamonds, one more opulent than the next. And, while no sunshine ever came into the cave, one could see in it all the same. The little girl was waited on as the princess that she was. There was a chambermaid to undress her, one to dress her, one to bathe her, one to comb her hair, one to bring her breakfast, one to serve her lunch, and one to put her to bed. Soon she got used to it, and she did not mind living that way.

The werewolf snored every day, and at night he went out. The child screamed with fear every time she saw him, so he seldom showed himself to her; he did not wish to frighten her.

Meanwhile, she grew into a beautiful young girl.

One evening when she went to bed, she could not sleep. Hearing that the werewolf was preparing to leave, she listened carefully. With his husky voice, the werewolf shouted:

"Call the cook."

The cook came.

I believe the time has come," he said, "she looks as tasty as a quail."

"I need to see for myself," said the cook.

The princess heard them gently turn the door knob.

Alas! So, what did he want of her? He wanted to eat her!

*Le si accapponò la pelle, sfido io! Si fece piccina piccina, e
finse di dormire. Il Lupo Mannaro s'accostava al letto,
svoltava le coperte con cautela, e il cuoco cominciava a
tastarla tutta, come gallina da tirargli il collo.*
*- Ancora una settimana, - disse il cuoco - e sarà un boccone
reale.*
Come intese queste parole, la Reginotta si sentì rinascere:
*- Otto giorni! Oh, quella quaglia il Lupo Mannaro non
l'avrebbe mangiata; no, no!*
*Pensa e ripensa, le venne un'idea. La mattina, saltata giù
dal letto, appostossi alla bocca della grotta, dentro il collo del
pozzo, ed aspettò che venisse gente ad attinger acqua. La
carrucola stride, la secchia fa un tonfo, ed ecco la Reginotta
che s'afferra alla corda, puntando i piedini sull'orlo della
secchia. La tiravano su lentamente; era un po' pesa. A un
tratto la corda si rompe, e secchia e Reginotta, patatunfete,
giù!*
Accorsero le cameriere e la ritirarono dall'acqua.
*- Ebbi un capogiro e cascai. Non ne fate motto, per carità; il
Lupo Mannaro mi picchierebbe.*
E passò un giorno.
*Il secondo giorno, aspetta aspetta, la secchia non venne giù.
Bisognava trovare un altro mezzo: ma non era come dirlo.
Quale? La grotta non aveva che quell'unica uscita.*
E passò un altro giorno.
*La Reginotta non si perdette d'animo. Appena aggiornava,
era al suo posto; ma la secchia non calava.*
E passarono altri due giorni.
*Una mattina, mentre lei piangeva dirottamente, guardando
fisso nell'acqua vide lì un pesciolino rosso, che parea d'oro,
colla coda bianca come l'argento, e con tre macchie nere sulla
schiena.*
*- Ah! Pesciolino, tu sei felice! Tu sei libero in mezzo
all'acqua, ed io qui sola, senza parenti né amici!*

She covered herself, and no wonder! She rolled herself into a little ball and pretended to sleep. The werewolf drew near to the bed, pulled back the covers carefully, and the cook began to touch her all over, just as he might wring the neck of a hen.

"Wait another week," said the cook "and she will make a snack fit for a king."

When she heard these last words, the princess felt revived.

"Eight days! The werewolf would never eat this quail; no, no!"

She thought and thought, and then she got an idea. In the morning, hopping out of bed, she hid at the mouth of the cave, inside the well, and she waited for people to come and draw water. The pulley screeched, the bucket made a thud, and the princess grabbed the rope, placing her feet on the rim of the bucket. They pulled her up slowly, for she was a bit heavy. At one point, the rope broke, and both the bucket and the princes fell down like a load of potatoes.

The servants came quickly and took her out of the water.

But she felt dizzy and she fell down. "Please, don't say a word. The werewolf will beat me."

And a day passed.

The second day, she waited and waited, but the bucket did not come down. She needed to find another way; but that was easier said than done. The cave had only one exit.

And another day passed.

The princess did not lose heart. As soon as morning came, she was at her place; but the bucket did not come down.

And another two days went by.

One morning, while she was crying distractedly and staring at the water, she saw a little red minnow, which looked as if he were made of gold, with a tail as white as silver, and with three black spots on his back.

"Oh minnow, you are happy, "said the princess. "You are free to swim in the middle of the water, and I am here alone without family or friends."

Il pesciolino montava a fior d'acqua, dimenando la coda, aprendo e chiudendo la bocca; pareva l'avesse sentita:

- Ah! Pesciolino, tu sei felice! Tu sei libero in mezzo all'acqua, ed io qui sola, senza parenti né amici. Fra quattro giorni sarò mangiata!

Il pesciolino rosso, dalla coda bianca e dalle tre macchie nere sulla schiena, s'era accostato alla sponda:

- Se tu fossi di sangue reale e volessi sposarmi, saremmo liberi tutti e due. Per vincere il mio incanto non ci vuol altro.

- Son sangue reale, pesciolino d'oro, e son tua sposa fino da questo momento.

- Cavalcami sulla schiena e tieni forte.

La Reginotta si mise a cavalcioni del pesciolino e gli si afferrò alle branchie; e il pesciolino, nuota, nuota, la portò in fondo al pozzo. Di lì passava un fiume, sotto terra. Il pesciolino infilò diritto la corrente e la Reginotta gli si tenne sempre ben afferrata alle branchie.

Ma ecco, in un punto, un pesce grossissimo, con tanto di bocca spalancata, che voleva ingoiarli:

- Pagate il pedaggio, o di qui non si passa.

La Reginotta si strappò un'orecchia e gliela buttò. Nuota, nuota, ecco un altro pesce più grosso del primo, con tanto di bocca spalancata e una foresta di denti:

- Pagate il pedaggio, o di qui non si passa.

La Reginotta si strappava l'altra orecchia e gliela buttava.

Quando la corrente sboccò all'aria aperta, il pesciolino depose la Reginotta sulla sponda e diè un salto fuor dell'acqua. Era diventato un bel giovane, con tre piccoli nèi sulla faccia. Lei disse:

- Andiamo a presentarci al Re mio padre. Son tredici anni che non mi vede.

Al portone del palazzo reale non volevano lasciarla passare.

- Sono la Reginotta! Son la figliuola del Re!

The minnow rose to just below the surface of the water, wagged his tail, opened and closed his mouth; he seemed to have heard her.

"Oh minnow, you are happy!" said the princes. "You are free to swim in the middle of the water, and I am here alone without family or friends. Within four days, I will be eaten."

The red minnow with the white tail and the three black marks on his back neared the side of the well.

"If you are of royal blood and wish to marry me, we will be free. To break the spell I am under, nothing else will do."

"I am of royal blood, golden minnow, and from this moment I am your wife."

"Ride on my back and hold on tightly."

The princess got on the minnow and held onto his gills; the minnow, swam and swam, and brought her to the bottom of the well. An underground river passed through it. The minnow slipped into the current with the princess holding on tightly.

However, at one point, there appeared a very large fish that wanted to swallow them with his mouth wide open.

"Pay the toll, or you cannot pass," he said

The princess tore off one of her ears and threw it to him. She swam and swam; there appeared another fish even larger than the first, his mouth wide open showing a forest of teeth.

"Pay the toll, or you cannot pass," he said.

The princess tore off her other ear, and she tossed it to him. When the river emerged into the open air, the minnow put the princess down onto the bank and jumped out of the water. He had become a handsome young man with three small black spots on his face. She told him:

"Let's go meet the king, my father. It has been thirteen years since he saw me."

However, at the entrance to the royal palace, they would not let her pass.

"I am the princess! I am the daughter of the king!"

Non ci credeva nessuno, nemmeno il Re. Pure ordinò di fargliela venire dinanzi:

- Chi sa? Poteva anche darsi!

Il Re la guardò da capo a piedi: gli pareva e non gli pareva. Lei gli raccontò la sua storia; ma non disse nulla delle orecchie, per vergogna. Infatti nascondeva il suo difetto, tenendo
basse le trecce.

Ma un ministro se n'accorse:

- E le orecchie, figliuola mia? Dove le perdeste le orecchie?

Il Re, indignato, la condannava a rigovernare i piatti e le stoviglie della cucina reale. Il principe Pesciolino (lo chiamarono subito così) fu dannato a spazzar le stalle:

- Imparassero in tal modo a farsi beffa del Re!

Un giorno Sua Maestà volea mangiare del pesce. Ma in tutto il mercato c'era due pesci soltanto, e nessuno sapeva che razza di pesci si fossero, neppure i pesciaioli. Ed erano lì dal giorno avanti, e cominciavano a passare. Ma il Re volea del pesce ad ogni costo, e il cuoco li comprò:

- Maestà, non c'è che questi; nessuno sa che pesci siano, neppure i pesciaioli. Trovansi in mercato da due giorni e cominciano a passare.

- Sta bene, - disse il Re - portali in cucina.

In cucina il cuoco fa per sventrarli, e che gli trova nelle budella? Due orecchie di creatura umana, ancor stillanti sangue!

Chiamarono subito Senza-orecchie, come le aven messo il nomignolo:

- Senza-orecchie, Senza-orecchie, ecco roba per te!

No one believed her, not even the king. Yet, he ordered that she be brought before him:

"Who knows? It still might be true!"

The king looked her over from head to toe; it appeared to be her, and it didn't appear to be her. She told him her story; however, she said nothing of the ears, because she was ashamed.

As a matter of fact, she had concealed her defect by keeping her hair down.

However, one of the ministers noticed:

"And your ears, my child? Where did you lose your ears?"

Indignant, the king sentenced her to wash the dishes and the tableware in the kitchen of the royal palace. Prince Minnow (they immediately gave him that nickname) was ordered to clean the stables.

"That will teach them to play a joke on the king!"

One day, his majesty wanted to eat fish. However, in the entire market there were only two fish, and no one knew what type of fish they were, not even the fishermen. They had been there since the day before, and they had begun to go bad. However, the king wanted fish at all costs, and the cook bought them.

"Majesty, there are no others but these, and no one knows what kinds of fish they are, not even the fishermen. They have been in the market for two days, and they have begun to go bad.

"That is all right," said the king. "Bring them into the kitchen."

In the kitchen, the cook tried to clean the fish. But what did he find in their guts? Two human ears, still dripping blood!

Immediately, they called "No Ears," as they had nicknamed her.

"No Ears, No Ears, here is something for you."

La Reginotta accorse: eran davvero le sue orecchie.
Tremante dalla contentezza se le adattò al capo e le si
appiccicarono; il sangue avea servito da colla.
Colle orecchie, il Re suo padre raffigurolla ad un tratto:
- È lei! È la mia figliuola!
E bandì feste reali per otto giorni. Poi, siccome era vecchio,
volle lasciare il regno. E il re Pesciolino e la regina Senza-
orecchie regnarono a lungo dopo di lui.

Stretta la foglia, e larga la via,
Dite la vostra, ché ho detto la mia.

The princess ran in. They were truly her ears. Shaking with happiness, she fitted them onto her head and attached them; the blood served as a glue.

With her ears on, the king, her father, recognized her immediately.

"It is she. It is my daughter!"

And he announced a royal feast that was to last eight days. Then since he was old, he wanted to give up the throne.

So, King Minnow and Queen No-Ears ruled long after him.

The journey is long and the path is narrow.
I've told my story; tell yours tomorrow.

Il lupo mannaro

C'era una volta un Re e una Regina che non avevan figliuoli e pregavano i santi, giorno e notte, per ottenerne almeno uno. Intanto consultavano anche i dottori di Corte.

- Maestà, fate questo.

- Maestà, fate quello.

E pillole di qua, e beveroni di là; ma il sospirato figliuolo non arrivava a spuntare.

Una bella giornata ch'era freddino, la Regina s'era messa davanti il palazzo reale per riscaldarsi al sole. Passa una vecchiarella:

- Fate la carità!

Quella per la noia di cavar le mani di tasca rispose:

- Non ho nulla.

La vecchiarella andò via brontolando.

- Che cosa ha brontolato? - domandò la Regina.

- Maestà, ha detto che un giorno avrete bisogno di lei.

La Regina le fece correre una persona dietro, per richiamarla; ma la vecchiarella aveva svoltato cantonata ed era sparita.

Otto giorni dopo, si presentava un forestiero, chiedeva di parlare in segreto col Re:

-Maestà, ho il rimedio per guarir la Regina. Ma prima facciamo i. patti.

- Oh, bravo! Facciamo i patti.

- Se nascerà un maschio, lo terrete per voi.

- E se una femmina?

- Se una femmina quando avrà compiti i sette anni, dovrete condurla in cima a quella montagna e abbandonarla lassù: non ne saprete più nuova.

The Werewolf

Once upon a time there were a king and queen who had no children, and they prayed to the saints day and night to have at least one. Meanwhile, they consulted with the court doctors.

"Majesty, do this."

"Majesty, do that."

They took these pills and drank those potions, but the longed-for child never arrived.

One beautiful day when it was a bit chilly, the queen went out in front of the royal palace to warm herself in the sun. Before her passed an old woman.

"Give me some money, for pity's sake!

Annoyed, the queen put her hands in her pockets and answered:

"I don't have any."

The old woman went on her way grumbling.

"What was she grumbling about?" asked the queen.

"Majesty, she said that someday you will have need of her."

The queen ordered someone to run after her, to call her back; however, the old woman had turned the corner and disappeared.

Eight days later, there appeared a stranger who wished to speak with the king in private.

"Majesty, I have a way to enable the queen to have a baby. But first we need to make a pact."

"Wonderful," said the king, "let's make a pact."

"If a boy is born, you will keep him."

"And if it is a girl?"

"If it is a girl, when she reaches seven years of age, you must bring her to the peak of that mountain and abandon her up there. You will not hear from her again."

- Consulterò la Regina.
- Vuol dire che non ne farete nulla.
Stretto fra l'uscio e il muro, il Re accettò. Il forestiero cavò di tasca una boccettina, che gli spariva fra le dita e disse:
- Ecco il rimedio. Questa notte, appena la Regina sarà addormentata, Vostra Maestà glielo versi tutto intero in un orecchio. Basterà.
Infatti, dopo nove mesi, la Regina partorì e fece una bella bambina. A questa notizia il Re diede in uno scoppio di pianto:
- Povera figliolina, che mala sorte! Che mala sorte!
La Regina lo seppe:
- Maestà, perché avete pianto: Povera figliolina, che mala sorte?
- Non ne fate caso.
La Reginotta cresceva più bella del sole: il Re e la Regina n'erano matti. Quando entrò nei sette anni, il povero padre non sapeva darsi pace, pensando che presto doveva condurla in cima a quella montagna, abbandonarla lassù e non averne più nuove! Ma il patto era questo: bisognava osservarlo.
Il giorno che la Reginotta compì i sette anni, il Re disse alla Regina:
- Vo in campagna colla bimba; torneremo verso sera.
Cammina, cammina, giunsero a piè della montagna e cominciarono a salire. La Reginotta non potea arrampicarsi, e il Re se la tolse in collo.
- Babbo, che andiamo a fare lassù? Torniamo indietro.
Il Re non rispondeva, e si bevea le lagrime che gli rigavano la faccia.
- Babbo, che andiamo a fare lassù? Torniamo indietro.
Il Re non rispondeva, e si bevea le lagrime che gli rigavano la faccia.
- Babbo, che siam venuti a fare quassù? Torniamo indietro.

"I will discuss this with the queen," said the king.

"I guess that there is nothing else to do," said the queen

Having no other choice, the king agreed. The stranger took from his pocket a tiny bottle that he had hid in his fingers and said:

"Here is the cure. Tonight as soon as the queen is asleep, your majesty must pour all of its contents into her ear."

That's all that was needed. Sure enough, after nine months, the queen gave birth to a beautiful baby girl. At the news, the king burst into tears.

"My poor little daughter, what bad luck! What bad luck!"

"Majesty," asked his courtiers, "why are you crying 'My poor little daughter, what bad luck'?" But the queen knew why.

"This is no coincidence," said the king.

The princess grew up more beautiful than the sun, but the king and the queen were beside themselves. When the child reached the age of seven, the poor father did not know where to turn, knowing that they would soon have to bring her to the top of the mountain and to abandon her up there, never to hear from her again. But such was the pact: he had to honor it.

The day that the princess completed her seventh year, the king said to the queen: "I am going into the country with the child; we'll be back around evening."

After walking for some time, they came to the foot of the mountain, and they started to climb. The princess could not climb, so the king carried her on his shoulders.

"Daddy, why are we going up there? Let's go back."

The king did not respond, as tears streamed down his face.

"Daddy, why are we going up there? Let's go back."

The king did not respond, as tears streamed down his face.

"Daddy, why have we come up here? Let's go back."

- Siediti qui; aspetta un momento.

E l'abbandonò alla sua sorte.

Vedendolo tornar solo, la Regina cominciò a urlare:

- E la figliuola? E la figliuola?

- Calò giù un'aquila, l'afferrò cogli artigli e la portò via.

- Ah, figliuola mia! Non è vero!

- Le sbucò addosso un animale feroce e andò a divorarsela nel bosco.

- Ah, figliolina mia! Non è vero!

- Faceva chiasso in riva al fiume e la corrente la travolse.

- Non è vero! Non è vero!

Allora il Re le raccontò per filo e per segno ogni cosa.

E la Regina partì, come una pazza, per ritrovar la figliuola.

Salita in cima alla montagna, cercò, chiamò tre giorni e tre notti, ma non scoperse neppure un segnale; e tornò, desolata, al palazzo.

Eran passati sette anni. Della bimba non s'era più saputo nuova. Un giorno la Regina si affaccia al terrazzino e vede giù nella via quella vecchiarella tanto ricercata:

- Buona donna, buona donna, montate su. - Maestà, oggi ho fretta; verrò domani.

La Regina rimase male. E il giorno dopo stette tutta la mattinata ad aspettarla al terrazzino.

Come la vide passare:

- Buona donna, buona donna, montate su.

- Maestà, oggi ho fretta; verrò domani.

Il giorno dopo, la Regina, per far meglio, andò ad aspettarla innanzi il portone.

- Maestà, oggi ho fretta; verrò domani.

"Sit here; wait a moment."

And he abandoned her to her fate.

Seeing him return alone, the queen began to scream:

"And what of our little daughter? Our daughter?"

"An eagle swooped down, grabbed her with his talons, and took her away."

"Oh my little daughter! It's not true!"

"A ferocious animal sprang upon her and took her into the forest to devour her."

"Oh my little daughter! It's not true!"

"The river rose over its banks, and the current carried her away."

"It's not true! It's not true."

Thus the king recounted all that happened in every detail.

And the queen ran off like a madwoman to find her daughter.

Having climbed to the top of the mountain, she called out for the child for three days and nights, but she found no sign of her, and she returned to the palace depressed.

Seven years passed, but there was still no news of the child. One day the queen came out onto the balcony of the palace and saw below on the street the old woman she had searched for so long:

"Good woman, good woman, come up here."

"Majesty, today I am in a hurry; I'll come tomorrow."

The queen was disappointed. And the next day, she waited the entire morning on the balcony.

When she saw the old woman pass, she said:

"Good woman, good woman, come up here."

"Majesty, today I am in a hurry; I'll come tomorrow."

To make sure that she got to speak with her, the next day the queen went out and waited for the old woman at the front gate.

"Majesty, today I am in a hurry; I'll come tomorrow."

Ma la Regina la prese per una mano e non la lasciò andar via; e per le scale le domandò perdono di quella volta che non le aveva fatto l'elemosina.

- Buona donna, buona donna, fatemi ritrovar la mia figliuola!
- Maestà, che ne so io? Sono una povera femminuccia.
- Buona donna, buona donna, fatemi ritrovar la mia figliuola!
- Maestà, male nuove. La Reginotta è alle mani d'un Lupo Mannaro, quello stesso che diè il rimedio e fece il patto col Re. Fra un mese le domanderà: mi vuoi per marito? Se lei risponde di no, quello ne farà due bocconi. Bisogna avvertirla.
- E il Lupo Mannaro dov'abita?
- Maestà, sotto terra. Si scende tre giorni e tre notti, senza mangiare, né bere, né riposare, e al terzo giorno s'arriva. Prendete un coltellino, un gomitolo di refe e un pugno di grano, e venite con me.

La Regina prese tutto quello che la vecchiarella avea ordinato, e partì insieme con lei.

Giunsero ad una buca, che ci si passava appena. La vecchiarella attaccò un capo del refe a una piantina e disse:

- Chi semina raccolga, Chi ti attacca, quei ti sciolga.

Ed entrarono. Scendi, scendi, scendi, la Regina già si sentiva le ginocchia tutte rotte.

- Vecchiarella, riposiamo un tantino!
- Maestà, è impossibile.

Scendi, scendi, scendi, la Regina non si reggeva più dalla fame.

- Vecchiarella, prendiamo un boccone, mi sento svenire!
- Maestà, non è possibile.

Scendi, scendi, scendi, la Regina affogava di sete.

- Vecchiarella, per carità, un gocciolo di acqua!

However, the queen took her by the hand and did not let her go; and on the stairs she apologized for the time when she had not shown her charity.

"Good woman, good woman, let me find my daughter!"

"Majesty, what do I know of her? I am a poor old woman."

"Good woman, good woman, let me find my daughter!"

"Majesty, I have bad news. The princess is in the hands of a werewolf, the same one that gave you the cure and made a pact with the king. Within a month, he will ask her to marry him. If she answers no, he will eat her up in two bites. You need to warn her."

"And where does the werewolf live?"

"Under ground, Majesty. If you climb down for three days and nights without eating, drinking, or resting, you will arrive on the third day. Take a small knife, a ball of thread, and a handful of wheat, and come with me."

The queen got all that the little old woman had asked for, and she left with her.

They came to the mouth of a cave, which was so small that they could only just pass through it. The little old woman tied one end of the thread to a small tree and said:

"He who sows shall reap; he who ties you will loosen you."

They entered the cave, and as they descended deeper and deeper, the queen soon felt pains in her knees.

"Old woman, let's rest for a little bit!"

"Majesty, it's not possible."

Going down still farther, the queen became very hungry.

"Old woman, let's get a bite to eat; I feel faint."

"Majesty, it's not possible."

Continuing their journey downward, the queen became so thirsty that she was choking.

"Old woman, for pity's sake, let me have a drop of water."

- *Maestà, non è possibile.*

E sbucarono in una pianura. Il gomitolo del refe terminò. La vecchiarella attaccò quell'altro capo ad una pianticina, e disse:

- *Chi semina raccolga, Chi ti attacca, quei ti sciolga.*

Cominciarono ad inoltrarsi. Ad ogni passo la Regina dovea lasciar cadere in terra un chicco di grano e la vecchiarella diceva:

- *Grano, grano di Dio, Com'io ti semino, vo' mieterti io.*

Il grano nasceva e cresceva subito, colle spighe mature che penzolavano.

- *Maestà, ora piantate in terra il coltellino e sputate tre volte; siamo arrivati.*

La Regina piantò il coltellino e sputò tre volte; e la vecchiarella disse:

- *Coltellino, coltellino di Dio, Com'io ti pianto, vo' strapparti io.*

Lasciamo costoro e torniamo alla Reginotta.

Vistasi sola sola in cima alla montagna, s'era messa a piangere e a strillare; poi, povera bimba, s'era addormentata. Si svegliò in un gran palazzo; ma per quelle stanze e quei stanzoni non vedeva anima viva. Gira, rigira, era già stanca.

- *Reginotta, sedete, sedete!*

Le sedie parlavano

Si sedette, e dopo un pezzettino, cominciò a sentirsi appetito. Comparve una tavola apparecchiata, colle pietanze fumanti.

- *Reginotta, mangiate, mangiate!*

La tavola parlava.

Mangiò, bevve, e poco dopo le vennero le cascaggini.

- *Reginotta, dormite, dormite!*

Il letto parlava. Era uno stupore. Così tutti i giorni. Non le mancava nulla, ma s'annoiava a star lì senza vedere un viso di

"Majesty, it's not possible."

And then they emerged onto a plain. The ball of thread was spent, and the old woman tied the other end to a seedling and said:

"He who sows shall reap; he who ties you will loosen you."

And as they went forward, the queen had to drop a grain of wheat at every step, and the old woman said.

"Grain, grain of God. As I plant you, so will I reap you."

The grain sprouted and grew immediately with mature buds that hung down heavily:

"Majesty, now thrust the little knife into the ground and spit three times; we have arrived."

The queen thrust the little knife into the ground and spat three times, and the little old woman said:

"Knife, knife of God. As I thrust you into the ground, so will I pull you out again."

Now, let's leave these two and return to the princess.

Seeing herself alone at the top of the mountain, she began to cry and scream; afterward the poor child fell asleep. When she awoke, she was in a grand palace, but in those grand rooms and halls she saw not a living soul. She looked around and around, and she was soon tired.

"Sit down, princess, sit down!"

The chairs were speaking to her.

She sat down and, after a little while, she began to feel hungry. Suddenly there appeared a table on which steaming dishes of food had been placed.

"Eat, princess, eat!" said the table.

She ate, she drank, and, after a little while, she became sleepy.

"Sleep, princess, sleep!" said the bed.

It was a wonder, and every day was the same. She wanted for nothing, but she became bored, for she never saw the face

cristiano. Spesso piangeva, pensando al babbo e alla mamma; ed una volta si mise a chiamarli ad alta voce, tra i singhiozzi:
- Babbo mio! Mamma mia! Con che cuore mi lasciate qui, mammina mia!
Ma una vociona le gridò:
- Sta' zitta! Sta' zitta!
Ranicchiossi in un canto, e non ebbe animo di più fiatare.
Passato un anno, un bel giorno si sentì domandare:
- Vuoi vedermi?
E non era quella vociona. Rispose:
- Volentieri.
Ed ecco gli usci si spalancano da loro stessi, e di fondo alla fila delle stanze viene avanti un cosino alto un cubito, vestito d'una stoffa a trama d'oro, con un berrettino rosso e una bella piuma più alta di lui.
- Buon giorno.
- Buon giorno. Oh, bimbo mio, come sei bello!
E lo prese in braccio e cominciò a baciarlo, a carezzarlo, a farlo saltare in aria come una bambola.
- Mi vuoi per marito? Mi vuoi?
La Reginotta rideva:
- Ti voglio, ti voglio.
E un altro salto per aria, prendendolo fra le mani.
- Come ti chiami?
- Gomitetto.
- Che fai qui?
- Sono il padrone.
- Allora lasciami andare! Lasciami tornare a casa mia!
- No, no! Dobbiamo sposarci.
- Per ora bada a crescere!

of another human being. She often cried, thinking of her father and mother; and once, between her sobs, she began to call to them in a loud voice:

"Daddy! Mommy! Oh, how did you have the heart to leave me here, mother dear."

However, she heard a dreadful voice scream at her:

"Be quiet! Be quiet!"

Frightened to death, she cowered in a corner.

After a year had passed, one day she heard someone ask:

"Do you want to see me?"

But it wasn't that dreadful voice, and she responded:

"Of course."

Suddenly, the doors burst open by themselves; from the end of a long line of rooms, a small creature, only one cubit tall, approached her. He was dressed in a garment of spun gold and wore a red cap with a beautiful feather that was taller than he.

"Good day."

"Good day, my little one. How beautiful you are!"

And she took him in her arms and began to kiss him, to caress him, and to toss him into the air as if he were a doll.

"Will you take me as your husband? Do you want me?"

The princess laughed:

"I do want you; I do."

And taking him by the hands, she tossed him into the air again.

"What's your name?"

"Gomitetto" (the little elbow).

"And what do you do here?"

"I am the master here."

"Let me go then. Let me go back home!"

"No, no! We must get married!"

"But first you will need to grow!"

Gomitetto se l'ebbe a male ed andò via. E per un anno non si fece vivo. La Reginotta s'annoiava a star lì senza vedere un viso cristiano. Ogni giorno chiamava:
- *Gomitetto! Gomitetto!*

Ma Gomitetto non rispondeva. Un bel giorno le domandò di nuovo:
- *Vuoi vedermi?*
- *Volentieri.*

In un anno dovea esser cresciuto un pochino: ma gli usci si spalancarono, e le venne innanzi sempre lo stesso cosino alto un gomito, vestito di stoffa a trama d'oro, col berrettino rosso sormontato da quella bella piuma più alta di lui.
- *Buon giorno.*
- *Buon giorno.*

La Reginotta, nel vederlo lo stesso, rimase sorpresa. Lo prese in collo e cominciò a baciarlo, a carezzarlo, a farlo saltare in aria come una bambola.
- *Mi vuoi per marito? Mi vuoi?*

La Reginotta rideva:
- *Ti voglio! Ti voglio! Ma per ora bada a crescere.*

E qui un capitombolo per aria, prendendolo fra le mani. Gomitetto se l'ebbe a male e andò via.

Ogni anno così; ed eran passati sette anni. Intanto la Reginotta s'era fatta una ragazza, che ci volevan quattro paia d'occhi per guardarla. Una notte non potendo prender sonno, pensava al babbo e alla mamma:
- *Chi sa se più si ricordano di me? Forse mi credono morta!*

E piangeva sui guanciali; quand'ecco sente buttar dei sassolini all'imposta della finestra.

Chi poteva essere, a quell'ora?

Si fece coraggio, saltò giù dal letto, aperse adagino adagino l'impòsta, e domandò:

Gomitetto was insulted and went away. And for one year he was not seen again. The princess was bored, for she never saw the face of another human being. Each day she called him:

"Gomitetto! Gomitetto!"

But Gomitetto did not answer. One fine day, however, he asked again:

"Do you want to see me?"

"Of course."

In one year he should have grown a little; however, as soon as the doors opened wide there came the same little creature as before. He was dressed in a garment of spun gold and wore a red cap with a beautiful feather that was taller than he.

"Good day."

"Good day."

The princess was very surprised that he had not changed. She took him by the neck and began to kiss him, to caress him, and to toss him into the air as if he were a doll.

"Will you take me as your husband? Do you want me?"

The princess laughed:

"I do want you; I do. But first you will need to grow."

And taking him by the hands, she tossed him into the air.

Gomitetto was insulted and went away.

This happened every year for seven years. In the meantime, the princess had grown into a young lady, so beautiful that one would need four pairs of eyes to look at her. One night, she could not sleep, for she was thinking of her father and mother.

"Who knows if they still remember me? Perhaps they think that I am dead."

And she cried on her pillows. Suddenly she heard pebbles hitting the window shutter. Who could it be at that hour?

Summoning her courage, she got our of bed, slowly opened the shutter, and asked:

- Chi siete? Che cosa volete?
- Son io, figliuola mia; siam venute per te!
Dall'allegrezza stava per saltar dalla finestra.
- Ascolta, figliuola - disse la Regina sotto voce. - Quel Gomitetto è il Lupo Mannaro. Ti s'è mostrato a quel modo per non farti paura. Ma ora che sei grande, fra qualche giorno t'apparirà col suo vero aspetto. Figliuola mia, non atterrirti. E se ti domanda: Mi vuoi per marito? rispondi di sì; altrimenti sarai morta; ne farà due bocconi. La prossima notte a quest'ora ci rivedremo.
La mattina, la Reginotta udì la solita voce:
- Vuoi vedermi?
- Volentieri.
Si spalancarono gli usci, ma, invece di Gomitetto, venne avanti il Lupo Mannaro alto, grosso, peloso, con certi occhiacci e certe zanne, che Dio ne scampi ogni creatura! La Reginotta si sentì mancare.
- Mi vuoi per marito? Ti feci fare apposta per me.
Lei tremava come una foglia.
- Mi vuoi per marito?
Più la Reginotta sentiva quella vociaccia, e più tremava e si smarriva.
- Mi vuoi per marito?
Voleva rispondergli: sì! Ma le scappò detto:
- Oh, no! no!
- Allora vien qui!
E l'afferrò colle granfie per ingoiarsela.
- Mangiami almeno domani! Te lo chieggo per grazia!
Il Lupo Mannaro stette un momentino incerto, e poi rispose:
- Ti sia concesso! Sarai mangiata domani.
La notte, all'ora fissata, lei s'affacciò alla finestra:
- Ah, mammina mia! Mi scappò detto di no; sarò mangiata domani.

"Who are you? What do you want?"

"It is I, my daughter; we have come for you!"

She was so happy that she almost jumped from the window.

"Listen, child," whispered the queen. "That Gomitetto is the werewolf. He has shown himself as Gomitetto so as not to frighten you. But now that you have grown up, he will appear in his true form in a few days. Don't be frightened, child. If he asks you to marry him, say yes. Otherwise, you will die; he will eat you in two bites. Tomorrow night we will meet again at this time."

In the morning, the princess heard the usual voice:

"Do you want to see me?"

"Of course."

The doors opened wide, but instead of Gomitetto, it was the werewolf who appeared—big, tall, and hairy, with big ugly eyes and tusks, from which any of God's creatures would surely run! The princess felt faint.

"Do you want me for your husband? I had you made just for me."

She shook like a leaf.

"Do you want me for your husband?"

The more the princess heard that horrible voice, the more she shook and lost heart.

"Do you want me for your husband?"

She wanted to answer yes, but "Oh no! No!" slipped out of her mouth:

"Well then, come here," said the werewolf.

And he grabbed her with her claws in order to eat her.

"Wait until tomorrow to eat me! I beg of you!"

The werewolf wavered for a moment and then replied.

"I grant you this wish! I will eat you tomorrow."

That night, at the appointed hour, she went to the window.

"Oh, mother! The word 'no' slipped out of my mouth, and tomorrow he will eat me."

- Fatevi coraggio! - disse la vecchiarella.
E picchiò forte al portone.
- Chi è? Chi cercate?
All'urlo del Lupo Mannaro tutto il palazzo tremava.
- Son coltellino,
  Son piantato nella terra dura,
  Per difender la creatura.
Contro questa malìa, il Lupo Mannaro non poteva nulla. E la mattina, all'alba, venne fuori; e come vide il coltellino, si mordeva le mani:
- Se trovo chi l'ha piantato, ne faccio un boccone!
Cercò, frugò attorno, ma non trovò nessuno. All'ultimo chiamò la Reginotta:
- Vien qua, strappami di terra questo coltellino: non ti mangerò più.
La Reginotta gli credette, e strappò il coltellino.
- Ed ora vien qui!
E l'afferrò colle granfie per ingoiarsela.
- Mangiami almeno domani! Te lo chieggo per grazia.
Il Lupo Mannaro stette un momentino incerto, e poi rispose:
- Ti sia concesso.
La notte, la Reginotta s'affacciò alla finestra:
- Ah, mammina mia! Mi disse: strappa di terra questo coltellino, ed io glielo strappai. Domani sarò mangiata!
- Fatevi coraggio!
E la vecchiarella picchiò forte al portone.
- Chi è? Chi cercate?
All'urlo del Lupo Mannaro, tutto il palazzo tremava.
- Son frumentino,
  Son seminato nella terra scura,
  Per difender la creatura.

"Be brave," said the little old lady. And she banged loudly at the gate.

"Who is it and who are you looking for?"

The whole palace trembled at the sound of the werewolf's voice.

"I am the little knife.

I have been planted in the hard earth

To defend this child."

The werewolf could not fight against such sorcery, and in the morning, at dawn, he came out. As soon as he saw the little knife, he bit his hands in frustration:

"If I find the one who planted that knife in the ground, I will finish him off in one bite."

He searched, ransacked the place, but found no one. Finally, he called the princess.

"Come here; if you pull this little knife out of the ground, I will never eat you."

The princess believed him, and she removed the knife.

"And now come here," said the werewolf.

And he grabbed her with his claws to eat her.

"Wait until tomorrow to eat me! I beg of you!"

The werewolf hesitated for a moment and then responded:

"I grant you this wish! I will eat you tomorrow."

That night, the princess came to the window:

"Oh, mother! He told me to pull the little knife out of the ground, and I took it out. Tomorrow he will eat me!"

"Be brave!"

And the little old woman knocked loudly at the gate.

"Who is it and who are you looking for?"

The entire palace trembled at the sound of the werewolf's voice.

"I am a little stalk of wheat.

And I have been planted in the dark earth

To defend this child."

Contro questa malìa, il Lupo Mannaro non poteva nulla. E la mattina all'alba, venne fuori; e come vide il seminato colle spighe penzoloni, si mordeva le mani:

- Se trovo chi lo seminò, ne faccio un boccone.

Cercò, frugò intorno, ma non trovò nessuno. E la mattina dopo disse alla Reginotta:

- Vieni qua: mietimi questo frumento; non ti mangerò più.

La Reginotta gli credette, e si mise all'opera. Per lei non c'era malìa, e in una giornata poté facilmente terminare di mieterlo.

- Ed ora vien qui!

- Mangiami almeno domani! Te lo chieggo per grazia.

Quegli stette un momentino incerto, e poi rispose:

- Ti sia concesso, per l'ultima volta.

La notte, la Reginotta s'affacciò alla finestra:

- Ah, mammina mia! Mi disse: mieti questo frumento ed io glielo mietei. Domani sarò mangiata.

- Fatevi coraggio!

E la vecchiarella picchiò forte al portone.

- Chi è? - urlò il Lupo Mannaro.

- Son refe fino
  Son attaccato alla pianta matura,
  Per difender la creatura.

Contro questa malìa, il Lupo Mannaro non poteva nulla. E la mattina all'alba venne fuori, e come vide il capo del refe legato alla pianticina, si mordeva le mani:

- Vien qua; scioglimi questo refe dai due capi: non ti mangerò più.

La Reginotta era stata indettata dalla vecchiarella. Non doveva fermarsi un passo, né mangiare, né bere, ma aggomitolare, aggomitolare e andare avanti. Sciolse quel capo, e lei avanti, aggomitolando, il Lupo Mannaro dietro.

The werewolf could not fight against such sorcery, and in the morning, at dawn, he came out. When he saw many stalks hanging heavy with wheat, he bit his hands in frustration.

"If I find the one who planted this, I will finish him off in one bite."

He searched, ransacked the place, but found no one. And the morning after he said to the princess:

"Come here; cut down this wheat for me, and I will never eat you."

The princess believed him and went to work. For her, there was no spell; in a day, she could easily complete the harvest.

"And now, come here!" said the werewolf.

"Wait until tomorrow to eat me! I beg of you!"

The werewolf wavered for a moment and then replied.

"I grant you this wish, but for the last time."

That night, the princess went to the window.

"Oh, mother! He told me to harvest this wheat, and I did. Tomorrow, he will eat me."

"Be brave!"

And the little old lady knocked loudly at the gate.

"Who is it?" screamed the werewolf.

"I am a fine thread
 And I am tied to a grown tree.
 To defend this child."

The werewolf could not fight against such sorcery, and in the morning, at dawn, he came out. And as soon as he saw the end of the thread tied to the tree, he bit his hands in frustration:

"Come here; If you untie this thread for me at both ends, I will never eat you."

The princess had already been given instructions by the little old woman. She was not to stop to eat or drink, but to keep rolling the thread up into a ball and walking on. So she untied one end and she went ahead, rolling up the thread as the werewolf walked behind.

- *Ripòsati, ripòsati!*
- *Quando sarò stanca, mi riposerò.*
Lei avanti aggomitolando, e il Lupo Mannaro dietro.
- *Prendi un boccone, prendi un boccone!*
- *Quando avrò fame mangerò.*
Lei avanti aggomitolando, e il Lupo Mannaro dietro.
- *Bevi un gocciolino d'acqua, un gocciolino!*
- *Quando avrò sete, berrò.*
Eran già arrivati alla buca d'uscita. Come il Lupo Mannaro s'accorse che l'altro capo del refe era attaccato alla pianticina di fuori, cominciò a mordersi rabbiosamente le mani. E vista la vecchiarella, diventò bianco come un panno lavato.
- *Ah! La nemica mia! Son morto! Son morto!*
La Regina e la Reginotta si voltarono e, invece della vecchiarella, videro una bellissima signora, che pareva la stella del mattino. Era la Regina delle Fate. Figuriamoci che allegrezza!
La Regina delle Fate prendeva intanto dei sassi, e li metteva l'uno sull'altro davanti la buca.
- *Sassi, sassi di Dio, Io vi muro e vo' smurarvi io!*
Murata la buca, la Regina delle Fate sparì.
E quella brutta bestiaccia crepò di fame lì dentro.
La Regina e la Reginotta tornarono sane e salve al palazzo; e un anno dopo la Reginotta sposò il Re di Portogallo.

"Rest, rest!" said the werewolf.

"When I get tired, I will rest," answered the princess.

She kept rolling up the thread with the werewolf following.

"Have a bite to eat; have a bite to eat!" said the werewolf.

"When I get hungry, I will eat."

She kept rolling up the thread with the werewolf following.

"Take a sip of water; take a sip of water!" said the werewolf.

"When I get thirsty, I will drink."

Soon they came to the mouth of the cave. When the werewolf realized that the end of the thread was attached to a tree outside, he began to bite his hands angrily in frustration. And seeing the little old woman, he became as white as a newly washed sheet.

"Aha! My enemy! I am dead! I am dead!"

The queen and the princess turned around and, instead of the little old lady, they saw a beautiful woman, who looked like the morning star. She was the queen of the fairies. Imagine their joy!

In the meantime, the queen of the fairies had taken the pebbles and placed them in front of the mouth of the cave.

"Pebbles, pebbles of God. Seal up this cave, forever!"

Having walled up the mouth of the cave, the queen of the fairies disappeared.

And that ugly beast died of hunger inside.

The queen and the princess returned to the palace safe and sound, and a year later the princess married the king of Portugal.

Cecina

C'era una volta un Re, che amava pazzamente la caccia, e per essere più libero di andarvi tutti i giorni, non aveva voluto prender moglie.

I ministri gli dicevano:
- Maestà, il popolo desidera una Regina.
E lui rispondeva:
- Prenderò moglie l'anno venturo.
Passava l'anno, e i ministri da capo:
- Maestà, il popolo desidera una Regina.
E lui: - Prenderò moglie l'anno venturo.
Ma quest'anno non arrivava mai.

Ogni mattina, appena albeggiava, indossava la carniera, e col fucile sulla spalla, e coi cani, via pei forteti e pei boschi.

Chi avea da parlare col Re, doveva andare a trovarlo in mezzo ai boschi e ai forteti.

I ministri ripicchiavano:
- Maestà, il popolo desidera una Regina.

Talché finalmente il Re si decise, e mandò a chiedere la figlia del Re di Spagna.

Ma, andato per sposarla, si accorse che era un po' gobbina.
- Sposare una gobbina? No. Mai!
- Ma è bella, è virtuosa! - gli dicevano i ministri.
- È gobbina e basta: no, mai!
E tornò alla caccia, ai boschi e ai forteti.

Quella Reginotta gobbina aveva per comare una Fata.
La Fata, vedendola piangere pel rifiuto del Re, le disse:

The Little Chickpea

Once upon a time, there was a king who had a passion for hunting, and in order to be free to hunt each and every day, he never wished to marry.

His ministers said to him:

"Majesty, the people want a queen."

"I will get married next year," he responded.

However, after a year had passed, the ministers said once again:

"Majesty, the people want a queen."

Again he responded, "I will get married next year."

However, next year never came.

Every morning, before daybreak, he put on his game bag, put his gun on his shoulder, and with his dogs he walked into the fields and the forests.

Whoever needed to speak with the king had to go out and find him in the middle of the forests and fields.

The ministers repeated:

"Majesty, the people want a queen."

So, finally, the king gave in, and he sent out agents to inquire about the daughter of the king of Spain.

However, on his way to marry her, he learned that she was slightly hunchback.

"Marry a hunchback?" he exclaimed. "No! Never!"

"But she is beautiful and virtuous!" his ministers insisted.

"She is a hunchback, and that's all. No. Never!"

And so, he returned to hunting in the forests and the fields.

The hunchback princess had a fairy godmother. Seeing the princess cry over having been rejected by the king, the fairy said:

Sta' tranquilla: ti sposerà e dovrà venire a pregarti. Lascia fare a me.

IInfatti un giorno il Re, andando a caccia, incontrò una donnicciola magra, allampanata, che un soffio l'avrebbe portata via.

- Maestà, buona caccia!

Il Re, a quel viso di mal augurio, stizzito, fece una mossaccia, e non rispose nulla.

E per quel giorno non ammazzò neppure uno sgricciolo. Un'altra mattina, ecco di nuovo quella donnicciuola magra, allampanata, che un soffio l'avrebbe portata via:

- Maestà, buona caccia!

- Senti, strega - le disse il Re - se ti trovo un'altra volta per la strada, te la farò vedere io!

E per quel giorno non ammazzò neppure uno sgricciolo. Ma la mattina dopo, eccoti lì quella del malaugurio:

- Maestà, buona caccia!

- La buona caccia te la darò io!

Il Re avea condotto con sé le sue guardie, e ordinò che quella donna del malaugurio fosse chiusa in una prigione.

Da quel giorno in poi, tutte le volte che il Re andò a caccia, non poté tirare un sol colpo. La selvaggina era sparita, come per incanto, dai forteti e dai boschi. Non si trovava un coniglio o una lepre, neppure a pagarli a peso d'oro.

Gli accadde anche peggio.

Non potendo più fare il solito esercizio della caccia, il Re cominciò a ingrassare, a ingrassare, e in poco tempo diventò così grasso e grosso, da pesare due quintali con quel suo gran pancione che pareva una botte.

Quando avea fatto due passi per le stanze del palazzo reale, era come se avesse fatto cento miglia. Soffiava peggio di un mantice, sudava da allagare il pavimento; e doveva subito

"Don't worry: he will come to you and beg you to marry him. Let me handle it."

As a matter of fact, one day while hunting, the king met a woman so thin and lanky that a puff of wind might blow her away.

"Good hunting, Majesty, " she said.

At this sign of bad luck, the king became irritated, gave her a dirty look, and did not reply.

However, for that entire day, he killed nothing, not even a wren.

On another morning, that silly woman reappeared. She was so skinny and lanky that even a puff of wind might blow her away.

"Good hunting, Majesty."

"Listen, witch," said the king, "if I find you on this road again, I will make you regret it."

And that day, the king killed nothing, not even a wren.

But the next morning, he encountered that bad omen again.

"Good hunting, Majesty."

"I'll give you good hunting," said the king.

And he had the guards take her away and ordered that this woman of bad luck be locked in prison.

From that day forward, every time the king went hunting, he could not fire off a shot. The wildlife had disappeared, as if by a spell, from the fields and the forests. There wasn't a rabbit or a hare to be had, not even for a piece of gold.

But things got even worse.

Hunting had been the king's only exercise, and because he was unable to go hunting anymore, he began to gain weight. In a little while, he became so fat that he weighed two hundred kilos, and he had such a big stomach that he looked like a barrel.

When he walked through the rooms of the royal place twice, it was as if he had walked a hundred miles. He breathed worse than a bellows, and he sweated enough to flood the palace floor.

subitoriposarsi e mangiare anche qualche cosa di sostanza, per rimettersi in forze. Desolato, consultava i migliori dottori.
- Vorrei dimagrare.
I dottori scrivevano ricette sopra ricette. Non passava giorno, che lo speziale non mandasse a palazzo bicchieroni d'intrugli amari come il fiele, che dovevano guarire Sua Maestà.
Ma Sua Maestà, più intrugli prendeva e più grasso diventava.
Nel palazzo reale avevano già allargato tutti gli usci delle stanze, perché il Re potesse passare; e una volta gli architetti dissero che se non si fossero puntellati ben bene i solai, Sua Maestà col gran peso gli avrebbe sfondati.
Il povero Re si disperava:
- O che non c'era rimedio per lui?
E chiamava altri dottori; ma inutilmente. Più intrugli prendeva e più grasso diventava.
Un giorno si presentò una vecchia e disse al Re:
- Maestà, voi avete addosso una brutta malìa. Io potrei romperla; ma voi, in compenso, dovrete sposare la mia figliuola, che si chiama Cecina, perché è piccina come un cece.
- Sposerò la tua Cecina!
Il Re avrebbe anche fatto chi sa che cosa, pur di levarsi di dosso tutto quel grasso e quel pancione.
- Conducila qui.
La vecchia cacciò una mano nella tasca del grembiule, e ne tirò fuori la Cecina, che era alta appena una spanna, ma bellina e ben proporzionata. Come vide quel pancione, la Cecina scoppiò in una risata; e mentre quella la teneva sulla palma della mano per mostrarla al Re, lei spiccò un salto e si mise ad arrampicarsi su pel pancione, correndo di qua e di là, come se il pancione del Re fosse stato per lei una collina.

Moreover, he had to rest immediately and to eat something substantial in order to get his strength back. Desperate, he consulted the best doctors:

"I want to lose weight."

The doctors wrote prescription after prescription. A day did not pass when the specialists did not send to the palace large glasses of concoctions as bitter as bile to make the king better.

But the more of these concoctions he took, the fatter he got.

The exits to all of the rooms of the royal palace had already been enlarged to enable the king to pass. One time, the architects said that if the floors were not well reinforced, the great weight of his majesty would cause them to cave in.

The poor king was desperate.

"Oh, is there no remedy for this?"

So, he called other doctors, but to no avail. The more concoctions he took, the fatter he got.

One day an old woman came to him and said:

"Majesty, you are suffering under an evil spell. I can break it. However, in return you must marry my daughter, who is called Cecina because she is as small as a chickpea."

"I will marry your Cecina."

The king would have done whatever it took to lose all that weight and to get rid of that belly.

"Bring her here."

The old woman thrust a hand into the pocket of her apron, and from it took out Cecina, who was barely as high as a hand's breadth, but pretty and well proportioned. When she saw that belly, Cecina broke out in laughter. And while the old woman was holding her in the palm of her hand to show her to the king, she leapt up and she began to climb on to his stomach, running this way and that as if the belly of the king were for her a kind of hill.

Il Re, con quei piedini, sentiva farsi il solletico e voleva fermarla; ma quella, salta di qua, salta di là, peggio di una pulce, non si lasciava acchiappare. Pel solletico, il Re rideva, ah! ah! ah!, e il pancione gli faceva certi sbalzi buffi. Ah! ah! ah!

Allora la Cecina:

- Pancione del Re, Palazzo per me!

Il Re dal gran ridere, teneva aperta la bocca; la Cecina, dentro e giù per la gola:

- Pancione del Re, Palazzo per me!

Figuriamoci lo spavento di Sua Maestà e di tutta la corte! Nella confusione, la vecchia era sparita.

E la Cecina, che dal suo palazzo ordinava:

- Datemi da mangiare!

E il Re doveva mangiare anche per lei.

- Datemi da bere!

E il Re doveva bere anche per lei.

- Lasciatemi dormire!

E il Re dovea stare fermo e zitto, perché la Cecina dormisse.

- Maestà, - disse uno dei ministri - che sia una malìa di quella donna magra, allampanata, fatta mettere in prigione? Facciamola condurre qui.

I guardiani aprirono la prigione e la trovarono vuota. Quella donna dovea essere scappata pel buco della serratura!

- Ed ora che fare?

E la Cecina, dal suo palazzo del pancione:

- Datemi da mangiare! Datemi da bere!

Il popolo intanto mormorava per le tasse; giacché per riempire quel pancione del Re, ce ne volea della roba! E bisognava pagare.

Il Re fece un bando:

- Chi gli cavava la Cecina dallo stomaco, diventava principe reale e avrebbe avuto quattrini quanti ne voleva!

Her little feet tickled the king, and he wanted to stop her, but she jumped here and there, worse than a flea, and she would not let herself be caught. "I am ticklish," the king laughed, "ha! ha! ha!" And his stomach made several funny jerks.

"The king's stomach is my palace!" cried Cecina.

Because he was laughing so much, the king kept his mouth open, and Cecina jumped into his mouth and down his throat.

"The king's stomach is my palace."

Imagine the surprise of the king and of all of the court. In the confusion, the old woman disappeared.

In the meantime, Cecina gave orders from her palace.

"Feed me!"

And because of her, the king also had to eat.

"Give me something to drink!"

And because of her, the king also had to drink.

"Let me sleep."

And the king had to stay still because Cecina was sleeping.

"Majesty," said one of the ministers, "could this be a spell cast by that skinny, lanky woman whom you had put in jail? Let's bring her here."

The guards opened the jail, but they found it empty. That woman must have escaped through the hole in the lock.

"And now what is to be done?"

Still, Cecina commanded from her palace of the stomach:

"Feed me, and give me something to drink."

Meanwhile, the people were complaining about their taxes. It took a great deal to fill the stomach of the king! The people had to pay.

The king issued a proclamation.

"Whoever removed Cecina from his stomach would become a royal prince and would have as much money as he wanted!"

Ma i banditori andarono attorno inutilmente. E come la Cecina cresceva, per quanto poco crescesse, il pancione del Re si gonfiava e pareva dovesse scoppiare da un momento all'altro.

Il Re la pregava:- Cecina bella, vieni fuori, ti faccio Regina!

- Maestà, sto bene qui dentro. Datemi da mangiare.

- Cecina bella, vieni fuori, ti faccio Regina!

- Maestà, sto bene qui dentro. Datemi da bere.

Se non fosse stato il timore della morte, il Re si sarebbe spaccato il pancione colle proprie mani.

E il popolo che brontolava:

- Re pancione ingoiava tutto! Lavoravano per Re pancione!

Come se Re pancione ci avesse avuto il suo piacere! Lo sapeva soltanto lui, quello che pativa, con la Cecina dentro che comandava a bacchetta e voleva essere ubbidita!

Finalmente un giorno ricomparve la vecchia:

- Ah, vecchia scellerata! Cavami fuori la tua Cecina, o guai a te!

- Maestà, son venuta a posta coi miei dottori.

E i suoi dottori erano due uccellacci più grossi di un tacchino, con un becco lungo un braccio e forte come l'acciaio.

- Maestà, - disse la vecchia - dovete stendervi a pancia all'aria in mezzo a una pianura.

Il Re, che era ingrassato da non poter più fare neppure un passo, comandò:

- Ruzzolatemi.

E il popolo cominciò a ruzzolarlo come una botte, per le scale e per le vie; e, dalla fatica, sudavano. Arrivati nella pianura, e messo il Re a pancia all'aria, uno degli uccellacci gli diè una beccata sul pancione e, che ne schizzò fuori? Uno zampillo di vino schietto, tutto il vino che Sua Maestà aveva bevuto in tanti anni.

However, the proclamations were useless. And as Cecina grew, even as little as she could, the king's belly began to grow; it seemed as if it were going to explode at any moment.

The king begged her:

"My beautiful Cecina. Come out and I will make you queen!"

"Majesty, I am fine in here. Give me something to eat."

"My beautiful Cecina. Come out and I will make you queen!"

"Majesty, I am fine in here. Give me something to drink."

If he were not afraid of dying, the king would have broken open his stomach with his own hands.

Meanwhile, the people were muttering:

"The royal belly devours everything! We are slaves to it!"

Oh, if only the king's belly had taken some pleasure from this. Only he knew what he suffered, with Cecina inside of him ordering him around sternly and demanding to be obeyed.

Finally, one day the old woman reappeared.

"You wicked old woman! Get Cecina out of me, or woe is you!"

"Majesty, I have come with my doctors to do just that."

Her two doctors were two ugly birds larger than turkeys, with beaks as long as an arm and as strong as steel.

"Majesty," said the old woman, "you must stand on a plain with your stomach in the air."

The king was so fat that he could no longer take a step, so he commanded:

"Roll me."

And the people began to roll him like a bottle down the stairs and on his way. From all of this exertion, they perspired heavily. When he arrived on the plain and he stuck his belly out in the air, one of the birds gave his belly a peck. And what do you think spurted out? A spring of pure wine, all of the wine that his majesty had drunk those many years.

La gente riempiva botti, botticini, caratelli, tini, barili, fiaschi, boccali; non c'erano vasi che bastassero. Pareva di essere alla vendemmia. Tutti cioncavano e si ubriacavano.
   E il pancione del Re si sgonfiò un poco.
   Allora l'altro uccellaccio gli diè la sua beccata, ed ecco rigurgitar fuori tutto il ben di Dio mangiato dal Re in tanti anni; maccheroni, salsicciotti, polli arrosto, bistecche, pasticcini, frutta, insomma ogni cosa. La gente non sapeva più dove riporli. Tutti mangiarono a crepapancia, come fosse di carnovale.
   E il pancione del Re sgonfiò un altro poco.
   Allora il Re disse:
   - Cecina bella, vien fuori; ti faccio Regina!
   La Cecina affacciò la testa da uno dei buchi, e ridendo rispose:
   - Eccomi qua.
   E il Re tornò com'era prima.
   Si sposarono; ma il Re, con quella cosina alta una spanna, che era una moglie per chiasso, si credette libero di tornare a divertirsi colla caccia, e stava fuori intere settimane.
   La Cecina piangeva:

   - Ah, poverina me! Son Regina senza Re!

   Il Re per questo lamentìo, non la poteva soffrire. Andò da una Strega e le disse:
   - Che cosa debbo fare per levarmi di torno la Cecina?
   - Maestà,
     Spellarla, lessarla,
     O arrosto mangiarla.
   Mangiarla gli repugnava; pure, tornato a casa disse alla Cecina:
   - Domani ti condurrò a caccia, e ti divertirai.
   Voleva condurla in mezzo ai boschi, dove non potesse vederlo nessuno. Ma la Cecina rispose:

The people filled vats, bottles, carafes, tubs, barrels, flasks, and jars. There just weren't enough vessels to store the wine. It seemed like a grape harvest. Everyone took part in it, and they all got drunk!

And the king's belly subsided a little.

Then, the other bird gave him a peck, and all food that the king had eaten those many years came out: macaroni, sausages, roasted chickens, beefsteak, cakes, fruit—in short, everything. The people did not know where to put the food that had come from the crack in his belly; it seemed like carnival time.

And the king's belly subsided a little more.

And so the king said:

"My beautiful Cecina, come out and I'll make you a queen!"

Cecina stuck her head out of one of the two holes and laughed. "Here I am."

And the king returned to his former self.

They got married; however, being only a hand's breadth tall, she was a wife in name only. The king believed himself free to return to the pleasures of the hunt, and he stayed out for several weeks at a time.

Cecina cried and cried.

"Oh, poor me! I am a queen without a king!"

The king could not take this lamenting anymore. So, he went to the witch and asked:

"What must I do to get rid of Cecina?"

"Majesty, skin her
 Boil her,
 Or roast her and eat her."

To eat her would have disgusted the king; however, when he returned home he said to Cecina:

"Tomorrow, I will take you hunting, and you will have a good time."

He wanted to lead her into the middle of the forest, where no one would see him. But Cecina responded:

- *Spellarla, lessarla,*
  O arrosto mangiarla.

  - *Grazie, Maestà! Ah, poverina me! Son Regina senza Re!*
Il Re rimase stupito:
- *Come lo sapeva?*
Tornò dalla Strega e le raccontò la cosa.
  - *Maestà, quando la Cecina sarà addormentata, tagliatele occa di capelli e portatemela qui.*
Però, quella sera, la Cecina non avea voglia di andare a letto.
  - *Cecina, vieni a dormire.*
  - *Più tardi, Maestà; per ora non ho sonno.*
Il Re aspettò, aspettò, e si addormentò lui per il primo. La mattina, svegliatosi, vide che la Cecina era già levata.
  - *Cecina, non hai dormito?*
  - *Chi si guarda si salva. Grazie, Maestà.*
  - *Ah, poverina me! Son Regina senza Re!*
Il Re rimase stupito:
- *Come lo sapeva?*
Tornò dalla Strega e le raccontò la cosa.
  - *Maestà, invitate re Corvo; appena la vedrà, ne farà un sol boccone.*
Venne re Corvo:
  - *Cra! Cra! Cra! Cra!*
E come vide la Cecina, alta una spanna, cra! cra! ne fece un boccone.
  - *Mille grazie, re Corvo. Ora potete andar via.*
  - *Cra! Cra! Cra! Ma prima di andar via, debbo mangiarti gli occhi.*
E con due beccate gli cavò gli occhi.
Il povero Re piangeva sangue:

"Skin her, boil her,
  Or roast her and eat her."
"Thank you, Majesty! Oh poor me! I am a queen without a king!"
The king was stupefied:
"How did she know that?"
He returned to the witch and told her about this.
"Majesty, when Cecina is sleeping, cut a lock of her hair and bring it here to me."
  However, that night, Cecina would not go to bed.
"Cecina, come to bed."
"Later, Majesty; right now I am not sleepy."
The king waited and waited, and he fell asleep first. Getting up the next morning, he noticed that Cecina was already up.
"Haven't you slept, Cecina?"
"He who guards himself saves himself. Thank you, Majesty."
Oh poor me! I am a queen without a king!"
The king was stupefied:
"How did she know this?"
He returned to the witch and told her about this.
"Majesty, invite the raven king here; as soon as he sees her, he will eat her in one bite."
The raven king arrived: "Cra! Cra! Cra! Cra!"
And as soon as he saw Cecina, as tall as a hand's breadth, he devoured her in one bite. "Cra! Cra!"
"A thousand thanks, raven king. Now you can go," said the king.
"Cra! Cra! Cra! However, before I leave, I must eat your eyes."
And with two pecks, he pulled out the king's eyes.
The poor king cried tears of blood.

- *La Cecina morta, e lui senz'occhi! Ah, Cecina mia!*
Passato un po' di tempo, ricomparve la solita vecchia. Era la/ Fata comare della Reginotta di Spagna.
- *Maestà, non vi affliggete. La Cecina è viva, e i vostri occhi son riposti in buon luogo; son nella gobba della Reginotta di Spagna.*
Il Re si trascinò fino al palazzo reale, dove questa abitava, e cominciò a gridare pietosamente, dietro al portone:
- *Ah, Reginotta! Rendetemi gli occhi.*
La Reginotta, dalla finestra, rispondeva:
- *Sposare una gobbina! No, mai!*
- *Perdonatemi, Reginotta; e rendetemi gli occhi!*
La Reginotta dalla finestra rispondeva:
- *Spellarla, lessarla,*
  O arrosto mangiarla.
Allora il Re capì che la Reginotta di Spagna e la Cecina erano una sola persona; e si mise a gridare più forte:
- *Ah, Reginotta! Ah, Cecina mia! Rendetemi gli occhi.*
La Reginotta scese giù e gli disse:
- *Ecco gli occhi.*
Il Re la guardò sbalordito. La Reginotta non era più gobba e somigliava precisamente alla Cecina, benché fosse di giusta statura.
Così fu perdonato, e da lì a poco la sposò.
Lei, per ricordo, volle sempre essere chiamata Cecina.

Vissero lieti e contenti
E a noi si allegano i denti.

"Cecina is dead, and I have no eyes. Oh my Cecina!"

After a while, that same old woman reappeared. She was the fairy godmother of the princess of Spain.

"Majesty, don't trouble yourself. Cecina is alive, and your eyes are in a safe place; they are in the hump of the Princess of Spain."

The king dragged himself to the royal palace, where the princess lived, and he began to scream piteously at the front gate:

"Oh Princess! Give me back my eyes."

From the window, the princess answered.

"Marry a hunchback! No, never!"

"Forgive me, princess; and give back my eyes to me."

From the window, the Princess answered.

"Skin her, boil her,
  Or roast her and eat her."

And, therefore, the king realized that the Princess of Spain and Cecina were the same person, and he began to yell louder.

"Oh princess! Oh my Cecina! Give me back my eyes!"

The princess came down and said:

"Here are your eyes."

"The king looked at her in amazement. The princess was no longer a hunchback, and she looked exactly like Cecina except that she was of the right height.

And so he was forgiven, and in a little while he married the princess. In order to recall what had happened, she wanted to be called Cecina forever.

Happy and contented they lived together.
But about us they cared not a feather.

L'albero che parla

C'era una volta un Re che credeva d'aver raccolto nel suo palazzo tutte le cose più rare del mondo.

Un giorno venne un forestiere, e chiese di vederle. Osservò minutamente ogni cosa e poi disse:

- Maestà, vi manca il meglio.

- Che cosa mi manca?

- L'albero che parla.

Infatti, tra quelle rarità, l'albero che parlava non c'era.

Con questa pulce nell'orecchio, il Re non dormì più. Mandò corrieri per tutto il mondo in cerca dell'albero che parlava. Ma i corrieri tornarono colle mani vuote.

Il Re si credette canzonato da quel forestiere, e ordinò d'arrestarlo.

- Maestà, se i vostri corrieri han cercato male, che colpa ne ho io? Cerchino meglio.

- E tu l'hai veduto, coi tuoi occhi, l'albero che parla?

- L'ho veduto con questi occhi e l'ho sentito con queste orecchie.

- Dove?

- Non me ne rammento più.

- E che cosa diceva?

- Diceva "aspettare e non venire è una cosa da morire".

Era dunque vero! Il Re spedì di bel nuovo i suoi corrieri. Passa un anno, e questi ritornano da capo colle mani vuote.

Allora, sdegnato, ordinò che al forestiere si tagliasse la testa.

- Maestà, se i vostri corrieri han cercato male, che colpa ne ho io? Cerchino meglio.

Questa insistenza lo colpì. Chiamati i suoi ministri, disse che voleva andar lui in persona alla ricerca dell'albero che parlava.

The Talking Tree

Once upon a time, there was a king who believed that he had collected all of the rarest things in the world in his palace.

One day, there came a stranger who asked to see them. He inspected everything carefully and said:

"Majesty, you are missing the best thing of all."

"What am I missing?" responded the king.

"The talking tree."

In fact, among all those rare things, there was no talking tree.

With this bug in his ear, the king could no longer sleep. So, he sent out agents to all parts of the world in search of the talking tree. However, they returned empty handed.

The king believed that the stranger had made a fool of him and ordered his arrest.

"Majesty," said the stranger. "If your agents have searched badly, what fault is that of mine? They should search better."

"And have you seen this talking tree with your own eyes?" asked the king.

"I have seen it with these eyes and heard it with these ears."

"Where?"

"I don't remember any more."

"And what was the tree saying?"

"He told me "to wait and not to arrive is a terrible thing."

Therefore it was true! The king sent his agents out once again. Nevertheless, they returned a second time empty-handed..

Outraged, therefore, the king ordered that the stranger be beheaded.

"Majesty," said the stranger, "If your agents have searched badly, what fault is that of mine? They should search better."

The stranger's persistence convinced him. Calling upon his ministers, he told them that he wanted to search for the talking tree personally.

Finché non lo avesse nel suo palazzo, non si terrebbe per Re. E partì, travestito.

Cammina, cammina, dopo molti giorni la notte lo colse in una vallata dove non c'era anima viva. Sdraiossi per terra e stava per addormentarsi, quand'ecco una voce che pareva piangesse:

- Aspettare e non venire è una cosa da morire!

Si scosse e tese l'orecchio. Se l'era sognato?

- Aspettare e non venire è una cosa da morire!

Non se l'era sognato! E domandò subito:

- Chi sei tu?

Non rispondeva nessuno. Ma le parole erano, precise, quelle dell'albero che parlava.

- Chi sei tu?

Non rispondeva nessuno. La mattina, come aggiornò, vide lì vicino un bell'albero coi rami pendenti fino a terra:

- Doveva esser quello.

E per accertarsene, stese la mano e strappò due foglie.

- Ahi! Perché mi strappi?

Il Re, con tutto il suo gran coraggio, rimase atterrito.

- Chi sei tu? Se sei anima battezzata, rispondi, in nome di Dio!

- Son la figliuola del Re di Spagna.

- E in che modo ti trovi lì?

- Vidi una fontana limpida come il cristallo, e pensai di lavarmi. Tocca appena quell'acqua, rimasi incantata.

- Che posso fare per liberarti?

- Bisogna aver la fatatura e giurare di sposarmi.

Until he had it in his palace, he would not reveal himself as the king. And he left disguised.

Traveling for many days, one night he found himself in a valley where there wasn't a living soul. Lying on the ground and about to go to sleep, he heard a voice that seemed to be crying:

"To wait and not to arrive is a terrible thing."

He roused himself and stretched out his ear. Was he dreaming?

"To wait and not to arrive is a terrible thing."

He had not dreamt it. And he asked immediately.

"Who are you?"

No one responded. However, the words were exactly those of the talking tree.

"Who are you?"

No one responded. As soon as the sun came up, he saw close by a beautiful tree, its branches hanging down to the ground.

"That must be it."

To check, he stretched out his hand and pulled off two leaves.

"Ouch! Why are you pulling at me?"

Even with all of his great courage, the king was terrified.

"Who are you? If you are a Christian soul, answer me in the name of God."

"I am the dear daughter of the king of Spain."

"And how have you come to this?"

"I once saw a fountain as clear as glass, and I wanted to take a bath in it. As soon as I touched that water, however, I was bewitched."

"What can I do to free you?"

"You need to learn the magical spell, and you must promise to marry me."

- *Questo lo giuro subito, e la fatatura saprò procurarmela, dovessi andare in capo al mondo. Ma tu, perché non mi rispondevi la notte scorsa?*

- *C'era la Strega... Sta' zitto, allontanati; sento la Strega che ritorna. Se per disgrazia ti trovasse, incanterebbe anche te.*

Il Re corse a nascondersi dietro un muricciolo, e vide arrivar la Strega a cavallo del manico di una granata.

- *Con chi hai tu parlato?*

- *Col vento dell'aria.*

- *Veggo qui delle pedate.*

- *Son forse le vostre.*

- *Ah! Son le mie?*

La strega afferrava una mazza di ferro e:

- *Di dove vieni? Vengo dal mulino.*

- *Basta, per carità! Non lo farò più!*

- *Ah! Son le mie?*

- *E, di dove vieni?*

- *Vengo dal mulino.*

Il Re, angustiato, si persuase che era inutile il seguitare a star lì; bisognava procurarsi la fatatura. E tornò addietro.

Ma sbagliò strada. Quando s'accorse d'essersi smarrito in un gran bosco e non trovava più la via, pensò di montare in cima a un albero per passarvi la notte; altrimenti, le bestie feroci n'avrebbero fatto un boccone.

Ed ecco, a mezzanotte, un rumore assordante per tutto il bosco. Era un Orco che tornava a casa coi suoi cento mastini, che gli latravano dietro.

- *Oh, che buon odore di carne cristiana!*

L'Orco si fermò a piè dell'albero, e cominciò ad annusar l'aria:

- *Oh, che buon odore!*

"I swear this immediately, and I will learn the magic spell even if I have to go to the ends of the earth. However, why didn't you answer me last night?"

"The witch was here… Be quiet, and get away; I hear the witch returning. If, heaven forbid, she finds you, she will bewitch you as well."

The king ran off and concealed himself behind a small wall, and he saw the witch riding on a broomstick.

"With whom have you been talking?" the witch asked.

"With the wind."

"But I see a few footprints here."

"Perhaps they are your own."

"Oh, they are mine? Are they?"

The witch grabbed an iron club and asked:

"Where have you come from? I have come from the mill."

"Enough," said the tree. "For pity's sake, I won't do it again."

"Oh, they are mine? Are they? And, wehre are you coming from? I come from the mill."

Tormented, the king persuaded himself that it was useless for him to stay there; he needed to find the magic spell. And he went back.

However, he took the wrong road. When he realized that he had lost his way in a great forest, he thought about climbing onto a limb of a tree to spend the night. Otherwise, ferocious beasts might have made a meal of him.

And at midnight, a deafening noise sounded throughout the forest. It was a monster who was returning home with his hundred mastiffs, who were barking as they followed him.

"Oh what a lovely scent of Christian meat" said the monster.

He stopped at the foot of the tree and he began to sniff the air.

"O, what a lovely scent."

*Il Re aveva i brividi mentre i mastini frugavano latrando, fra
le macchie, e raspando il suolo dove fiutavan le pedate. Ma
per sua buona sorte era buio fitto; e l'Orco, cercato
inutilmente per un po' di tempo, andava via chiamandosi dietro
i mastini.*

- Té! Té!

*Quando fu giorno, il Re, che tremava ancora dalla paura,
scese da quell'albero e cominciò ad inoltrarsi cautamente.
Incontrò una bella ragazza.*

*- Bella ragazza, per carità, additatemi la via. Sono un
viandante smarrito.*

*- Ah, povero a te! Dove tu sei capitato! Fra poco ripasserà
mio padre e ti mangerà vivo, poverino!*

Infatti si sentivano i latrati dei mastini dell'Orco e la voce di
lui che se li chiamava dietro:

- Té! Té!

- Questa volta sono morto! - pensò il Re.

*- Vien qua, - disse la ragazza - bùttati carponi. Io mi sederò
sulla tua schiena, e la mia gonna ti coprirà. Non fiatare!*

L'Orco, vista la figliuola, si fermò.

- Che fai lì?

- Mi riposo.

- Oh, che buon odore di carne cristiana!

- Passava un ragazzino, e ne feci un bocconcino.

- Brava! E le ossa?

- Se le rosicchiarono i cani.

L'Orco non cessava d'annusar l'aria.

- Oh, che buon odore!

- Se volete arrivare alla marina, non indugiate per via.

*Partito che fu l'Orco, il Re raccontò alla ragazza, per filo e
per segno, tutta la sua storia.*

-Maestà, se volete sposarmi, la fatatura ve la darei io.

The king shivered while the barking mastiffs searched in the bushes and scratched at the soil where they sniffed the footprints. But, it was lucky for him that it was dark, and the monster, having searched unsuccessfully for a time, began to call back his mastiffs.

"Come, come!"

When day came, the king, who was trembling with fear, climbed down from the tree and began to move out cautously. He encountered a beautiful girl.

"Beautiful girl, for pity's sake, show me the way. I am a lost traveler."

"Woe is you. What have you gotten yourself into! In a little while, my father will return, he will eat you alive, poor man!"

In fact, the barks of the monster's mastiffs could be heard, as could his calling after them:

"Come, come!"

"This time I am dead," thought the king.

"Come here," said the girl. "Get down on all fours; I will sit on your back; my gown will cover you. Don't say anything."

Seeing his daughter, the monster stopped.

"What are you doing here?"

"I am resting."

"Oh what a lovely scent of Christian meat!"

"A young lad passed by, and I made a quick meal of him."

"Wonderful! And the bones?"

"The dogs gnawed them."

The monster continued to smell the air.

"Oh, what a lovely scent."

"If you are to get to the seashore," said the girl to her father, "you must not delay."

Once the monster had left, the King told her his story in every detail.

"Majesty, if you want to marry me, I will teach you the magic spell."

La ragazza era una bellezza; il Re l'avrebbe sposata volentieri.

- Ahimè, bella ragazza! Ho impegnato la parola.

- È la mia cattiva sorte! Ma non importa.

Lo condusse a casa, prese un barattolo e gli strofinò il petto con una pomata di suo padre. Il Re fu fatato.

- Ed ora, bella ragazza, dovreste prestarmi una scure.

- Eccola.

- Che cosa è quest'unto?

- È l'olio della cote dove è stata affilata.

Colla fatatura, ci volle un batter d'occhi per tornare al luogo dove trovavasi l'albero che parlava.

La Strega non c'era, e l'albero gli disse:

- Bada! Dentro il tronco c'è nascosto il mio cuore. Quando dovrai abbattermi non dar retta alla Strega. Se ti dirà di dar i colpi in su, e tu dàlli in giù. Se ti dirà di darli in giù, e tu dàlli in su; altrimenti m'ammazzeresti. Alla Stregaccia poi bisognerà spiccarle la testa con un sol colpo, o saresti spacciato; neppure la fatatura ti salverebbe.

Venne la Strega.

- Che cerchi da queste parti?

- Cerco un albero per far del carbone, e stavo osservando questo qui.

- Ti farebbe comodo? Te lo regalo, a patto che per atterrarlo tu dia colpi dove ti dirò io.

- Va bene.

Il Re brandì la scure, che tagliava meglio d'un rasoio e domandò:

- Dove?

- Qui.

The young woman was a beauty; the king would have gladly married her.

"Alas, beautiful girl I have already given my word."

"And that is my bad luck! However, it doesn't matter."

After taking him to her house, she took a pot and she scrubbed his chest with a potion that belonged to her father. The king was enchanted.

"And now, beautiful girl, you must lend me a hatchet."

"Here it is," she said.

"And what is this grease?"

"It is the oil from the whetstone on which the hatchet was sharpened."

"Under its spell, it takes only the blink of an eye to return to the place where you found the talking tree."

[When the King returned to the talking tree,] the witch was no longer there, and the tree said:

"Be careful. My heart is hidden within the trunk. When you are ready to chop me down, don't follow the witch's instructions. If she tells you to chop high, strike lower. If she tells you to chop low, strike higher; otherwise you will kill me. Then, you will have to split that dirty old witch's head with one stroke. Otherwise, you will be as good as dead; not even the spell will be able to save you.

When the witch returned, she asked the king:

"What are you searching for in these parts?"

"I am searching for a tree from which to make charcoal, and I was looking at this one here."

"Why not make yourself comfortable? I will give you the tree as a present, as long as you chop it down according to my instructions."

"Fine," said the king, and he took the hatchet, which cut better than a razor and asked:

"Where?"

"Here."

E lui, invece, diè lì.
- Ho sbagliato. Da capo. Dove?
- Lì.
E lui, invece, diè qui.- Ho sbagliato. Da capo.
Intanto non trovava il verso di assestare il colpo alla Strega:
essa stava guardinga. Il Re fece:
- Oooh!
- Che vedi?
- Una stella.
- Di giorno? È impossibile.
- Lassù, diritto a quel ramo: guardate!
E mentre la Strega gli voltava le spalle per guardare diritto
a quel ramo, lui le menò il colpo e le staccò, di netto, la testa.
Rotta così la malìa, dal tronco dell'albero uscì fuori una
donzella, che non poteva esser guardata fissa, tanto era bella!
Il Re, contentissimo, tornò insieme con lei al palazzo reale, e
ordinò che si preparassero subito magnifiche feste per gli
sponsali.
Arrivato quel giorno, mentre le dame di corte abbigliavano
da sposa la Regina, s'accorsero, con gran meraviglia, che avea
le carni dure come il legno. Una di esse volò dal Re:
- Maestà, la Regina ha le carni dure come il legno!
- Possibile?
Il Re e i ministri andarono ad osservare. La cosa era
sorprendente. Alla vista parevano carni da ingannare
chiunque; a toccarle, era legno! Lei intanto parlava e si
muoveva. I ministri dissero che il Re non poteva sposare una
bambola, quantunque essa parlasse e si muovesse; e
contromandaron le feste.
- Qui c'è un altro incanto! - pensò il Re, che si ricordò
dell'unto della scure.

Instead, he struck at another spot.

"I have made a mistake," said the king. "Once again, where?"

"Here" said the witch.

Instead, he struck at another spot.

"I have made a mistake," said the king. "Once again, where?"

In the meantime, he did not have the opportunity to deal a blow to the witch; she was watching him carefully.

"Oh" exclaimed the king.

"What do you see?" asked the witch.

"A star"

"During the day? That's impossible."

"Up there, right over that branch: look!"

And while the witch turned her shoulders to look directly at the branch, he dealt her a blow and cleanly cut off her head.

The spell was broken, and from the trunk of the tree emerged a maiden. So beautiful was she that no one could stare at her!

Contented, the king returned with her to his royal palace and ordered that a great wedding feast be prepared immediately.

One day, as the ladies of court were helping the queen put on her wedding gown, they noticed with great astonishment that her flesh was as hard as wood. One of them ran to the king.

"Majesty, the Queen has flesh as hard as wood."

"Is that possible?" he said.

The king and the ministers went to look. It was amazing. In appearance it looked so like flesh that it would fool anyone. However, it felt like wood! At the same time, she was able to speak and to move. The ministers told the king that he could not marry a doll, even though she could talk and move, and they cancelled the wedding.

"Here there is another spell" thought the king, who remembered the grease of the hatchet.

Prese un pezzetto di carne e lo tagliuzzò con questa. Aveva indovinato! I pezzettini, alla vista, parevan carne da ingannare chiunque; a toccarli, eran legno. Il tradimento gliel'aveva fatto la figliuola dell'Orco, per gelosia.

Il Re disse ai ministri:

- Vado e torno.

E si trovò nel bosco, dove aveva incontrato quella ragazza.

- Maestà, da queste parti? Che buon vento vi mena?

- Son venuto apposta per te.

La figlia dell'Orco non volea credergli:

- Parola di Re, che siete venuto apposta per me?

- Parola di Re!

Ed era vero; ma lei s'immaginava per le nozze.

Si presero a braccetto ed entrarono in casa.

- Questa è la scure che tu mi prestasti.

Nel porgergliela, il Re fece in maniera di ferirla in una mano.

- Ah, Maestà, che avete fatto! Son diventata di legno!

Il Re si fingeva afflittissimo di quell'accidente:

- E non si può rimediare?

- Aprite quell'armadio, prendete quel barattolo, ungetemi tutta coll'olio che è lì dentro, e sarò subito guarita.

Il Re prese il barattolo:

- Aspetta che io torni!

Lei capì e si messe a urlare:

- Tradimento! Tradimento!

E gli scatenò dietro i cento mastini di suo padre.

He took a small piece of flesh and he cut it up into little bits with the hatchet. He guessed it! At first sight, anyone would believe these little pieces were flesh; touching them, however, revealed that they were wood. This treachery was the work of the monster's daughter, out of jealousy.

The king said to his ministers:

"I go, but I will return." And he found himself in the forest where he had met that girl.

"Majesty, what are you doing here? What kind wind sent you?"

"I have come just for you," said the king.

The monster's daughter did not want to believe him.

Is this truly the word of the king? Have you come just for me?

"It is true," said the king.

And it was true. But she believed he had come to marry her.

They took each other arm in arm and went into the house.

"This is the hatchet that you lent me," said the king.

When he handed it to her, the king pretended to strike one of her hands.

"Oh, Majesty, what have you done? I have turned into wood!"

The king pretended to be troubled: "And can this not be remedied?" he asked.

Open that closet, take out that pot, and smear the oil in it all over me. And I will recover immediately.

The king took out the pot.

"Wait, " he said, "I will return."

However, she realized what was going on and began to scream.

"Treachery! Treachery!"

With that, she sent her father's hundred mastiffs after him.

Ma sì!... il Re era sparito. Con quell'olio le carni della Regina tornarono subito morbide, e si poterono celebrare le nozze.

Furono fatte feste reali per otto giorni,
e a noialtri non dettero neppure un corno.

But, of course, the king had already disappeared. With the oil he had taken, the flesh of the queen suddenly became soft, and they were able to get married.

The royal celebration lasted for eight days.
But to us, they gave not even a fig!

I tre anelli

C'era una volta un sarto, che aveva tre figliuole, una più bella dell'altra. Sua moglie era morta da un pezzo, e lui si stillava il cervello per riuscire a maritarle. Le ragazze non avevano dote, e senza dote un marito è un po' difficile a trovarsi.

Un giorno questo povero padre pensò d'andarsene in una pianura e chiamare la Sorte:

- Sorte, o Sorte!

Gli apparve una vecchia, colla conocchia e col fuso:

- Perché mi hai tu chiamata?

- Ti ho chiamata per le mie figliuole.

- Menale qui ad una ad una; si sceglieranno la sorte colle loro mani.

Il buon uomo, tornato a casa tutto contento, disse alle figliuole:

- La vostra fortuna è trovata!

E raccontò ogni cosa. Allora la maggiore si fece avanti, ringalluzzita:

- La prima scelta tocca a me. Sceglierò il meglio!

Il giorno dopo, padre e figliuola si avviarono per quella pianura:

- Sorte, o Sorte!

Gli apparve una vecchia, colla conocchia e col fuso:

- Perché m'hai tu chiamata?

- Ecco la mia figliuola maggiore.

La vecchia cavò di tasca tre anelli, uno d'oro, uno d'argento, uno di ferro e li mise sulla palma della mano:

- Scegli, e Dio t'aiuti!

- Questo qui.

Naturalmente prese l'anello d'oro.

- Maestà, vi saluto!

La vecchia le fece un inchino e sparì.

The Three Rings

Once upon a time, there was a tailor who had three daughters, one more beautiful than the other. His wife had been dead for some time, and he wracked his brain to get them married. These girls had no dowry, and finding a husband for them would be difficult.

One day this poor old father went out upon a wide plain and called out to Fate;

"Oh, Fate, Oh Fate!"

There appeared an old woman with a with a staff and a spindle.

"Why have you called me?"

"I have called you because of my daughters."

"Send them here, one by one; they shall choose their fates by their own hands."

The good man went home happy and said to his daughters:

"Your fortune is assured!"

And he told them everything. Therefore, the oldest came forward boldly.

"The first choice belongs to me. I will choose the best."

The next day, father and daughter went on to the plain.

"Fate, Oh Fate!"

To them appeared an old woman with a staff and a spindle.

"Why have you called me?"

"This is my oldest daughter."

The old woman took three rings from her pocket—one of gold, one of silver, and one of iron—and she put them into the palm of her hand.

"Choose, and may God help you!"

"This one here," said the girl.

Naturally, she took the golden ring.

"Majesty, I salute you!" said the old woman.

Then she made a bow and disappeared.

Tornati a casa, la sorella maggiore, pavoneggiandosi, disse alle altre due:

- Diventerò Regina! E voi reggerete lo strascico del manto reale!

Il giorno dopo andò col padre l'altra figlia.

Comparve la vecchia colla conocchia e col fuso, e cavò di tasca due anelli, uno d'argento ed uno di ferro:

- Scegli, e Dio t'aiuti!

- Questo qui.

E, s'intende, prese quello d'argento.

- Principessa vi saluto!

La vecchia le fece un inchino e sparì.

Tornata a casa, quella disse alla maggiore:

- Se tu sarai Regina, io sarò Principessa!

E tutt'e due si diedero a canzonare la sorella minore:

- Che volete? Chi tardi arriva male alloggia. Dovea venire al mondo prima.

Lei zitta.

Il giorno dopo andò col padre la figliuola minore.

Comparve la vecchia colla conocchia e col fuso e cavò di tasca, come la prima volta, tre anelli, uno d'oro, uno d'argento e uno di ferro:

- Scegli, e Dio t'aiuti!

- Questo qui.

Con gran rabbia di suo padre, avea preso quello di ferro.

La vecchia non le disse nulla, e sparì.

Per la strada il sarto continuò a brontolare:

- Perché non quello d'oro?

- Il Signore m'ispirò così.

Le due sorelle, curiose, vennero ad incontrarla per le scale.

- Facci vedere! Facci vedere!

Back home, the oldest sister arrogantly addressed the other two:

"I will become a queen! And you will carry the train of my royal cloak!"

The next day the second daughter went with the father.

Once again, there appeared the old woman with a staff and a spindle. She took from her pocket two rings, one of silver and one of iron:

"Choose, and may God help you!"

"This one here," said the girl.

And, of course, she took the silver one.

"Princess, I salute you!" said the old woman.

Then, she made a bow and disappeared.

Back home, this daughter said to the oldest sister:

"If you are going to be a queen, I am going to be a princess."

And both of them began to tease their younger sister:

"What do you expect? She who arrives late finds bad lodgings. You should have come into the world first."

But the youngest daughter remained silent.

The next day, the youngest daughter went with her father.

Once again, there appeared the old woman with the staff and the spindle, and, like the first time, she took from her pocket three rings: one of gold, one of silver, and one of iron.

"Choose, and may God help you!"

"This one here," said the girl.

When she chose the iron ring, her father became furious with her.

The old woman said nothing and disappeared.

On the road home, the tailor continued to complain.

"Why didn't you choose the golden ring?"

"The Lord inspired me to choose the iron one."

The other two other sisters were curious, and they came to meet her on the stairs when she got back.

"Let's see! Let's see!"

Come videro l'anello di ferro, si contorcevano dalle risa e la canzonavano. Saputo poi che lo avea scelto fra uno d'oro e uno d'argento, per grulla la presero e per grulla la lasciarono.

E lei, zitta.

Intanto si sparse la voce che le tre belle figliuole del sarto avevano gli anelli della buona sorte. Il Re del Portogallo dovea prender moglie e venne a vederle. Rimase ammaliato dalla maggiore:

- Siate Regina del Portogallo!

La sposò con grandi feste e la menò via.

Poco dopo venne un Principe. Rimase ammaliato dalla seconda.

- Siate Principessa!

La sposò con grandi feste e la menò via.

Restava l'ultima. Non la chiedeva nessuno.

Un giorno, finalmente, si presentò un pecoraio:

- Volete darmi questa figliuola?

Il sarto, che ne aveva una Regina ed una Principessa, era montato in superbia e rispose:

- Il pecoraio, scusate, noi per ora ce l'abbiamo.

Stava per passare un altr'anno. La minore restava sempre in casa, e il padre non faceva altro che brontolare giorno e notte:

- Le stava bene, stupidona! Sarebbe rimasta in un canto, con quel suo anello di ferro.

E all'anno appunto, tornò a presentarsi il pecoraio:

- Volete darmi quella figliuola?

- Prendila - rispose il sarto. - Non si merita altro!

Si sposarono, senza feste e senza nulla, e la menò via.

Allora il sarto disse:

- Voglio andar a visitare la mia figliuola Regina.

When they saw the iron ring, they doubled up with laughter and began to tease her. Learning that she had chosen it over the gold and silver ones, they took her for a fool and left her.

But she remained silent.

Meanwhile, the rumor got out that that the tailor's three beautiful daughters had the three rings of good fortune. The king of Portugal needed to get married, and he came to see them. He fell in love with the oldest.

He proclaimed her "queen of Portugal!"

He married her, they had a grand celebration, and he took her away.

A little while after, came a prince who fell in love with the second daughter.

"My princess!" he declared.

He married her, they had a grand celebration, and he took her away.

Only the last daughter remained. No one wanted her.

Finally, one day, a shepherd arrived and asked the tailor:

"Will you give me this daughter?"

The tailor, who was now the father of a queen and a princess, had become haughty, and he responded:

Shepherd, excuse me, but for now we will keep her.

When nearly a year had passed, the youngest daughter was still at home and her father complained day and night:

"Oh, this is fine! You stupid girl! Now you will remain in a corner with your ring of iron."

And exactly one year later, the shepherd returned:

"Will you give me your daughter?"

"Take her," responded the tailor. "She doesn't deserve anything better."

They married, without a wedding feast or any other celebration, and he took her away.

Thereupon, the tailor said: "I want to visit my daughter the queen."

La trovò che piangeva.

- Che cos'hai, figliuola mia?

- Sono disgraziata! Il Re vorrebbe un figliuolo, ed io non posso farne. I figliuoli li dà Dio.- Ma l'anello della buona fortuna non giova a nulla?

- Non giova a nulla. Il Re mi ha detto: "Se fra un anno non avrò un figliuolo, guai a te!". Son certa, babbo mio, che mi farà tagliar la testa.

Quel povero padre, come potea rimediare? E partì per far visita alla figliuola Principessa. La trovò che piangeva.

- Che cos'hai, figliuola mia?

- Sono disgraziata! Tutti i figliuoli che faccio mi muoiono dopo due giorni.

- E l'anello della buona fortuna non giova a nulla?

- Non giova a nulla. Il Principe mi ha detto: "Se questo che hai nel seno morrà anche lui, guai a te!". Son certa, babbo mio, che mi farà scacciar di casa!

Quel povero padre che potea farci? E partì.

Per via gli nacque il pensiero d'andar a vedere l'altra figliuola, quella del pecoraio. Ma aveva vergogna di presentarsi. Si travestì da mercante, prese con sé quattro ninnoli da vendere e, cammina, cammina, arrivò finalmente in quelle contrade lontane.

Vide un magnifico palazzo stralucente, e domandò a chi appartenesse.

- È il palazzo del re Sole.

Mentre stava lì a guardare, stupito, sentì chiamarsi da una finestra:

- Mercante, se portate bella roba, montate su. La Regina vuol comprare.

Montò su, e chi era mai la Regina? La sua figliuola minore, la moglie del pecoraio. Quello rimase di sasso; non potea neppure aprir le cassette degli oggetti da vendere.

When he found her, she was crying.

"What's wrong, my child?"

"I am miserable. The king would like a son, and I cannot make one. Sons are given by God."

"But is the ring of good fortune of no use?"

"It is of no use. The king has told me: 'Unless I have a son within a year, woe to you!' I am certain, my father, that he will cut off my head."

What could the poor father do? And he left to pay a visit to his daughter, the princess. But he found her crying as well.

"What's the matter, my child?"

"I am wretched! All of the children I had died after two days."

"But is the ring of good fortune of no use?"

"It is of no use." The prince has told me: 'If the child that you have in your womb also dies, woe to you.' I am certain, my father, that he will turn me out of the house."

What could the poor father do? And he left.

On the way, he decided to visit the other daughter, the one who had married the shepherd. However, he was ashamed to show himself. So, he disguised himself as a merchant, took with him three baubles to sell and, walking for some time, finally arrived in that distant land.

He saw a magnificent palace all lit up, and he asked to whom it belonged.

"It is the palace of the Sun King," he was told.

Staring at it in astonishment, he heard someone calling him from the window.

"Merchant, if you have beautiful things to sell, come up. The queen wishes to buy."

He went up. To his amazement he saw that the queen was none other than his youngest daughter, the wife of the shepherd. He was so dumbfounded that he couldn't even open the case to take out the things he was selling.

- *Vi sentite male, poverino? - gli disse la Regina.*
- *Figliuola mia, sono tuo padre! E ti chiedo perdono!*
*Lei, che l'aveva riconosciuto, non permise che le si gettasse
ai piedi, e lo ricevé tra le braccia:*
- *Siate il ben venuto! Ho dimenticato ogni cosa. Mangiate e
bevete, ma prima di sera andate via. Se re Sole vi trovasse,
rimarreste incenerito.*
*Dopo che quello ebbe mangiato e bevuto, la figliuola gli
disse:*
- *Questi doni son per voi. Questa nocciuola è per la sorella
maggiore: questa boccettina di acqua per l'altra. La nocciuola,
dee inghiottirsela col guscio; l'acqua, dee berne una stilla al
giorno, non più. E che badino, babbo!*
*Quando le due sorelle intesero la bella fortuna toccata alla
minore e videro quella sorta di regali che loro inviava, arsero
d'invidia e di dispetto:*
- *Si beffava di loro con quella nocciuola e con quell'acqua!*
*La maggiore buttò la nocciuola in terra, e la pestò col
calcagno. La nocciuola schizzò sangue. C'era dentro un
bambino piccino piccino: lei gli aveva schiacciata la testa!*
Il Re, visto quell'atto di superbia e il bambino schiacciato:
- *Olà! - gridò - levatemela d'innanzi; mozzatele il capo!*
E, senza pietà né misericordia, la fece mettere a morte.
*L'altra, nello stesso tempo, avea cavato il turacciolo alla
boccetta e, affacciatasi a una finestra, n'avea versata tutta
l'acqua.*
*Sotto la finestra passavano dei ragazzi che trascinavano un
gatto morto. L'acqua cadde su questo, e il gatto risuscitò.*
- *Ah, scellerata! - urlò il Principe. - Hai tolto la sorte ai
nostri figliuoli!*
E in quel momento di furore, la strangolò colle sue mani.

"Are you ill, poor man?" asked the queen.

"Oh, my daughter, I am your father. And I beg your forgiveness."

His daughter recognized him. She did not let him bow before her and, instead, she embraced him.

"You are welcome here. I forgive everything. Eat and drink, but before night comes you must be on your way. If the Sun King finds you, you will be burned to ashes."

After he had eaten and drunk, his daughter said:

"These gifts are for you. This hazelnut is for my oldest sister, and this small bottle of water is for my other sister. The hazelnut must be swallowed with the shell; the water must be drunk one drop per day, no more. And with care, father!"

When the other two sisters heard about the good fortune that had befallen their younger sister and saw what kinds of gifts she had sent, they became envious and spiteful.

"She mocks us by sending this hazelnut and this water," they said.

The elder sister threw the hazelnut on the ground, and she crushed it with her heel. The hazelnut spurted blood. Inside there was a tiny baby; she had crushed its head.

Seeing this arrogance and the crushed child, the king screamed:

"Oh, get her out of my sight; off with her head!"

And without pity or mercy, he had her put to death.

At the same time, the other sister had pulled the stopper from the bottle and had thrown all of the water out of a window.

Under the window two young boys were dragging a dead cat. The water fell on it, and the cat was brought back to life.

"Oh, wicked one," screamed the prince. "You have wasted the water and condemned our children!"

And in that moment of madness, he strangled her with his own hands.

Il babbo tornò dalla figliuola minore, e raccontò, piangendo, quelle disgrazie.

- *Babbo mio, mangiate e bevete, e prima di sera andate via. Se re Sole vi trovasse, rimarreste incenerito. Appena avrò buone notizie, vi manderò a chiamare.*

La sera tornò re Sole, e lei gli domandò:
- *Maestà, che cosa avete visto nel vostro viaggio?*

- *Ho visto tagliar la testa a una Regina e strangolare una Principessa. Se lo meritavano.*

- *Ah, Maestà, eran le mie sorelle! Ma voi potete risuscitarle; non mi negate questa grazia!*

- *Vedremo! - rispose re Sole.*

Il giorno dopo, appena fu giunto nel luogo dov'era seppellita la Regina, picchiò sulla fossa e disse:
- *Tu che stai sotto terra,*
  Mi manda la tua sorella;
  Se dal buio volessi uscire,
  Del mal fatto ti déi pentire.

- *Rispondo a mia sorella:*
  Sto bene sotto terra.
  Dio gli dia male e malanno!
  Vo' la nuova avanti l'anno!

- *Resta lì, donnaccia infame!*

E il re Sole continuò il suo viaggio. Arrivato dov'era stata sepolta la Principessa, picchiò sulla fossa e disse:
- *Tu che stai sotto terra,*
  Mi manda la tua sorella;
  Se vuoi tornare da morte a vita,
  Del mal fatto sii pentita!

- *Rispondo a mia sorella:*
  Sto bene sotto terra.
  Male occulto o mal palese,
  Vo' la nuova avanti un mese!

The father returned to his youngest daughter and, crying, told her of the tragedies.

"Father, come eat and drink, but before night comes you must leave. If the Sun King finds you, you will be burned to ashes. As soon as I have good news, I will call for you."

At night, the Sun King returned, and she asked him:

"Majesty, what have you seen on your journey?"

"I have seen a queen get her head cut off and a princess strangled. They deserved it."

"Oh, Majesty, they were my sisters! But you can revive them; don't deny me this request!"

"We will see!" responded the Sun King.

The next day, as soon as he had reached the tomb in which the queen was buried, he tapped on the ground and said:

"You who are under the ground,
   I am sent by your sister;
   If you want to emerge from the darkness,
   You must repent your sins."

"Tell my sister this:
   'I am happy to stay under ground.'
   May God visit evil and sickness upon her
   Before the year is out."

"Then stay there, you ugly, evil woman!" he replied.

And the Sun King continued his journey. When he reached the place where the princess was buried, he tapped on the ground and said:

"You who are under the ground,
   I am sent by your sister;
   If you want to come back from the dead and live again,
   Repent your sins!"

"Tell my sister this:
   'I am happy to stay under ground.'
   May evil befall her—hidden or known—
   Before the month is out!"

- Resta lì, donnaccia infame!
Re Sole continuò il suo viaggio, e quelle due sorelle se le
mangiarono i vermi.

Stretta è la foglia, larga è la via.
Dite la vostra, ché ho detto la mia.

"Stay, there, you ugly, evil woman!" he replied.

And so, the Sun King continued on his journey and left the two sisters to be eaten by worms.

The journey is long and the path is narrow.
I've told my story; tell yours tomorrow.

La vecchina

C'era una volta un Re molto giovane, che voleva prender moglie, ma voleva sposare la più bella ragazza del mondo.

- E se non è di sangue reale? - gli domandarono i ministri.

- Non me n'importa nulla.

Allora sappiate, Maestà, che la più bella ragazza del mondo è la figliuola di un ciaba. Ma il popolo, che è maligno, potrebbe chiamarla: la regina Ciabatta... Maestà, non sta bene: rifletteteci meglio.

Il Re rispose: - La figliuola del ciaba è la più bella ragazza del mondo? La figliuola del ciaba sarà dunque mia sposa e Regina. Andrò a vederla senza farmi conoscere; partirò domani.

Ordinò che gli si sellasse uno dei suoi cavalli, e, accompagnato da un solo servitore, s'incamminò per quel paese, dove il ciaba abitava.

Per via incontrarono una vecchia che domandava l'elemosina:

- Fate la carità! Fate la carità!

Il Re non se ne dava per inteso.

La vecchina arrancava dietro il cavallo.

- Fate la carità! Fate la carità!

Il cavallo del Re s'adombrò, e urtò la vecchina che cadde per terra.

Il Re, senza punto curarsene, tirò innanzi; ma il servitore, impietosito, scese da cavallo, la sollevò, e visto che non s'era fatta nulla di male, cavò di tasca le poche monete che aveva e gliele mise in mano:

- Vecchina mia, non ho altro.

- Grazie, figliuolo; si vede il buon cuore. Accetta in ricambio questo anellino e portalo al dito; sarà la tua fortuna.

The Old Woman

There once was a very young king who wanted to take a wife, but he would marry only the most beautiful girl in the world.

"And what if she is not of royal blood?" asked his ministers.

"That does not concern me in the least," responded the king.

"Then you should know, Majesty, that the most beautiful girl in the world is the daughter of a cobbler. But the people, who are malicious, will call her the 'cobbler queen.' Majesty, this is not good. Think carefully about this."

The king responded: "The most beautiful girl in the world is the daughter of a cobbler? Very well, she shall be my wife and my queen. I will go to see her without identifying myself to her. I leave tomorrow."

He ordered that one of his horses be saddled and, accompanied by only one servant, he made his way to the town in which the cobbler lived.

On the way, he encountered an old woman who was begging.

"Please show me some charity," she implored.

But the king paid her no mind.

As the old woman hobbled behind the king's horse, she continued to beg for his charity.

At the sound of her cries, the king's horse reared up and smashed into the old woman, who fell to the ground.

Without paying any attention, the king rode on. But the servant was moved to pity and helped her up. Seeing that she had not been hurt, he took the few coins he had and gave them to her.

"My dear lady, this is all I have," said the servant.

"Thank you, my son," she replied. "I can see that you have a good heart. Accept in return this small ring and wear it on your finger. It will bring you good luck."

Arrivati in quel paese, il Re accompagnato dal servitore passò e ripassò davanti la bottega del ciaba, finché non gli riuscì di vedere la bella ragazza, che era la più bella del mondo. Rimase abbagliato!

E, senza por tempo in mezzo, disse al ciaba:

- Io sono il Re: vo' la tua figliuola per moglie.

- Maestà, c'è un intoppo. La mia figliuola ha una malìa: chi le parlerà la prima volta e le farà provare una puntura al dito mignolo, quello dovrà essere il suo sposo. Possiamo provare.

Il Re a questa notizia rimase un po' turbato; ma poi pensò:

- Se questa malìa è la sua buona sorte, costei dev'essere destinata a sposare un regnante.

E tutto allegro, disse al ciaba:

- Proviamo.

Il ciaba chiamò la figliuola, senza dirle del Re; e come questi se la vide dinanzi, restò più abbagliato di prima.

- Buon giorno, bella ragazza.

- Buon giorno, signore.

Lei non sapeva nulla della malìa. Suo padre, che sarebbe stato felice di vederla Regina, le domandò:

- Non ti senti nulla?

- Nulla. Che cosa dovrei sentirmi?

Il povero Re, gli parve di morire a quella risposta. E stava per andarsene zitto zitto; quando il servitore, ch'era rimasto in un canto, credette opportuno di dire sottovoce alla ragazza: - Badate, è Sua Maestà!

- Ahi! Ahi! Ahi!

La ragazza si sentiva un'atroce puntura al dito mignolo, e scoteva la mano:

- Ahi! Ahi! Ahi!

Figuriamoci il viso del Re, come capì che quella ragazza, la più bella del mondo, era destinata a quel tanghero del suo servitore!

When he arrived in the land to which he was traveling, the king, accompanied by his servant, walked back and forth in front of the cobbler's shop until he finally succeeded in seeing that beautiful maiden, the most beautiful in all the world. The king was dazzled by her beauty.

And without wasting a moment, he said to the cobbler.

"I am the king, and I want to marry your daughter."

"Majesty," said the cobbler, "there is a problem. My daughter is under a spell. He who speaks to her for the first time and makes her feel a sting in her little finger will be her husband. We can try."

At this news, the king became a bit angry, but then he thought:

"If this spell is lucky, she is destined to marry royalty."

Happy again, he said to the cobbler: "Let's try."

The cobbler called his daughter without telling her of the king. As soon as he saw her before him, he was even more dazzled than ever.

"Good day, beautiful girl."

"Good day, sir."

She knew nothing of the spell. Her father, who would have been very happy to see her become a queen, asked her: "Don't you feel anything?"

"Nothing," she said. "What should I feel?"

The poor king looked as if her were going to die when he heard this response. And he remained very quiet while the servant, who was standing in a corner, took the opportunity to tell the girl under his breath: "Listen, he is your lord."

"Ouch! Ouch! Ouch!" cried the young woman. She felt a horrible sting in her little finger and her hand hurt.

"Ouch! Ouch! Ouch!"

Imagine the look on the king's face when he realized that the young lady, the most beautiful women in the world, was destined for that lout of a servant!

Prese in disparte il ciaba e gli disse:
- Lascia fare a me; la tua figliuola sarà Regina.
Tornato al palazzo reale, chiamò il servitore:
- Prima che tu sposi la figliuola del ciaba, devi rendermi un servigio: mi fido soltanto di te. Portami questa lettera al Re di Spagna, e attendi la risposta; ma nessuno deve sapere dove tu vada e perché.
- Maestà, sarà fatto. Prese la lettera e partì.
A metà di strada incontrò quella vecchina:
- Dove vai, figliuolo mio?
- Dove mi portan le gambe.
- Ah, poverino! Tu non sai quel che ti aspetta. Quella lettera è un tradimento! Se tu la presenti al Re, sarai subito ammazzato. Portagli questa, invece: farà un altro effetto.
Allora lui prese la lettera della vecchina, e quella del Re la buttò via. Ringraziò e proseguì il viaggio.
Era già passato un anno, e non si era saputo più nuova di lui.
Il Re tornò dal ciaba, e disse alla ragazza:
- Quell'uomo dev'essere morto: è già passato un anno e non si sa nuova di lui. Il meglio che possiamo fare è lo sposarci noialtri.
- Maestà, come voi volete.
Il Re fece i preparativi delle nozze, e quando fu quel giorno, andò insieme coi ministri a rilevare la sposa con la carrozza di gala.
In casa del ciaba trovarono una granata ritta in mezzo alla stanza, e il Re disse ai ministri:
- Ecco Sua Maestà la Regina!
I ministri, stupefatti, si guardarono in viso senza osar di rispondere.
- Maestà, è una granata

He took the cobbler aside and he said:

"Leave it to me, and your daughter will be a queen."

On returning to the royal palace, he summoned the servant.

"Before you marry the daughter of the cobbler, you must render me a service. I trust only you. Take this letter to the king of Spain, and wait for a reply. However, no one must know where you are going or why."

"Master, it is done." He took the letter and departed.

On the way, however, the servant met the old woman who had given him the ring.

"Where are you going, my son?" she asked

"Wherever my legs take me."

"Oh, my poor boy!" she cried. "You do not know what awaits you. That letter is a betrayal. If you present it to the king of Spain, you will be killed immediately. Take this one instead for a better result."

Therefore, he took the letter from the old woman and threw the king's letter away. He thanked her and went on his way.

A year later, however, there was no news of him.

So, the king returned to the cobbler and said to his daughter:

"The servant must be dead. A year has already passed, and there is no news of him. The best thing we can do is to get married."

"As you will, Majesty," replied the young woman.

The king made preparations for the wedding, and when the day came he went with his ministers to take away the bride in a luxurious coach.

In the cobbler's house, they found a broom standing erect in the middle of a room, and the king said to his ministers: "Here is her majesty, the queen."

The ministers were stupefied, and they looked at each other without daring to respond.

But then they said: "Majesty, that is a broom!"

Il Re in quella granata ci vedeva la figliuola del ciaba, la più bella ragazza del mondo; e, presala pel manico (lui credeva di prenderla per la mano) la portò in carrozza e cominciò a dirle tante belle cose.

I ministri erano costernati e si sussurravano nell'orecchio:

- Che disgrazia! Il Re è ammattito! Il Re è ammattito!

Però, prima di arrivare in città, dove il popolo aspettava l'entrata della Regina, si fecero coraggio; e uno di loro gli disse:

- Maestà, perdonate!... Ma questa qui è una granata!

Il Re montò sulle furie; la prese per un'offesa alla Regina. Fece fermar la carrozza e ordinò ai soldati che legassero quell'impertinente alla coda di un cavallo, e così lo trascinassero fino al palazzo reale.

Gli altri, vista la mala parata, stettero zitti. E il Re, giunto al palazzo reale, si affacciò alla finestra per mostrare al popolo la Regina:

- Ecco la vostra Regina!

Non avea finito di dirlo, che gli cadde come una benda dagli occhi e si vide lì, colla granata in mano, mentre tutto il popolo rideva, perché Sua Maestà pareva proprio uno spazzino.

Con chi prendersela? La colpa era della sua cattiva stella, e di quella malìa della ragazza!

Ma intanto s'incaponiva di più nel volerla per moglie.

Il servitore tornò sano e salvo, colmo di regali.

- Che rispose il Re di Spagna?

- Maestà, il Re di Spagna rispose: Fai, fai, fai, Non l'hai avuta e non l'avrai.

Il Re fece finta di esserne contento, ma chiamò un Mago e gli raccontò ogni cosa:

- Come va questa faccenda?

But in this broom, the king saw the cobbler's daughter, the most beautiful girl in the world. He took the broom by the handle, thinking that he was taking the young woman by the hand, put it into the carriage, and began to speak sweetly to it.

Bewildered, the ministers whispered in each other's ears: "What a tragedy. The king is mad! The king is mad!"

However, before arriving in the city, where the people awaited the queen's entrance, one of them found the courage to say:

"Pardon us Majesty, but that is a broom."

The king became furious, for he took the comment as an offense to the queen. He ordered the carriage to stop and told the soldiers to tie the impertinent minister to the tail of a horse. In this way he dragged him all the way to the royal palace.

Seeing this terrible outcome, the others remained silent. Near the royal palace, the king came to the window of the carriage to show the people their new queen.

"Here is your queen!" he shouted.

Before he had even finished saying this, however, everything became clear to him, as if a bandage had fallen from his eyes, and he saw himself with a broom in his hand. The people laughed, for the king looked like a street cleaner.

Who was to blame? The fault was surely that of his unlucky star and of the spell that had been placed on the girl.

Nonetheless, he wanted to marry the young woman even more than before.

Then, the servant returned from Spain safe and sound, and loaded with gifts.

"What response from the king of Spain?" asked the king.

"Majesty, the king of Spain says: 'Fai, fai, fai; you don't have her now and you never will.'"

The king pretended to be content, but he called a magician and told him everything.

"What goes on here?" he asked

- Maestà, la faccenda è piana. Quell'uomo possiede l'anello incantato della fata Regina, e finché lo avrà al dito, non vi sbarazzerete di lui. Bisogna trovare un'astuzia per portargli via quell'anello: la forza non vale.

Pensa e ripensa, un giorno il Re, visto che il suo servitore era tutto sudato dal gran lavorare che aveva fatto:

- Vien qua, - gli disse - vo' darti un bicchiere del mio vino; te lo meriti.

Quel vino era conciato coll'oppio, e il pover'uomo non l'ebbe bevuto, che cadde in un profondissimo sonno.

Sua Maestà gli cavò l'anello dal dito, se lo mise nel suo, e così andò a presentarsi alla figliuola del ciaba:

- Buon giorno, bella ragazza!

- Ahi! Ahi! Ahi!

La ragazza sentiva un'atroce puntura al dito mignolo e scuoteva la mano!

- Ahi! Ahi! Ahi!

Ora la cosa andava bene, e il Re ordinò di bel nuovo i preparativi per le nozze. E quando fu quel giorno, andò a rilevare la sposa colla carrozza di gala.

Giunti al palazzo reale, disse alla Regina:

- Maestà, questo è il vostro appartamento.

Ma, poco dopo, quando il Re volle andare a vederla, gira di qua, gira di là, non trovava l'uscio e vedeva scritto sui muri:

Fai, fai, fai,

Non l'hai avuta e non l'avrai.

La Regina veniva ai ricevimenti di corte, veniva nella sala da pranzo dove c'erano molti invitati; poi si ritirava nel suo appartamento.

Il Re voleva andare a vederla; ma, gira di qua, gira di là, non trovava mai l'uscio e vedeva sempre scritto sui muri:

Fai, fai, fai,

Non l'hai avuta e non l'avrai.

"Majesty, the matter is plain. That man possesses the fairy queen's magic ring, and as long as he has it on his finger, you will not be rid of him. You need to find some trick to get that ring. All of your power will do you no good."

Racking his brain, one day the king noticed that his servant was perspiring from some hard work he had just finished.

"Come here," he told him. "I want to give you a glass of my wine. You deserve it."

This wine was tainted with opium, and no sooner had the poor man drunk it than he fell into a deep sleep.

His Majesty pulled the ring from his finger, and put it on his own, and thus went to present himself to the daughter of the cobbler.

"Good day, beautiful lady."

"Ouch! Ouch! Ouch!" she cried, for she felt a terrible stabbing in her little finger and her hand stung.

"Ouch! Ouch! Ouch!"

Now things were going well, and the king ordered that preparations for the wedding be made anew. And when the day came, he picked up the bride in an elegant carriage.

Once at the royal palace, he showed the queen to her apartment.

However, in a little while, when the king wanted to see her, he turned this way, he turned that way, but he could not find the door to her apartment. Instead, he saw written on the wall:

"Fai, fai, fai.

You don't have her now, and you never will."

The queen came to court receptions, to the dining room where many people had been invited; then she returned to her apartment.

The king wanted to see her. He turned this way, he turned that way, but he could never find the door to her apartment. Instead, he always saw written on the wall:

"Fai, fai, fai.

You don't have her now and you never will."

Si disperava, ma non diceva nulla a nessuno; non volea sentirsi canzonare.

Quel pover'uomo del servitore, dopo un sonno di due giorni, appena aperti gli occhi, si era subito accorto che gli era stato rubato l'anello, ed era uscito dal palazzo reale, piangendo la sua sventura.

Fuori le porte della città avea trovato la vecchina:

- Ah, vecchina mia! Mi han rubato l'anello.

- Non ti disperare, non è nulla. Quando il Re avrà sposato, appena la Regina sarà entrata nel suo appartamento, pianta questo chiodo sulla soglia dell'uscio e vedrai.

Perciò il Re non trovava mai l'uscio, quando voleva entrare nelle stanze della Regina. C'era quel chiodo piantato lì, che glielo impediva.

Il Re scoppiava dalla rabbia. Fece chiamare novamente il Mago, e gli raccontò in segreto ogni cosa.

- Come va questa faccenda?

- Maestà, la faccenda è piana. Quell'uomo ha avuto un chiodo incantato dalla fata Regina, e l'ha piantato sulla soglia. E questa volta, Maestà, non c'è astuzia che valga: rimarrete un marito senza moglie.

- Ma che offesa ho io fatto a codesta fata Regina? Non la conosco neppur di vista!

- No, Maestà. Vi rammentate d'una vecchina che vi domandò l'elemosina il giorno che voi andavate la prima volta dal ciaba? Vi ricordate che la urtaste col cavallo e cadde per terra?

- Sì.

Era lei, la fata Regina.

Il Re dovette persuadersi che era inutile lottare con una Fata, e si rassegnò a sposare una bella ragazza, sì, ma non la più bella del mondo. Sposò la Reginotta di Francia.

He despaired, but he said nothing to anyone, for he did not want to be ridiculed.

Meanwhile, after having slept for two days, the servant woke up, and he immediately realized that he had been robbed of the ring and thrown out of the royal palace. He bemoaned his fate.

Outside of the city gate, he found the old woman.

"Oh, my dear old lady. They have stolen my ring," he said.

"Don't despair," she said. "It is nothing. After the king has been married and as soon as the queen enters her apartment, place this nail on the door's threshold and you'll see."

So, the King never found the door when he wanted to enter the queen's rooms. A nail, planted on the threshold, always stopped him.

Bursting with anger, the king had the magician called again, and he recounted everything, swearing the magician to secrecy.

"What goes on here?" he asked

"Majesty," said the magician, "things are plain. That man got a magical nail from the fairy queen, and he placed it on the threshold. And this time, majesty, there is no trick that will work. You will remain a husband without a wife."

"But what offense have I committed against this fairy queen? I don't know her, nor have I ever seen her."

"No, Majesty. Do you remember an old woman who asked you for some kindness the day who you first traveled to the cobbler's? Do you recall crashing into her with your horse and her falling to the ground?"

"Yes," said the king.

"It was she, the fairy queen."

The king had to persuade himself that it was useless to battle a fairy, and he resigned himself to marry a woman who was, yes, beautiful, but not the most beautiful woman in the world. She was the princess of France.

Il servitore sposò la figliuola del ciaba; e il Re gli diè una ricca dote e lo fece intendente di casa reale.

Re e servitore ebbero molti figliuoli:
E noi restiamo da cetriuoli.

The servant married the daughter of the cobbler. The king gave them a rich dowry and made him the superintendent of the royal palace.

Many a child had both servant and king.
So ends our story of the old woman and her magical ring.

La fontana della bellezza

C'era una volta un Re e una Regina, che avevano una figliuola bruttissima e contraffatta nella persona, e non se ne davano pace.

La tenevan rinchiusa, sola sola, in una camera appartata e, un giorno il Re, un giorno la Regina, le portavan da mangiare in una cesta. Quando erano lì, sfogavansi a piangere.

- Figliuola sventurata! Sei nata Regina, e non puoi godere della tua sorte!

Diventata grande, a sedici anni, lei disse al padre:

- Maestà, perché tenermi rinchiusa qui? Lasciatemi andar pel mondo. Il cuore mi presagisce che troverò la mia fortuna.

Il Re non voleva acconsentire:

- Dove sarebbe andata, così sola e inesperta? Era impossibile!

- Lasciatemi andare, o m'ammazzo!

A questa minaccia disperata, il Re non seppe resistere:

- Figliuola mia, parti pure!

La diè quattrini a sufficienza, e una notte, mentre tutti nel palazzo reale dormivano, la Reginotta si messe in via. Cammina, cammina, arrivò in una campagna. Il sole, al meriggio, scottava; e lei riparossi sotto un albero. Di lì a poco ecco un lamentìo:

- Ahi! Ahi! Ahi!

Lei, dalla paura, si voltò di qua e di là, ma non vide nessuno.

- Ahi! Ahi! Ahi!

Allora, fattasi coraggio, avvicinossi a quel punto d'onde il lamento partiva, e tra l'erba scoperse una lucertolina, che agitava il moncherino della coda e nicchiava a quel modo.

- Che cosa è stato, lucertolina?

The Fountain of Beauty

Once upon a time, there were a king and queen who had a very ugly daughter. Her personality was no better, and she never gave her parents any peace.

They kept her hidden, alone, in a secluded room. One day the king, then another day the queen brought her food in a basket. When they were there, they gave themselves over to crying.

"Unfortunate daughter! You have been born a queen, and you can not enjoy your fate."

She grew older, and at sixteen years she said to her father:

"Lord, why do you keep me shut away? Let me go into the world. My heart predicts that I will find my fortune."

The king did not wish to consent:

"Where will you go, alone and inexperienced? It's impossible."

"Let me go or I will kill myself."

Hearing this desperate threat, the king didn't know how to resist.

"Go, then, my daughter."

He gave her enough money, and while all in the royal palace were sleeping, the princess went on her way. She walked for a long time and came to a rural area. The sun was just rising above the horizon, and she rested under a tree. There, in a little while she heard a lament.

"Ahi! Ahi! Ahi!"

Out of fear, she turned this way and that, but she saw no one.

"Ahi! Ahi! Ahi!"

So, taking courage, she neared the place from where the lament was coming, and across the grass sprang a small lizard, which shook the stump of his tail hesitantly.

"What has happened, lizard?"

*- Mi hanno rotto la coda e non ritrovo il pezzettino. O, se tu
me lo trovassi, ti farei un gran regalo.*

*La Reginotta, impietosita, si dié a frugare: e fruga e rifruga
in mezzo a quell'erbe, finalmente eccolo lì!*

- Grazie, ragazza mia. Pel tuo regalo, scava qui sotto.

*Scavato un tantino, la Reginotta tirò fuori una cipolla poco
più grossa d'una nocciuola.*

- Che cosa debbo farne?

- Tienla cara. Un giorno, forse, ti servirà.

La Reginotta se la mise in tasca.

*Strada facendo, incontrò una povera vecchia con un sacco
di grano sulle spalle. A un tratto si rompe il sacco, e tutto il
grano le va per terra. La vecchia cominciò a pelarsi dalla
stizza.*

Non è nulla disse la Reginotta. Ve lo raccatterò io.

*Ah, i chicchi son contati! Se ne mancasse uno solo, mio
marito mi ammazzerebbe!*

*E la Reginotta, con una santa pazienza, glielo raccattò tutto,
chicco per chicco, senza che ne mancasse uno solo.*

- Grazie, buona figliuola; non posso darti altro che questo.

*E le dette un coltellino da due soldi, di quelli col manico di
ferro.*

- Che cosa volete che ne faccia?

- Tienlo caro. Un giorno, forse, ti servirà.

La Reginotta se lo mise in tasca.

*Cammina, cammina, arrivò all'orlo d'un fosso profondo.
Sentiva un belato tremolante. Guardò e vide laggiù una
capretta:*

- Capretta, che cosa è stato?

- Son cascata nel fosso e mi son rotta una gamba.

"They have broken off my tail, and I can't find the remainder of it. Oh, if you find it for me, I will give you a great gift."

Impetuously, the princess began to search, and she searched and searched through the grass and finally found it.

"Thank you, my girl. For your gift, dig under here."

Digging a little while, the princess pulled out an onion a little larger than a hazel nut.

"What am I to do with this?"

"Hold on to it always. Maybe, one day it will come in handy."

The princess put it in her pocket.

Traveling a while, she met a poor old woman carrying a sack of grain on her shoulders. All at once, the sack broke, and all the grain fell to the ground. The woman became very agitated.

"This is nothing," said the princess. "I will pick them up for you."

"Oh, the beans are counted. Even if only one is missing, my husband will kill me."

And, having the patience of a saint, the princess picked them all up, bean by bean, without missing even one.

"Thank you, dear child; however, I can't give you anything but this."

And she gave her a small pocketknife with an iron handle.

"What am I to do with this?"

"Hold on to it always. Maybe, one day it will come in handy."

The princess put the knife in her pocket.

After walking for some time, she came upon the edge of a deep hole and heard a fearful bleating. Looking down, she saw a baby goat.

"Little goat, what has happened?"

"I have fallen into the hole and have broken my leg."

Scese laggiù, la prese in collo, e poi la fasciò così bene con un fazzoletto, che quella, alla meglio, zoppicando, poté camminare.

- Grazie, ragazza. Che darti? Il mio sonaglino.

- Che cosa vuoi me ne faccia?

- Tienlo caro. Un giorno, forse, ti servirà.

La Reginotta le staccò dal collare il sonaglino e se lo mise in tasca, insieme con la cipolletta e il coltellino da due soldi.

Cammina, cammina, una sera capitò presso una fattoria fuori di mano.

- Anime cristiane, datemi alloggio per questa notte!

La padrona pareva una buona donna, e si misero a ragionare in cucina, mentre la pentola bolliva.

- Chi siete? Dove andate?

La Reginotta cominciò a raccontarle la sua storia.

- Zitta, zitta, chiacchierona! Zitta, zitta!

Era la pentola che brontolava; ma la sentiva lei sola.

Non le diè retta e continuò un altro pochino, fino al punto della sua partenza del palazzo reale.

- Zitta, zitta, chiacchierona! Zitta, zitta!

Era la pentola che brontolava; ma la sentiva lei sola. Rimase colpita; e si fermò.

- E dopo? - domandò la donna.

- Eccomi qui.

Quando giunse il marito, quella donna gli riferì minutamente ogni cosa.

- Sai che ho pensato, marito mio? Noi abbiamo una figliuola che è un sole: conduciamola dal Re. Gli diremo che è la sua figliuola, resa così bella da una Fata. La Reginotta la chiuderemo nel granaio e ve la lasceremo morire.

Ma il Re come potrà crederlo?

- Ci ho tutti i segnali.

She climbed down, took the kid by the neck, and afterward she bound up his leg with a handkerchief, so that, somehow, he was able to hobble along.

"Thank you, young lady," said the kid. "What shall I give you? My bell."

"And what am I to do with it?"

"Hold on to it. One day it may come in handy."

The princess removed the bell from the kid's collar and put it in her pocket along with the onion and the pocketknife with the iron handle.

After traveling on, one night she came to an isolated farmhouse.

"Christian souls," she said, "give me lodging tonight."

The mistress of the farm seemed to be a good woman, and they began to talk in the kitchen while the pot was boiling.

"Who are you and where are you going?" asked the mistress.

The princess began to tell her story.

"Quiet, quiet, chatterbox. Quiet, quiet," mumbled the pot, but only she could hear it.

However, she didn't pay any attention and continued on for a while, until she came to the time when she had left the palace.

"Quiet, quiet, chatterbox. Quiet, quiet" mumbled the pot, but only she could hear it.

She was struck with fear, and she stopped speaking.

"And then?" asked the lady

At that point, the woman's husband came home. "Here I am," he said. And the woman recounted everything the princess had told her in minute detail.

"Do you know what I have been thinking husband? We have a daughter who is as beautiful as the sun. Let's take her to the king and tell him that she is his daughter made this beautiful by a fairy. We'll lock up the princess in the barn and let her die. "

"But will the king ever believe this?"

"I have a plan."

Così fecero. Nel mezzo della notte, afferrarono la povera Reginotta, la chiusero in un granaio, e il giorno dopo condussero la loro figliuola al palazzo reale.

Il Re e la Regina, sentita quella storia della Fata, rimanevano ancora incerti. Allora la ragazza, indettata, disse:

- Maestà, non vi ricordate di quando venivate nella mia camera colla cesta, e poi vi mettevate a dire piangendo: "Figliuola sventurata, sei nata Regina e non puoi godere della tua sorte"?

Il Re e la Regina rimasero. Quelle parole non potea saperle nessun altro, che la loro figliuola! Abbracciarono la ragazza, e bandirono feste reali.

Ai due che l'avean condotta regalarono un monte di monete d'oro.

Intanto la povera Reginotta, dopo essersi per tre giorni stemperata in lagrime, cominciò a sentire anche fame. Chiamò più volte, domandando per carità almeno un tozzo di pan duro!

Non accorreva anima viva. Allora rammentossi della cipolletta:

- Poteva ingannare un po' lo stomaco!

E la cavò di tasca.

- Comanda! Comanda!

- Da mangiare!

Ed ecco pietanze fumanti, tovagliuolo, posata, coltello, bottiglia e bicchiere.

Terminato di mangiare, ogni cosa sparì.

Cavò di tasca il coltellino.

- Comanda! Comanda!

- Spacca quell'uscio per legna.

E, in un attimo, l'uscio fu ridotto un mucchio di legna. Cava di tasca il sonaglino e si mette a suonarlo. Ed ecco una mandria di capre, che non poteva contarsi.

- Comanda! Comanda!

- Pascolate per questi campi, finché ci sia un filo d'erba.

This is what they did: In the middle of the night, they grabbed the poor princess, shut her up in a barn and took their own daughter to the royal palace.

Hearing the story of the fairy, the king and queen remained unconvinced. So, the girl provided the following details:

"Majesty, don't you remember when you came to my room carrying a basket, crying 'Oh, unfortunate daughter. You have been born a queen, and you cannot enjoy your fate'"?

The king and queen were astounded. No one but their own daughter could know these words. Thus, they embraced the girl, and they ordered a royal festival.

To the two who had brought her, they gave a pile of gold coins.

Meanwhile, after having dissolved into tears for three days, the poor princess began to be hungry. She called out several times begging for at least a crust of hard bread.

But not a living soul heard her. Then, she remembered the little onion. Perhaps it might help relieve her hunger. And she took it out of her pocket.

"What is your command?" said the onion.

"I want to eat," said the princess. And there appeared several steaming dishes of food, napkins, silverware, a knife, a bottle, and glasses.

As soon as she finished eating, everything disappeared. Then, she took the little knife from her pocket.

"What is your command?"

"Break that wooden door into pieces!"

And in a moment the door was reduced to a heap of wood.

Then, she took the bell out of her pocket, and she began to ring it. Suddenly, a flock of goats appeared, so large that they could not be counted.

"What is your command?"

Graze over these fields, until there is not a blade of grass left.

E in un minuto i seminati, le vigne, gli alberi di quella fattoria eran distrutti.

La Reginotta partì e arrivò in una città, dove c'era un Re che avea l'unico suo figliuolo gravemente ammalato. Tutti i medici del mondo, i più dotti, i più valenti, non n'avean saputo conoscere la malattia. Dicevano ch'era matto: ma egli ragionava benissimo. Aveva soltanto dei capricci, e dimagrava, dimagrava a segno che era ridotto una lanterna.

Un giorno il Reuccio trovossi affacciato a una finestra del palazzo reale, e vide passar la Reginotta.

- Oh! Com'è brutta! La voglio qui! La voglio qui!

Il Re la fece chiamare:

- Ragazza, vorresti entrare a servizio?

- Maestà, volentieri.

- Dovresti servire il Reuccio.

E si mise a servire il Reuccio.

- Bruttona, fai questo! Bruttona, fai quello.

Il Reuccio non la comandava altrimenti: volea perfino che rigovernasse i piatti.

Una volta al Reuccio gli venne la voglia dei bacelli; ed era d'autunno! Dove andare a pescarli?

Bacelli! Bacelli!

Non diceva altro, e rifiutava di mangiare. Il Re avrebbe pagato quei bacelli a peso d'oro.

La Reginotta rammentossi della cipolletta e la cavò di tasca.

- Comanda! Comanda!

- Un bel piatto di bacelli!

Ed ecco un bel piatto di bacelli.

Il Reuccio se li mangiò con gran gusto, e dopo disse:

- Mi sento meglio!

Un'altra volta gli venne voglia d'un pasticcio di lumache. Ma non era la stagione.

And in one minute, the plants, the vines, and the trees of that farm were destroyed!

The princess left and went to a city where there was a king whose only son was gravely ill. All the doctors of the world, even the most learned and the most skillful, could not diagnose his illness. They said that he was mad; nonetheless, he reasoned very well. He was simply given to whims of fancy. He had lost weight to the point that he resembled a beam of light.

One day, as the prince was looking out a window in the royal palace, he saw the princess pass by.

"Oh, how ugly she is! I want her here. I want her here."

And so the king had her summoned.

"Young lady, do you want to enter my service?" asked the king.

"Of course, Majesty," she replied

"Well, then, you will serve the prince."

And so she became a servant of the prince.

"Ugly one, do this! Ugly one, do that." The prince commanded her in this manner; in fact, he even wanted her to wash dishes.

One time, the prince had an urge to eat peapods. However, it was autumn. Where were they to find them?

"Peapods! Peapods!"

He wanted nothing else, and he refused to eat. The king would have paid for the peapods with their weight in gold.

The princess remembered the little onion, and she took it out of her pocket.

"What is your command?"

"A big plate of peapods."

And suddenly there appeared a big plate of peapods. The prince ate them with great relish, and afterward, he said "I feel better."

Another time, he had a yearning for snails baked in a pie. But it wasn't summer.

- Pasticcino di lumache! Pasticcino di lumache!
Non diceva altro, e rifiutava di mangiare. Il Re avrebbe
pagato quelle lumache a peso d'oro.
La Reginotta corse di bel nuovo alla cipolletta.
- Comanda! Comanda!
- Un pasticcino di lumache!
Il Reuccio se lo mangiò con gran gusto, e dopo disse:
- Mi sento assai meglio.
Infatti, s'era rimesso un po' in carne.
Un'altra volta finalmente gli venne la voglia delle polpettine
di rondine. Non era la stagione. Dove andare a pescarle?
- Polpettine di rondine! Polpettine di rondine!
Il Re quelle rondini le avrebbe pagate a peso d'oro.
La Reginotta, al solito, cavò di tasca la cipolletta.
- Comanda! Comanda!
- Polpettine di rondine!
Il Reuccio se le mangiò con gran gusto e dopo disse:
- Sto benissimo.
Era diventato fresco come una rosa: non si rammentava
neppure d'essere stato malato. E, un giorno, vista la Reginotta:
- Oh, come è brutta! - esclamò. - Ma chi è costei?
Cacciatela via!
La Reginotta andò via piangendo:
- La sua stella voleva così!
E incontrò la vecchia, quella del grano.
- Che cosa è accaduto, figliuola?
In poche parole le raccontò l'accaduto.
- Sta' allegra, figliuola mia! Ti aiuterò io. Vieni con me.
E la condusse davanti a una grotta.

Where to find them? "Snails baked in a pie! Snails baked in a pie!" he demanded!

He wanted nothing else and he refused to eat. The king would have paid for the snails with their weight in gold.

The princess turned once again to the little onion.

"What is your command?"

"Snails baked in a pie."

The prince ate them with great relish, and afterward he said: "I feel much better."

In fact, he was starting to put on weight.

Finally, another time he had a yen for swallow eggs. But it was not summer. Where to find them?

"Swallow eggs! Swallow eggs!" he demanded.

The king would have paid for the swallow eggs with their weight in gold.

As before, the princess took the little onion from her pocket.

"What is your command?"

"Swallow eggs!"

The prince ate them with great relish and said: "I feel wonderful!"

He had become as fresh as a rose, and he did not remember ever having been ill. And one day he visited the princess.

"Oh, how ugly she is," he exclaimed. "Who is this woman? Throw her out!"

The princess went away crying; this was her destiny.

And then she encountered the old woman whom she had met in the wheat field.

"What has happened, daughter?" she asked.

In a few words, the princess explained it all.

"Be happy, my daughter," said the old woman. "I will help you. Come with me."

And she brought her to the opening of a grotto.

- *Ascolta: lì dentro c'è la fontana della bellezza. Chi può tuffarvisi a un tratto, diventa bella quanto il sole. Ed ora, bada bene: questa grotta ha quattro stanze. Nella prima c'è un drago: buttagli in gola la cipolletta, e ti lascerà passare. Nella seconda c'è un gigante tutto coperto d'acciaio, con una mazza di ferro brandita: mostragli la lama del coltellino, e ti lascerà passare. Nella terza c'è un leone affamato: appena ti viene incontro, scuoti il sonaglino: non ti toccherà neppur esso. Ma non bisogna aver paura; se no, addio; sei spacciata. Nella quarta stanza c'è la fontana. Appena entrata lì, senza esitare un momento, tùffati dentro l'acqua con tutte le vesti.*

La Reginotta entrò. Ed ecco il drago con tanto di bocca, che stendeva il collo per inghiottirsela. Gli butta in gola la cipolletta, e quello si ritira, si attorciglia chetamente, e si mette a dormire.

Lei passa oltre. Ed ecco il gigante tutto coperto d'acciaio, che si slancia incontro brandendo la mazza, cacciando terribili urli. Gli mostra la lama del coltellino, e il gigante va a rannicchiarsi in un canto.

La Reginotta passa oltre nella terza stanza. Ed ecco il leone, colle fauci spalancate, colla coda rizzata che faceva tremar l'aria. Lei scuote il sonaglino e sbuca un branco di capre. Il leone si slancia su di esse, le sbrana e se le divora.

E lei passa oltre. Vede la fontana, e vi si tuffa dentro con tutte le vesti. Si sentì diventar un'altra: lei stessa non si riconosceva. Da che il mondo è mondo, non s'era mai vista una bellezza pari a quella.

Tornò nella città, dov'era il Reuccio, e prese a pigione una casa dirimpetto al palazzo reale.

Il Reuccio rimase sbalordito:

- *Oh, che bellezza! Oh, che bellezza! Se fosse sangue reale, la prenderei per moglie.*

"Listen. In there, you will find the fountain of beauty. If you plunge into it you will instantly become as beautiful as the sun. Now, pay close attention. This grotto has four rooms. In the first, there is a dragon. Throw the little onion into his mouth, and he will let you pass. In the second, there is a giant covered in steel, wielding an iron cudgel. Show him the blade of the little knife, and he will let you pass. In the third, there is a hungry lion. As soon as he comes up to you, ring the little bell, and he will not touch you either. But do not fear; otherwise, all is lost. In the fourth room is the fountain. As soon as you enter, do not hesitate. Plunge into the water with all of your clothes on."

The princess entered, and immediately she saw a dragon with a huge mouth, extending his neck to devour her. So, she threw the little onion down his throat, and he stepped back, coiled himself up quietly, and fell asleep.

She went on. And before her she saw a giant in armor of steel, who lurched toward her wielding a cudgel and uttering frightening screams. She showed him the blade of the little knife, and the giant cowered in a corner.

The princess then went into the third room. There she saw a lion whose jaws were open and whose tail was raised high in the air. She rang the bell, and there appeared a herd of goats. The lion rushed upon them, tore them to pieces, and ate them.

And so, the princess moved into another room where she saw a fountain into which she threw herself with all of her clothes on. Suddenly she felt as if she had become another person. In fact, she did not recognize herself. From one end of the earth to the other there had never been seen one as beautiful as she.

She returned to the city where the prince lived, and she rented a house across from the royal palace.

The prince was amazed.

"Oh what a beauty. Oh what a beauty. If only she were of royal blood, I would marry her."

Il Re, che voleva bene al figliuolo quanto alla pupilla degli occhi suoi, mandò subito un ministro a domandarle se mai fosse di sangue reale.

- Sono. Ma se il Reuccio mi vuole, dovrà farmi tre regali.

- Che regali dovrebbe fare?

- La cresta del gallo d'oro, la pelle del re Moro, il pesce senza fiele. Gli do tempo tre anni. Se no, non mi può avere.

Il Reuccio partì alla ricerca del gallo d'oro, che si trovava in certi boschi pieni di animali feroci. E c'era un gran pericolo: chi lo sentiva cantare, moriva. Dopo mille fatiche e mille stenti, una mattina il Reuccio scoperse il gallo d'oro appollaiato su d'un albero. Tirargli e ammazzarlo fu tutt'una. E tornò trionfante.

- Va bene - disse la Reginotta. - Mettetelo lì. Aspetto la pelle del re Moro.

Il re Moro era terribile. Con lui, fin allora non ce n'avea potuto nessun guerriero. Il Reuccio mandò a sfidarlo: ne voleva la pelle.

- Venga a prendersela.

Si combatterono colle spade, e il re Moro lo aveva conciato così bene, che il Reuccio grondava sangue da tutte le parti.

Ma in un punto questi ebbe l'agio d'assestargli un colpo al cuore.

- Son morto!

Il Reuccio lo scorticò con diligenza e portò la pelle alla Reginotta.

- Va bene: mettetela là. Aspetto il pesce senza fiele.

Questo era più difficile. Fra tante migliaia di pesci va a pescare per l'appunto quello lì! Eppure bisognava pescarlo.

The king loved his son as much as the pupils of his own eyes, so he quickly sent a minister to the princess to ask her if she was of royal blood.

"I am," she said. "However, if the prince wants me, he will have to give me three gifts."

"What gifts are these?" asked the minister.

"The crest of a golden rooster, the skin of a Moorish king, and a fish without bile. I will give him three years. If he doesn't bring these gifts, he will not have me."

The prince left in search of a golden rooster, which was in a forest full of ferocious animals. And there was great danger, for whoever heard the rooster crow died. After a thousand labors and a thousand difficulties, one morning he found the rooster perched in a tree. All at once, he pulled him down from the tree and killed him.

"Very well," said the princess. "Put him here. I await the skin of a Moorish king."

The Moorish king was ferocious. Until now, no one had been able to defeat him. However, the prince sent him a challenge. He wanted his skin.

"Come and get it!" said the Moor.

They fought with swords, and the Moorish king wounded the prince badly, so that he was bleeding from many parts of his body.

However, the prince was able to stab him in the heart.

"I am dead!" cried the Moor

The prince skinned him carefully and brought his hide to the princess.

"Very well, put it here," said the princess. "I await the fish without bile."

This was more difficult. Among the many thousands of fish in the sea, he had to catch precisely the one she wanted. Yet he had to try.

Prese canna, lenza ed amo, e se n'andò in riva al mare.

Stette mesi e mesi: tempo perduto! E a compire i tre anni restavano intanto soli otto giorni!

L'ultimo giorno, tirò fuori un pesciolino di meschina apparenza. La fortuna lo aveva aiutato: era il pesce senza fiele.

- Va bene - disse la Reginotta; - mettetelo lì. Ora si mandi dal Re mio padre. Senza il suo consenso, non voglio sposarmi.

Spedirono un ambasciatore, ma l'ambasciatore tornò presto:

- Quello dice che siamo matti. La sua figliuola l'ha lì,·chi volesse vederla.

- Dunque tu ci hai corbellati. E la misero in prigione.

Le rimaneva in tasca il sonaglino. Disperata, si diè a sonarlo furiosamente. Accorse la capretta.

- Ah, capretta, capretta! Guarda a che sono arrivata! Non ho che te, per aiutarmi.

- Prendi quest'erba, masticala bene e trattienila in bocca.

E intanto che masticava, la Reginotta ritornava bruttissima e contraffatta nella persona come una volta.

- Per ritornar bella, ti basterà sputarla fuori. Ora zitta, e vienmi dietro.

Uscirono di prigione senza che le guardie e i carcerieri se n'accorgessero, e la Reginotta in quattro salti andò a presentarsi ai suoi genitori.

Come la videro, il Re e la Regina capiron subito l'inganno. E sentito il tradimento di quel marito e quella moglie, li mandarono ad arrestare e, insieme con la loro figliuola, li fecero buttare in prigione.

La Reginotta sputò fuori l'erba e ridiventò bellissima.

Da che il mondo è mondo non si era mai vista una bellezza pari a quella!

Fu mandato a chiamare il Reuccio, si sposarono, e vissero fino a vecchi felici e contenti.

He took his fishing pool, his line and hook, and he went to the seashore. He stayed there for months. It was time wasted. And then only eight days remained to complete the three years.

On the last day, he caught a small fish that looked unhealthy. Fortune had smiled on him; it was a fish without bile.

"Very well," said the princess. "Place it here. Now if you will call my father, who is also a king. Without his permission, I will not marry."

They sent out an ambassador, but he returned right away.

"The king says that we are mad. His daughter is with him, for all to see."

"You have tried to make fools of us." So, they put her in jail.

Then she remembered the little bell. Desperate, she began to ring it furiously.

And there suddenly appeared a little goat.

"Oh, little goat. Look at what has happened. I have only you to help me."

"Take this grass, chew it well, and keep it in your mouth.".

And as soon as she chewed it, the princess became ugly again, the opposite of the person she had once been.

"To become beautiful again, all you need to do is to spit out the grass. For now, keep quiet and follow me."

They escaped the prison without the guards or the jailors noticing, and the princess ran off to present herself to her parents.

As soon as they saw her, the king and queen understood the deception. Realizing the treachery of that husband and wife, they had them arrested and imprisoned together with their own daughter.

Then the princess, spit out the grass and became beautiful again. From one end of the earth to the other, there had never been seen one as beautiful as she.

The prince was sent for, they got married, and they lived happily and contented for the rest of their lives.

Il cavallo di bronzo

*C'era una volta un Re e una Regina, che avevano una figliuola
più bella della luna e del sole, e le volevano bene come alla
pupilla degli occhi.*

Un giorno venne uno, e disse al Re:

*- Maestà, passavo pel bosco qui vicino, e incontrai l'Uomo
selvaggio. Mi disse: "Vai dal Re, e digli che voglio la
Reginotta per moglie. Se non l'avrò qui fra tre giorni, guai a
lui!"*

*Il Re, sentendo questo, fu molto costernato e radunò il
Consiglio di corona:*

*- Che cosa doveva fare? L'Uomo selvaggio era terribile:
poteva devastare tutto il regno.*

*- Maestà, - disse uno dei ministri - cerchiamo una bella
ragazza, vestiamola come la Reginotta e mandiamola lì:
l'Uomo selvaggio sarà contento.*

*Trovarono una ragazza bella come la Reginotta, le fecero
indossare uno dei più ricchi abiti di lei, e la mandarono nel
bosco. Dovea dire che lei era la figlia del Re.*

Il giorno appresso quella ragazza tornò indietro.

-Che cosa è stato?

*- Maestà, trovai l'Uomo selvaggio, e mi domandò: "Chi
sei?". "Sono la Reginotta." "Lasciami vedere." Mi sbottonò la
manica del braccio sinistro e urlò: "Non è vero! La Reginotta"
dice "ha una voglia in quel braccio!" e mi ha rimandato. Se fra
due giorni non avrà lì la sposa, guai a voi!*

*Il Re non sapeva che cosa fare, e radunò di bel nuovo il
Consiglio di corona:*

*- L'Uomo selvaggio sa che la Reginotta ha una voglia nel
braccio sinistro; è impossibile ingannarlo.*

The Bronze Horse

There once was a king and queen who had a daughter more beautiful than the moon and the sun, and they loved her as much as the pupils of their own eyes.

One day, someone came and said to the king:

"Majesty, I was traveling through the nearby forest and I met the savage. He said: 'Tell the king that I want to marry the princess. If she is not here within three days, woe to him!'"

Hearing this, the king was very concerned, and he called together the royal council.

What was he to do? The savage was terrifying; he could devastate the entire kingdom.

"Majesty," said one of the ministers, "let's find a beautiful young girl, dress her up to look like the princess, and send her to him; the savage will be happy."

They found a girl as beautiful as the princess. They had her put on one of the most expensive of the princess's outfits, and they sent her into the forest. She was told to say that she was the daughter of the king.

The next day, the girl returned to the palace.

"What happened?" asked the king.

"Majesty, I found the savage, and he asked me: 'Who are you?' 'I am the princess.' 'Let me see,' he said, and he unbuttoned the sleeve of my left arm and screamed: 'It's not true! The princess has a birthmark on this arm!' and he sent me back. If the princess is not with him within two days, woe is you!"

The king did not know what to do, and he called the royal council together again:

"The savage knows that the princess has a birthmark on her left arm; it is impossible to fool him."

- *Maestà, - disse il ministro - cerchiamo un'altra ragazza, chiamiamo un pittore che le dipinga una voglia simile a quella della Reginotta, vestiamola con uno dei suoi vestiti, e mandiamola lì. Questa volta l'Uomo selvaggio non avrà da ridire.*

Trovarono un'altra bella ragazza, le fecero dipingere una voglia sul braccio, simile a quella della Reginotta, l'abbigliarono con uno dei più ricchi abiti di lei e la mandarono nel bosco. Doveva dire che lei era la figlia del Re. Ma, il giorno appresso, quella ragazza tornò indietro.

- *Che cosa è stato?*

- *Maestà, trovai l'Uomo selvaggio e mi domandò: "Chi sei?". "Sono la Reginotta." "Lasciami vedere." Mi osservò tra i capelli e urlò: "Non è vero! La Reginotta" dice "ha tre capelli bianchi sulla nuca". Se domani la sposa non sarà lì, guai a voi.*

Il povero Re e la povera Regina avrebbero battuto il capo nel muro. Dunque dovean buttare quella gioia di figliuola in braccio all'Uomo selvaggio?

- *Maestà, - dissero i ministri - facciamo un ultimo tentativo. Cerchiamo un'altra ragazza. Il pittore le dipingerà la voglia sul braccio, le tingerà di bianco tre capelli sulla nuca; poi le metteremo indosso uno dei vestiti della Reginotta e la manderemo lì. Questa volta l'Uomo selvaggio non avrà più da ridire.*

Ma il giorno appresso ecco quella ragazza che torna indietro anch'essa.

- *Che cosa è stato?*

"Majesty," said one of the ministers, "let's find another young woman; we will paint a birthmark on her similar to the princess's. Let's dress her in one of the princess's outfits, and send her to him. This time the savage won't complain."

They found another beautiful young woman and, on her arm, they had painted a birthmark similar to the princess's. They dressed her in one of the princess's most expensive outfits, and they sent her into the forest. She was to say that she was the daughter of the king. However, the next day, the young woman came back.

"What happened?" asked the king.

"Majesty, I found the savage, and he asked me: 'Who are you?' 'I am the princess.' 'Let me see.' He looked through my hair and screamed: 'It's not true; the princess has three white hairs on the nape of her neck.' If the bride is not with him to-morrow, woe to you."

The poor king and the poor queen wanted to beat their heads against the wall. Why should they throw that joy of a daughter into the arms of the savage?

"Majesty," said the ministers, "let's make one last try. We will look for another young woman. The artist will paint the birthmark on her arm, and will dye three hairs on the nape of her neck white. Then, we will have her wear one of the princess's dresses, and we will send her to him. The savage will not know the difference.

But the next day, even this young woman came back.

"What happened?" said the king?

- *Maestà, trovai l'Uomo selvaggio e mi domandò: "Chi sei?". "Sono la Reginotta." "Lasciami vedere." Mi osservò il braccio sinistro: "Va bene!". Mi osservò tra i capelli, sulla nuca: "Va bene!". Poi prese un paio di scarpine ricamate e mi ordinò: "Calza queste qui". E siccome i miei piedi non c'entravano, urlò: "Non è vero!". E mi ha rimandato dicendo: "Guai! Guai!"*

Allora i ministri:

- *Maestà, ora succede certamente un disastro! Per la salvezza del regno, bisogna sacrificare la Reginotta!*

Il Re non sapeva rassegnarsi: avrebbe dato anche il sangue delle sue vene invece della figliuola! Ma il destino voleva così, e bisognava piegare il capo.

La Reginotta si mostrava più coraggiosa di tutti: infine l'Uomo selvaggio non l'avrebbe mangiata!

Indossò l'abito da sposa, e accompagnata dal Re, dalla Regina, dalla corte e da un popolo immenso, tra pianti ed urli strazianti, s'avviò verso il bosco.

Arrivata lì, abbracciò il Re e la Regina confortandoli che sarebbe tornata a vederli, e sparì tra gli alberi e le macchie folte. Non si seppe più nuova di lei né dell'Uomo selvaggio. Passato un anno, un mese e un giorno, arriva a corte un forestiero, che chiede di parlare col Re. Era un nanetto alto due spanne, gobbo e sbilenco, con un naso che pareva un becco di barbagianni e certi occhietti piccini piccini. Il Re non aveva voglia di ridere; ma come vide quello sgorbio non seppe frenarsi.

- *Che cosa voleva?*

- *Maestà, - disse il Nano - vengo a farvi una proposta. Se mi darete mezzo regno e la Reginotta per moglie, io andrò a liberarla dalle mani dell'Uomo selvaggio.*

- *Magari! - rispose il Re. - Non mezzo, caro amico, ma ti darei il regno intero.*

"Majesty, I found the savage and he asked me: 'Who are you?' 'I am the princess.' 'Let me see.' He looked at my left arm: "Very well!' he said. He looked through the hair on the nape of my neck. 'Very well!' Then he took a pair of embroidered slippers and commanded: 'Put these on.' And because my feet would not fit into them, he yelled: 'It's not true!' And he sent me back saying 'Woe! Woe!'"

Therefore the ministers said: "Majesty, a tragedy is sure to occur! In order to save the kingdom, you will have to sacrifice the princess!"

The king could not resign himself to this; he would rather sacrifice the blood of his own veins than give up his daughter. But fate would have it this way, and he had to submit.

The princess showed herself to be more courageous than them all. After all, the savage would not eat her!

She put on a wedding gown, and accompanied by the king, the queen, members of the court, and an immense number of subjects, she made her way toward the forest amid weeping and heart-rending cries.

Once she arrived, she embraced the king and queen, assuring them that she would return and see them, and she disappeared among the trees and the thick bushes. From that point, nothing was heard about her or about the savage. However, after a year, a month, and a day, there came to court a stranger who wished to speak with the king. He was a dwarf, about eighteen inches tall, hunchbacked and lop-sided, with a nose that looked like a barn owl's and with beady little eyes. The king did not want to laugh, but he could not restrain himself when he saw this runt.

"What do you want?"

"Majesty," said the dwarf, "I have come to make a deal. If you give me half the kingdom as well as the hand of the princess in marriage, I will free her from the hands of the savage."

"Of course!" answered the king. "And not just half, dear friend; I will give you the entire kingdom."

- Parola di Re non si ritira.

- Parola di Re!

Il Nano partì.

E non era trascorsa una settimana, che il Re riceveva un avviso:

"Domani, allo spuntar del sole, si trovasse presso il bosco, colla Regina, con la corte e con tutto il popolo, per far festa alla sua figliuola, che ritornava!"

Il Re e la Regina non osavano credere: dubitavano che quello sgorbio si facesse beffa di loro: pure andarono. E allo spuntar del sole, ecco il Nanetto gobbo e sbilenco, che conduceva per mano la Reginotta vestita da sposa, come quando era entrata nel bosco per l'Uomo selvaggio.

Figuriamoci che allegrezza!

Le feste e i banchetti non ebbero a finir più. Ma di nozze non se ne parlava, e della metà del regno nemmeno.

Il Re, ora che aveva lì la figliuola, e che l'Uomo selvaggio era stato ucciso dal Nano, non intendeva più saperne di mantener la sua parola. Il Nano, di quando in quando, gli domandava:

- Maestà, e le mie nozze?

Ma quello cambiava discorso: da quell'orecchio non ci sentiva.

- Maestà, e la mia metà del regno?

Ma quello cambiava discorso: da quell'altro non ci sentiva neppure.

- Bella parola di Re! - gli disse il Nano una volta.

- Ah, nanaccio impertinente!

E il Re gli tirò un calcio alla schiena, che lo fece saltare dalla finestra.

- Doveva esser morto!

Andarono a vedere in istrada; ma il Nano non c'era più. Si era rizzato di terra, si era ripulito il vestitino, ed era andato via, lesto lesto, come se nulla fosse stato.

"A king cannot break his promise."

"I give you my promise."

And the dwarf left.

Before a week had passed, the king received a message:

"Tomorrow at sunrise, come to the edge of the forest with the queen, the court, and all of the people to celebrate the return of your daughter!"

The king and queen did not dare to believe it. They thought this runt was trying to trick them. Yet they went. And at sunrise, there appeared the hunchbacked, lop-sided dwarf, leading the princess by the hand. She was dressed as a bride, just as she had been when she entered the forest to meet the savage.

Imagine what happiness!

The celebrations and the banquets never ended. However, no one ever spoke of the wedding or of giving half the kingdom away.

Now that he had his daughter and the savage had been killed by the dwarf, the king no longer knew how to keep his word. From time to time, the dwarf asked him:

"And what about my wedding, Majesty?"

But he always changed the subject; he would hear none of that.

"And what about my half of the kingdom, Majesty?"

But he always changed the subject; he would hear none of that either.

"The king's promise is worthless!" once said the dwarf.

"Oh, impertinent dwarf!" said the king, and he threw a shoe at his backside so hard that it made him jump out of the window.

"I hope he dies!"

They went to search for him in the street, but he was gone. He had gotten up from the ground, had cleaned himself off and had run off very quickly. It was as if he had never been there.

- *Buon viaggio! - disse il Re tutto contento.*
Ma la Reginotta, da quel giorno in poi, diventò di malumore; non diceva una parola, non rideva più, andava perdendo il colorito.
- *Che cosa ti senti, figliuola mia?*
- *Maestà, non mi sento nulla; ma... chi dà la sua parola la dovrebbe mantenere.*
- *Come? Lei dunque voleva quel Nano gobbo e sbilenco?*
- *Non intendevo dir questo; ma... chi dà la sua parola la dovrebbe mantenere.*
Anche la Regina non viveva tranquilla:
- *Quel Nano era potente: aveva vinto l'Uomo selvaggio; doveva tramare qualche brutta vendetta!*
Il Re rispondeva con una spallucciata:
- *Se quello sgorbio gli veniva un'altra volta dinanzi!*
Ma la Reginotta ripeteva:
- *Chi dà la sua parola, la dovrebbe mantenere!*
Intanto essendosi sparsa la notizia che la Reginotta era stata liberata dalle mani dell'Uomo selvaggio, il Reuccio del Portogallo mandò a domandarla per moglie.
La Reginotta non disse né di sì, né di no; ma il Re e la Regina non vedevano l'ora di celebrare le nozze.
Il Reuccio di Portogallo si mise in viaggio, e per via incontrò un uomo, che conduceva un gran carro con su un cavallo di bronzo, che pareva proprio vivo.
- *O quell'uomo, dove lo portate cotesto cavallo di bronzo?*
- *Lo porto a vendere.*
Il Reuccio lo comprò e ne fece un regalo a suo suocero.
Il giorno delle nozze era vicino. La gente accorreva in folla nel giardino del Re, dove il cavallo di bronzo era stato collocato su un magnifico piedistallo. Restarono tutti meravigliati:
- *Par proprio vivo! Par di sentirlo nitrire!*
Scese a vederlo anche il Re con la corte; e tutti:

"Have a good trip!" said the king quite happily.

However, from that day forward, the princess became melancholic. She refused to speak and to laugh, and she had lost the color in her cheeks.

"What's wrong, my daughter?"

"Majesty, nothing is wrong with me, but one who gives his word should keep it."

"What? Did you want that hunchbacked, lopsided dwarf?"

"I am not saying that, but one who gives his word should keep it."

Even the queen wasn't happy.

"That dwarf was powerful; he defeated the savage. He might very well seek a terrible revenge!"

The king responded with a shrug of his shoulders: "If that hunchback comes back here again, I will take care of him!"

But the princess repeated: "One who gives his word should keep it!"

In the meantime, the news spread that the princess had been freed from the hands of the savage. The prince of Portugal sent word that he wanted to marry the princess.

The princess said neither yes nor no, but the king and queen could not wait to celebrate the marriage.

The prince of Portugal started his journey, and on the way he met a man who was driving a large cart in which was a bronze horse. It looked as if it were alive.

"Dear sir, where are you taking that bronze horse?"

"I am going to sell him."

The prince bought the horse and gave it to his father-in-law.

The day of the wedding neared. The people flocked to the king's garden, where the bronze horse had been placed on a magnificent pedestal. They were all astonished:

"He looks as if he were alive, as if we could hear him neigh."

Even the king came down with the court to see him; and all of them said:

- *Par proprio vivo! Par di sentirlo nitrire!*
Solo la Reginotta non diceva nulla.
Il Reuccio, stupito, le domandò:
- *Reginotta, non vi piace?*
- *Mi piace tanto, - rispose lei - che sento una gran voglia di cavalcarlo.*
Fecero portare una scala, e la Reginotta montò sul cavallo di bronzo. Gli tastava il ciuffo, gli accarezzava il collo, lo spronava leggermente col tacco; e intanto diceva scherzando:

- *Cavallo, mio cavallo,*
  Salta dal piedistallo;
  Non metter piede in fallo,
  Cavallo, mio cavallo.

Non ebbe finito di dir così, che il cavallo di bronzo si scosse, agitò la criniera, dette fuori un nitrito, e via con un salto per l'aria. In un batter d'occhio cavallo e Reginotta non si videro più.
Tutti erano atterriti; non osavano fiatare. Ma in mezzo a quel silenzio scoppia a un tratto una risatina, una risatina di canzonatura!
- *Ah! Ah! Ah!*
Il Re guardò, e vide il Nano che si contorceva dalle risa con quella sua gobbetta e quelle sue gambine sbilenche. Capì subito che quel cavallo fatato era opera del Nano.
- *Ah! Nano, nanuccio - gli disse pentito; - se tu mi rendi la mia figliuola, essa sarà tua sposa, con mezzo regno per dote.*
Il Nano continuava a contorcersi dalle risa:
- *Ah! Ah! Ah!*
E a vedergli fare a quel modo, tutta quella gente ch'era lì, cominciarono a ridere anch'essi, e poi perfino la Regina:
- *Ah! Ah! Ah!*

"He looks as if he were alive, as if we could hear him neigh."

Only the princess said nothing.

Amazed, the prince asked her: "Princess, don't you like him?

"I like him a lot," she answered, "so much so that I really want to ride him."

They called for a ladder, and the princess mounted the bronze horse. She stroked his forelock, she caressed his neck, she spurred him lightly with her heel, and all the while she said jokingly:

"My horse, my horse,
  Jump from the pedestal;
  Don't slip,
  My horse, my horse."

She hadn't stopped saying this before the bronze horse rose up, shook his mane, gave out a mighty neigh, and went off with a leap into the air. In the wink of a eye, the horse and the princess were no longer to be seen.

Everyone was frightened; they didn't dare say a thing. But in the middle of this silence all of a sudden they heard a giggle, a little mocking chuckle.

"Ah, ha, ha!"

The king watched, and he saw the dwarf who was writhing with laughter, he with his little hump and his crooked little legs. He knew right away that what the horse had done was the work of the dwarf.

Sorrowfully, the king said: "Oh dwarf, little dwarf, if you bring back my daughter, she shall be your wife and you shall have half the kingdom as a dowry.

But the dwarf continued to writhe with laughter:

"Ah, ha, ha!"

And seeing him react in that way, everyone began to laugh.

And finally, even the queen began to laugh.

"Ah, ha, ha!"

Si tenevano i fianchi, non ne potevano più. Soltanto quel povero Re rimase così afflitto e scornato, che faceva pietà.

- Ah! Nano, nanino bello; se tu mi rendi la mia figliuola, essa sarà tua sposa con mezzo regno per dote.

- Maestà, se dite per davvero, - rispose il Nano prima dovete riprendervi quel che mi deste l'altra volta.

- Che cosa ti diedi?

- Un bel calcio nella schiena.

Il Re esitava: avea vergogna di ricevere un calcio in quel posto, davanti al popolo e la corte. Ma l'amore della figliuola gli fece dire di sì.

Si rivoltò colle spalle al Nano e stette ad aspettare la pedata: però il Nano volle mostrarsi più generoso di lui; e invece di menargli il calcio, disse:

- Cavallo, mio cavallo,
  Non metter piede in fallo;
Torna sul piedistallo,
Cavallo, mio cavallo.

In un batter d'occhio, cavallo e Reginotta furono lì.

Allora il Nano disse al Re:

- Maestà, datemi un pugno sulla gobba! Non abbiate paura.

Il Re gli diede un pugno sulla gobba e questa sparì.

- Maestà, datemi una tiratina alle gambe! Non abbiate paura!

Il Re gli diede una tiratina alle gambine, e queste, di bòtto, si raddrizzarono.

- Maestà, afferratemi bene, la Regina per le braccia e voi pei piedi, e tiratemi forte.

Il Re e la Regina lo afferrarono l'uno pei piedi, l'altra per le braccia, e tira, tira, tira, il Nano, da nano che era, diventò un bel giovine di alta statura.

Il Reuccio del Portogallo si persuase ch'era di troppo e disse:

They held their sides, and they couldn't stand it any longer. Only the poor king felt scorned and humiliated, a pitiful sight.

"Oh dwarf, dear dwarf; if you return my daughter, she shall be your wife and you shall have half of the kingdom as a dowry."

"Majesty, if you are telling the truth," responded the dwarf, "you must first take back what you gave me the last time."

"And what was that?"

"A good kick in the backside."

The king hesitated; he was ashamed to have someone kick him in that place, especially in front of all of his people and his court. However, his love for his daughter made him consent.

He turned his back to the dwarf and waited for the kick; however, the dwarf wanted to show himself to be more generous than he and, instead of kicking him, he said:

"My horse, my horse,

Don't slip;

Return to the pedestal,

My horse, my horse."

In the blink of an eye, the horse and the princess reappeared. Then, the dwarf said:

"Majesty, punch me in my hump! Don't be afraid."

The king punched him in his hump, and it disappeared.

"Majesty, give my legs a little pull! Don't be afraid!"

And the king gave the tiny legs a little pull, and suddenly they straightened out.

"Majesty, take hold of me—the queen by the arms and you by the feet—and pull me hard."

The king and the queen grabbed hold of him, one by the feet and the other by the arms, and they pulled and pulled. With that, the dwarf ceased to be a dwarf and became a tall, handsome young man.

The prince of Portugal realized that he could not marry the princess, and he said:

- *Datemi almeno quel cavallo: farò la strada più presto.*
Montò sul cavallo di bronzo, e dette le parole fatate, in un colpo sparì.

La Reginotta e il Nano (lo chiamarono sempre così) furono moglie e marito.

E noi restiamo a leccarci le dita.

"At least give me the horse so I can travel home faster."

He mounted the bronze horse, said the magic words, and disappeared in one fell swoop.

The princess and the dwarf (they always called him that) became husband and wife.

And here we remain, just licking our fingers.

L'uovo nero

C'era una volta una vecchia che campava di elemosina, e tutto quello che buscava, lo divideva esattamente: metà lei, metà la sua gallina.

Ogni giorno, all'alba, la gallina si metteva a schiamazzare; avea fatto l'uovo. La vecchia lo vendeva un soldo, e si comprava un soldo di pane. La crosta la sminuzzava a quella, la midolla se la mangiava lei: poi andava attorno per l'elemosina.

Ma venne una mal'annata. Un giorno la vecchina tornò a casa senza nulla.

- Ah, gallettina mia! Oggi resteremo a gozzo vuoto.

- *Pazienza ci vuole! Mangeremo domani.*

Il giorno appresso, sul far dell'alba, la gallina si mise a schiamazzare. Invece d'un uovo, ne aveva fatti due, uno bianco e l'altro nero.

La vecchia andò fuori per venderli. Quello bianco lo vendé subito; quello nero, nessuno voleva credere che fosse uovo di gallina. La vecchina comprò il solito soldo di pane, e tornò a casa:

- *Ah, gallinetta mia! L'uovo nero non lo vuol nessuno.*

- *Portatelo al Re.*

La vecchia lo portò al Re.

- *Che uovo è questo?*

- *Maestà, di gallina.*

- *Quanto lo fai?*

- *Maestà, quello che il cuore v'ispira.*

- *Datele cento lire.*

La vecchina, con quelle cento lire, si credette più ricca di Sua Maestà.

Giusto in quei giorni la Regina avea posta una gallina, e alle uova messe a covare aggiunse anche quello. Ma la chioccia non lo covò.

The Black Egg

Once upon a time, there was an old woman who lived by begging, and she divided everything she got equally: half for her, half for her chicken.

One day, at dawn, the chicken began to cackle; she had laid an egg. The old woman sold it for a penny, she and bought a penny's worth of bread. She broke the crust into small pieces and gave them to the chicken; the middle she ate herself. Then, she returned to begging.

But then misfortune visited. One day the old woman came home with nothing.

"Oh, my dear chicken! Today, our stomachs will be empty."

"We need patience," said the chicken. "We will eat tomorrow."

The next day, at around dawn, the chicken began to cackle. Instead of laying one egg, she had laid two, one white and the other black.

The old woman went out to sell them. She sold the white one quickly, but no one believed that the black one was the egg of a chicken. The old woman bought a piece of bread and went home.

"Ah, my dear chicken! No one wants the black egg."

"Bring it to the king."

The old woman brought it to the king.

"What egg is this?" asked the king.

"The egg of a chicken, Majesty."

"How much do you want for it?"

"Majesty, whatever you think is fair."

"Give her one hundred lire," said the king.

With a hundred lire, the old woman thought herself richer than his majesty.

On that very day, the queen had brought in a chicken and, to the eggs that she was sitting on, was added this one. However, the hen would not sit on it.

Il Re fece chiamare la vecchia:

- Quell'uovo era barlaccio.

- Maestà, non può essere; la gallina l'avea fatto lo stesso giorno.

- Eppure non è nato.

- Bisognava lo covasse la Regina.

La cosa parve strana. Ma la Regina, curiosa, disse:

- Lo coverò io.

E se lo mise in seno. Dopo ventidue giorni, sentì rompersi il guscio. Venne fuori un pulcino bianco ch'era una bellezza.

- Maestà, Maestà! Fatemi la zuppa col vino.

E pigolava.

- Sei galletto o pollastra?

- Maestà, son galletto.

- Canta.

- Chicchirichì!

Era proprio galletto. E diventò il divertimento di tutta la corte. Ma più cresceva e più si faceva impertinente. A tavola beccava nei piatti del Re e della Regina; razzolava, come se nulla fosse, nei piatti dei Ministri, che non osavano dirgli sciò per rispetto del Re; girava di qua e di là per tutte le stanze del palazzo reale, s'appollaiava dovunque, e insudiciava e riempiva ogni cosa di pollìna. E poi tutto il giorno:

- Chicchirichì! Chicchirichì!

Rintronava le orecchie. La gente del palazzo reale non ne poteva più.

Un giorno la Regina s'era fatta un vestito nuovo ch'era una meraviglia, ed era costato un sacco di quattrini. Prima che lo indossasse, va il galletto e glielo insudicia.

La Regina montò sulle furie:

- Sporco galletto! Per questa volta passi. Un'altra volta te la farò vedere io!

The king summoned the old woman.

"That egg was rotten."

"Majesty, that cannot be; the chicken laid it just this morning."

"And yet it has not hatched."

"The queen must do it."

It seemed strange, but the queen, who was curious, said: "I will do it."

And she put the egg in her bosom. After twenty-one days, she felt the shell break. And out came a beautiful white chick.

"Majesty, Majesty, make me some wine soup," he peeped.

"Are you a rooster or a hen?" asked the king.

"Majesty, I am a rooster."

"Sing."

"Cock-a-doodle-do"

He was truly a rooster. And he became the delight of the entire court. However, the more he grew, the more he became impertinent. At the table, he pecked at the dishes of the king and queen; he scratched around, as if it were nothing, in the plates of the ministers, who didn't dare shoo him away because of their respect for the king. The rooster went through all of the rooms in the royal palace, he roosted everywhere, and he soiled everything and covered it with his droppings. All day long, he cackled:

"Cock-a-doodle-do! Cock-a-doodle-do!"

He hurt everyone's ears. The people in the royal palace could not take it anymore.

One day the queen had a marvelous new dress made for herself; it cost a great deal of money. Before she put it on, however, the rooster soiled it.

The queen was furious.

"Dirty rooster! This time, I will let you get away with it. But next time, you will pay dearly for it."

E ordinò alla sarta un altro vestito più ricco di quello. La sarta ci si messe con impegno; figuriamoci che vestito!... Ma prima che la Regina lo indossasse, va il galletto e glielo insudicia.

La Regina perdé il lume degli occhi:

- Sporco galletto! Ora ti concio io. Chiamatemi il cuoco.

Il cuoco si presentò.

- Mi si faccia con cotesto galletto una buona tazza di brodo.

In cucina gli tirarono il collo e lo messero a lessare. Appena la pentola diè il primo bollore:

- Chicchirichì!

Il galletto era scappato fuori, come se non gli avessero mai tirato il collo e non lo avessero mai pelato e abbrustolito.

Il cuoco corse dalla Regina:

- Maestà, il galletto è risuscitato!

La cosa era troppo strana, e il galletto diventò prezioso. Tutti lo guardavano con rispetto; qualcuno anche con un po' di paura. Ed esso se n'abusava. A tavola beccava peggio di prima, nei piatti del Re e della Regina; razzolava, come se nulla fosse, nei piatti dei Ministri che non osavano dirgli sciò per rispetto del Re; s'appollaiava dovunque, insudiciava perfino il soglio reale e lo riempiva di pollìna. E poi, notte e giorno: chicchirichì! chicchirichì! Rintronava gli orecchi. E il popolo imprecava a denti stretti:

- Accidempoli al galletto e a chi lo fa allevare!

Un giorno Sua Maestà dovea scrivere a un altro Re. Prese carta, penna e calamaio, fece la lettera e la lasciò sul tavolino ad asciugare. Va il galletto e gliela insudicia, proprio dov'era la firma.

- Sporco galletto! Per questa volta passi. Un'altra volta te la farò vedere io!

And she ordered the dressmaker to make her a dress even more expensive than the first. The dressmaker got busy; imagine what a dress! But before the queen put it on, the rooster dirtied it.

The queen was beside herself with anger!

"Dirty rooster! Now, I'll dirty you! Call the cook."

When the cook came, the queen said:

"Use this rooster to make me a nice chicken soup!"

The cook pulled off the rooster's neck and put him in the pot, but before it started to boil, they heard:

"Cock-a doodle-do!"

The rooster had escaped, and he remained as if his neck had never been torn off, as if he had never been plucked or burned.

The cook ran to the queen.

"Majesty, the rooster has come back to life."

This was very strange, and the rooster became very valuable. Everyone looked on him with respect; some even regarded him a little fearfully. And he took advantage. At table, he pecked at the plates of the king and queen worse than ever. He scratched around, as if it were nothing, in the plates of the ministers, who dared not shoo him away because of their respect for the king. He roosted everywhere, soiling even the royal throne and covering it with his droppings. Moreover, night and day he cried: "Cock-a-doodle-do! Cock-a-doodle-do!" He hurt everyone's ears. The people cursed him between clenched teeth:

"Damn that rooster and whoever is keeping him."

One day, the king had to write to another king. With paper, pen, and ink, he wrote the letter and left it on the table for the ink to dry. The rooster went to it and soiled it, right on his signature.

"Dirty rooster! This time, you'll get away with it. But next time, you will pay dearly for it."

Il Re scrisse di bel nuovo la lettera, e la lasciò sul tavolino ad asciugare. Va il galletto, e gliela insudicia, proprio dov'era la firma.

Il Re perdé il lume degli occhi:
- Sporco galletto! Ora ti concio io! Chiamatemi il cuoco.
Il cuoco si presentò.
- Mi si faccia arrosto pel pranzo.
In cucina gli tirarono il collo e lo infilzarono nello spiedo.
Quando fu l'ora del pranzo, il cuoco lo servì in tavola. Sua Maestà cominciò a dividerlo, a chi un'ala, a chi una coscia, a chi un po' di petto, a chi il codione: serbò per sé il collo e la testa colla cresta e coi bargigli.

Avea terminato appena di mangiare, che dal fondo del suo stomaco sente scoppiare:
- Chicchirichì!

Fu una costernazione generale. Chiamarono tosto i medici di corte.

Bisognerebbe spaccar la pancia del Re; ma chi ci si mette?

E il galletto, di tanto in tanto, dal fondo dello stomaco di Sua Maestà, dava la voce:
- Chicchirichì!
- Chiamatemi la vecchia - disse il Re.

Appunto essa veniva a domandar l'elemosina al palazzo reale, e la condussero su.

- Strega del diavolo! Che malìa hai tu fatta a quell'uovo? Ho mangiato la testa del galletto, ed esso mi canta dentro lo stomaco. Se non me ne liberi, tienti per morta!

- Maestà, datemi un giorno di tempo.

E tornò subito a casa:
- Ah, gallettina mia! Sono stata chiamata dal Re: "Ho mangiato la testa del galletto, ed esso mi canta dentro lo stomaco". Se non lo libero, sarò morta!

The king wrote the letter again and left it on the table for the ink to dry. The rooster went to it and soiled it, right on his signature.

The king was beside himself with anger.

"Dirty rooster! Now I'll dirty you! Call the cook!"

When the cook came, he told him:

"Roast him for my lunch."

In the kitchen, they pulled off his neck and strung him up on a spit.

When lunchtime came, the cook served him at the table. His majesty began to break him apart, pulling off a wing here, a leg there, a little bit of the breast, and then the tail. He saved the neck and the head with the crest and the wattle for himself.

Just as he finished eating, he heard a noise coming from his stomach:

"Cock-a-doodle-do!"

There was great a consternation. Immediately, they called for the court doctors.

They needed to open the king's belly, but who would do it?

And from time to time, the rooster crowed from the bottom of his majesty's stomach:

"Cock-a-doodle-do!"

"Call the old woman," said the king.

At that very time, she had come to the royal palace to beg, and they brought her to the king.

"Witch of the devil! What spell did you put on that egg? I have eaten the head of the rooster, and still he crows within my stomach. If you don't free me of him, consider yourself dead!"

"Majesty, give me one day."

And she quickly returned home.

"Oh, my dear chicken! I have been summoned by the king, who said: 'I have eaten the head of the rooster, and still he crows within my stomach.' If can't get that rooster out of him, he will have me killed."

- Vecchia mia, questo è nulla. Domani prenderai un po' di becchime, tornerai dal Re e farai: billi! billi! Sentendo la tua voce, il galletto verrà fuori.

E così fu.

La cosa era troppo strana. Il galletto diventò famoso, e tornò a fare peggio di prima.

Una mattina, avanti l'alba:

- Chicchirichì! Maestà, vo' una gallina.

- E diamogli una gallina!

Il giorno appresso, avanti l'alba:

- Chicchirichì! Maestà, vo' un'altra gallina.

- E diamogli un'altra gallina!

Insomma, ne volle due dozzine.

Un'altra mattina, avanti l'alba:

- Chicchirichì! Maestà, vo' gli sproni d'oro.

E sproni d'oro siano!

Il galletto, ch'era diventato un bel gallo, con quegli sproni d'oro si pavoneggiava attorno, beccando questo e quello.

Un'altra volta, avanti l'alba:

- Chicchirichì! Maestà, vo' la cresta doppia d'oro.

- E cresta doppia d'oro sia!

Il Re cominciava a stufarsi; ma il gallo, con quegli sproni d'oro e quella cresta doppia d'oro, si pavoneggiava attorno, beccando questo e quello.

Finalmente un'altra mattina, avanti l'alba:

- Chicchirichì! Maestà, vo' mezzo regno; ho corona al par di voi!

Al Re scappò la pazienza:

- Levatemelo di torno, questo gallaccio impertinente!

"Oh, my dear old lady," said the chicken, "this is nothing. Tomorrow, take a little bit of bird seed, return to the king, and call: 'Billi! Billi!' Hearing your voice, the rooster will come out."

And so it was.

This was very strange. The rooster became famous, but he behaved worse than ever.

One morning before dawn:

"Cock-a-doodle-do! Majesty, I want a hen."

"Give him a hen!"

The day after, before dawn, the rooster crowed.

"Cock-a-doodle-do! Majesty, I want another hen."

"Give him another hen!" said the king.

In all, he wanted two dozen.

Another morning, before dawn, he crowed:

"Cock-a-doodle-do! Majesty, I want golden spurs."

And golden spurs there were!

The young cock, who had now become a beautiful rooster, strutted about wearing the golden spurs pecking here and there.

Another time, before dawn, he crowed:

"Cock-a-doodle-do, I want a thick golden crest."

"And a thick golden crest there will be!" said the king.

However, the king began to lose patience; but the rooster, with those golden spurs and that thick golden crest, strutted about, pecking here and there.

Finally, one morning before dawn, he again cried:

"Cock-a-doodle-do! Majesty, I want half of the kingdom and a crown just like yours."

The king was fed up.

"Get rid of this impertinent rooster!"

*Ma come fare? Ammazzarlo era inutile; risuscitava sempre.
Portarlo lontano non concludeva nulla: sarebbe tornato.
Prenderlo colle buone era peggio; rispondeva canzonando: -
Chicchirichì! Il Re, disperato, mandò a chiamare la vecchia:*
— *Se non mi liberi del gallo, ti fo mozzare la testa!*
— *Maestà, datemi un giorno di tempo.*
E tornò subito a casa:
— *Ah, gallinetta mia! Sono stata chiamata dal Re: "Se non mi
liberi del gallo, ti fo mozzare la testa". Che debbo rispondere?*
— *Rispondi: "Maestà, voi non avete figliuoli; adottatelo per
figliuolo, si cheterà".*
*Il Re, messo colle spalle al muro, risolvette di adottarlo. Ma
giovò poco.*
*Con tutte quelle galline, il palazzo reale era diventato un
pollaio. Il Re, la Regina, i Ministri, le dame di corte, i
servitori, tutti si sentivan pieni di pollìna dalla testa ai piedi, e
non potevano reggere. E poi, schiamazzate di qua, chicchiriate
di là; aveano il capo come un cestone.*
Il popolo imprecava a denti stretti:
— *Accidempoli al gallo, alle galline e a che li fa allevare!*
— *Senti, strega - disse il Re. - Se fra un giorno non mi spazzi
gallo e galline, pagherai con la tua testa.*
— *Maestà, qui ci vuole la fata Morgana; mandatela a
chiamare.*
Il Re mandò a chiamare la fata Morgana. La Fata rispose:
— *Chi vuole vada, chi non vuole mandi.*
E il Re dovette andarci egli stesso in persona.
— *Maestà, finché quel gallo non sarà diventato un uomo al
pari di voi, non avrete mai pace.*
— *Ma che cosa ci vuole, perché diventi un uomo al pari di
me?*
— *Ci vuol tre sorta di becchime. Fate tre solchi colle vostre
mani, e spargete queste tre sementi. Mietete, trebbiate, senza
mescolare il grano, e poi dite:*

But how was that to be done? It was useless to try to kill him; he always revived. Taking him far away would solve nothing; he always returned. Treating him well was even worse, for he would respond by mocking: "Cock-a-doodle-do!" Desperate, the king sent for the old woman.

"If you don't rid me of this rooster, I will have your head!"

"Majesty, give me one day."

And she immediately went home.

"Oh, my little chicken. If I do not rid the king of the rooster, he will have my head. How shall I answer?"

"Respond this way: 'Majesty, you do not have sons; if you adopt him as your son, he will quiet down.'"

Having his back against the wall, the king decided to adopt him. But it did little good.

With all those chickens, the royal palace became a hen house. The king, queen, ministers, court ladies, servants, all felt overwhelmed by chickens; they could not take it. The cackling here and the cock-a-doodle-doing there made their heads ache.

The people cursed under their breath. "Damn that rooster, the chickens, and whoever is keeping them!"

"Listen, witch," said the king. "If you don't rid me of rooster and chickens within one day, you will pay with your head."

"Majesty, only Morgan, the fairy, can help; have her summoned."

The king summoned Morgan, the fairy. But she responded: "Who wishes will go; who does not will stay."

And the king had to go to her in person.

Majesty, until the rooster becomes a man just like you, you will never have peace."

"But what must be done to make him a man just like me?"

"Three kinds of birdseed must be used. Make three furrows with your own hands, and sprinkle these three seeds. Then, reap the grain, thresh it without mixing it up, and then say:

- Billi, billi!
    Chi gli piace se ne pigli!
E spargerete per terra questo grano qui. Quando non ne rimarrà più un chicco:
    - Billi, billi!
    Chi gli piace se ne pigli!
E spargerete per terra quest'altro grano. Quando non ne rimarrà più un chicco:
    - Billi, billi!
    Chi gli piace se ne pigli!
E spargerete per terra l'ultimo grano.
Il Re s'ingegnò di far tutto a puntino. Quando fu il momento:
- Billi, billi!
    Chi gli piace se ne pigli!
E una metà delle galline morì.
- Billi, billi!
    Chi gli piace se ne pigli!
E il resto delle galline morì.
- Billi, billi!
    Chi gli piace se ne pigli!
Il gallo si mise a beccare lui solo, e appena beccato l'ultimo grano, si ritirò, s'allungò, chicchirichì! Si scosse le penne d'addosso e diventò un giovane alto e bello. Di gallo gli eran rimasti soltanto la cresta e gli sproni. Ma non importava.
    Il Re disse al popolo:
- Non ho figliuoli, e questo qui sarà il Reuccio. Rispettatelo per tale.
    - Viva il Reuccio! Viva il Reuccio!
Ma, sottovoce, dicevano:
- Staremo a vedere. Chi gallo nasce dee chicchiriare.

'Billi, billi!
 Whoever likes it can take it.'"
"Now, sprinkle this first type of grain on the ground. When not a bit of it is left, say:
 'Billi, billi!
 Whoever likes it can take it.'"
"Then, sprinkle this other grain on the ground. When not a bit of it is left, say:
 'Billi, billi!
 Whoever likes it can take it.'"
And, then, sprinkle the last of the three grains on the ground:
The king strove to do exactly as she said. When the moment came:
 "Billi, billi!
 Whoever likes it can take it."
 And half of the chickens died.
 "Billi, billi!
 Whoever likes it can take it."
 And the rest of the chickens died.
 "Billi, billi!
 Whoever likes it can take it."
The rooster began to peck by himself, and after eating the last grain, he shrank, then he grew: "Cock-a-doodle-do." He shook off his feathers and he became a tall, handsome young man. Of the rooster, only the crest and the spurs were left. But it did not matter.
The king said to the people:
"I have no son, and this one shall be the prince. Respect him as such."
"Long live the prince! Long live the prince!"
However, under their breath they were saying:
"It remains to be seen what kind of rooster has been born from that cock-a-doodle-do."

244 Luigi Capuana

Il Reuccio, dopo parecchi mesi, diventò malinconico. Voleva star solo, non parlava con nessuno.

- Che cosa avete, figliuolo mio?

- Maestà, nulla.

Non lo voleva dire, provava rossore, ma sentiva una gran voglia di far chicchirichì!

Chiamarono i medici di corte; chiamarono anche quelli fuori del regno, i più valenti. Non ci capivano niente.

- Forse il Reuccio voleva moglie?

Non voleva moglie.

Ma dunque che cosa voleva? Qualunque cosa avesse voluto, gli sarebbe stata concessa.

- Vorrei... fare chicchirichì!

Bisognò permetterglielo: e si sfogò tutta la giornata.

Allora gli tagliarono la cresta, e quella voglia non la ebbe più.

E il popolo:

- Staremo a vedere! Chi da gallina nasce convien che razzoli.

Dopo parecchi mesi il Reuccio tornò ad essere malinconico. Voleva star solo, non parlava con nessuno.

- Che cosa avete, figliuolo mio?

- Maestà, nulla.

Non lo voleva dire, provava rossore, ma sentiva una gran voglia d'uscir fuori a razzolare.

Tornarono a chiamare i dottori, ma non ci capivano niente.

- Forse il Reuccio voleva moglie?

- Non voleva moglie.

- Ma dunque che cosa voleva? Qualunque cosa avesse chiesta, gli sarebbe stata concessa.

- Vorrei... uscir fuori a razzolare

After a few months, the prince became melancholic. He wanted to be alone, and he spoke to no one.

"What's the matter, my son?"

"Nothing, majesty."

He was ashamed to admit it, but he had a great yearning to crow!

They called the court doctor; they even called doctors from outside the kingdom, but they did not understand the problem.

"Perhaps the prince wants to get married?"

But he did not want to get married.

What, then, did he want? He must have wanted something that would make him happy.

"I would like to cry cock-a-doodle-do!"

They had to let him do so, and he crowed all day long.

So, they cut off his crest, and he no longer desired to crow.

But the people said:

"We will see. He who is born of a chicken is sure to scratch about."

After a few months, the prince became melancholic again. He wanted to be alone; he spoke to no one.

"What is the matter, my son?"

"Nothing, Majesty."

He was ashamed to admit it, but he had a great desire to go outside and scratch about.

Again they called the doctors, but they didn't know what to do.

"Perhaps the prince wants to get married?"

But he did not want to get married.

What, then, did he want? He must have wanted something that would make him happy.

"I want to go outside and scratch about!"

E bisognò permetterglielo.

Allora gli strapparono gli sproni, e quella voglia non la ebbe più.

Venne il tempo di dargli moglie:

- Vi piacerebbe, figliuolo mio, la Reginotta di Spagna?

- Maestà, dovendo sposare,... vorrei sposare una pollastra!

Si era dunque sempre daccapo?

Il Re quel giorno avea le paturne. Tira fuori la sciabola e gli taglia la testa.

Ma, invece di sangue d'uomo, gli uscì fuori sangue di pollo.

Si presentò allora la vecchina:

- Maestà, ecco, è finita.

Gli riappiccicò il capo collo sputo, e il Reuccio tornò vivo.

Ora ch'era un uomo davvero stette tranquillo, e di lì a poco si sposò colla Reginotta di Spagna. Poi diventarono Re e Regina, e fecero un po' di bene.

E la fiaba finisce.

And they had to let him do so.

Thereupon, they ripped off his spurs, and he no longer had that desire.

There came a time when he was to marry.

"My son, would the princess of Spain please you?"

"Majesty, I need to get married, but I want to marry a pullet!"

Was he always to be as before?

One day the king was in a bad mood. He drew his saber and cu off the prince's head.

However, instead of human blood, chicken's blood came out.

The old woman then appeared.

"Look, Majesty, it is over."

She reattached his head with her spittle, and the prince came alive.

Now that he was truly a man, he was happy, and in a little while he married the princess of Spain. Later, they became king and queen and lived happily ever after.

And now our tale has come to and end.

La figlia del re

C'era una volta un Re e una Regina, che avevano una figlia unica, e le volevano più bene che alla pupilla de' loro occhi.

Mandò il Re di Francia per domandarla in sposa.

Il Re e la Regina, che non sapeano staccarsi dalla figliuola, risposero:

- È ancora bambina.

Un anno dopo, mandò il Re di Spagna.

Quelli si scusarono allo stesso modo:

- È ancora bambina.

Ma i due regnanti se l'ebbero a male. Si misero d'accordo e chiamarono un Mago:

- Devi farci un incanto per la figlia del Re, il peggiore incanto che ci sia.

- Fra un mese l'avrete.

Passato il mese, il Mago si presentò:

- Ecco qui. Regalatele questo anello; quando lo avrà portato in dito per ventiquattr'ore, ne vedrete l'effetto.

Regalarglielo non potevano, perché s'eran già guastati coi parenti di lei. Come fare?

- Ci penserò io.

Il Re di Spagna si travestì da gioielliere, e aperse una bottega dirimpetto al palazzo reale.

La Regina volea comprar delle gioie e lo mandò a chiamare.

Quello andò, e in uno scatolino a parte ci avea l'anello.

Dopo che la Regina ebbe comprato parecchie cose, domandò alla figliuola:

- O tu, non vuoi nulla?

- Non c'è niente di bello - rispose la Reginotta.

- Ci ho qui un anello raro; le piacerà.

E il finto gioielliere mostrò l'anello incantato.

The King's Daughter

Once upon a time, there were king and queen who had only one child, a daughter they loved more than the pupils in their eyes.

One day, the king of France asked for her hand in marriage.

But the king and queen did not know how to tear themselves away from their daughter, and so they responded:

"She's still a child."

One year later, the king of Spain asked for her hand.

They excused themselves in the same way:

"She's still a child."

But the two rulers were offended, and together they called upon a magician.

"You must cast a spell on the daughter of the king, the worst spell possible."

"Within a month, you shall have your spell."

When a month had passed, the magician appeared:

"Look here. Give her this ring. After she has worn it for twenty-four hours, you will see the effect."

But they could not give her the ring, for they had quarreled with her parents. What to do?

"I'll take care of it," said the king of Spain.

So, he disguised himself as a jeweler and opened a shop in front of the royal palace.

The queen wished to buy some jewelry, and she sent for him.

He went to the palace carrying a small box containing the ring.

After the queen had bought some things, she asked her daughter:

"And don't you want anything?"

"There is nothing beautiful here," responded the princess.

"There is a precious ring, which is sure to please you."

And the false jeweler showed her the enchanted ring.

- Oh, che bellezza! Oh, che bellezza! Quanto lo fate?
- Reginotta, non ha prezzo, ma prenderò quel che vorrete.
Gli diedero una gran somma e quello andò via.
La Reginotta s'era messo in dito l'anello e lo ammirava ogni momento:
- Oh, che bellezza! Oh, che bellezza!
Ma dopo ventiquattr'ore (era di sera):
- Ahi! Ahi! Ahi!
Accorsero il Re, la Regina, le dame di corte, coi lumi in mano.
- Scostatevi! Scostatevi! Son diventata di stoppa.
Infatti la povera Reginotta avea le carni tutte di stoppa.
Il Re e la Regina erano proprio inconsolabili. Radunarono il Consiglio della Corona.
- Che cosa poteva farsi?
- Maestà, fate un bando: Chi guarisce la Reginotta sarà genero del Re.
E i banditori partirono per tutto il regno, con tamburi e trombette.
- Chi guarisce la Reginotta sarà genero del Re!
In una città c'era un giovinotto, figlio d'un ciabattino. Un giorno, vedendo che in casa sua si moriva di fame, disse a suo padre:
- Babbo, datemi la santa benedizione: vo' andare a cercar fortuna pel mondo.
- Il cielo ti benedica, figliuolo mio!
E il giovinotto si mise in viaggio.
Uscito pei campi, in una viottola incontrò una frotta di ragazzi che, urlando, tiravan sassate a un rospo per ammazzarlo.
-   Che male vi ha fatto? È anch'esso creatura di Dio: lasciatelo stare.

"Oh, how beautiful! Oh, how beautiful! How much is it?"

"Princess, the ring has no price; I will take what you want."

She gave him a great amount of money, and he went away.

The princess put the ring on her finger and admired it constantly.

"Oh, how beautiful! Oh, how beautiful!"

However, after twenty-four hours, she cried out during the night:

"Ah! Ah! Ah!"

The king, the queen, and the ladies of the court came running with lamps in their hands.

"Stay away, stay away! I have become a bunch of straw."

The flesh of the poor princess had actually turned into straw.

The king and the queen were inconsolable. They called together the royal council.

"What can be done?"

"Majesty, issue a proclamation: whoever heals the princess will become the king's son-in-law."

And the heralds went throughout the kingdom announcing to the sounds of drums and trumpets:

"Whoever heals the princess will become the king's son-in-law!"

In one city, lived a young man, the son of a cobbler. One day, because his family was impoverished, he said to his father:

"Father, give me you blessing to seek my fortune in the world."

"Heaven bless you, my son!"

And the young man went on his way. On a path through the fields, he came upon a gang of boys who were yelling at a toad and trying to kill it with stones.

"What harm has the toad done to you?" asked the young man. "Even this is a creature of God; leave him alone."

Vedendo che quei ragazzacci non smettevano, saltò in mezzo ad essi, diè uno scapaccione a questo, un pugno a quello, e li sbandò: il rospo ebbe agio di ficcarsi in un buco.

Cammina, cammina, il giovinotto incontrò i banditori che, a suon di tamburi e di trombette, andavan gridando:

- Chi guarisce la Reginotta, sarà genero del Re.

- Che male ha la Reginotta?

- È diventata di stoppa.

Salutò e continuò per la sua strada, finché non gli annottò in una pianura. Guardava attorno per vedere di trovar un posto dove riposarsi: si volta, e scorge al suo fianco una bella signora. Trasalì.

- Non aver paura: sono una Fata, e son venuta per ringraziarti.

- Ringraziarmi di che?

- Tu m'hai salvato la vita. Il mio destino è questo: di giorno son rospo, di notte son Fata. Ai tuoi comandi!

- Buona Fata, c'è la Reginotta ch'è diventata di stoppa, e chi la guarisce sarà genero del Re. Insegnatemi il rimedio: mi basterà.

- Prendi in mano questa spada e vai avanti, vai avanti. Arriverai in un bosco tutto pieno di serpenti e di animali feroci. Non lasciarti impaurire: vai sempre avanti, fino al palazzo del Mago. Quando sarai giunto lì, picchia tre volte al portone.

Insomma gli disse minutamente come dovea fare:

- Se avrai bisogno di me, vieni a trovarmi.

Il giovinotto la ringraziò, e si mise in cammino. Cammina. cammina, si trovò dentro il bosco, fra gli animali feroci. Era uno spavento! Urlavano, digrignavano i denti, spalancavano le

Seeing that these boys would not stop, he jumped into the middle of them. He boxed one of the boys' ears, and he punched another. They disbanded, and the toad was able to jump into a hole.

Walking on, the young man came upon the king's heralds, who, to the sounds of drums and trumpets, went around shouting:

"Whoever heals the princess will become the king's son-in-law."

"What's the matter with the princess?" asked the young man.

"She's turned to straw."

He greeted them and continued on his way until he came to a heath where he no longer heard them. He looked about to find a place to rest, and turning around he was startled at the sight of a beautiful woman at his side. He jumped up.

"Don't be afraid; I am a fairy, and I have come to thank you."

"Thank me for what?"

"You saved my life. My fate is to be a toad during the day and a fairy at night. I am at your service!"

"Good fairy, there is a princess who has turned to straw, and whoever cures her will become the king's son-in-law. Teach me the remedy; that's all I need."

"Take this sword and travel far. You will come to a forest filled with snakes and other ferocious beasts. Do not let them frighten you; keep going until you reach the magician's palace. When you arrive there, knock three times at the portal."

In short, she told him what to do in every detail.

"If you need me, come and find me."

The young man thanked her and went on his way. After a while, he found himself in a forest among ferocious beasts. It was frightening! They growled, bared their teeth, and opened

254   Luigi Capuana

bocche; ma quello sempre avanti, senza curarsene. Finalmente giunse al palazzo del Mago, e picchiò tre volte al portone.
-Temerario, temerario! Che cosa vieni a fare fin qui?
- Se tu sei Mago davvero, devi batterti con me.
Il Mago s'infuriò e venne fuori armato fino ai denti: ma, come gli vide in mano quella spada, urlò:
- Povero me! E si buttò ginocchioni:
- Salvami almeno la vita!
- Sciogli l'incanto della Reginotta, e avrai salva la vita.
Il Mago trasse di tasca un anello, e gli disse:
- Prendi; va' a metterglielo nel dito mignolo della mano sinistra e l'incanto sarà disfatto.
Il giovanotto, tutto contento, si presenta al Re:
- Maestà, è vero che chi guarisce la Reginotta sarà genero del Re?
- Vero, verissimo.
- Allora son pronto a guarirla.
Chiamaron la Reginotta, e tutti quelli della corte gli s'affollarono attorno; ma le avea appena messo in dito l'anello, che la Reginotta divampò, tutta una fiamma! Fu un urlo. Nella confusione, il giovanotto poté scappare, e non si fermò finché non giunse dove gli era apparsa la Fata:
- Fata, dove sei?
- Ai tuoi comandi.
Le narrò la disgrazia.
- Ti sei lasciato canzonare! Tieni questo pugnale e ritorna dal Mago: vedrai che questa volta non si farà beffa di te.
E gli disse minutamente come dovea regolarsi.
Il giovinotto andò subito, e picchiò tre volte al portone.
- Temerario, temerario! Che cosa vieni a fare fin qui?
- Se tu sei Mago davvero, devi batterti con me.

wide their mouths. However, the young man kept going, without paying attention. Finally, he reached the palace of the magician and knocked three times at the portal.

"Oh foolish boy! Why have you come this far?"

"If you are truly a magician, you must fight me."

The magician was infuriated, and he came out armed to the teeth. However, as soon as he saw the young man with the sword in this hand, he cried:

"Woe is me!" And he dropped to his knees.

"At least spare my life, " said the magician.

"Remove the spell you placed on the princess, and your life will be spared."

The magician took a ring from his pocket and said:

"Take this; place it on the pinkie of her left hand, and the spell will be removed."

Happy as could be, the young man went to the king:

"Majesty, is it true that the one who heals the princess will become the king's son-in-law?"

"True, very true."

"And so, I am ready to cure her."

They summoned the princess, and all the people of the court gathered around her. However, when he placed the ring on her finger, the princess burst into flames. There was a great outcry. In the confusion, the young man escaped, and he did not stop until he reached the place where the fairy had appeared to him.

"Fairy, where are you?"

"At your service," she said.

He told her of the misfortune.

"You have been tricked! Take this dagger and return to the magician. This time, see that the magician does not fool you."

And she told him what to do in every detail.

The young man left immediately, and he knocked at the portal.

"Oh foolish boy! Why have you come this far?"

"If you are truly a magician, you must fight me."

Il Mago s'infuriò e venne fuori, armato fino ai denti. Ma come gli vide in mano quel pugnale, si buttò ginocchioni:
- Salvami almeno la vita!
- Mago scellerato, ti sei fatto beffa di me! Ora starai lì incatenato, finché l'incanto non sia rotto.
Lo legò bene, piantò il pugnale in terra, e vi attaccò la catena. Il Mago non poteva muoversi.
- Sei più potente, lo veggo! Torna dalla Reginotta, cavale di dito l'anello del gioielliere e l'incanto sarà disfatto.
Il giovinotto non avea viso di presentarsi al Re; ma saputo che la Reginotta se l'era cavata con poche scottature, perché tutti quei della corte aveano spento le fiamme, si fece coraggio e si presentò:
- Maestà, perdonate; la colpa non fu mia; fu del Mago traditore. Ora è un'altra cosa. Caviamo di dito alla Reginotta quell'anello del gioielliere, e l'incanto sarà disfatto.
Così fu. La Reginotta diventò nuovamente di carne, ma pareva un tronco: non avea lingua, né occhi, né orecchi; era rovinata dalle fiamme. E se lui non la guariva intieramente, non potea diventar genero del Re.
Partì e andò in quella pianura dove gli era apparsa la Fata:
- Fata, dove sei?
- Ai tuoi comandi.
Le narrò la disgrazia.
- Ti sei lasciato canzonare!
E gli disse, minutamente, come dovea regolarsi.
Il giovanotto tornò dal Mago:
- Mago scellerato, ti sei fatto beffa di me! Lingua per lingua, occhio per occhio!
- Per carità, lasciami stare! Vai dalle mie sorelle, che stanno un po' più in là. Devi fare così e così.

The magician was infuriated, and he came out armed to the teeth. However, as soon as he saw the young man with the dagger in this hand, he dropped to his knees.

"At least spare my life."

"Wicked magician, you made a fool of me! Now you will remain chained until the spell is broken."

He chained him well, stuck the dagger in the ground, and attached the chain to it. The magician could not move.

"I see you are more powerful than I! Return to the princess. Take the jeweler's ring from her finger; the spell will be broken."

The young man was afraid to face the king. However, knowing that the princess had not been burned much—for all of the people of the court had put out the flames—he screwed up his courage and presented himself:

"Majesty, pardon me; the fault was not mine. It was that wicked magician's. I have another remedy. If we remove the jeweler's ring from the princess's finger, the spell will be broken."

And so it was. The princess was restored to flesh, but she looked like a torso, with no tongue, eyes, or ears. She had been ruined by the fire. And if the young man did not make her whole, he could not become the king's son-in-law.

He went to the plain where the fairy had appeared to him.

"Fairy, where are you?"

"At your service."

He told her about the misfortune.

"You have been tricked!"

And she told him what to do in every detail.

The young man returned to the magician.

"Wicked magician, you have made a fool of me! Now it's an eye for an eye, a tooth for a tooth."

"Leave me alone, for pity's sake! Go to my sisters who live a little farther on." And he told him what to do.

Cammina, cammina, arriva in una campagna dove c'era un palazzo simile a quello del Mago. Picchiò al portone.
- *Chi sei? Chi cerchi?*
- *Cerco Cornino d'oro.*
- *Capisco: ti manda mio fratello. Che cosa vuole da me?*
- *Vuole un pezzettino di panno rosso; gli si è bucato il mantello.*
- *Che seccatura! Prendi qua.*
E gli buttò dalla finestra un pezzettino di panno rosso, tagliato a foggia di lingua.

Andò avanti, e arrivò a piè d'una montagna dove, a mezza costa, c'era un palazzo simile a quello del Mago. Picchiò al portone.
- *Chi sei? Chi cerchi?*
- *Cerco Manina d'oro.*
- *Capisco: ti manda mio fratello. Che cosa vuole da me?*
- *Vuole due grani di lenti per la minestra.*
- *Che seccatura! Prendi qua.*
E gli buttò dalla finestra due grani di lenti, involtati in un pezzettino di carta.

Andò avanti, e arrivò in una valle, dove c'era un altro palazzo simile a quello del Mago. Picchiò al portone.
- *Chi sei? Chi cerchi?*
- *Cerco Piedino d'oro.*
- *Capisco: ti manda mio fratello! Che cosa vuole da me?*
- *Vuole due lumachine per mangiarsele a cena.*
- *Che seccatura! Prendi qua.*
E gli buttò dalla finestra le lumachine richieste.
Il giovanotto tornò dal Mago:
- *Ho portato ogni cosa.*

He walked on until he came to a meadow where there was a palace like the magician's. He knocked at the portal

"Who is it? Who are you looking for?"

"I am looking for a golden horn."

"I understand; my brother sent you. What does he want from me?"

"He wants a small piece of red cloth; his cape has worn out."

"What a bother! Take this."

And from the window, she threw him a small piece of red cloth cut in the shape of a tongue.

He walked on and came to the foot of a mountain where, half way up, there was a palace like the magician's. He knocked at the portal.

"Who is it? Who are you looking for?"

"I am looking for a golden hand."

"I understand; my brother sent you. What does he want from me?"

"He wants two lentils for soup."

"What a nuisance! Take these."

And from the window, she threw him two lentils, wrapped in a small piece of paper.

He walked on and came to valley, where there was another palace like the magician's. He knocked at the portal.

"Who is it? Who are you looking for?"

"I am seeking a golden foot."

"I understand; my brother sent you. What does he want from me?"

"He wants two snails to eat at dinner."

"What a nuisance! Take these."

And from the window she threw him the snails he had requested.

The young man then returned to the magician.

"I have brought everything."

Il Mago gli disse come doveva fare, e il giovanotto stava per andarsene:

- *Mi lasci qui incatenato?*

- *Lo meriteresti, ma ti sciolgo. Se mi hai ingannato, guai a te!*

Il giovane si presentò al palazzo reale e si fece condurre dalla Reginotta.

Le aperse la bocca, vi mise dentro quel pezzettino di panno rosso, e la Reginotta ebbe la lingua. Ma le prime parole che disse furon contro di lui:

- *Miserabile ciabattino! Via di qua! Via di qua!*

Il povero giovane rimase confuso:

- *Questa è opera del Mago!*

Senza curarsene, prese i due semi di lenti, con un po' di saliva glieli applicò sulle pupille spente, e la Reginotta ebbe la vista. Ma appena lo guardò, si coprì gli occhi colle mani:

- *Dio, com'è brutto! Com'è brutto!*

Il povero giovane rimase:

- *Questa è opera del Mago!*

Ma, senza curarsene, prese i gusci delle lumachine che aveva già vuotati, e con un po' di saliva glieli applicò bellamente dov'era il posto degli orecchi: la Reginotta ebbe gli orecchi.

Il giovane si rivolse al Re e disse:

- *Maestà, son vostro genero.*

Come intese quella voce, la Reginotta cominciò a urlare:

- *Mi ha detto: Strega! Mi ha detto: Strega!*

Il povero giovane, a questa nuova uscita, sbalordì:

- *È opera del Mago!*

- *E tornò dalla Fata.*

- *Fata, dove sei?*

- *Ai tuoi comandi.*

The magician told him what to do, and he was about to leave:

"Are you leaving me here chained?"

"You deserve it, but I will unchain you. However if you have deceived me, woe is you!"

The young man presented himself at the royal palace and had himself led to the princess.

He opened her mouth, placed the small piece of red cloth into it, and the princess had a tongue. However, with her first words she attacked the young man.

"You wicked cobbler. Get out of here! Get out of here!"

The poor young man was confused.

"This is the work of the magician!"

Without hesitation, he took the two lentils and applied them with a little saliva on the pupils that had been burned out. And so, the princess's sight was restored. However, as soon as she looked upon him, she covered her eyes with her hands:

"God, how ugly he is! How ugly he is!"

The poor young man was stunned.

"This is the work of the magician!"

However, without hesitation, he took the shells of the snails, which he had already emptied, and he placed them nicely on the place where the ears should be. And so, the princess's ears were restored.

The young man turned to the king and said:

"Majesty, I am your son-in-law."

As soon as she heard his voice, the princess began to scream:

"He called me a witch! He called me a witch!"

Upon hearing this, the poor young man was astonished:

"This is the work of the magician! And I am going back to the fairy."

"Fairy, where are you?"

"At your service."

Le narrò la sua disgrazia.
La Fata sorrise e gli domandò:
- Le hai tu tolto di dito l'altro anello del Mago?
- Mi pare di no.
Vai a vedere; sarà questo.
Come la Reginotta ebbe tolto di dito quell'altro anello, tornò gentile e tranquilla.
Allora il Re le disse:
- Questi è il tuo sposo.
La Reginotta e il giovanotto si abbracciarono alla presenza di tutti, e pochi giorni dopo furono celebrate le nozze.

E furono marito e moglie;
E a lui il frutto e a noi le foglie.

He told her about his misfortune.

The fairy smiled and asked him:

"Have you removed the magician's other ring from her finger?"

"I don't think so."

"Go and see; that must be the problem."

As soon as the ring was removed from the princess's finger, she became gentle and peaceful.

Thus, the king said:

"This is your husband."

The princess and the young man embraced in front of all of the people, and a few days later they celebrated their wedding.

They became husband and wife.
May we all live as happy a life.

Serpentina

C'era una volta un Re e una Regina. La Regina era incinta.
Un giorno passò una di quelle zingare che van dicendo la buona ventura, e il Re la fece chiamare:
- Che partorirà la Regina?
- Maestà, un serpente.
Quelli trasecolarono.
- E che dovevano farne? Ammazzarlo appena nato? Allevarlo?
- Dovevano allevarlo.
La povera Regina dette in un pianto dirotto:
-Chi avrebbe allattato una bestia così schifosa? Lei sarebbe morta dal terrore! E poi, se le mordeva il seno?
- Maestà, non abbiate paura. Avrà un dente soltanto, un dente d'oro.
Infatti la Regina partorì un bel serpentello verde-nero, che subito, appena nato, sguizzò di mano alla levatrice, attaccossi alla poppa della mamma e si mise a poppare.
Quando fu addormentato, il Re gli aperse la bocca e vide che avea davvero un dente soltanto, un dente d'oro. Però, siccome non voleva che quella loro disgrazia si risapesse, fece dire che la Regina avea partorito una bella bimba, ed era stata chiamata Serpentina.
Serpentina cresceva rapidamente, e quando apriva la bocca, il suo dente d'oro stralucciava.
Un giorno ripassò quella zingara, e il Re la fece chiamare:
- Dimmi la ventura di Serpentina.
- Buona o cattiva, Maestà?
- Buona o cattiva.
La zingara prese in mano la coda di Serpentina e si messe ad osservarla attentamente. Scrollava la testa.
- Zingara, che cosa vedi da farti scrollare la testa?
- Maestà, veggo guai!

Serpentina

Once upon a time, there lived a king and a queen. The queen was going to have a baby.

One day there passed by one of those gypsies who go around telling people's fortunes, and the king had her summoned.

"What will the queen have?" asked the king.

"A serpent, Majesty."

They were astounded.

And what were they to do with it? Kill it as soon as it was born, or raise it? They had to raise it.

Weeping uncontrollably, the poor queen said:

"Who will suckle such a disgusting animal?"

She would die of fear! And then what if it bit her breast?

"Majesty, don't worry. It has only one tooth, a golden tooth."

Sure enough, the queen gave birth to a beautiful little green snake, which immediately jumped out of the midwife's hand and attached itself to its mother's breast and began to suck.

When the snake fell asleep, the king opened its mouth and saw that, indeed, it did have only one tooth, a golden tooth. However, because he did not want word of this tragedy to get out, he had it reported that the queen had given birth to a baby girl, who was named Serpentina.

Serpentina grew rapidly and, when she opened her mouth, her golden tooth sparkled brightly.

One day that same gypsy passed by again, and the king had her summoned.

"Reveal Serpentina's fortune to me."

"Good or ill, Majesty?"

"Good or ill."

The gypsy took Serpentina's tail in her hand and began to observe her closely. She shook her head.

"Gypsy, what makes you shake your head?"

"Majesty, I see trouble."

- E non c'è rimedio?

- Maestà, bisognerebbe interrogare una più sapiente di me: la Fata gobba.

- O dove trovare questa Fata gobba?

- Prendete del pane e del vino per otto giorni e camminate sempre diritto, badiamo! Senza voltarvi in dietro. All'ottavo giorno vi troverete avanti a una grotta: la Fata gobba abita lì.

- Va bene, - disse il Re - partirò domani.

Prese le provviste per otto giorni, e si mise in cammino. Quando fu a mezza strada:

- Maestà! Maestà!

Stava per voltarsi, ma si ricordò della raccomandazione della zingara, e tirò diritto.

Un altro giorno, ecco dietro a lui un urlo di creatura umana:

- Ahi! M'ammazzano! Ahi!

Il Re si fermò, irresoluto; quel grido strappava l'anima!... E stava per voltarsi; ma si ricordò della raccomandazione, e tirò diritto.

Un altro giorno, ecco alle sue spalle un gran rumore, come di cavalli che corrano di galoppo.

- Bada! Bada!

Spaventato, stava per voltarsi; ma si ricordò della raccomandazione della zingara, e tirò diritto.

Giunto davanti alla grotta, cominciò a chiamare:

- Fata gobba! Fata gobba!

- Gobbo sarai te! - rispose una voce.

E il povero Re, sentitosi un po' di peso sulle spalle, si tastò. Gli era proprio spuntata la gobba.

Ed ora che fare? Come tornare indietro con quella mostruosità?

-Risolse di tornar di notte, perché nessuno lo vedesse. La Regina, accortasi di quel gonfiore sulle spalle, gli domandò:

"And is there no remedy for it?"

"Majesty, you need to ask someone more knowledgeable than I: the hunchbacked fairy."

"And where shall I find this hunchbacked fairy?"

"Pack enough bread and wine for a journey of eight days. Make sure you walk straight ahead! Don't turn around. On the eighth day, you will find yourself in a grotto: the hunchbacked fairy lives there."

"Very well," said the king, "I will leave tomorrow."

He took provisions for eight days, and he began to walk. When he was half way, he heard:

"Majesty! Majesty!"

He was about to turn around, but he remembered the gypsy's advice, and he went straight ahead.

Another day, he heard behind him the shriek of a human being.

"Oh, they have killed me. Oh!"

The king stopped, and he wavered. That cry tore at his soul, and he was about to turn, but he remembered the gypsy's advice, and he went straight ahead.

Another day, over his shoulder he heard a loud noise, like the galloping of horses.

"Careful! Careful!"

Frightened, he was about to turn, but he remembered the gypsy's advice, and he went straight ahead.

Once he reached the grotto, he began to call:

"Hunchbacked fairy! Hunchbacked fairy!"

"You will be a hunchback," responded a voice. Feeling that his shoulder had grown heavier, the poor king touched a swelling that had actually grown there.

"And now, what shall I do? How can I return home with this monstrosity on my shoulder?"

He decided to return at night, for no one would see him then. However, as soon as the queen saw that swelling on his shoulder, she asked:

- Maestà, che portate addosso?
- Porto la mia disgrazia!
E raccontò com'era andata.
La Regina risolse di tentar lei:
- Fra loro donne si sarebbero intese meglio.
Fece le sue provviste di pane e vino per otto giorni, e partì.
A metà strada:
- Maestà! Maestà!
Lei, sbadatamente, si volta, e si trova tornata al punto d'onde era partita.
- Pazienza! Ricomincerò.
La seconda volta, più in là di mezza strada, ecco alle sue spalle un gran rumore, come di cavalli che corrano di galoppo:
- Bada! Bada!
Presa dallo spavento, si volta, e si trova di nuovo al punto d'onde era partita.
Allora, da scaltra, disse al Re:
- Maestà, turatemi le orecchie col cotone e versatevi su della cera. Così non sentirò nulla, e potrò arrivare dalla Fata gobba: altrimenti non ci sarà verso.
Il Re le turò le orecchie a quel modo, e lei partì.
Giunta davanti la grotta, si sturò le orecchie, e picchiò. Picchia, ripicchia, non rispondeva nessuno. Lei non voleva chiamare, e dava all'uscio col bastone, a due mani.
- Chi è? - urlò finalmente una voce - Chi cercate?
- Son io: cerco la Fata.
- Quale Fata? Delle Fate ce n'è tante!
- La Fata gobba.
Le scappò di bocca.
- Gobba sarai tu!

"Majesty, what are you carrying?"

"I am carrying my misfortune."

And he explained how this had happened.

The queen decided to attempt the trip herself:

"Women understand each other if they talk among themselves," she said.

She took bread and wine for a journey of eight days and left.

At the half-way point, however, she heard:

"Majesty! Majesty!"

Carelessly, she turned around, and she found herself at the point from which she had departed.

"Patience! I will begin again," she said.

The second time, more than half way there, over her shoulder she heard a loud noise, like the galloping of horses:

"Careful! Careful!"

Seized by fear, she turned, and she found herself once again at the point from which she had departed.

So, having learned her lesson, she said to the king:

"Majesty, plug up my ears with cotton and pour wax over it. This way I will hear nothing, and I will be able to reach the hunchbacked fairy; there is no other way."

The king stopped up her ears in this manner, and she departed.

Arriving at the grotto, she unplugged her ears, and she began to knock. She knocked and knocked, but no one answered. She did not want to call out, and she rapped at the door with a cudgel that she held in both hands.

"Who is it?" someone finally shouted. "Whom are you seeking?"

"It is I," said the queen. "I am looking for the fairy."

"Which fairy? There are lots of fairies."

"The hunchbacked fairy," said the queen.

The words slipped from her mouth.

"You will be a hunchback!"

*La Regina si tastò subito le spalle. Le era proprio spuntata
la gobba.*

*Tornò di notte, per non esser veduta; e il Re, prima di ogni
cosa, le guardò dietro.*

- Maestà, che portate addosso?

- Porto la mia disgrazia!

E raccontò com'era andata.

*- E tutto questo per Serpentina! Schiacciamogli la testa! La
mala fortuna ci vien per lei.*

Il Re non sapea risolversi:

Non era sangue loro?

- Farò di mio capo - disse fra sé la Regina.

E, di nascosto al Re, chiamò una guardia di palazzo:

*- Prendi questa cassettina e vattene in un bosco. Quando
sarai lì, farai una catasta di legna, ve la metterai su e darai
fuoco. Finché non sia consumata, non dovrai tornare indietro.*

- Maestà, sarà fatto.

Intanto il Re ordinava gli si chiamasse la zingara:

- Dimmi la ventura di Serpentina.

- Buona o cattiva, Maestà?

- Buona o cattiva.

*- Maestà, Serpentina corre pericolo di morte: E se muore
Serpentina, tutto il regno va in rovina.*

- Che pericolo può correre nelle stanze reali?

- Maestà, non è più lì.

*Quando il Re apprese quello che sua moglie avea fatto,
cominciò a strapparsi i capelli:*

*- La loro rovina era compiuta. Ah! Povera Serpentina, dove
tu sei?*

E una voce lontana, lontana:

- Maestà, sono nel bosco.

- E che tu fai?

-   Sento strani rumori.

Immediately, the queen touched her shoulder. On it, a swelling had grown.

She returned at night so that no one would see her. However, the first thing that the king did was to look behind her.

"Majesty, what are you carrying?"

"I am carrying my misfortune," said the queen.

And she explained how this had happened.

"And all of this because of Serpentina! We should squash her head! She has brought us bad luck."

The king did not know how to solve the problem.

After all, wasn't this his flesh and blood?

"I will work this out," said the queen to herself.

And, concealing her plan from the king, she called a palace guard.

"Take this little box and go into the forest. When you are there, make a pile of wood, place the box in it, and set it on fire. Do not return until it is consumed by the flames.

"Majesty, it will be done."

Meanwhile, the king ordered that the gypsy be brought to him.

"Reveal Serpentina's fortune to me."

"Good or ill, Majesty?"

"Good or ill."

"Majesty, Serpentina is in mortal danger. And if she dies, your entire realm will be destroyed."

"What danger can she face in the royal apartments?"

"Majesty, she is no longer there."

When the king realized what his wife had done, he began to pull his hair.

"Our ruin is assured. Oh, poor Serpentina, where are you?"

From far away, he heard a voice: "Majesty, I am in the forest."

"And what are you doing?"

"I hear strange noises."

Il Re ordinò:
- Mi si selli il miglior cavallo della mia scuderia!
Montò a cavallo e via, come un fulmine, per la strada del bosco. Di tanto in tanto si fermava:
- Serpentina, dove tu sei?
- Maestà, in mezzo al bosco.
Ora la voce era più vicina.
- E che tu fai?
- Maestà, ho troppo caldo.
Il Re conficcava gli sproni nei fianchi del cavallo: avrebbe voluto che volasse. Ma quando fu in mezzo al bosco, vide una gran fiamma:
- Serpentina, dove tu sei?
- Maestà, in mezzo al bosco.
La voce era vicinissima.
- E che tu fai?
- Pelle nuova, Maestà!
Il Re corse alla catasta in fiamme, e senza curar di scottarsi, tirò la cassettina fuori della brace. L'aperse in fretta e furia, e vide scappar fuori una ragazza di belle forme; se non che avea la pelle tutta squamosa, come quella d'un serpente.
- Troppa fretta, Maestà! Ora non potrò più maritarmi!
Serpentina non avea avuto il tempo di far pelle nuova. E dava in un dirotto pianto; era inconsolabile:
- Lasciatemi qui sola. Anderò dalla Fata gobba.
Non potendola persuadere altrimenti, il Re l'abbandonò in mezzo al bosco e tornò al palazzo reale.
Ma Serpentina, gira di qua, gira di là, non trovava l'uscita. Vide uno scarafaggio:
- Scarafaggio, bel scarafaggio! Se mi conduci dalla Fata gobba, ti faccio un magnifico regalo.
- Non la conosco.

The king commanded:

"Saddle the best horse in my stable."

He mounted the horse and, like a flash of lightning, set out for the forest road. Now and again, he stopped.

"Serpentina, where are you?"

"Majesty, I am deep in the forest."

Now, the voice was closer.

"And what are you doing?"

"Majesty, it is too hot in here."

The king stuck his spurs into the sides of the horse; he wished he could fly. However, when he was in the forest, he saw a great fire:

"Serpentina, where are you?"

"Majesty, deep in the forest."

The voice was very close.

"And what are you doing?"

"I am growing a new skin, Majesty!"

The king ran to the flaming heap and, without fear of being burned, he pulled the small box from the flames. He opened it in haste and rage, and he watched a beautiful young woman escape; however, her skin was covered with scales, just like a serpent's.

"You have saved me too soon, Majesty. Now I can no longer get married!"

Serpentina had not had the time to grow a new skin. And she fell into an uncontrollable sobbing. She was inconsolable:

"Leave me here alone. I will go to the hunchbacked fairy."

Unable to convince her to do otherwise, the king left her deep in the forest and returned to the royal palace.

Serpentina turned this way and that, but she could not find a way out of the forest. But then she spotted a cockroach:

"Cockroach, dear cockroach! If you lead me to the hunchbacked fairy, I will give you a magnificent present."

"I don't know her," said the cockroach.

E tirò via.

Più in là, vide un topolino:

- Topolino, bel topolino! Se mi conduci dalla Fata gobba, ti faccio un magnifico regalo.

- Non la conosco.

E tirò via.

Più in là ancora, vide un usignuolo in cima a un albero:

- Usignuolo, bell'usignuolo! Se mi conduci dalla Fata gobba, ti faccio un magnifico regalo.

- Mi dispiace, ma non posso. Aspetto la bella dal dente d'oro che deve passare di qui.

- Usignuolo, bell'usignuolo! Sono io la bella dal dente d'oro.

E mostrò il dente.

- O Reginotta mia! Son tant'anni che t'aspetto.

L'usignuolo divenne, tutt'a un tratto, il più bel giovane che si fosse mai visto, la prese per mano e la condusse fuor del bosco.

Giunti davanti alla grotta, il bel giovane picchiò.

- Chi siete?

- Son io e Serpentina.

- Chi volete?

- La Fata regina.

La grotta si spalancò, e si vide il gran palazzo della Fata gobba; ma bisognava dirle Fata regina; se no, se l'avea a male.

- Ben venuta, figliuola mia! T'aspettavo da un pezzo. Questo giovine è figlio d'un regnante. Una Maga gli aveva fatto l'incantesimo, e per romperlo ci voleva la ragazza dal dente d'oro. Ora dovrete sposarvi.

La Reginotta, con quella pelle squamosa, era un orrore. La Fata gobba cominciò a strusciarla da capo a piedi, e in poco

And he went on his way.

In a little while, she saw a little mouse:

"Little mouse, dear little mouse! If you lead me to the hunchbacked fairy, I will give you a magnificent present."

"I don't know her."

And he went on his way.

A little later, she saw a nightingale on the limb of a tree.

" Nightingale, dear nightingale! If you lead me to the hunchbacked fairy, I will give you a magnificent present."

"I am sorry, but I can't. I am waiting for the beauty with a golden tooth who should pass by."

"Nightingale, dear nightingale! I am the beauty with the golden tooth."

And she showed the nightingale the tooth.

"Oh, my princess! I have been waiting many years for you."

All of a sudden, the nightingale became the most handsome young man who has ever been seen. He took her by the hand and led her out of the forest.

Once they were before the grotto, the young man began to knock.

"Who are you?"

"It is I and Serpentina."

"What do you want?"

"The queen of the fairies."

The grotto opened, and the great palace of the hunchbacked fairy was revealed; however, one had to call her the fairy queen; otherwise there would be trouble.

"Welcome, my child! I have been waiting for you for a while. This young man is the son of a king. An enchantress put a spell on him, which only the girl with the golden tooth could break. Now you should get married."

With her scaly skin, the princess looked like a horror. The hunchbacked fairy began to peel off her scales from head to foot.

*d'ora la mondò, in guisa che non pareva più lei. Era così bella,
che abbagliava.*

*La Regina, come intese che Serpentina stava per tornare,
montò sulle furie:*

- Se vien lei, partirò io! È la nostra cattiva sorte!

*Ma, saputo che quella recava l'unguento da far sparire le
gobbe, le andò incontro col Re e con tutta la corte.*

*Fecero grandi feste, e vissero tutti felici e contenti.
E noi citrulli ci nettiamo i denti.*

In a little while, she changed her so much that she no longer looked like herself. In fact, she was so beautiful that she dazzled onlookers.

When the queen heard that Serpentina was about to return to the royal palace, she became angry.

"If she comes, I go! That is our evil fate!"

However, realizing that Serpentina had brought with her an ointment that would cause the humps to disappear, she and the king went to meet her with their entire court.

They enjoyed a great celebration.

And all were filled with contentment and joy.
So may it be for us, each girl and boy.

Il soldo bucato

C'era una volta una povera donna rimasta vedova con un figliolino al petto. Era di cattiva salute, e con quel bimbo da allattare poteva lavorare pochino. Faceva dei piccoli servigi alle vicine, e così lei e la sua creatura non morivano di fame.

Quel figliolino era bello come il sole; e la sua mamma, ogni mattina, dopo averlo rifasciato, lavato e pettinato, un po' per buon augurio, un po' per chiasso, soleva dirgli:

- Bimbo mio, tu sarai barone!

  Bimbo mio, tu sarai duca!

  Bimbo mio, tu sarai principe!

  Bimbo mio, tu sarai Re!

E ogni volta che lei gli diceva: tu sarai Re, il bimbo accennava di sì colla testina, come se avesse capito.

Un giorno si trovò a passare proprio il Re, e sentito:

- Bimbo mio, tu sarai Re.

La prese in mala parte, perché non aveva avuto ancora figliuoli e ne era accorato assai.

- Comarina, - le disse - non vi arrischiate più a dire così, o guai a voi!

La povera donna, dalla paura, non disse più nulla. Però quel figliolino, ora che la sua mamma stava zitta, ogni mattina, appena rifasciato, lavato e pettinato, si metteva a piangere e strillare.

Lei gli ripeteva:

- Bimbo mio, tu sarai barone!... Tu sarai duca!... Tu sarai principe!...

Ma il bimbo non si chetava. Talché una volta, per prova, tornò a dirgli sottovoce:

- Bimbo mio, tu sarai Re!

Il bimbo accennò di sì colla testina, come se avesse capito, e non strillò più.

The Penny with a Hole in It

There once was a poor widow with an infant at her breast. She
was in poor health and, with a nursing child, she could work
very little. She performed small services for her neighbors
and, in that way, she and her child did not die of hunger.

The little boy was as beautiful as the sun; every morning, after his mother had changed him, bathed him, and combed his
hair, she said, both for good luck and to cheer him up:

"My child, you shall be a baron!
 My child, you shall be a duke!
 My child, you shall be a prince!'
 My child, you shall be king!"

And each time that she said "you shall be king," the child
nodded "yes" with his little head, as if he had understood.

One day, the king himself happened to pass by and heard:

"My child, you shall be king!"

He took it badly, for he did not yet have any children, and he
was very discouraged about it.

"Little neighbor," he said, "don't dare say that again, or woe
to you!"

Out of fear, the poor woman didn't say this again. However,
now that his mother was silent, every morning after being
changed, bathed, and combed, the little boy began to cry and
scream.

So, over and over she said to him:

"My child, you shall be a baron! My child, you shall be a
duke! My child, you shall be a prince!"

However, the child did not quiet, so one time the mother
tried saying under her breath:

"My child, you shall be king!"

The child nodded "yes" with his little head as if he had understood, and he stopped screaming.

Allora la povera donna si persuase che quel figliolino doveva avere una gran fortuna; e temendo la collera del Re, già pensava di mutar paese.

Intanto, poiché il figliuolo era spoppato, quando le capitava di fare qualche servizio, pregava una vicina:

- Comare, tenetemi d'occhio il bambino; vado e torno in due minuti.

Un giorno le accadde di tardare. La vicina era seccata di tenere in braccio quel cattivello che piangeva perché voleva la mamma. In quel punto comparve un cenciaiolo:

- Cenci, donnine, cenci!

- Lo volete questo cencio qui?

- Se ci si combina, lo prendo.

- Ve lo do per un soldo.

Il cenciaiuolo le tolse il bimbo di braccio e le mise in mano un soldo bucato.

A quella scena lei e le altre vicine presenti ridevano: il cenciaiuolo in questo mentre svoltava la cantonata e spariva. Corri, cerca, chiama... L'avete più visto?

Figuriamoci che pianto, quella povera mamma, quando apprese la sua disgrazia!

Corse subito dal Re:

- Giustizia, Maestà!... Mi han rapito il bambino!

- Bimbo mio, tu sarai Re! - le rispose il Re facendole il verso, per canzonarla.

E la mandò via, tutto contento che quel malaugurio per la sua discendenza fosse sparito.

Gli occhi della povera donna parevano un fiume. Andava attorno tutta la giornata, fermando la gente:

- Buona gente, incontraste per caso il cenciaiuolo che mi ha rubato il mio bambino?

Le persone, che non ne sapevano nulla, la prendevano per matta e le ridevano in viso.

So, the poor woman convinced herself that this little child would have great luck, and fearing the anger of the king, she now thought about going to another country.

Meanwhile, because the child was still nursing, when the poor woman had a job, she asked a neighbor:

"Dear friend, keep an eye on the baby; I will be right back."

One day, she happened to be late. The neighbor was tired of holding the little thing in her arms, for he was crying for his mother. At that moment, there appeared a junk peddler.

"Rags, ladies, rags."

"Do you want this rag?" asked the neighbor.

"If we can strike a deal, I will buy him," said the man.

"I will sell him to you for a penny."

The peddler took the child from her arms and gave her a penny with a hole in it.

With this, she and the other neighbors there laughed. Meanwhile, the peddler turned the corner and disappeared. She ran after him, searched, and called out: "Have you seen him?"

Imagine the pain of that poor mother when she learned about this great misfortune.

She ran quickly to the king:

"Justice, Majesty! They have stolen my baby!"

"My little child, you shall be king!" responded the king, as he made a face to mock her.

And he sent her away, satisfied that this evil omen on his descendants had disappeared.

The poor woman's eyes ran with tears like a river. She went about all day long stopping people:

"Good folks, have you by any chance encountered the peddler who stole my baby?"

The people, who knew nothing, took her for a madwoman and laughed in her face.

Quel giorno della disgrazia, la vicina le aveva dato il soldo bucato messole in mano dal cenciaiuolo; ma la povera donna, dalla gran rabbia che aveva, lo buttò via.

La mattina dopo, apre un cassetto... il soldo bucato era lì.

- Soldaccio maledetto! Non ti voglio neppur vedere!

E lo buttò nuovamente via dalla finestra.

Ma la mattina dopo, torna ad aprire quel cassetto e che vede? Il soldo bucato.

Richiuse il cassetto con stizza.

- Fossero almeno dieci lire...! Mi comprerei uno straccio di veste!

Non avea finito di dirlo, che sentì lì dentro un suono di soldi rimescolati. Stupita, riapre. Pareva che il soldo avesse figliato. Oltre a quello, c'erano lì tanti soldi, da fare giusto dieci lire.

Da allora in poi, quando avea bisogno di denaro, le bastava che dicesse:

- Soldino mio, vo' cento lire, vo' mille lire!

Le cento lire, le mille lire erano subito lì.

La buona donna non si teneva questa fortuna per sé sola; faceva spesso la carità a tutte le persone bisognose al par di lei, ed era già diventata una benedizione del cielo.

Ma quel bene lei lo faceva sempre col pensiero al figliolino perduto. Che le importava di tanta fortuna, senza il suo figliolino? E sperava sempre che, un giorno o l'altro, il cielo l'avrebbe consolata.

In quel tempo il Re ebbe il capriccio di comprarsi un magnifico cavallo. Conchiuso il negozio, andò per prendere il denaro dallo scrigno ove solea tenerlo riposto, e si accorse che mancava una bella somma.

Appostò lì due guardie per acchiappare il ladro; e, passati alquanti giorni, tornò a guardare: mancava un'altra bella somma!

The day of the misfortune, the neighbor had given her the penny with the hole, which the peddler had given her. However, in her rage, the poor woman had thrown it away.

The next morning, however, she opened a small box and found the penny with the hole inside

"Evil penny! I never want to see you again!" And she threw it from the window once again.

But the next morning, upon opening the box again, what did she see? The penny with the hole in it.

She angrily closed the box.

"If it were at least 10 lire, I would buy myself a rag of a dress."

She had not yet finished saying this when she heard inside the box the sound of money being stirred up. Amazed, she opened it again. It seemed as if the money had reproduced. In addition to the penny, there was enough money to make 10 lire.

From that point on, when she had need of money, she needed only to say:

"My little penny, I want 100 lire, I want 1000 lire!"

And the 100 lire, the 1000 lire were there immediately.

The good woman did not keep this fortune for herself. She often gave it to the needy people around her, and she soon came to be seen as a blessing from heaven.

However, as she did these good deeds, the thought of her lost son weighed on her mind. What good did so much wealth do her without her little boy? And she always hoped that, one day or another, heaven would console her.

At that time, the king had a yearning to buy himself a magnificent horse. Having concluded the deal, he went to get money from the treasure box where he had secretly hid it. But he realized that a good portion of it was missing!

He posted two guards there to catch the thief. After several days, he returned to see: there was still more money missing.

Si mise in agguato lui stesso; cominciava a sospettare dei suoi Ministri Una mattina, ecco una voce nell'aria, lontana, lontana:

- Soldino mio, vo' mille lire!

E, subito, un rimescolìo nello scrigno, come se qualcuno vi prendesse quattrini a manate.

Apre in fretta in fretta... Le mille lire mancavano, ma lì dentro non c'era nessuno!

- Come andava questa faccenda?

Il Re ci perdeva la testa.

Però, benché fosse un po' avaro, gli dispiaceva di più dover morire senza figliuoli. Se la prendeva colla Regina, come se la colpa fosse stata di lei, e la maltrattava:

- Non era buona a fargli un figliuolo, neppure di terra cotta!

La Regina, indispettita, gli fece colle sue mani un bel puttino di terra cotta.

- Ecco, se era buona!

Tutti accorrevano al palazzo reale per vedere quel puttino di terra cotta, che era una meraviglia, e vi andò anche quella povera donna.

- Oh Dio! È tutto il mio bambino!... Ma non era così che ti volevo Re, figliolino mio!

E si mise a piangere.

Il Re, a quelle parole, montò in furore. Diè un calcio al puttino di terra cotta e lo ridusse in mille pezzi.

Alla povera donna parve di vedersi squarciare sotto gli occhi il figliolino perduto. Ma che poteva dire a Sua Maestà? Dovette ingozzare anche quell'amarezza, e tornarsene a casa zitta zitta.

Intanto nello scrigno del Re i quattrini continuavano a mancare; e sempre quella voce nell'aria, lontana lontana:

- Soldino mio, vo' cento lire, vo' mille lire!

E quanti diceva la voce, tanti il Re ne sentiva prendere dalla mano del ladro invisibile.

So he himself stood watch; he began to suspect one of his ministers.

One morning, a distant voice was heard crying in the air:

"My little penny, I want a thousand lire."

And quickly, there was a shuffling within the treasure box as if someone were taking out the coins in handfuls.

He opened it frantically. The 1000 lire were missing, but inside there was no one.

"How can this be?" said the king.

He was losing his mind.

However, although he was a bit avaricious, he was even more worried about dying without having children. So, he took it out on the queen, as if it were her fault, and he maltreated her.

"She is not capable of producing a son," said the king, "not even one made of terra cotta!"

Irritated, the queen made with her own hands a beautiful little cherub of terra cotta.

"See if this is to your liking," she said.

Everyone hurried to the royal palace to see the terra cotta cherub, which was a marvel. And so did that poor woman.

"Oh, Lord, he looks exactly like my baby! But this is not how I wanted you to become king, my little boy."

And she began to cry.

At these words, the king became furious. He kicked the little terra cotta cherub and broke it into a thousand pieces.

To the poor woman, it seemed as if she were seeing her little lost boy being torn apart before her eyes. But what could she say to his majesty? She had to swallow even this bitterness, and she returned home without a word.

Meanwhile, from the king's treasure chest, the money continued to disappear. Always there was a distant voice in the air:

"My little penny, I want 100 lire, I want 1000 lire!"

And whatever amount the voice uttered, that's how much the king heard the invisible thief take.

Il Re mise le sue spie per scoprire di chi fosse quella voce: e un giorno le spie gli condussero dinanzi ammanettata la donna del bambino rubato:

Era lei che aveva detto: "Soldino mio, vo' cento lire!".

Il Re non volle neppure ascoltare la povera donna, che voleva raccontargli come stesse la cosa, e la fece gettare in un fondo di carcere.

Ma da quel giorno egli non ebbe più pace.

Voleva andare a letto? E gli strappavano le coperte:

- Maestà, non si dorme!

Chi era? Non si vedeva nessuno.

Si sedeva a tavola per mangiare? E gli portavano via il piatto:

- Maestà, non si mangia!

Chi era? Non si vedeva nessuno.

Se durava un altro po', il Re moriva d'inedia. Perciò mandò a consultare un vecchio Mago.

Il Mago (che poi era quel cenciaiuolo che avea rapito il bambino per proteggerlo) rispose soltanto:

- Bimbo mio, tu sarai Re!

Visto che il destino era quello, e non volendo morire d'inedia, il Re cominciò dallo scarcerare la povera donna, e tornò a mandare dal Mago:

- Come rintracciare il bimbo? Lo avea rapito un cenciaiuolo e non se ne sapeva più notizia.

Il Mago rispose:

- Raccatti i cocci di quel puttino di terra cotta e li saldi insieme collo sputo.

Il Re, sebbene di mala voglia, raccattò i cocci del puttino e li saldò collo sputo.

- Ed ora?

- Ed ora - rispose il Mago - prepari una bella festa e faccia così e così.

The king posted his spies to discover the source of the voice: and one day, the spies brought before him in manacles the poor woman whose baby had been stolen.

It was she who had said: "My little penny, I want 100 lire!"

The king would not listen to the poor woman, who wanted to explain what had happened, and had he had her thrown into the bottom of a prison.

But from that day, he had no peace.

If he wanted to sleep, the covers would tangle him up:

"Majesty, you cannot sleep."

But who had said that? There was no one to be seen.

If he sat at table to eat, his plate would magically float away.

"Majesty, you cannot eat!"

But who had said that? There was no one to be seen.

If this lasted much longer, the king would die of starvation. So, he decided to consult an old magician.

The magician, who was that same peddler who had stolen the baby to protect him, said only:

"My little child, you shall be king!"

Seeing that his fate was determined and not wanting to starve to death, the king ordered the poor woman released, and he called on the magician again:

"How shall we find the child? A peddler abducted him, and there has been no news of him ever since."

The magician responded:

"Pick up the pieces of the little terra cotta cherub and stick him together with saliva."

Although he was mean spirited, the king stuck all the pieces of the cherub back together with saliva.

"And now?" he said

"And now," responded the magician, "prepare a great feast and follow my instructions."

Il Re fece dei grandi preparativi, poi, secondo le istruzioni del Mago, mandò a chiamare la mamma del bimbo a palazzo reale e la fece sedere a lato della Regina.

Il puttino di terra cotta bello e saldato si vedeva collocato nel mezzo del salone e, attorno attorno, ministri, principi, cavalieri in gran gala che aspettavano.

Quando fu l'ora, s'intese nella via:

- Cenci, donnine, cenci!

A questo grido il puttino di terra cotta scoppiò, e ne uscì fuori un bel giovinotto fra un gran rovesciarsi di monete, che ruzzolavano da tutte le parti.

Il Re, contento anche perché riacquistava tutti i suoi quattrini, voleva abbracciarlo come un figliuolo; ma quello corse prima dalla sua mamma e non sapeva staccarsela dal petto:

- Bimbo mio, tu sarai Re!

Ed era già Reuccio, poiché il Re lo adottava!

Qui entrò una guardia e disse:

- Maestà, c'è di là un cenciaiuolo; rivuole il suo soldo bucato.

Il Re non ne sapeva nulla; ma la povera donna rispose subito:

- Eccolo qui.

Sentita la storia di quel soldo, il Re pensò ch'era meglio tenerselo per sé. Andò di là, bucò un altro soldo e diede questo in cambio di quello al cenciaiuolo.

Ma gliene incolse male.

La prima volta che disse:

- Soldino mio, vo' mille lire!

Invece di mille lire furono mille nerbate, che lo conciarono per le feste, tanto che morì.

- Bimbo mio, tu sarai Re!

E si era avverato.

Stretta è la foglia, larga è la via,
Dite la vostra, ché ho detto la mia.

The king made grand preparations. Then, following the magician's instructions, he summoned the mother of the little boy to the royal palace and had her seated next to the queen.

The beautiful, restored terra cotta cherub was displayed in the middle of the salon and all around it waited ministers, princes, and knights in a grand assembly. When the time came, along the way could be heard:

"Rags, Ladies, rags!"

At this sound, the terra cotta cherub exploded, and out sprang a handsome young man in a pile of coins that overflowed on all sides.

Happy over having recovered all of his money, the king wanted to embrace him like a son, but the young man ran first to his mother and could not break away from her embrace:

"My little child, you shall be king!"

And he was already a prince, for the king had adopted him!

At that moment, a guard entered and said

"Majesty, there is in the other room a peddler; he wants his penny with the hole in it."

The king knew nothing about this, but the poor woman quickly replied:

"Here it is."

Hearing the story of the penny, the king thought it better to keep it for himself. He went inside, got another penny, and gave this one to the peddler in its place.

But it turned out badly for him the first time he said:

"My little penny, I want 1000 lire!"

Instead of 1000 lire, he received 1000 lashes, which hurt him so badly that he died.

"My little child, you shall be king!"

And her wish had come true.

The journey is long and the path is narrow.
I've told my story; tell yours tomorrow.

Tì, tìriti, tì

C'era una volta un contadino che aveva un campicello tutto sassi, e largo quanto la palma della mano. Vi era rizzato un pagliaio e viveva lì, da un anno all'altro, zappando, seminando, sarchiando, insomma facendo tutti i lavori campestri.

Nelle ore di riposo cavava di tasca un zufolo e, tì, tìriti, tì, si divertiva a fare una sonatina, sempre la stessa; poi riprendeva il lavoro.

Intanto quel campicello sassoso gli fruttava più di un podere. Se i vicini raccoglievano venti, e lui raccoglieva cento, per lo meno. I vicini si rodevano. Una volta quel campicello non lo avrebbero accettato neanche in regalo: da che lo aveva lui, non sapevan che cosa fare per strapparglielo di mano.

- Compare, volete disfarvi di questi quattro sassi? C'è chi li pagherebbe tre volte più della stima.

- Questi sassi son per me:
Non li cederei neppure al Re.

- Compare, volete disfarvi di questi quattro sassi? C'è chi li pagherebbe dieci volte più della stima.

- Questi sassi son per me:
Non li cederei neppure al Re.

Una volta, per caso, passò di lì anche il Re, accompagnato dai ministri. Vedendo quel campicello, che pareva un giardino, coi seminati verdi e vegeti, mentre quelli dei campi attorno somigliavano a setole di spazzola, gialli, stenti, si fermò, colpito dalla meraviglia e disse ai ministri:

- È proprio una bellezza! Lo comprerei volentieri.

- Maestà, non si vende. Il padrone di esso è un uomo strano. Risponde a tutti:

- Questi sassi son per me:
Non li cederei neppure al Re.

- Oh! Voglio vederlo.

E fece chiamare il contadino.

Tì, tìriti, tì

There once was a farmer who had a field that was full of rocks and was very small. There he had raised a straw hut, in which he lived from year to year. He plowed, sowed, and weeded. In short, he did all the work that farmers do.

When it came time to rest, he took a pipe out of his pocket and played "tì, tìriti, tì." He amused himself always by playing the same little tune; then, he went back to work.

Meanwhile, that stony little field yielded more than a farm would. If his neighbors reaped twenty, he would reap at least one hundred. The neighbors were jealous to say the least. At one time, they had thought that the little farm was worthless, but since the farmer was so successful with it they desperately wanted to tear it from his hands.

"Neighbor, do you want to get rid of this land? There is someone who will pay three times its worth."

"These stones are for me."

He wouldn't even let the king have them.

"Neighbor, do you want to get rid of this land? There is someone who will pay ten times its worth."

"These stones are for me."

He wouldn't even let the king have them.

Once, by chance, the king actually passed by accompanied by his ministers. To him, the little farm looked like a garden with the crops green and thriving, while those in the fields around them looked like bristles on a brush—yellow and bare. The king stopped and was astonished by the sight.

"It is truly a beauty! I would certainly buy it."

"Majesty, it is not for sale. Its owner is a strange man. He tells everyone: 'These stones are for me.'"

He wouldn't even let the king have them.

"I want to see him," said the king.

And he summoned the farmer.

- È vero che questo campicello tu non lo cederesti neppure al Re?

- Sua Maestà ha tanti poderi! Che se ne farebbe dei miei sassi?

- Ma se lui li volesse?

- Se lui li volesse?

- Questi sassi son per me:

Non li cederei neppure al Re.

Il Re fece finta di non aversela avuta a male, e la notte dopo mandò cento guardie a scalpicciare, zitte zitte, quel seminato, da non lasciar ritto neanche un filo d'erba.

La mattina, il contadino esce fuor del pagliaio, e che vede? Uno spettacolo! E tutti i vicini che stavano a guardare, con gusto, quantunque si mostrassero addolorati.

- Ah, compare, compare! Se voi aveste venduto quei quattro sassi, ora questa disgrazia non vi sarebbe accaduta.

Ma quegli zitto, dinoccolato, come se non dicessero a lui.

Quando i vicini furono andati pei fatti loro, cavò di tasca lo zufolo, e tì, tìriti, tì, il seminato cominciava a rizzarsi; tì, tìriti, tì, il seminato si rizzava come se nulla fosse stato.

Il Re, sicuro del fatto suo, lo aveva mandato a chiamare:

- C'è qualcuno che ti vuol male. So che la notte scorsa ti han mezzo distrutto il seminato. Vendi a me quei quattro sassi. La gente, quando saprà che son miei, li guarderà da lontano.

- Maestà, non è vero nulla. Il mio seminato è più bello di prima.

Il Re si morse il labbro:

- Dunque i suoi ordini non erano stati eseguiti!

E se la prese coi Ministri. Ma appena questi gli riferirono che le povere guardie, dal gran scalpicciare di quella nottata, non si poteano neppur muovere, il Re rimase!

"Is it true that you won't even let the king have this little field?"

"Your majesty has so many fields! What will you do with my stones?"

"But what if I wanted them?"

"What if you wanted them? Well, these stones are for me."

He wouldn't even let the king have them.

The king made believe not to be offended, but the next night he sent a hundred soldiers to sneak silently into the field and destroy the crop, leaving not one blade of grass standing.

That morning, the farmer left his hut and saw a terrible sight! The neighbors were standing around and looking at the scene with great satisfaction, although they appeared to be sorry.

"Oh, neighbor, neighbor! If you had sold your land, this tragedy would not have befallen you."

However, he remained silent, relaxed, as if they were not talking to him.

When the neighbors left, he took the pipe out of his pocket and began to play "tì, tìriti, tì," and the crops began to revive; "tì, tìriti, tì."— the crops revived as if nothing had ever happened.

Feeling self-assured, the king summoned the farmer.

"There is someone who wishes you evil. I know that last night he destroyed your crop. Sell me this little piece of land. When the people know it is mine, they will not come near it."

"Majesty, none of this is true. My crop is more beautiful than before."

The king bit his lip.

Well then, his orders had not been carried out!

And he took it up with the ministers. However, as soon as they reported that the poor guards were so exhausted from their labor the night before that they could not even move, the king was stunned!

- Quest'altra notte, ad ora tarda, si mandi lì tutto l'armento.
La mattina, il contadino esce fuori dal pagliaio, e che vede?
Uno spettacolo: il terreno brucato raso!
I vicini:
- Ah, compare, compare! Se voi aveste venduto quei quattro
sassi, questa nuova disgrazia non vi sarebbe accaduta.
E quegli zitto, dinoccolato, come se non dicessero a lui.
Quando i vicini furono andati via pei fatti loro, cavava di
tasca lo zufolo, e tì, tìriti, tì, il seminato ripullulava; e tì, tìriti,
tì, il seminato era bell'e cresciuto come se nulla fosse stato.
Il Re, questa volta, era sicuro di aver buono in mano. Volea
vederlo, quell'uomo! Chi sa che grugno!
E appena l'ebbe alla sua presenza:
- C'è qualcuno che ti vuol male. So che la notte scorsa ti
hanno, a dirittura, distrutto ogni cosa. Vendi a me quei quattro
sassi. La gente, quando saprà che sono miei, li guarderà da
lontano.
- Maestà, non è vero nulla. Il mio seminato è più bello di
prima.
Il Re si morse il labbro:
Dunque i suoi ordini non erano stati eseguiti!
E se la prese coi Ministri. Ma quando questi gli riferirono
che tutto l'armento, dal gran mangime di quella nottata, avean
le pance che gli scoppiavano e che metà eran già morti di
ripienezza, il Re rimase!
- Qui c'è un mistero! Bisogna scoprirlo. Vi do tempo tre
giorni.
Col Re non si scherzava. I Ministri cominciarono dal
grattarsi il capo, e, pensa e ripensa, uno di essi propose di
andare, la notte, ad appostarsi dietro il pagliaio di quel
maledetto contadino e star lì fino all'alba. Chi sa? Qualcosa
avrebbero visto.
- Benone!

"Late tonight, send out the entire guard," he ordered.

The next morning, the farmer came out of his hut, and he saw a terrible sight!

The crop was burned to the ground! The neighbors said:

"Oh, neighbor, neighbor! If you had sold your land, this tragedy would not have befallen you."

However, he remained silent, relaxed, as if they were not talking to him.

When the neighbors left, he took the pipe out of his pocket and began to play "tì, tìriti, tì," and the crop rose again; and "tì, tìriti, tì"—it grew beautifully, as if nothing had ever happened.

This time, the king was sure that he had everything in hand. He wanted to see the farmer and to look him right in the face!

And right away he had the man before him.

"Someone wishes you evil. I know that last night, at his direction, everything in your garden was destroyed.

Sell me this land. When the people know it is mine, they will not come near it."

"Majesty, none of this is true. My crop is more beautiful than before."

And the king bit his lip.

Well then, his orders had not been carried out!

And he took this up with his ministers. However, when they reported that the bellies of the guards were bursting full with the grain they had eaten that night and that half of them had already died from being so full, the king was stunned.

"This is a mystery! There must be an explanation. You have three days to find it," the king told his ministers.

The king was not to be fooled with. The ministers began to scratch their heads, and thinking it over, one of them suggested that they go out at night, hide themselves behind that evil farmer's hut, and stay there until dawn. Who knows? They might see something.

"Very well!"

296 Luigi Capuana

*Andarono; e siccome nel pagliaio c'erano parecchie fessure,
si misero a spiare attraverso a queste.*

*Il Re non avea potuto chiuder occhio pensando
all'accaduto: e la mattina, di buon'ora, fece chiamare i
ministri.*

- Maestà, oh! Che abbiamo visto! Che abbiamo visto!

- Che cosa avete mai visto?

*- Quel contadino ha uno zufolo, e appena si mette a
sonarlo, tì, tìriti, tì, il suo pagliaio, di botto, diventa una
reggia.*

- E poi?

*- E poi vien fuori una ragazza più bella della luna e del sole,
e lui, tì, tìriti, tì, la fa ballare con quella sonata; e dopo le dice:*

-Bella figliuola, se il Re ti vuole,

Dee star sette anni alla pioggia e al sole.

E se sette anni alla pioggia e al sole non sta,

Bella figliuola, il Re non ti avrà.

- E poi?

*E poi smette di sonare e quella reggia, di botto, ridiventa
pagliaio.*

*- Glieli darò io la pioggia e il sole! - disse il Re, toccato sul
vivo.*

- Ma prima vediamo codesto miracolo di bellezza!

E andò la notte dopo, accompagnato dai Ministri.

*Ed ecco il contadino cava di tasca il suo zufolo, e tì, tìriti, tì,
di botto il pagliaio diventa una reggia; e tì, tìriti, tì, compare la
ragazza e si mette a ballare. A quella vista il Re ammattì:*

- Oh, che bellezza! Dovrà esser mia! Dovrà esser mia!

*E, senza metter tempo in mezzo, picchia all'uscio a più
riprese.*

*Il contadino cessò di suonare; di botto la reggia ridivenne
pagliaio, ma di aprire non se ne parlò neppure: e il Re, che
bruciava dall'impazienza, dovette tornarsene a palazzo. Prima
che albeggiasse, spedì un corriere a spron battuto:*

They went out, and since there were several cracks in the hut, they positioned themselves to spy through them.

The king had not been able to close his eyes because he was thinking about what had occurred. And early in the morning he summoned the ministers.

"Oh, Majesty, what we have seen! What we have seen! That farmer has a pipe and, as soon as he begins to play 'tì, tìriti, tì,' his hut suddenly becomes a palace."

"And then?"

"And then a young woman comes out who is more beautiful than the moon and the sun, and he has her dance to his little song, 'tì, tìriti, tì.' And later he says:

'Beautiful child, if the king wants you,

He must spend seven years in rain and sun.

And if he doesn't spend seven years in rain and sun,

The king will not have you.'"

"And then?"

"And then he begins to play, and immediately the palace turns back into a hut."

"I'll give him rain and sun!" said the king, for their story had touched a raw nerve.

"But first let's see this beautiful miracle!"

So, he went out the next night accompanied by the ministers.

And as soon as the farmer took the pipe out of his pocket and played "tì, tìriti, tì," the hut turned into a palace; and "tì, tìriti, tì," the young woman began to dance. At the sight of her, the king went wild!

"Oh what a beauty. She must be mine! She must be mine!"

And without wasting any time, he knocked at the door repeatedly.

The farmer stopped playing. Immediately, the palace turned back into a hut, but he did not open the door. And the king, who was burning up with impatience, had to go back to the palace. Before dawn, however, he sent a courier at full speed:

- Lo voleva il Re, subito subito.
Il contadino andò a presentarsi:
- Sua Maestà che cosa comandava?
- Comando e voglio la tua figliuola per sposa. Lei diventerà
Regina e tu Ministro di palazzo reale.
- Maestà, c'è una condizione:
  Chi vuole la mia figliuola
  Dee star sette anni alla pioggia e al sole;
  E se sette anni alla pioggia e al sole non sta,
  Fosse chi fosse, non l'otterrà.
*Il Re avrebbe voluto darglieli lui la pioggia e il sole! Ma
c'era di mezzo la ragazza. Si strinse nelle spalle e rispose:*
- Starò sette anni alla pioggia e al sole.
  *Lasciò il governo ai Ministri, per tutto il tempo che sarebbe
stato assente, e andò ad abitare col contadino, scottandosi la
pelle al solleone e restando sotto la pioggia anche quando
veniva giù a catinelle.*
  *Dopo poco tempo, povero Re, non si riconosceva più; parea
fatto di terra cotta, colla pelle bruciata a quel modo. Ma avea
un compenso. Di tanto in tanto, la notte, il contadino cavava
di tasca lo zufolo, e prima di sonare, gli diceva:*
- Maestà, rammentatevi bene:
  Chi tocca stronca,
  Chi parla falla!
  *E tì, tìriti, tì, di botto il pagliaio diventava una reggia; e tì,
tìriti, tì, compariva la ragazza più bella della luna e del sole.*
  *Il Re se la divorava cogli occhi, mentre quella ballava.
Dovea fare proprio un grande sforzo per non slanciarsi ad
abbracciarla e non dirle: "Sarai Regina!". La passione lo con-
teneva.*

"The king wants you, right away."

The farmer went off to present himself at court.

"Your majesty, what is your command?

"I command that you give me your daughter in marriage. She will become the queen, and you a minister of the royal palace.

"Majesty, there is one condition:

  Whoever wants my daughter

   Must spend seven years in rain and sun;

   And if he doesn't spend seven years in rain and sun,

   Come what may, he will not have her."

The king wanted to put him in the rain and the sun! But there was the young woman to consider. So, he shrugged his shoulders and answered:

"I will spend seven years in rain and sun."

He left the government in the hands of the ministers for the time he would be away, and he went to live with the farmer, getting sunburned in the summer heat and remaining in the rain even when it came down in buckets.

After a while, one could not recognize the poor king; he appeared to be made of terra cotta with his skin so sunburned. But there was one consolation. From time to time, at night, the farmer took his pipe out of his pocket, and before playing said to the king:

"Majesty, remember well:

  He who touches will fall.

  He who speaks will fail."

And as soon as he started to play "tì, tìriti, tì," the shed became a palace; and as he played, there appeared the young woman who was as beautiful as the moon and the sun.

The king devoured her with his eyes as she danced. He had to make a great effort not to throw her into his arms and to say "you will be queen," so great was his passion for her.

Eran passati sei anni, sei mesi e sei giorni. Il Re, dalla contentezza, si fregava le mani.

Fra poco quella ragazza più bella della luna e del sole sarebbe stata sua sposa! E lui se ne tornerebbe al palazzo reale, Re come prima e più beato di prima!

Ma la sua disgrazia volle che una notte il contadino cavasse di tasca lo zufolo, e si mettesse a sonare senza ripetergli:

- Maestà, rammentatevi: chi tocca stronca, chi parla falla.

Quando, tì, tìriti, tì... apparve la ragazza più bella della luna e del sole, e si messe a ballare, il Re non seppe più frenarsi, le corse incontro e l'abbracciò, gridando:

- Sarai Regina! Sarai Regina!

Fu un lampo. E, invece della ragazza, che cosa si trovò fra le braccia? Un ceppo bitorzoluto!

- Maestà, ve l'avevo pur detto io:
Chi tocca stronca,
Chi parla falla!

Il Re pareva di sasso:

- Bisognava ricominciare?

- Bisognava ricominciare!

E ricominciò.

Si abbrustoliva al sole:

- Sole, bel sole
Patisco per amore!

Si lasciava conciare dalla pioggia.

- Pioggia, pioggia bella,
Patisco per la donzella!

E quando il contadino cavava di tasca lo zufolo e, tì, tìriti, tì, la ragazza ricompariva e si metteva a ballare, lui se la divorava cogli occhi, da un cantuccio, zitto e cheto come l'olio.

After six years, six months, and six days had passed, the king rubbed his hands joyfully.

Soon, the young woman who was more beautiful than the moon and the sun would be his bride. He wanted to return to the palace, king just as before, and even happier than before!

But as fate would have it, one night, the farmer took his pipe out of his pocket and he began to play without stopping:

"Majesty, remember:

He who touches will fall.

He who speaks will fail."

When he played "tì, tìriti, tì," there appeared the young woman who was more beautiful than the moon and the sun, and she started to dance. The king did not know how to restrain himself; he ran after her, and he embraced her, yelling:

"You will be queen! You will be queen!"

What happened next was amazing. Instead of finding the young woman in his arms, he found a log, ugly and gnarled!

"Majesty, I told you this would happen:

He who touches will fall.

He who speaks will fail."

The king was stunned:

"Do I need to begin again?"

"You need to begin again!"

And he started all over again.

He roasted in the sun.

"Sun, beautiful sun,

I suffer for love!"

He allowed himself to be soaked by the rain.

"Rain , beautiful rain,

I suffer for the sake of that maiden!"

And when the farmer took the pipe out of his pocket and played "tì, tìriti, tì," the young woman reappeared and started to dance. The king devoured her with his eyes from a little

Non se la sentiva di ricominciare.

Eran passati novamente sei anni, sei mesi e sei giorni, e il Re, dalla contentezza, già si fregava le mani.

Ma la sua disgrazia volle che una notte il contadino cavasse di tasca lo zufolo e, tì, tìriti, tì, comparisse la ragazza e si mettesse a ballare come non aveva ballato mai, con una grazia, con una sveltezza! Il povero Re non poté più frenarsi e le corse incontro e l'abbracciò:

- Sarai Regina! Sarai Regina!

E che cosa si trovò fra le braccia? Un ceppo bitorzoluto.

- Ah, Maestà, Maestà!

Chi tocca stronca,

Chi parla falla!

Il Re pareva di sasso:

- Bisognava ricominciare?

- Bisognava ricominciare!

E ricominciò:

- Sole, bel sole,

Patisco per amore;

Pioggia, pioggia bella,

Patisco per la donzella!

Questa volta però stette bene in guardia, e ai sette anni fissati ebbe finalmente la ragazza, più bella della luna e del sole. Non gli parea neppur vero! Intanto che cosa era accaduto? Era accaduto che i suoi Ministri e il popolo ritenendolo per matto, si erano dimenticati di lui e avevan dato, da parecchi anni, la corona reale a un suo parente.

Il Re, infatti, si presenta al palazzo reale colla sposa sotto braccio e i soldati di sentinella:

- Non si passa! Non si passa!

- Sono il Re! Chiamate i miei Ministri!

corner, as quiet and still as oil. He certainly did not want to start all over again.

When another six years, six months, and six days had passed, the king rubbed his hands joyfully.

But as fate would have it, one night the farmer took the pipe out of his pocket and, when he played "tì, tìriti, tì," the young woman reappeared and began to dance as she had never danced before, quickly and gracefully. The king did not know how to restrain himself; he ran after her, and he embraced her:

"You will be queen! You will be queen!"

What happened next was amazing. Instead of finding the young woman in his arms, he found a log ugly and gnarled!

"Oh, Majesty, Majesty!

  He who touches will fall.

  He who speaks will fail."

The king was stunned:

"Do I need to begin again?"

"You need to begin again!"

And he started all over again.

"Sun, beautiful sun,

  I suffer for love!

  Rain , beautiful rain,

  I suffer for the sake of that maiden!"

This time, however, he was very careful. When seven years were up, he finally had the young woman who was more beautiful than the moon and the sun. He couldn't believe it! Meanwhile, however, his ministers and his people believed that he had gone mad. They had forgotten about him, and after a few years, they had given the royal crown to one of his relatives.

Sure enough the king presented himself at the royal palace with his bride on his arm.

When the guards saw him, they said:

"You cannot pass! You cannot pass!"

"I am the king! Call my ministers!"

Che Ministri? I vecchi eran morti e quelli del nuovo Re lo lasciavano cantare.

Si rivolge al popolo:

- Come? Non riconoscete il vostro Re?

Il popolo gli ride in faccia e non gli dà retta.

Disperato, ritorna al campicello, dal contadino. Dov'era il pagliaio, vede, con sorpresa, un palazzo che pareva una reggia. Monta le scale, e invece del contadino, gli viene incontro un bel vecchio con tanto di barba bianca: era il gran mago Sabino.

- Non ti scoraggiare! - gli disse questi.

E lo prese per mano, e lo condusse in una magnifica stanza, dove c'era un catino pieno di acqua. Il Gran Mago afferra quel catino e glielo riversa sulla testa, e il Re, da un po' invecchiato che già era, rinverdisce, a un tratto, di vent'anni.

Allora il vecchio:

- Affàcciati a quella finestra, suona questo zufolo e vedrai.

Il Re si affaccia, si mette a sonare, tì, tìriti, tì, ed ecco un esercito armato di tutto punto, fitto come la nebbia, su pei colli e per la pianura. Intimata la guerra, mentre i soldati combattevano lui, in cima a un poggio, sonava tì, tìriti, tì, senza cessare finché la battaglia non fu vinta.

Tornò a palazzo reale vittorioso e trionfante, perdonò a tutti, e all'occasione dei suoi sponsali diè un mese di feste per tutto il regno.

E presto ebbe un erede;
E noi scalzi d'un piede.

What ministers? The old ministers were dead, and those of the new king ignored him.

He turned to his people.

"What? Don't you recognize your king?"

The people laughed in his face and took no notice of him.

Desperate, he returned to the little farm. Where the hut had been—what a surprise! There now appeared what looked like a royal palace. He climbed the stairs and, instead of the farmer, he met an old man with a long, white beard. He was Sabino, the great magician.

"Don't be discouraged!" he said to the king.

And he took him by the hand and led him into a magnificent room where there was a basin full of water. The great magician grabbed the basin and dumped it on the king's head. The king, who had grown somewhat old during this time, was made younger by twenty years.

And so, the old man said:

"Look out of this window, play this pipe, and see what happens."

The king looked out of the window, began to play "tì, tìriti, tì," and there appeared an army fully equipped and thick as fog over the hills and the plain. He ordered the attack and, while the soldiers were fighting, he sat on the top of a hill and played "tì, tìriti, tì" without end until the battle was won.

He returned to the palace victorious and triumphant, forgave everyone and, on the occasion of his wedding, he declared a month of celebration throughout the kingdom.

Very quickly, he had an heir.
And now ends our story fair.

Testa di rospo

*C'era una volta un Re e una Regina. La Regina partorì e fece
una bambina più bella del sole. Insuperbita di questa figliolina
così bella, spesso diceva:*

- Neppur le Fate potrebbero farne un'altra come questa.

*Ma una mattina, va per levarla di culla e la trova
contraffatta, con una testa di rospo.*

- Oh Dio, che orrore!

*Benché fosse figlia unica e le volesse un gran bene, quella
testa di rospo le facea schifo, e non volle più allattarla.*

Il Re, angustiato, disse a un servitore:

*- Prendila e portala giù; mettila fra i cagnolini figliati dalla
cagna. Però se morisse, sarebbe meglio per lei!*

*Non morì. La cagna, tre, quattro volte il giorno tralasciava
di dar latte ai cagnolini, e porgeva le poppe a Testa-di-rospo.
La leccava, la ripuliva, la scalducciava tenendosela accosto, e
non permetteva che alcuno stendesse la mano a toccarla.*

*Quando il Re e la Regina scendevano giù per vedere, la
cagna ringhiava, mostrava i denti; e un giorno che la Regina
fece atto di voler riprendere la figliuola, le saltò addosso e le
morse mani e gambe.*

*Testa-di-rospo nel canile prosperava. Quando crebbe, non
volle più lasciarlo. Durante la giornata abitava su nelle stanze
reali; pranzava a tavola col Re, colla Regina, con tutta la
corte, e prima di toccar le pietanze, metteva da parte i meglio
bocconi; poi ne riempiva il grembiule e scendeva giù, nel
canile.*

- Mamma cagna, mangiate; la mia vera mamma siete voi!

*La notte dormiva lì, con mamma cagna. Non c'era mai stato
verso di indurla a dormire nel suo letto.*

Toad Head

There once were a king and queen. The queen gave birth to a baby girl, who was more beautiful than the sun. Boasting of such a beautiful child, she often said:

"Not even the fairies can make another like this one."

But one morning, taking her out of the crib, she found that she had been transformed and now had the head of a toad.

"Oh, Lord, what a horror!"

Although she was an only child and was greatly loved, her toad's head disgusted the queen, and she no longer wanted to breast feed her.

Anguished, the king told a servant:

"Bring her down here and place her with the dog's puppies. However, if she dies, it would be better for her."

But she did not die. Three or four times a day, the dog came out to feed the puppies, and she also gave one of her teats to Toad-Head. She licked her, cleaned her, kept her warm by holding her close, and she did not allow anyone to stretch out a hand and touch her.

When the king and queen came down to see her, the dog showed her teeth and snarled. One day when the queen made a gesture as if to take back the child, the dog jumped on her and bit her on her hands and her legs.

Toad-head prospered in the kennel. After she grew up, she did not want to leave it. During the day she lived in the royal apartments; she had lunch at the table with the king, the queen, and the entire court, but before she touched her dish, she put aside the best morsels. Then she filled up her apron and carried them down to the kennel.

"Mamma dog, eat; you are my real mother!"

At night she slept with the mother dog. There was never any way to persuade her to sleep in her own bed.

La Regina, sentendole ripetere ogni giorno: - Mamma
cagna, mangiate; la mia vera mamma siete voi! -, cominciò a
odiarla terribilmente, come se non fosse stata sua figliuola.

E una volta disse al Re:

- Maestà, no, costei non è la nostra figliuola. Ce la
scambiarono quand'era in culla. Che ne facciamo di questo
mostro? Io direi di farla ammazzare.

Il Re non ebbe animo di commettere questa crudeltà:

- Mostro o non mostro, è una creatura di Dio.

Talché la Regina giurò di disfarsene in segreto.

E che pensò? Pensò di dar ad intendere al Re che era
nuovamente gravida e, quando fu l'ora, gli fece presentare una
bambina nata di fresco, che lei aveva fatto comprare a peso
d'oro in un altro paese.

Il Re fu molto contento; e alla bambina mise nome
Gigliolina; perché era bianca come un giglio.

Allora la Regina gli disse:

- Ora che abbiamo quest'altra figliuola, che ne facciamo di
quel mostro? Io direi di farla ammazzare.

Per amore di quest'altra figliuola, il Re, benché a
malincuore acconsentì.

Ma come andarono per prendere Testa-di-rospo e farla
ammazzare, sulla soglia del canile trovarono mamma cagna,
che abbaiava e ringhiava mostrando i denti.

E Testa-di-rospo non voleva uscir fuori.

- Perché non vieni fuori?

- Perché mi farete ammazzare.

- E chi ti ha detto questo?

- Me l'ha detto mamma cagna.

La Regina, maliziosa, voleva indurla colle buone:

- Non è vero, sciocchina. Vieni su, vieni a vedere che bella
sorellina ti è nata.

Hearing her repeat every day "Mamma dog, eat; you are my real mother!" the queen began to hate her, as if she were not her own daughter.

And, one day, she told the king:

"Majesty, this girl is not our daughter. She must have been switched in the crib. What shall we do with this monster? I say let's have her killed."

The king did not have the heart for such cruelty:

"Monster or not, she is a creature of God."

Therefore, the queen swore to undo things in secret.

And what was she thinking? She thought she would fool the king into believing that she was pregnant once again, and when the hour came, she presented him with a newborn baby girl, whom she had bought with a piece of gold in another country.

The king was very happy; and he gave the baby the name Little Lily, for she was as white as a lily.

Thus, the queen said:

"Now that we have this other daughter, what shall we do with this monster? I say have her killed."

For the love of this other child, the king consented, although with a heavy heart.

But when they went to get Toad-Head in order to kill her, on the threshold of the kennel they found mamma dog, who was barking, snarling, and showing her teeth.

And Toad-Head did not want to leave.

"Why don't you come out?" they asked.

"Because you will have me killed."

"And who has told you that?"

"Mamma dog told me that."

Although she meant her evil, the queen wanted to persuade her with kindness:

"It's not true, silly. Come see your beautiful little sister."

- Sorellina non me n'è nata,
A peso d'oro fu comprata.
Mamma cagna, mamma cagna,
Siete voi la vera mamma.
- Che significa? - domandò il Re.
- O che gli date retta? Testa-di-rospo parla da bestia.
Ma il Re disse:
- Chi tocca Testa-di-rospo l'ha da fare con me. Mostro o
non mostro, è una creatura di Dio. Lei è la vera Reginotta,
perché nata la prima.
La Regina, arrabbiata per lo smacco, che pensò? Pensò di
ricorrere ad una Strega:
- Fammi due vestiti compagni, tutti oro e diamanti; ma uno
dev'essere incantato: deve bruciare addosso a chi se lo mette.
- Fra un anno li avrete.
In questo mentre la Regina fingeva di voler bene egualmente
alle due figliuole; anzi, se comprava un balocco, un ninnolo
per la Gigliolina, ne comprava uno più bello per Testa-di-
rospo.
La Gigliolina, vedendo il regalo più bello, si metteva a
strillare:
- Quello lì lo voglio io!
E Testa-di-rospo glielo dava.
Passato l'anno, la Regina tornò alla Strega.
- Maestà, i vestiti sono pronti; ma badate di non scambiarli.
Per non sbagliare in questo incantato ci ho messo un diamante
di più.
- Ho capito.
Chiamò le due figliuole e disse:
- Ecco due bei vestiti; provateveli subito, per vedere se
vanno bene. Questo è il tuo, Testa-di-rospo.
Ma la Gigliolina, contati i diamanti e visto che in quello di
Testa-di-rospo ce n'era uno di più, comincia a strillare:

"No sister has been born to me.
   She was bought with a piece of gold.
   Mamma dog, mamma dog,
    You are my true mother. "
"What does this mean?" asked the king.
"Don't pay attention to her; she's talking about the animals."
However, the king said:
"Whoever touches Toad-Head will answer to me. Monster or no monster, she is a creature of God. She is the true princess, for she is the first born."
Angry over her humiliation, what did the queen think? She thought about seeking out a witch.
"Make me two dresses that look alike, all gold and diamonds. But one must be enchanted so as to burn the one who wears it."
"You will have them within a year," said the witch.
In the meantime, the queen pretended to love the two daughters equally; in fact, if she bought a toy or bauble for Little Lily, she bought a more beautiful one for Toad-Head.
Seeing that her sister had gotten the more beautiful gift, Little Lily would start to scream:
"I want that one!"
And Toad-Head would give it to her.
After a year, the queen returned to the witch.
"Majesty, the dresses are ready; however, be careful not to mistake one for the other. In order to distinguish them, I have added an extra diamond to the enchanted one."
"I understand," said the queen.
She called her two daughters and said:
"Here are two lovely dresses. Try them on right away to see if they fit. Toad-Head, this one is yours."
However, Little Lily, having counted the diamonds and seeing that Toad-Head's dress had one more than hers, began to scream:

- Quello lì lo voglio io!

La Regina non permise che lo toccasse.

Intanto la Gigliolina continuava a strillare, e pestare coi piedi:

- Quello lì lo voglio io! Quello lì lo voglio io!

Accorse il Re e disse:

- Non ti persuadi che quello è un po' più grande? Provalo, e vedrai.

E stava per infilarglielo.

- No, Maestà - disse Testa-di-rospo.

Vestito bello, fatto da poco,

   Vestito nuovo fatto di fuoco,

   Mamma cagna, mamma cagna,

   Siete voi la vera mamma.

- Che significa? - domandò il Re.

- O che gli date retta. Testa-di-rospo parla da bestia.

Ma il Re disse:

- Chi fa danno a Testa-di-rospo, fa il proprio danno. Lei è la vera Reginotta, perché nata la prima.

La Regina, arrabbiata per quest'altro smacco, non sapeva più che inventare.

E la sua rabbia si accrebbe quando vide arrivare a corte il Reuccio del Portogallo, che andava cercando una principessa reale per moglie.

La Regina disse al Re:

- Almeno facciamogli vedere tutte e due le figliuole; così sceglierà.

Il Re, per contentarla, rispose:

- Sia pure.

Il Reuccio voleva visitare le principesse negli appartamenti ov'esse abitavano; e la Regina lo condusse prima nel magnifico appartamento della Gigliolina. La Gigliolina, vestita cogli abiti più sfarzosi, sfolgorava come una stella.

"I want that one!"

The queen did not let her touch it.

Meanwhile, Little Lily continued to scream and stamp her feet.

"I want that one! I want that one!"

The king rushed in and said:

"If you are not sure that yours is the best, try on the other one and see."

And she began to slip it on.

"No, Majesty," said Toad-Head.

"The true dress is made of fewer diamonds.

The other is made of fire.

Mamma dog, mamma dog,

You are my true mother."

"What does this mean?" asked the king.

"Oh, don't pay any attention to her; she's referring to the animals."

But the king said:

"Whoever harms Toad-Head will pay dearly. She is the true princess, for she is the first born."

Angry over this other humiliation, the queen did not know what else to do.

And her anger became more bitter when she saw the prince of Portugal arrive at court in search of a royal princess to marry.

The queen told the king:

"At least let him see both daughters. That way, he can choose."

To please her, the king said,

"As you wish."

The prince wanted to visit the princesses in their apartments. And the queen led him first to the magnificent apartment of Little Lily. Dressed in the most magnificent clothes, Little Lily shined like a star.

Il Reuccio disse:
- È mai possibile che l'altra principessa sia bella quanto questa? Andiamo a vederla. Ma dove andiamo?
- Nel canile. L'altra abita nel canile.
Il Reuccio, stupito, scese giù insieme col Re e con la Regina, e trovò Testa-di-rospo nel canile:
- Reuccio, entrate voi solo; c'è posto soltanto per uno.
Il Reuccio entrò, e Testa-di-rospo chiuse lo portello.
Mamma cagna si accovacciò lì dietro, ringhiando.
Aspetta un'ora, aspetta due, il Reuccio non compariva. La Regina, sopra tutti, era impaziente pel ritardo:
- Chi sa che brutto scherzo Testa-di-rospo stava per farle!
Il brutto scherzo fu che il Reuccio, uscito dal canile, disse al Re:
- Maestà, vi chieggo la mano di Testa-di-rospo.
La Regina non rinveniva dallo sbalordimento:
- Ma che cosa avete fatto tante ore lì dentro?
- Ho visitato tutto il palazzo. Di fronte al palazzo di Testa-di-rospo, il palazzo reale sembrerebbe una stalla.
Il Re e la Regina si guardarono, meravigliati.
- Reuccio, dite davvero?
- Dico davvero.
La Regina dovette inghiottire quest'altra pillola amara, e che pensò? Pensò di accertarsi coi suoi occhi di quello che il Reuccio aveva detto:
- Testa-di-rospo, vorrei vedere il tuo palazzo.
- Maestà, quel canile lo chiamate palazzo?
- Testa-di-rospo, una notte vorrei dormire con te.
- Chiedetene il permesso a mamma cagna: è lei la padrona.
La Regina andò a trovare mamma cagna:
- Mamma cagna, vorrei visitare il vostro palazzo.
- Bau! Bau!

The prince said:

"Is it possible that the other princess is as beautiful as this one? Let's go see her. But where are we going?"

"To the kennel. The other one lives in the kennel."

Stunned, the prince went down with the king and queen and found Toad-Head there.

"Prince, enter by yourself, for there is room for only one."

The prince entered, and Toad-Head closed the gate.

Mamma dog crouched in the back of the kennel and snarled.

After one hour, then another, the prince still had not come out. The queen was impatient over the delay more than anyone else.

"Who knows what a terrible joke Toad-Head is playing."

The terrible joke was that when the prince came out of the kennel, he told the king:

"Majesty, I ask you for the hand of Toad-Head."

The queen was astonished.

"But what have you been doing in there for so many hours?"

"I have visited her entire palace. Compared with Toad-Head's palace, the royal palace looks like a stable."

The king and queen stared at each other in amazement.

"Prince, are you telling the truth?"

"Yes, "I am telling the truth."

What did the queen think at having to swallow this other bitter pill? She wanted to see with her own eyes what the prince had described.

"Toad-Head, I want to see your palace."

"Majesty, do you call that kennel a palace?"

"Toad-Head, I would like to sleep with you one night."

"You will have to ask mamma dog for permission, for she rules the kennel."

The queen went to find mamma dog:

"Mamma dog, I want to visit your palace."

"Bow, wow!"

- *Che cosa dice?*
- *Dice di sì.*
- *Mamma cagna, una notte vorrei dormire con Testa-di-rospo.*
- *Bau! Bau!*
- *Che cosa dice?*
- *Dice di sì.*

La Regina, per entrare nel canile, dovette quasi piegarsi in due.

- *Ed è questo il tuo gran palazzo?*
- *Questo: non ve lo dicevo?*

La Regina, indispettita, uscì fuori brontolando contro il Reuccio, che le avea dato ad intendere tante sciocchezze; e appena fuori, cominciò a sentire per tutto il corpo un brulichio e un brucìo insoffribile. Era, da capo a piedi, ripiena di pulci; e, siccome montava a corsa le scale e scoteva le vesti, ne seminava per terra cataste che annerivano il pavimento.

Così per le stanze del palazzo; ma più scoteva e più gliene brulicavano addosso e se la rodevano viva viva.

In un momento, Re, ministri, dame di corte, gente di palazzo, tutti si videro assaliti da quelle bestiole affamate, che davano morsi da portar via la pelle; e tutti urlavano:

- *Accidempoli alla Regina, che volle entrare nel canile!*

Il Re corse subito da Testa-di-rospo:

- *Figliuola mia, dàcci aiuto!*
- *Mamma cagna, dategli aiuto!*

Mamma cagna si mise a girellare per le stanze:

- *Bau, bau! Bau, bau!*

E sentendola abbaiare, tutte le pulci saltavano addosso a lei.

La Regina non si stimò castigata abbastanza e insistette:

- *Testa-di-rospo, questa notte vengo a dormire con te.*
- *Maestà, in un giaciglio!*
- *Per una volta, potrò provare.*

"What is she saying?"
"She says yes."
"Mamma dog, I want to sleep with Toad-Head one night."
"Bow, wow!
"What is she saying?"
"She says yes."
In order to enter the kennel, the queen nearly had to double up.
"And is this your grand palace?"
"It is; didn't I tell you?"
Vexed, the queen came out grumbling against the prince, who had led her to believe such silliness. But as soon as she was out, she began to feel a swarming and a burning all over her body. From head to foot, she was covered with fleas. She climbed the stairs running and, as she threw off her clothes, she spread piles of them onto the floor, which turned black.
In this way, she ran about the palace, but the more she shook, the more they burned her and ate her alive.
In a moment, the king, the ladies of the court and the gentlemen of the palace were all assaulted by these hungry little creatures, which bit so hard that they flayed the skin. And everyone yelled:
"Curses on the queen, who wants to sleep in the kennel."
The king ran quickly to Toad-Head.
"Daughter, help her."
"Mamma dog, help them," said the princess.
Mamma dog began to walk from room to room.
"Bow, wow! Bow, wow!"
And hearing her bark, all of the fleas jumped right on her.
However, the queen was not repentant, and she insisted:
"Toad-Head, tonight I will come sleep with you."
"In a straw bed, Majesty?"
"I would like to try it once."

Si acconciò alla meglio, e finse di dormire. In quel canile ci doveva essere un mistero; voleva scoprirlo.

Verso mezzanotte, sentì un romore come di un crollo di muro. Aprì gli occhi, e rimase abbagliata.

Avea davanti una fila di stanze, così ricche e così splendide, che quelle del palazzo reale, in confronto, sarebbero parse vere stalle; e Testa-di-rospo che dormiva, in fondo, sopra un letto lavorato d'oro e di pietre preziose, con cortinaggi di seta e lenzuola bianche più della spuma.

E non aveva più quella schifosa testa di rospo; ma era così bella, che, al paragone, la Gigliolina, bella e bianca come un giglio, sarebbe parsa proprio una megera.

Accecata dal furore, la Regina pensò:

- Ora entro, e mentre dorme, la strozzo colle mie mani.

Ma il muro si richiuse a un tratto, e lei vi batté la faccia e si ammaccò il naso.

Senza aspettare che facesse giorno, tornò su in camera.

Sentiva nelle carni un brucìo, un gonfiore!... Stende una mano, e si scorge che, da capo a piedi, era piena di zecche.

Si sveglia il Re: è pieno di zecche anche lui.

Si svegliano i ministri, le dame di corte, insomma tutte le persone del palazzo reale; son tutti, da capo a piedi, pieni di zecche; e, dal prurito e dal dolore, non possono reggere:

- Accidempoli alla Regina, che volle dormire nel canile!

Il Re corse di nuovo da Testa-di-rospo.

- Figliuola mia, dàcci aiuto!

- Mamma cagna, dategli aiuto!

Mamma cagna, Bau, bau! No, no! Non ne vuol sapere.

-   Figliuola mia, dàcci aiuto!

That night, the queen settled herself as best she could, and she pretended to sleep. There had to be some mystery in this kennel, and she wanted to discover it.

Around midnight, she heard a noise as if a wall had collapsed. She opened her eyes and she was dazzled.

She had before her a corridor of rooms so rich and splendid that, by comparison, the rooms of the royal palace would have truly seemed like stables. And there was Toad-Head sleeping at the end of the corridor on a bed made of gold and precious stones, with curtains of silk and sheets as white as sea foam.

And she no longer had the disgusting head of a toad; instead, she was so beautiful that, in comparison, Little Lily, who was as beautiful and as white as a lily, looked exactly like a hag.

Blinded by anger, the queen thought:

"I will now enter and, while she is sleeping, I will strangle her with my own hands."

However, the wall closed suddenly, and she banged her face and smashed her nose against it.

Without waiting for daybreak, she returned to her room.

She felt a burning, a swelling in her flesh. Stretching out her hand, she realized she was covered with ticks from head to toe.

The king awoke, and he too was full of ticks.

The ministers awoke, the ladies of the court awoke; in fact, all of the people in the royal palace awoke. All of them were covered from head to foot with ticks, and they could not stand the itching and the pain.

"Curses on the queen, who wants to sleep in the kennel."

The king ran once again to Toad-Head.

"Help her, my daughter."

"Mamma dog, help them," said the princess.

But mamma dog said "Bow, wow! No, no!" She would not hear of it.

"Help her, my daughter," said the king.

Che aiuto poteva dargli? Mamma cagna rispondeva sempre:
- Bau, bau! No, no!

Intanto tornava il Reuccio per sposare Testa-di-rospo.

Tutti erano occupati a tagliar le zecche, colle forbici, perché strappare non si potevano; facevano più male. E più ne tagliavano e più ne rimaneva da tagliare:

- Accidempoli alla Regina, che volle dormire nel canile!

Allora il Re montò in furore. Afferrò la Regina pel collo, e disse:

- Trista femmina, che cosa hai tu fatto, da attirarci addosso tanti guai?

La Regina non ne poteva più e confessò ogni cosa: che avea detto come le Fate non potrebbero farne una pari; che avea comprato quella bambina a peso di oro; che avea fatto fare il vestito incantato per bruciare viva Testa-di-rospo.

- Ora son proprio pentita, e domando perdono alla Fata!

Disse appena così, che alla Reginotta cadde giù quella schifosa testa di rospo, e la Gigliolina si trovò vestita come una figliuola di contadini, qual era. La Reginotta splendeva come il sole, sicché, per guardarla, bisognava mettersi una mano agli occhi. Le zecche erano sparite, e non se ne vedeva neppure il segno.

Il Reuccio di Portogallo e la Reginotta si sposarono; e se ne stettero e se la godettero e a noialtri nulla dettero.

*But what help could she give? Mamma dog always an-
swered:*

"Bow, wow! No, no!"

Meanwhile, the prince returned to marry Toad-Head.

Everyone was busy cutting off the ticks with scissors because they couldn't pull them off. That made things worse. And
the more they cut the more there remained to be cut:

"Curses on the queen, who wants to sleep in the kennel."

Thereupon, the king became furious. He grabbed the queen
by the neck and said:

"Unhappy woman, what have you done to draw so much
misery on yourself?"

The queen could no longer be quiet, and she confessed all:
that she had said that the fairies could not make a child like
hers; that she had bought the other baby for a piece of gold;
and that she had the enchanted dress made in order to burn
Toad-Head alive.

"I am now truly sorry, and I ask the pardon of the fairies."

As soon as she said this, the disgusting toad head dropped
from the princess, and Little Lily found herself dressed like the
child of peasants that she was. The princess shined like the sun,
so much so that one had to place a hand over his or her eyes
just to look upon her. The ticks were gone, and no longer could
one see the marks they had made.

The prince of Portugal and the princess got married.

The enjoyed their lives, so rich and sweet.
But to us they gave not even one small treat!

Topolino

C'era una volta un Re, che più non viveva tranquillo, dal giorno in cui una vecchia indovina gli aveva detto:
- Maestà, ascoltate bene:

Topolino non vuol ricotta;
vuol sposare la Reginotta;
E se il Re non gliela dà,
Topolino lo ammazzerà.

Il Re consultò subito i suoi ministri; ed uno di loro disse:
- Maestà, è mai possibile che un topolino voglia sposare la Reginotta? Io credo che quella donna si sia beffata di voi.
Ma gli altri non furono dello stesso parere.
- Per evitare la disgrazia, bisogna distruggere tutti i topi del regno, mentre la Reginotta trovasi ancora nelle fasce.
Perciò il Re messe fuori un decreto:
- Pena la vita a chi non teneva uno o più gatti, secondo che avesse casa o palazzo. Chi ammazzava cento topi diventava barone.
Il Re diè l'esempio egli il primo; e il palazzo reale fu pieno di gatti, tenuti assai meglio dei cortigiani e anche dei ministri. Inoltre, a tutti gli usci venivano appostate guardie con una granata in mano, invece di sciabola, che dovevano gridare all'armi appena visto un topo.
Sulle prime, con quella caccia ai topi per diventare barone, fu uno spasso per tutto il regno.
Il Re, ogni volta che gli portavano al palazzo un centinaio di topi uccisi, traeva un respiro dal profondo del petto.
- Voi siete barone!
- Che mi vale, Maestà, l'esser barone, se non ho da mangiare? disse una volta un contadino, che, invece di cento, ne aveva portati un mezzo migliaio.
- È giusto - rispose il Re.

Topolino

Once upon a time, there was a king who had not lived in peace
ever since the day that an old fortune teller had told him:

"Majesty, listen well to this riddle:

'It is not cheese that pleases this mouse.

He wants the princess as his spouse.

And if the King does not comply,

The mouse will surely make him die.'"

The king consulted his ministers right away; one of them
said:

"Majesty, is it possible that a little mouse wants to marry the
princess? I think the old woman wants to make a fool of you."

But the others were not of the same opinion.

"In order to avoid this tragedy, it is necessary to destroy all
of the mice in the kingdom while the princess is still a baby."

Therefore, the king issued a decree:

"On pain of death, everyone must have one or more cats,
whether he lives in a house or a palace. Anyone who kills one
hundred mice will become a baron."

The king set the example; and the royal palace was filled
with cats, cared for better than the ladies of the court and even
the ministers. Furthermore, at each entrance were posted
guards holding brooms rather than swords. They were supposed to sound the alarm as soon as they saw a mouse.
At first, the idea of becoming a baron by hunting mice swept
the kingdom.

Each time that someone brought a hundred dead mice to the
place, the king took a deep breath and said:

"You are a baron!"

"But what good is being a baron, Majesty, if I don't have
anything to eat?" once said a peasant who, instead of bringing a
hundred mice, had brought five hundred.

"You are right," responded the king.

E gli fece un bel regalo.

Saputasi la cosa, tutti quelli che accorrevano al palazzo reale, ripetevano la stessa storia:

- Che mi vale, Maestà, l'esser barone, se non ho da mangiare?

Ma il Re, ch'era un po' tirchio, si seccò presto a dover far tanti regali; e all'ultimo rispose:

- Il decreto dice soltanto: sarete baroni.

E il popolo ne fu scontento; molto più che, con tutti quei gatti per la casa, i quali miagolavano da mattina a sera, si viveva una vitaccia d'inferno. Ma Sua Maestà ordinava così; era forza ubbidirgli!

Da lì a qualche anno, non si trovava un topo in tutto il regno, neppure a pagarlo un milione.

Il Re già cominciava a rassicurarsi; e siccome la Reginotta era cresciuta, egli pensava di darle marito. Parecchi Principi l'avevano chiesta. Ma la Reginotta, quasi lo facesse a posta, a ogni domanda di matrimonio, rispondeva:

- Maestà, chiedo un altr'anno di tempo.

Intanto era accaduto questo: in un paesotto del regno, nascosto fra le montagne, una povera donna aveva partorito un bambino mostruoso, col viso d'uomo e il resto del corpo di vero topolino, con le sue zampine e con la sua codina.

Al vederlo, la mamma e la levatrice rimasero trasecolate: e la levatrice, che provava ribrezzo a toccare quel mostricino, aveva consigliato di soffocarlo.

La mamma non n'ebbe il cuore, e pregò:

- Non ne fiatare con anima viva, comare!

Infatti nessuno ne seppe nulla; e il bambino crebbe vegeto e vispo da quel topolino ch'egli era. Camminava su due gambe, come un uomo; solamente la mamma lo vestiva in maniera, che del suo corpo non si potesse vedere altro che il volto. Alle zampine anteriori gli metteva sempre i guanti.

And he gave him a beautiful gift.

Hearing this, all of those who came to the royal palace said the same thing:

"What good is being a baron, Majesty, if I have nothing to eat?"

But the king, who was a bit stingy, soon got tired of giving so many gifts, and he finally responded:

"The decree said only that you would be barons."

But the people were unhappy, so much so that, with all of those cats in their houses, which meowed from morning until night, their existence became a living hell. However, his majesty had ordered this, and he was going to be obeyed!

For several years thereafter, not one mouse could be found in the entire kingdom, not even for a million lire.

The king began to be reassured, and since the princess had grown up, he thought about finding her a husband. Several princes had asked for her hand. But the princess responded to every proposal in this way (perhaps she was just stalling):

"Majesty, I want to wait another year."

Meanwhile, this occurred: in a small village of the kingdom, which was hidden in the mountains, a poor woman had given birth to a monstrous baby, with the face of a human being but the body of a mouse, and with paws and a little tail.

Upon seeing him, the mother and the midwife were astonished, and the midwife, who was sickened by this monstrosity, advised the mother to suffocate it.

But the mother did not have the heart to do so; she pleaded:

"Don't say a word to a living soul, neighbor!"

Sure enough, no one heard anything, and the baby grew lively and vigorously as the mouse that he was. However, he walked on two legs like a man, and his mother dressed him in such a way that of his body only his face could be seen. On his front paws, she always placed gloves.

Gli aveva posto nome Beppe, e così lo chiamavano tutti; ma quando non c'era nessuno, ella, per tenerezza, lo chiamava Topolino.

- Topolino, fa' questo; Topolino, fa' quest'altro!

E Topolino non le dava mai il menomo dispiacere, e faceva questo e faceva quello.

- Dio t'aiuterà, Topolino!

E un giorno Topolino disse:

- Mamma, voglio fare il soldato.

La poveretta che gli voleva bene, piangendo rispose:

- Ed io, come rimango sola sola? Ora sono vecchia, e non posso più lavorare.

- Vi lascerò la mia coda. Quando avrete bisogno di qualcosa, direte:

- Codina, codina
   Servi la tua mammina!

Ed essa vi servirà, come se fossi io stesso in persona. Se non v'ubbidirà, vorrà dire che in quel momento io corro un gran pericolo. Allora, lasciatevi guidare da essa e venite a trovarmi. Così fece, e partì. Quella coda era fatata.

Al Re era stata mossa guerra da un altro Re, offeso dal rifiuto della Reginotta. Uscito, con tutto l'esercito a combattere, in ogni battaglia ne toccava.

Mutava generali, chiamava nuova gente sotto le armi, veniva alle mani, faceva prodezze straordinarie, ma rimaneva vinto sempre; e una volta poté salvarsi, scappando sul suo cavallo a rotta di collo.

Si presentò Topolino, ch'era alla guerra anche lui:

- Maestà, se mi date il comando in capo, vi faccio uscire vittorioso.

- E tu chi sei?

She named him Beppe, and that's what everyone called him; however, when no one was around, she called him "Topolino" (Little Mouse)" out of tenderness.

"Topolino, do this; Topolino, do that!"

And Topolino never displeased her; he did just what she wanted. .

"God help you, Topolino!"

And one day Topolino said:

"Mamma, I want to be a soldier."

The poor woman, who loved him very much, said tearfully:

"And I, how will I live all alone? I am old now, and I can't work anymore."

"I will leave you my little tail; when you need something, say:

"Little tail, little tail,
   Come help your mama!"

"And it will help you, as if I were here in person. If it does not obey you, you will know that at that moment I am great danger. Therefore, be guided by this little tail, and come to find me."

Having said this, he left. That tail was enchanted.

The king had gone to war with another king, who had been offended by the princess's rejection of his proposal of marriage. Despite having gone out with his entire army to fight, he had not won a battle.

He changed generals, put additional men under arms, fought bravely in hand-to-hand combat himself, but he was always defeated. And once in order to save himself, he had to ride away on his horse at breakneck speed.

To him, came Topolino, who was also in the war:

"Majesty, if you make me commander, I will make you victorious."

"And who are you?"

- *Mi chiamo Niente-con-Nulla; ma non vuol dire. Mettetemi alla prova.*

- *Niente-con-Nulla sia comandante!*

I generali dell'esercito credettero che Sua Maestà fosse ammattito:

- *Affidare il comando in capo a quel cosino, ch'era davvero Niente-con-Nulla!*

Non rinvenivano dallo stupore. Ma quando fu l'ora della battaglia, Topolino impartì gli ordini, fece sonare le trombe, e in un batter d'occhio l'esercito nemico fu spazzato via.

- *Viva Niente-con-Nulla! Viva Niente-con-Nulla.*

Non si sentiva acclamare altro. Nessuno più gridava: "Viva il Re!", tanto che Sua Maestà cominciò a esserne seccato, e pensava di levarsi di torno Niente-con-Nulla, che ci mancava poco non contasse più di lui.

- *Come fare per levarselo di torno? Occorreva un pretesto.*

Il pretesto lo trovò una mattina, che la Reginotta venne a dirgli:

- *Maestà, volete ch'io sposi? Datemi Niente-con-Nulla per marito.*

Il Re montò sulle furie. Ma, per far la cosa zitto e queto, deliberò di sbarazzarsi di Niente-con-Nulla per mezzo del veleno.

Invitatolo a pranzo, verso la fine gli fece porre davanti un piatto d'oro con su una torta di ricotta avvelenata.

- *Questo piatto è per voi solo, per farvi onore. Niente-con-Nulla, mangiate.*

Ma Niente-con-Nulla, levatosi da tavola e fatto un inchino a Sua Maestà, rispose:

- *Topolino non vuol ricotta;*
    Vuol sposare la Reginotta!

E andò via.

Il Re e i Ministri rimasero strabiliati:

"My name is Nothing-with-Nothing; but that doesn't mean anything. Put me to the test."

"Nothing-with-Nothing, you are in command!" said the king.

The generals of the army believed his Majesty was mad: "to entrust command to this truly Nothing-with-Nothing!"

They could not overcome their amazement. However, when the hour of battle came, Topolino gave orders, had the trumpets sound and, in the blink of an eye, the enemy was sent packing.

"Long live Nothing-with-Nothing! Long live Nothing-with-Nothing!" everyone shouted.

They could not bring themselves to cheer anyone else. No one cheered "Long live the king" any more. The king began to become annoyed, and he thought about getting rid of Nothing-with-Nothing, who had become almost as important as himself.

"How shall I get rid of him?" thought the king. An excuse was needed.

He found that excuse one morning when the princess said:

"Majesty, do you want me to marry? Let me take Nothing-with-Nothing for my husband."

The king became furious. However, to work this evil quietly and calmly, he thought about getting rid of Nothing-with-Nothing by poisoning him.

Inviting him to lunch, toward the end of the meal, he put before him a golden plate on which there was a poisoned ricotta cake.

"This plate is for you alone, so as to honor you. Eat, Nothing-with-Nothing."

However, rising from the table and bowing to the king, Nothing-with-Nothing responded:

"Over dessert, I will not tarry,
    It is the princess I want to marry."

And he went away.

The king and the ministers remained astounded.

- Giacché Topolino è lui, - disse un Ministro - facciamolo arrestare, rinchiudiamolo in una stanza con tutti i gatti del palazzo reale, e così sarà divorato vivo vivo.

Lo fecero arrestare, lo spogliarono, lo rinchiusero in uno stanzone insieme con un centinaio di gatti affamati, e stettero ad aspettare. Quando riapersero la stanza, Topolino non c'era più. E i gatti si leccavano i baffi, come se avessero desinato saporitamente.

Il Re, dalla contentezza, ordinò una festa di ballo.
Va per indossare il manto reale, e lo trova interamente rosicchiato dai topi. I generali, le dame di corte, gl'invitati, nel momento d'abbigliarsi per la festa, tutti avevano trovato le loro uniformi e gli abiti rosicchiati dai topi!

Ma questo non fu nulla. I Ministri portavano al Re i decreti da firmare; e, il giorno dopo, le carte trovavansi rosicchiate proprio dov'era la firma. A poco a poco, nel palazzo reale, delle materasse, delle lenzuola, delle coperte, della biancheria, degli arnesi, dei mobili non rimase più intatto un solo capo; pareva che un esercito di topi fosse stato a divertirvisi coi suoi dentini distruttori. Né valeva il rinnovare ogni cosa; quello che oggi compravano, domani era bell'e rosicchiato.

Centinaia di gatti, intanto, passeggiavano su e giù per le stanze, miagolando, o si stendevano al sole facendo le fusa. Soltanto i vestiti e i mobili della Reginotta non erano rosi.

Il Re, i Ministri, tutta la corte non sapevano dove dare il capo.

- Questa è opera di Topolino!

- Maestà, - disse il Ministro che aveva suggerito di far divorare Topolino dai gatti - si costruisca una gran trappola, che abbia l'aspetto della camera della Reginotta, e cerchisi un Mago capace di fare una bambola grande al naturale, somigliantissima a lei, con un congegno da poter chiamare:

"Since he is a little mouse," said a minister, "let's have him arrested and lock him in a room with all of the cats in the royal palace, and in this way he will be eaten alive."

They had him arrested, they undressed him, and they locked him in a room with one hundred hungry cats, and then they waited. When they opened the door, Topolino was no longer there. And the cats were licking their whiskers, as if they had just had a tasty dinner.

Content, the king ordered that a celebratory ball be held.

However, when he put on his royal cloak, he found that mice had nibbled their way through it. When the generals, the ladies of the court, and the other guests got dressed for the ball, they all found that their uniforms and clothing were eaten by mice!

But that wasn't all. The ministers had brought the king a decree to sign, and the next day they found the paper nibbled through exactly where the signature was. Little by little, in the royal palace, nothing of the mattresses, sheets, blankets, linens, and other materials or of the furniture was left intact; it looked like an army of mice had enjoyed itself with its destructive teeth. They were bent on ruining everything. Indeed, whatever was bought one day would surely be eaten the next.

Meanwhile, hundreds of cats walked back and forth through the palace rooms, meowing or stretching themselves out in the sun. Only the clothing and the furniture of the princess were not eaten.

The king, the ministers, and all the court did not know where to turn.

"This is the work of Topolino!"

"Majesty," said the minister who had suggested that Topolino be devoured by cats, "why not build a large mouse trap that looks like the princess's room? Then you can find a magician to make a large life-like doll looking exactly like the

"Topolino! Topolino!" con lo stesso tono della voce di lei.
Sono sicuro che Topolino cascherà nell'inganno. Quando
l'avremo in mano penseremo al da farsi.

L'idea parve eccellente. Senza che ne trapelasse nulla, i
magnagni di corte costruirono una trappola, che simulava la
camera della Reginotta; e un famoso Mago fece una bambola
grande al naturale, da scambiarsi colla Reginotta in carne e
ossa, e che diceva: "Topolino! Topolino!" con lo stesso tono
della voce di questa. Collocarono la trappola nel giardino
reale, ed aspettarono fino alla dimane.

Tutta la notte, il congegno della bambola chiamò:
"Topolino! Topolino!". Ma chi sa dove lucevano gli occhi di
Topolino in quel punto?

Per sei notti l'inganno non giovò. Alla settima, il povero
Topolino, lusingato dalla somiglianza, era accorso alla
trappola e c'era rimasto.

Figuriamoci il tripudio del Re e dei Ministri, la mattina
quando lo trovarono acquattato in un cantuccio presso la
bambola!

- Rosicchia, Topolino! Sposa la Reginotta, Topolino!

Lo beffeggiavano senza pietà; e Topolino, acquattato nel suo
cantuccio, li guardava e non rispondeva nulla.

Giusto in quel giorno, la sua mamma, avendo bisogno d'un
servigio, aveva detto:·

- Codina, codina,
Servi la tua mammina!
Ma la codina non si era mossa.

- Ah, codina, codina! - esclamò quella mamma desolata: -
Topolino è in pericolo; andiamo a soccorrerlo, presto!

E si avviarono, la codina avanti, e lei dietro, finché non
giunsero alla capitale del regno e non entrarono nel giardino
reale, mischiati alla folla che accorreva per la curiosità di

princess with a device that calls 'Topolino! Topolino!' in the same voice as she. I am sure Topolino will fall for the trick. When we have him in our hands, we can think about what to do."

This seemed like an excellent idea. Without letting anyone else know, the nobles of the court constructed a trap that looked like the princess's room. And a famous magician made a large life-like doll that looked like the princess in the flesh and that said: "Topolino! Topolino!" in the same tone of voice as she. They placed the trap in the royal garden, and they waited until the next day.

All night the device within the doll cried: "Topolino! Topolino!" But who knew where Topolino was at that point?

For six nights, the trick produced no results. On the seventh, poor Topolino, deceived by the likeness of the princess, was drawn into the trap and was captured.

Imagine the jubilation of the king and the ministers the morning that they found him crouching in a corner near the doll!

"Keep nibbling, Topolino! Of course you will marry the princess," they mocked.

In fact, they taunted him without mercy, and, crouching in his corner, Toppolino watched them but said nothing.

On that very day, his mother needed some help and she said:
"Little tail, little tail,
    Come help your mother."
But the little tail did not move.

"Oh little tail, little tail," exclaimed the distressed mother. "Topolino is in danger; let's go to his aid immediately!"

And they started off, the little tail in front and she behind until they reached the capital of the kingdom and entered the royal garden. They mixed in with the crowd that, out of

*osservare Topolino dentro la trappola. Quel giorno Topolino
doveva esser bruciato. La trappola era stata unta tutta d'olio e
di grasso; s'aspettava il Re e la corte per appiccargli fuoco.*

*La codina spiccò un salto e andò ad appiccicarsi al codone
di Topolino.*

- Topolino ha la coda! Lascia vedere la coda, Topolino!

*E Topolino, che si era subito ringalluzzito, si voltava
compiacente e dimenava la coda come se non avesse capito la
condanna che gli stava sul capo. La gente rideva e batteva le
mani. Ora che Topolino era cascato in disgrazia, nessuno più
si rammentava del bene ch'egli aveva fatto, quando si
chiamava Niente-con-Nulla: il mondo è così! Al suono delle
trombe, ecco il Re e i Ministri e la corte, tutti vestiti in gran
gala, preceduti dal carnefice, con una torcia accesa in pugno.
La Reginotta era rimasta al palazzo.*

Il Re, per scherno, allora disse:

- Topolino, prima di morire, che grazia chiedi?

E Topolino, senza scomporsi, rispose:

- Maestà:

-Topolino non vuol ricotta
  Vuol sposare la Reginotta;
  E se il Re non gliela dà,
  Topolino lo ammazzerà.

E si lisciava la coda.

- Date fuoco! - ordinò il Re inviperito.

*Ma non appena il carnefice ebbe accostata la torcia alla
trappola, ecco che insieme con la trappola scoppia in fiamme
il trono reale. Le vampe avvolsero il Re e i Ministri, che non
trovarono scampo.*

*La gente fuggiva, atterrita; ma Topolino, trasformato in
bellissimo giovane, usciva fuori sano e salvo.*

*Agli urli, alle strida, accorse subito la Reginotta; e, visto il
disastro, si mise a piangere:*

- Topolino, se mi vuoi bene, risuscita mio padre!

curiosity, was running to see Topolino in the trap. That day, he
was to be burned. The trap was covered with oil and grease; the
crowd was waiting for the king and his court to set it on fire.

Then the little tail leaped up and stuck itself to Topolino.

"Topolino has a tail! Let's see your tail, Topolino!"

Then, as if emboldened, Topolino turned around and wagged
his tail as if he didn't understand that he had been condemned
to death. The people laughed and clapped their hands. Now
that Topolino had fallen into disfavor, no one remembered the
good that he had done when he was called Nothing-with-
Nothing. That's the way of the world. At the sound of the
trumpets, the king and the ministers of the court entered, all
dressed in elegant clothes, proceeded by an executioner with a
torch clutched in his fist. The princess was still in the palace.

Sneering, the king said:

"Topolino, before you die, what is your last wish?"

Without hesitation, Topolino responded:

"Majesty:

It is not cheese that pleases this mouse.
He wants the princess as his spouse.
And if the king does not comply,
The mouse will surely make him die."

And he groomed his tail.

"Burn him!" ordered the King angrily.

But as soon as the executioner had put the torch to the trap,
the royal throne and the trap burst into flames. The flames en-
veloped the king and the ministers, who could find no escape.

The people were terrified and fled; however, Topolino,
transformed into a handsome young man, came out safe and
sound.

Hearing the cries and screams, the princess ran out immediately and, seeing the disaster, began to cry.

"Topolino, if you love me, bring my father back to life!"

Topolino esitava. Allora si fece avanti sua madre:
- Topolino, te ne prego anch'io, risuscita il Re!
Poteva dire di no alla mamma e alla sua cara Reginotta?
Toccò colle mani il cadavere mezzo carbonizzato del Re, e lo fece risuscitare. Ma il Re era diventato un altro. Domandò umilmente perdono del male che gli aveva fatto, e conchiuse:
- Giacché questo è il volere di Dio, sposatevi e siate felici!

Il popolo fece grandi feste.
Dei Ministri bruciati nessuno si diè pensiero.

Topolino hesitated. At that point, his mother came before him:

"Topolino, I too beg you to bring the king back to life!"

Could he say no to his mother and to his beloved princess?

He placed his hands on the half-burned body of the king, and he brought him back to life. But the king had become another. Humbly, he asked for pardon for the evil he had done, and he concluded:

"Since this is the will of God, get married and be happy!"

The people then made a great celebration.

However, no one cared about the ministers who had been burned.

Il racconta-fiabe

C'era una volta un povero diavolo, che aveva fatto tutti i mestieri e non era riuscito in nessuno.

Un giorno gli venne l'idea di andare attorno, a raccontare fiabe ai bambini. Gli pareva un mestiere facile, da divertircisi anche lui. Perciò si mise in viaggio, e la prima città che incontrò, cominciò a gridare per le vie:

- Fiabe, bambini, fiabe! Chi vuol sentir le fiabe?

I bambini accorsero da tutte le parti, e gli fecero ressa attorno. Lui cominciò:

-C'era una volta un Re e una Regina, che non avevano figliuoli, e facevano voti e pellegrinaggi...

- To'! Questa la sappiamo a mente, - dissero i bambini - è la fiaba della Bella addormentata nel bosco. Un'altra! Un'altra!

- Ve ne dirò un'altra.

E cominciò:

-C'era una volta una bambina, che aveva la mamma matta e la nonna più matta di lei. La nonna le fece un cappuccetto rosso...

- To'! Questa la sappiamo a mente: è la fiaba di Cappuccetto rosso.

- Un'altra! Un'altra!

Quel povero diavolo, un po' seccato, cominciò da capo:

-C'era una volta un signore che aveva una figliuola. Gli era morta la moglie e ne aveva presa un'altra, vedova con due figlie...

- To'! È la fiaba di Cenerentola. Sappiamo a mente anche questa.

E visto che era buono a raccontare soltanto fiabe vecchie, i bambini gli voltarono le spalle e lo piantarono come un grullo.

Partì e andò in un'altra città. E, appena arrivato, si messe a gridare per le vie:

The Teller of Tales

There was once a poor fellow who had tried every craft but had succeeded at none of them.

One day he got the idea of going around and telling fairy tales to children. To him this seemed like and easy job, at which he would also enjoy himself. So, he began to travel about and, at the first city that he came to, he began to shout as he went:

"Fairy tales, children! Who wants to hear fairy tales?"

The children ran to him from everywhere, and they circled around him. Thus, he began:

"There were once a king and queen who had no children, and they made offerings and pilgrimages...."

"Hey! We know that one by heart," said the children—"it is the tale of Sleeping Beauty of the forest. Tell us another! Another! Another!"

And he began, again:

"There was once a little girl whose mother was insane and whose grandmother was more insane than she. He grandmother made her a little red hood...."

"Hey! We know that one by heart; it is the story of Little Red Riding Hood."

"Another! Another!"

The poor man was a little annoyed, but he started over again:

"There once was a gentlemen who had a daughter. His wife had died, and he had taken another, a widow with two children."

"Hey! That's the story of Cinderella. We know that one by heart as well."

And realizing that he was good at telling only old tales, the children turned their backs and made fun of him.

So, he left and went to another city. And as soon as he arrived, he began to shout as he went:

- *Fiabe, bambini, fiabe! Chi vuol sentire le fiabe?*
*I bambini accorsero da tutte le parti e gli fecero ressa
attorno. Ma non cominciava una fiaba, che quelli non
urlassero tosto:*
- *La sappiamo! La sappiamo!*
*E visto che era buono a raccontare soltanto fiabe vecchie,
gli voltarono le spalle e lo piantarono come un grullo.*

*Quando ebbe provato più volte e sempre con lo stesso
cattivo successo, quel povero diavolo si perdette d'animo, e
non sapeva più dove dare di capo.*

*Angustiato, si mise a camminare senza sapere dove lo
portassero i piedi, e si trovò in mezzo a un bosco.*

*Sopravvenuta la notte, si stese sull'erba, sotto un albero, per
dormire; ma non poté chiuder occhio: aveva una gran paura.*
*Gli pareva che le piante, collo stormire delle fronde,
parlassero sotto voce fra loro; gli pareva che le bestie e gli
uccelli notturni, con quei loro strani gridi e canti, tramassero
qualche cosa contro di lui.*

*Il cuore gli batteva forte nel petto, e non vedeva l'ora che
fosse giorno.*

*lla mezzanotte in punto, che vede? Vede una gran luce pel
bosco, e da ogni pianta sbucava gente che rideva, che cantava,
che ballava; e intanto da tutte le parti venivano rizzate
prestamente tante bellissime tende e tavole piene di cose non
mai viste, che luccicavano più dell'oro. S'accòrse di essere
capitato in mezzo alla fiera delle Fate; si fece coraggio e si
levò. Avea pensato:*

- *Le Fate debbono vendere anche delle belle fiabe, nuove di
zecca: vo' veder di comprarle.*

*E accostatosi a una che vendeva roba sotto una ricca tenda
là vicino, le disse:*

- *Ci avete fiabe nuove?*
- *Fiabe nuove non ce n'è più; se n'è perduto il seme.*

"Fairy tales, children, fairy tales! Who wants to hear fairy tales?"

The children ran from everywhere and circled around him. However, he had hardly begun a tale when they began to shout:

"We know that one! We know that one!"

And realizing that he was good at telling only old tales, the children turned their backs and made fun of him.

When he tried several times with no success, the poor man felt desperate and no longer knew where to turn next.

Depressed, he began to walk without knowing where his feet were taking him; he found himself in the middle of a forest.

When night fell, he lay under a tree and tried to fall asleep on the grass; however, he could not close an eye, for he was very afraid. It appeared that when shaking their leaves the plants were talking to themselves under their breaths. It also seemed as if the animals and the birds of the night, with their strange shrieks and songs, were plotting something against him.

His heart beat quickly in his chest, and he did not believe he would make it through the night.

At the stroke of midnight, he saw a great light through the forest. From each plant appeared people laughing, singing, and dancing. Meanwhile, from everywhere popped up many beautiful tents and tables filled with things never seen before, which shone more brightly than gold. He realized he was at the fair of the fairies. Encouraged, he stood up and began to think:

"The fairies must also sell beautiful fairy tales that are brand new. I will go and see if I can buy them."

And he approached a woman who was selling things under an elegant tent nearby.

"Do you have any new fairy tales?" he asked.

"There are no more new fairy tales; the seed to grow them has been lost."

Poco persuaso di questa risposta, andò da un'altra Fata che teneva in mostra sulla tavola e nei barattoli tante bellissime cose, che la prima non aveva:

- Ci avete fiabe nuove?

- Fiabe nuove non ce n'è più; se n'è perduto il seme.

E due!

Girò attorno un altro pezzo, osservando qua e là; e come vide una tenda, che gli parve la più ricca di tutte, si accostò alla Fata venditrice e le domandò timidamente:

- Ci avete fiabe nuove?

- Fiabe nuove non ce n'è più; se n'è perduto il seme.

E tre!

Vedendolo rimasto male, quella Fata gli disse:

- Sapete, quell'uomo, che dovreste voi fare? Dovreste andare dal mago Tre-Pi che n'ha pieni i magazzini.

- E dove si trova cotesto mago Tre-Pi?

- Lontan lontano, fra' suoi boschi di aranci.

Prima dell'alba, la fiera finì. Le Fate, le tende, ogni cosa disparve; e quelpovero diavolo si trovò solo in mezzo al bosco, e non sapeva se fosse stato sveglio o pure avesse sognato.

Cammina, cammina, incontrò un viandante:

- Compare, sapreste dirmi dove sono i boschi di aranci del mago Tre-Pi?

- Andate avanti, sempre avanti.

Cammina, cammina, incontrò una vecchia:

- Comare, sapreste dirmi dove sono i boschi di aranci del mago Tre Pi?

- Andate avanti, sempre avanti.

Non si arrivava mai!

Finalmente, ecco i boschi di aranci. Ma c'erano i muri attorno, e si doveva entrare da un piccolo cancello guardato da un mastino.

Not happy with this answer, he went to another fairy who displayed on the table and in jars many beautiful things that the first one did not have.

"Do you have any new fairy tales?" he asked.

"There are no more new fairy tales; the seed to grow them has been lost."

And that made two!

He wandered around a bit more, observing what was there. And when he saw a tent that seemed richer than all the rest, he approached the fairy vendor and asked timidly:

"Do you have any new fairy tales?"

"There are no more new fairy tales; the seed to grow them has been lost."

And that made three!

Seeing him become sad, that fairy told him:

"Do you know, sir, what you should do? You ought to go to Tre-Pi, the magician, who has storehouses full."

"And where can one find Tre-Pi, the magician?"

"Far, far away, in his forest of orange trees."

The fair ended before dawn. Fairies, tents, and everything else disappeared. He found himself alone in the middle of the forest, and he didn't know whether he was awake or had dreamt it all.

He walked and walked, and he met a wayfarer.

"Neighbor, can you tell me where I can find the forest of oranges of Tre-Pi, the magician?"

"Straight ahead, always straight ahead."

He walked and walked, and he met an old woman:

"Neighbor, can you tell me where I can find the forest of oranges of Tre-Pi, the magician?"

"Straight ahead, always straight ahead."

However, he never seemed to get there!

Finally, the forest of orange trees appeared. However, it was surrounded by walls, and it could be entered only through a small gate guarded by a mastiff.

- Chi cerchi da questa parte? - gli domandò il mastino.
- Cerco il mago Tre-Pi.
- È fuori: aspetta.
*Ed ecco, sul tardi, il mago Tre-Pi, nero come il pepe, con
una barbona nera e certi occhi neri che schizzavano fuoco.*
- Ah, buon mago Tre-Pi, dovreste farmi un favore!
- Parla, che cosa vuoi?
*- Vorrei delle fiabe nuove. Voi, che ne avete dei magazzini,
dovreste darmene qualcuna.*
*- Fiabe nuove non ce n'è più: se n'è perduto il seme. Di
quelle che ho io tu non sapresti che fartene. E poi, servono a
me, per conservarle imbalsamate. Vuoi vederle?*
E lo condusse dentro, nei magazzini
*C'erano tutte le fiabe del mondo, situate nei cassetti fatti a
posta, classate e numerate; e il mago Tre-Pi gli guardava
sempre le mani, per paura che quello non gliene portasse via
qualcuna.*
- Ma non c'è proprio verso di poterne trovare delle nuove?
*- Le nuove, - rispose il mago - forse le sa una vecchia Fata,
fata Fantasia: ma non vuol dirle a nessuno. Vive sola in una
grotta, e bisognerebbe andarci in compagnia della Bella
addormentata nel bosco, di Cappuccetto rosso, di Cenerentola,
di Pelosina, di Pulcettino e simil gente. Prova; però ti dico che
è fatica sprecata.*
- Non importa; proverò.
Tornò addietro e andò dalla Bella addormentata nel bosco:
- O Bella addormentata, vi prego, venite con me.
- Volentieri.
- O Cappuccetto rosso, ti prego, vieni con me.
- Volentieri.
- O buona Cenerentola, ti prego, vieni con me.
- Volentieri.

"What are you searching for in these parts?" asked the mastiff.

"I am searching for Tre-Pi, the magician."

"He's out now; wait."

And later in the day, appeared Tri-Pi, the magician, as black as pepper, with a long black beard and black eyes that shot fire.

"Oh good magician Tre-Pi, please do me a favor!"

"Tell me; what do you want?"

"I want some new fairy tales. You, who have them in your storehouses, should give me a few."

"There are no more new fairy tales; the seed to grow them has been lost. And you won't know what to do with the ones I have. Besides, I need to preserve them forever. Do you want to see them?"

And he led him inside to the storehouses.

Inside were all of the fairy tales of the world, placed in cases made especially for them, classified and numbered. And Tre-Pi, the magician, watched his hands closely, for he feared that he might steal one of them.

"But, isn't there any way to find new fairy tales?"

"Perhaps," responded the magician, "the new ones are known by an old fairy, named Fantasia, but she doesn't want to tell them to anyone. She lives alone in a cave, and you have to go to her only in the company of Sleeping Beauty, Little Red Riding Hood, Cinderella, Rapunzel, Pulcinetto and other such folks. You can try, but I think it is a futile effort."

"That's not important; I'll try."

He turned back and went to Sleeping Beauty in the forest:

"Oh Sleeping Beauty, I beg you to come with me."

"Gladly," she said.

"Oh, Little Red Riding Hood, I beg you to come with me."

"Gladly," she said.

"Oh, Cinderella, I beg you to come with me."

"Gladly," she said.

Insomma li radunò tutti, e si misero in via. Quelli sapevano il posto della grotta dove la vecchia Fata viveva rinchiusa, e ve lo condussero facilmente. Picchiarono all'uscio.
- *Chi siete?*
- *Siamo noi.*
Fata Fantasia li riconobbe alla voce, e venne ad aprire.
- *Che cosa volete? E chi è costui? Temerario, come osi di venire da me!*
E voleva scacciarlo via.
Quelli la rabbonirono e le esposero il motivo della loro venuta:
- *Questo povero disgraziato ha tentato tutti i mestieri e non è riuscito in nessuno. Si era anche messo a fare il raccontafiabe; ma i bambini, che già sanno a mente le nostre storie, ora vorrebbero delle fiabe nuove, e non gli prestano attenzione. Bella fata Fantasia, aiutatelo voi!*
- *Fiabe nuove non ce n'è più; se n'è perduto il seme.*
- *Bella fata Fantasia, aiutatemi voi!*
Sentendosi pregare colle lagrime agli occhi, fata Fantasia s'intenerì:
- *Vado e vengo.*
Rientrò nella grotta, e dopo un pezzetto, ricomparve col grembiule ricolmo:
- *Tieni; con questa roba forse ti riescirà.*
- *E gli diede una stiacciata, un'arancia d'oro, un ranocchino, una serpicina, un uovo nero, tre anelli, insomma tante cose strane.*
- *Che debbo farne?*
- *Portali teco e vedrai.*
Ringraziò, tutto contento, accompagnò quegli altri alle case loro e, la prima città che incontrò, si messe a gridare per la via:
- *Fiabe, bambini, fiabe! Chi vuol sentire le fiabe?*

In short, he gathered them all, and they went on their way. They knew the location of the cave where the old fairy lived alone, and they led him there easily. They knocked at the door.

"Who's there?"

"It's us."

Fairy Fantasia recognized their voices, and she came to the door.

"What do you want? And who is with you? Oh, foolish one, how dare you come to me!"

And she wanted to throw him out.

But the others calmed her down, and they explained the reason for their visit.

"This poor, unfortunate fellow has tried many trades, but he has succeeded at none of them. He even tried telling fairy tales; however, the children, who know our stories by heart, now want new fairy tales, and they paid no attention to him. Dear fairy Fantasia, please help him!"

"There are no more new fairy tales; the seed to grow them has been lost."

"Dear fairy Fantasia, please help me!" said the poor fellow.

Hearing these tearful pleas, fairy Fantasia began to soften.

"I'll be right back."

She went back into the cave, and, after a little while, she reappeared with her apron full.

"Take these things; perhaps they will help you."

And she gave him a roll, a golden orange, a little frog, a little snake, a black egg, three rings—in short, many strange things.

"What should I do with these things?"

"Take them with you and go."

Grateful and content, he went with the others back home. At the first city that he came upon, he began to shout as he went:

"Fairy tales, children, fairy tales! Who wants to hear fairy tales?"

I bambini accorsero da tutte le parti e gli fecero ressa attorno.

Lui prese la stiacciata in mano e cominciò:

- C'era una volta...

Non sapeva neppure una parola di quel che dovea raccontare; ma, aperta la bocca, la fiaba gli usciva filata, come se l'avesse saputa a mente da gran tempo. E fu la fiaba di Spera di sole.

La fiaba piacque ai bambini:

- Un'altra! Un'altra!

E quello, preso a caso uno dei regali della Fata, che portava seco in una borsa, cominciò:

- C'era una volta...

Non sapeva neppure una parola di quel che dovea raccontare; ma, aperta la bocca, la fiaba gli usciva filata, come se l'avesse saputa a mente da gran tempo.

E raccontò la fiaba di Ranocchino, porgi il ditino.

La fiaba piacque ai bambini:

- Un'altra! Un'altra!

E così di seguito; ne raccontò più di una dozzina, e lui ci si divertiva più dei bambini.

Poi andò in un'altra città:

- Fiabe, bambini, fiabe! Chi vuol sentire le fiabe?

E ricominciò da capo. I bambini contentissimi.

Ma, infine, erano sempre quelle: Spera di sole, Ranocchino, Cecina, Il cavallo di bronzo, Serpentina, Testa-di-rospo... Sicché, all'ultimo, i bambini si seccarono, e appena cominciava:

"C'era una volta..." lo interrompevano:

- La sappiamo, la sappiamo a mente!

Che cosa farne di quelle fiabe, ora che i bambini non volevano più sentirle, perché le sapevano tutte a mente?

Pensò di regalarle al mago Tre-Pi, per metterle nei cassetti, colle altre fiabe imbalsamate.

The children ran from everywhere and circled around him.

He took the roll in his hand and began:

"Once upon a time…"

He did not know one word of the tale that he was going to tell, but, opening his mouth, the tale came out without hesitation, as if he had known it by heart for a long time. It was the tale called "Ray of Sunshine."

The tale pleased the children.

"Another! Another!" they cried.

And from the bag that he carried with him, he pulled out one of the gifts the fairy had given him. And he began:

"Once upon a time…."

He did not know one word of the tale that he was going to tell but, when he opened his mouth, the tale came out without hesitation, as if he had known it by heart for a long time.

And he told a tale of "The Little Frog," who points his finger.

The tale pleased the children.

"Another! Another!" they cried.

And thus he continued; he told more than a dozen, and he enjoyed himself even more than the children did.

He traveled on to another city:

"Fairy tales, children, fairy tales! Who wants to hear fairy tales?"

And he started all over again. The children were very happy.

However, the tales were always the same. "Ray of Sunshine," "The Little Frog," "The Little Chickpea," "The Bronze Horse," "Serpentina," "Toad Head".… Eventually, the children became bored and, as soon as he began, "Once upon a time…," they interrupted him:

"We know that one; we know it by heart!"

What was he to do with those tales now that the children did not want to hear them anymore, for they knew them by heart?

He thought he would give the to Tre-Pi, the magician so he could put them in the cases with the other preserved tales.

E andò a trovarlo.

Al cancello c'era il solito mastino:

- Chi cerchi da queste parti?

- Cerco il mago Tre-Pi.

- È fuori: aspetta.

Sul tardi, ecco il mago Tre-Pi, nero come il pepe, col suo barbone nero e quei suoi occhi neri che schizzavano fuoco:

- Sei tornato di nuovo? Che vuoi da me?

- Nulla, buon Mago; vengo anzi a farvi un regalo. Queste son fiabe nuove e nei vostri cassetti non ce le avete. Ora che tutti i bambini le sanno a mente, ho pensato di regalarvele per metterle insieme colle altre imbalsamate.

- Ah, sciocco! Sciocco! - rispose il Mago. - Non vedi che cosa hai in mano?

Il racconta-fiabe guardò: aveva in mano un pugno di mosche!

E tornò addietro scornato, e di fiabe non ne volle più sapere. Perciò si conchiude:

Fiabe nuove non ce n'è più; se n'è perduto il seme!

Come e perché, cari bambini, lo saprete facilmente quando sarete più grandi.

And he went to find him.

At the gate there was that lone mastiff:

"What are you searching for in these parts?" asked the mastiff.

"I am searching for Tre-Pi, the magician.

"He's out now: wait."

And later in the day, appeared Tri-Pi, the magician, as black as pepper, with a long black beard and black eyes that shot fire.

"Have you come back again? What do you wish from me?"

"Nothing, good magician. In fact, I have come to give you a gift. These are new fairy tales, which are not stored in your boxes. Since all of the children know them by heart, I thought I would give them to you to put away them with the others."

"Oh fool! Fool! Don't you see what you have in your hand?"

The teller of tales looked; he held in his hand a fistful of flies!

He returned in shame, not wanting to know anything more of fairy tales. Therefore, we can conclude:

"There are no more new fairy tales; the seed to grow them has been lost."

And why this is so, dear children, you will know only when you are older.

La reginotta

C'era una volta un Re e una Regina che avevano una figliuola più bella della luna e del sole.

Un giorno, dopo il pranzo, il Re disse alla Regina:

- Maestà, guardate qui, tra I capelli. Sento qualche cosa che mi morde.

La Regina osservò, scostando I capelli colle dita, e trovò un pidocchio che era uno stupore. Stava per ischiacciarlo.

- No- disse il Re.- Proviamo d'allevarlo.

E misero il pidocchio in uno scatolino piccino piccino.

Gli davan da mangiare ogni giorno, e quello cresceva e ingrassava. Presto dovettero levarlo via di lì perché non ci capiva più, così grosso s'era fatto. Il Re, curioso di vedere fin dove sarebbe arrivato, lo trattava bene, e insieme alla Regina, andava tutti i giorni ad osservarlo in quella stanza del palazzo reale dove lo tenevano nascosto. Il pidocchio cresceva, cresceva. Furon costretti a levarlo via anche da quell'altro scatolino; era più grosso d'un pugno: si stentava a riconoscere che fosse un pidocchio. Insomma, cresci, cresci, diventò quanto una gallina e poteva appena muoversi, dalla gran ciccia che avea addosso.

Allora il Re lo ammazzò, lo scorticò e ne conciò la pelle. E fece un bando:

- Chi indovina che pelle di animale sia questa, avrà la Reginotta mia figliuola in isposa. Chi non sa indovinarlo, gli si taglia la testa.

Le Reginotta eara angustiata.

- Che marito le sarebbe toccato in sorte?

E piangeva. Ma il Re voleva così e bisognava ubbidire!

Accorsero parecchie persone da tutti i punti del regno. Chi disse la pelle essere d'un animale, chi d'un altro; ed ebbero, senza misericordia, tagliate le teste.

The Princess

Once upon a time, there was a king and a queen who had a daughter more beautiful than the moon and the sun.

One day, after lunch, the king said to the queen: "Majesty, look through my hair. I feel something biting me."

The queen searched through his hair with her finger and found a big, fat louse. She was about to crush it.

"No," said the king. "Let's try to remove it."

And they put the louse in a tiny box.

They fed it every day, and it got bigger and fatter. Soon, they had to remove it because it no longer fit in the box; it had become so fat. Curious to see where this would end, the king treated the louse well, and, together with the queen, went to observe it every day in the room of the royal palace where they kept it hidden. The louse grew and grew. They were forced to remove it even from this other box; it was larger than a person's fist. It was hard to believe that it was a louse. In short, it grew and grew, becoming the size of a chicken, and it could barely move because of all the weight it had gained.

Therefore, the king killed it, skinned it, and tanned its pelt. And he announced the following:

"Whoever can guess from what animal this pelt is taken will marry my daughter. Whoever guesses wrong, will have his head cut off."

The princess became very upset.

"What kind of husband am I destined to have?"

And she cried. However, the king wanted it to be so, and he had to be obeyed.

Many people from all over the kingdom rushed to the palace. Some said that the pelt was from one animal; others that it came from another. And, without mercy, they all had their heads cut off.

Si provarono altri. L'idea di sposar la Reginotta era una gran tentazione, e pareva cosa facile il conoscere una pelle d'animale. Però, quand'erano lì, rimanevano. E il Re, senza misericordia, gli faceva tagliare le teste.

Finalmente, ecco un bel giovane.

- Peccato! Verrà fatta la festa anche a lui!

Tutti ne aveano compassione vedendolo così giovane e così bello. Perfino il Re gli disse di pensarci due volte prima d'esporsi al cimento. Ma quegli, ostinato, entrava nella sala dov'era esposta la pelle.

- È pelle di pidocchio!

- Bravo! - gli disse il Re.

- Tu sposerai la Reginotta.

L'abbracciò, lo ritenne a pranzo e ordinò feste per tutto il regno.

La Reginotta era contenta. Lo sposo, giovane e bello, pareva anche d'alto lignaggio.

- Chi sei? - gli domandò il Re a tavola.

- Son carne battezzata e ho sangue reale nelle vene.

- E dov'è il tuo paese?

- Il mio paese? È lontano, lontano. Per andarvi ci si mette un anno, un mese e un giorno, e chi ci arriva non fa più ritorno.

La Reginotta sgomentossi.

Il Re e la Regina piangevano, pensando che la loro figliuola doveva vivere in quel paese lontano, lontano, che per andarvi ci si metteva un anno, un mese e un giorno, e chi ci arriva non fa più ritorno. Ma parola di Re non va indietro.

E fatte le nozze, la Reginotta e il bel giovane, con un gran seguito, si misero in viaggio. Centinaia di carri e di cavalli portavano la dote di lei, tutta in gioie e quattrini, e il corredo e i magnifici regali ricevuti dal Re e dalla Regina.

Cammina, cammina, cammina, non arrivavano mai!

Tempted by the idea of marrying the princess, others tried as well. It seemed easy to recognize the pelt of an animal. However, when they came there, they were dumbfounded. And, without mercy, the king had their heads cut off.

Finally, a handsome young man arrived.

"What a shame! Even you will take part in this terrible celebration."

Everyone pitied him, seeing that he was so young and handsome. Even the king told him to think it over twice before exposing himself to danger. However, he was persistent, and he entered the room where the pelt was hanging.

"It's the pelt of a louse!"

"Bravo!" the king said to him. "You will marry the princess"

He embraced him, invited him to lunch, and ordered a celebration for the entire kingdom.

The princess was happy. The groom, young and handsome, also seemed to be of noble lineage.

"Who are you?" the king asked him at the table.

"My flesh is baptized, and royal blood runs through my veins."

"And where is your country?"

"My country? It is very far away. It takes a year, a month, and a day to get there, and whoever arrives can never return." The princess became frightened.

The king and queen wept. Their daughter would have to live in a far-away land, which took a year, a month, and day to get to and from which no one ever returned. However, a king cannot go back on his word.

And having gotten married, the princess and the handsome young man began their journey, a great crowd following them. Hundreds of wagons and horses carried the bride's dowry, all in jewels and coins, as well as the trousseau and the magnificent gifts given by the king and queen. They journeyed and journeyed, but still they did not arrive!

- *Dov'è il tuo paese?*
- *Dietro quelle montagne.*

Oltrepassaron le montagne e non s'arrivava ancora!

- *Dov'è il tuo paese?*
- *Più in là di quelle foreste.*

Oltrepassaron le foreste e non s'arrivava ancora!

- *Dov'è il tuo paese?*
- *In fondo a quella pianura.*

Traversarono la pianura e non si arrivava ancora!

La Reginotta intanto non si dava pace. Pensava al babbo e alla mamma che non avrebbe più riveduti.

Quel paese, così lontano lontano che non ci s'arrivava mai, le metteva un grande sgomento.

- *Vuoi tu fare in fretta? - le disse lo sposo.*
- *Sì.*
- *Ti prenderò in collo e vedrai.*

E la Reginotta lo lasciò fare. E non gli si è attaccata al collo colle braccia, che il bel giovane si trasforma in un Orco, alto, grosso, peloso, dagli occhi di brace, con certe zanne e certe *granfie!*

- *Ah, Vergine santa! Ah, mamma mia!*

La Reginotta avea chiuso gli occhi, si sentiva come portar via da un vento furioso.

L'Orco, nella sua corsa, faceva rintronar le vallate e le montagne:

- *Auhiii! Auhiii!*

Pareva un terremoto dovunque passasse, pareva un tempesta.

Quando la Reginotta aperse gli occhi, capì che era già arrivata nel castello dell'Orco suo sposo.

Si sentì stringere il cuore.

"Where is your country?"

"Behind those mountains."

They passed over the mountains, but they still didn't arrive!

"Where is your country?"

"Beyond these woods."

They traveled beyond the woods, but they still did not arrive!

"Where is your country?"

"On the other side of this plane."

They crossed the plane, but they still did not arrive!

Meanwhile, the princess was troubled. She kept thinking about her father and mother, whom she would never see again.

This far-away country, where one never arrives, caused her great distress.

"Are you in a hurry?" said the groom.

"Yes."

"I will grab you by the neck and you will see how fast you get there."

And the princess allowed him to do so, but as soon as he put his arms around her neck, the young man turned into an ogre, huge, hairy, with fiery eyes and great scary fangs and claws!

"Oh, Holy Virgin! Oh, mamma!"

The princess closed her eyes, and she felt as if she had been blown away by some fierce wind.

On the way, the ogre made the valleys and mountains thunder.

"Auhiii! Auhiii!"

Wherever he went, it seemed as if there had been an earthquake or great storm.

When the princess opened her eyes, she realized that she had arrived at the castle of her husband, the ogre.

She was heartbroken.

Il castello era tutto circondato da mura così alte che si vedeva a mala pena un po' di cielo. Stanzoni freddi e bui; catenacci dappertutto; dappertutto ceffi di guardie che avrebero messo spavento anche al più coraggioso del mondo.

- Che fare? Bisognava rassegnarsi!

L'Orco le usava grandi riguardi. La mattina andava via per la caccia e tornava la sera carico di preda. La Reginotta riconosceva quell'alito a dieci miglia di distanza. La preda consisteva sempre in poveri cristiani, parte uccisi, parte vivi, che l'Orco poi divorava mezzo crudi, uno a colazione, uno a pranzo, uno a cena. Per la Reginotta invece portava pietanze squisite, pasticcini, torte, dolciumi di ogni sorta.

- Mangia! Hai paura?

- No.

- Mangia dunque!

- Non ho appetito.

- Mangia!!...

E bisognava mangiare, perché l'Orco s'offendeva del rifiuto e digrignava i denti.

-Bevi! Hai paura?

- No.

- Bevi dunque!

- Non ho sete.

- Bevi!!...

E bisognava bere, perché l'Orco s'offendeva del rifiuto e digrignava i denti.

Ma torniamo al Re e alla Regina.

Un giorno, dopo che il vincitore e la Reginotta eran partiti, arrivò un giovinetto: voleva, anche lui, tentar la prova della pelle.

- Troppo tardi, bel giovinetto! La prova fu vinta.

- E da chi, Sacra Maestà?

The castle was completely surrounded by walls so high that one could hardly even see a bit of sky. The large rooms were cold and dark. There were locks everywhere and sinsister looking guards who would have frightened the bravest person in the world.

"What can I do? I must resign myself!"

In the morning the ogre went hunting; he returned at night loaded with his catch. The princess could smell his breath from ten miles away. His catch always consisted of unfortunate people, half dead and half alive, whom the ogre devoured still a little raw, one for breakfast, one for lunch, and one for dinner. But the ogre showed the princess great respect. He brought her exquisite dishes, pastries, cakes, and sweets of all kinds.

"Eat! Are you afraid?"

"No."

"Then, eat!"

"I'm not hungry."

"Eat!"

And she had to eat because the ogre was offended by her refusal, and he would grind his teeth.

"Drink! Are you afraid?"

"No."

"Then drink!"

"I'm not thirsty."

"Drink!"

And she had to drink because the ogre was offended by her refusal, and he would grind his teeth.

But, now, let's return to the king and queen.

One day, after the winner of the contest and the princess had left, a young man arrived; he too wanted to try to identify the pelt.

"Too late, young man! The contest has been won."

"And by whom, Holy Majesty?"

-Da uno che abita un paese così lontano, che per andarci ci si mette un anno, un mese e un giorno, e chi ci arriva non fa più ritorno

- È un Orco! Ahimè, la Reginotta è alle mani d'un Orco!

Figuriamoci il dolore del Re, della Regina e di tutta la corte a questa brutta notizia!

Il giovinetto andò via lamentandosi che la sua cattiva sorte lo avesse fatto arrivare troppo tardi. Era innamorato della Reginotta soltanto perché gli avevano detto che era più bella della luna e del sole; ed ora, pensando che lei si trovava alle mani di quella bestiaccia, provava un dolore di morte.

E camminava, senza saper dove andasse: i suoi occhi parevano due fontane.

Giunto in una pianura, stanco del cammino fatto, si sedette sopra un sasso, continuando a rammaricarsi.

Passava una vecchia con un fastello di legna sulle spalle.

- Che hai bel giovinetto?

- Che volete che abbia, vecchiarella mia?

E narrò il tristo caso della Reginotta e dell'Orco.

La vecchia non rispose nulla e riprese il cammino col suo fastello sulle spalle.

- Voi siete stanca, povera donna - disse il giovinetto.

- Date a me cotesto fastello. Faremo strada insieme.

- Grazie, figliuolo!

Il giovinetto si caricò il fastello e riprese la via insieme alla vecchia. Quel fastello era pesante.

- Nonna, la vostra abitazione è molto lontana di qui?

- Un albero che balla e un uccellin che parla; appena gli avremo incontrati e saremo giunti a casa mia.

Il fastello aumentava di peso. Il giovinetto stentava a reggerlo, sudava, ansava. E intanto il sole era tramontato; faceva già scuro.

- Nonna, la vostra abitazione è molto lontana di qui?

"By one who lives in a land so far away that it takes one year, one month, and one day to get there. And from this land no one ever returns."

"He's an ogre! Alas, the princess is in the hands of an ogre!"

Imagine the pain of the king, of the queen, and of the entire court over this terrible news.

The young man went on his way lamenting that his bad luck had caused him to arrive too late. He was in love with the princess, for he had heard that she was more beautiful than the moon and the sun. And now, thinking that she was in the hands of that beast, he felt a deadly pain.

And so he walked on, without knowing where he was going; his eyes resembled two fountains.

Arriving on a plain, and tired after his journey, he sat on a rock, continuing to lament his fate.

An old woman passed by carrying a bundle of wood on her shoulders.

"What's the matter, young man?"

"What's the matter with me, my dear lady?"

And he told her the sad story of the princess and the ogre.

The old lady said nothing and continued to walk with her bundle on her shoulders.

"You are tired, poor woman," said the young man.

"Give me this bundle. We will travel together."

"Thank you, my son!"

The young man lifted the bundle and continued along with the old woman. The bundle was heavy.

"Grandma, is your home very far from here?"

"A tree that dances and a little bird that talks; as soon as we find them, we will be at my house."

The bundle got heavier. The young man was hardly able to carry it; he was sweating and gasping. Meanwhile, the sun had set and it was dark.

"Grandma, is your home very far from here?"

- *Un albero che balla e un uccellin che parla; appena gli avremo incontrati e saremo giunti a casa mia.*

Era notte; ci si vedeva poco. Ed ecco pel prato un albero che andava saltelloni e pareva ballasse, come se fosse stato una persona viva.

- *Hai fatto buona guardia, ora basta* - *gli disse la vecchia.*

E l'albero cessò di saltellare. Il giovinetto si era fermato, stupito.

- *Avanti, figliuolo; c'è ancora qualche tratto.*

Intanto il fastello aumentava di peso.

Il giovinetto non ne poteva più!

Stava per maledire l'ora e il punto che lui avea fatto quella carità a quella vecchia, quand'ecco uno sbatter di ali.

Era l'uccellino che parlava.

- *Bene arrivata la mammina mia! Bene arrivato chi viene con lei!*

Il giovinetto, dalla paura, cominciò a tremare.

- *Siamo giunti* - *disse la vecchia.*

Ed entrarono in casa.

Quello si tolse di spalla il fastello, ch'era ridiventato leggiero, e lo posò accanto al focolare.

Allora la vecchia prendeva due ramicelli di legna, accendeva il fuoco, preparava la minestra; poi stendeva la tovaglia e metteva i piatti sulla tavola.

E quando tutto fu pronto:

- *Cricrì, cricrì, cricrì!*

L'uccellino diventava una bella ragazza.

Si misero a mangiare.

Il giovinetto aveva ribrezzo di toccar le pietanze; temeva non fossero incantate.

- *Dove vai, giovinetto, così sperso pel mondo? Se tu volessi fermarti qui, ti darei le mie ricchezze e questa bella figliuola in isposa.*

"A tree that dances and a little bird that talks; as soon as we find them, we will be at my house."

It was night and hard to see anything. But in the meadow they saw a tree that went skipping along and seemed to be dancing, as if it were a living person.

"You have guarded well, but now enough," the old woman told him.

And the tree stopped skipping. The young man stood still, amazed at the sight.

"Onward, my son. We still have a way to go."

Meanwhile, the bundle got heavier.

The young man couldn't carry it any longer.

He was about to curse the hour and place that he had offered the old woman his help, but then he heard a beating of wings.

It was the little bird that spoke.

"Welcome, my little mamma! And welcome to the one who comes with you!"

The young man began to tremble from fear.

"We're here," said the old woman.

And they entered the house.

Off his shoulders he took the bundle, which had become light again, and he placed it next to the fireplace.

The old woman then took two branches, lit the fire, and made soup. Next, she spread the tablecloth and placed the dishes on the table.

And when everything was ready: "Chirp, chirp, chirp!"

The little bird had become a beautiful young lady.

They started to eat.

However, the young man was hesitant to touch the food because he feared a spell may have been placed on it.

"Where are you going, young man, wandering lost through the world? If you want to stay here, I will give you my wealth and this beautiful daughter in marriage."

- Ah, nonna mia, lasciatemi andare! Cerco la Reginotta del mio cuore e vo' trovarla, ad ogni costo. Se non la troverò monaco mi farò.

- Poverino! Ma tu non sai la via del paese dell'Orco. È lontano, lontano! Per andarvi ci si mette un anno, un mese e un giorno, e chi ci arriva non fa più ritorno!

- Che importa? La mia vita è della Reginotta; se morrò per lei, tanto meglio! Datemi un cantuccio per dormire, e domani svegliatemi all'alba; vo' mettermi in cammino.

La vecchia lo condusse in una cameretta così bella da star bene anche in una reggia. Ma il giovinetto non poteva dormire. Pensava alla sua Reginotta e a quell'Orco, si svoltava di qua e di là fra le lenzuola e sospirava.

- Cricrì, cricrì, cricrì!

Entrava in camera l'uccellino e subito diventava una bella ragazza, quella di poco prima.

- Perché non dormi, giovinetto? Perché sospiri?

- Penso alla Reginotta del mio cuore e non posso chiuder occhio.

- Prendi me. Sono bella, sono ricca, sono di sangue reale. Dove vorresti trovare una fortuna migliore?

- Ah, ragazza mia, lasciatemi andare! La mia sorte vuol così.

- Cricrì! Cricrì! Cricrì!

La bella ragazza ritornava uccellino.

- Strappa una penna da questa coda, strappa due penne da queste ali. Nei momenti di gran pericolo, prendine una in mano e comanda. Sarai ubbidito.

Il giovinetto esitava:

- Poteva essere un tranello!

Ma quello, di nuovo:

- Strappa una penna da questa coda, strappa due penne da queste ali. Nei momenti di gran pericolo, prendine una in mano e comanda. Sarai ubbidito.

"Oh, Grandma, let me go! I am searching for the princess of my heart, and I want to find her at any cost. If I don't find her, I will become a monk."

"Poor boy! But you don't know the way to the land of the ogre. It is very far. To get there, it takes a year, a month, and a day, and whoever goes there can never return."

"What does it matter? My life belongs to the princess; if I die for her, all the better! Give me a corner where I can sleep, and tomorrow wake me at dawn. I want to be on my way."

The old woman took him to a room as good as one in any palace. But the young man couldn't sleep. He thought only of the princess and that ogre. He turned this way and that between the sheets, and he sighed all night.

"Chirp, chirp, chirp!"

Into the room came the small bird, and all of a sudden it became the beautiful young lady whom he had just met.

"Why aren't you sleeping, young man? Why do you sigh so?"

"I am thinking about the princess of my heart, and I can't sleep."

"Marry me. I am beautiful, I am rich, and I am of royal blood. Where will you find a better fate?"

"Oh, my dear girl, let me be. My fate is sealed."

"Chrip! Chirp! Chirp"

And the beautiful young girl turned back into a little bird.

"Tear a feather from this tail; tear two feathers from these wings. When you are in great danger, hold one in your hand and call for my help. You will be obeyed."

The young man hesitated:

"This might be a trick!"

But she repeated:

"Tear a feather from this tail; tear two feathers from these wings. When you are in great danger, hold one in your hand and call for my help. You will be obeyed."

- *Allora!...- disse il giovinetto.*

E, rassicurato, gli strappò quelle penne dalla coda e dalle ali e se le mise in serbo nelle tasche.

La notte era lunga e lui non poteva conciliar sonno. Pensava alla sua Reginotta e a quell'Orco, si rivoltava di qua e di là fra le lenzuola e sospirava.

Entrò in camera la vecchia.

- *Perché non dormi, giovinetto? Perché sospiri?*

- *Penso alla Reginotta del mio cuore e non posso chiuder occhio.*

- *Sposa la mia figliuola. È bella, è straricca, è di sangue reale.*

- *Ah, nonna, lasciatemi andare! La mia sorte vuol così.*

- *Tu sei un cuore fedele! Prendi questa nocciuola. Nei momenti di gran pericolo schiacciala fra i denti e comanda. Sarai ubbidito.*

All'alba il giovinetto partì.

Cammina, cammina, giorno e notte, arrivava in mezzo a una foresta dove non c'era un segno di strada. Alberi di qua, alberi di là, macchie, siepi, spine. Non poteva più andare né avanti, né indietro.

- *Ah!... Questo è il paese dell'Orco! - esclamava ad un tratto.*

Provò una grande allegrezza. Prese in mano quella penna della coda dell'uccellin che parlava, e:

- *Penna mia, penna mia, presto, aprimi la via!*

Il bosco s'aperse. Ed ecco una strada larga, diritta, che non finiva mai. Più lui s'inoltrava e più la strada s'allungava. Il giovinetto avea terminato il pane e l'acqua portati con sé; e lì non c'era acqua, non c'era frutta, nulla! Cominciava già a provare tutti gli strazii della fame. Intanto annottava; una notte senza stelle, buio come in gola; e si sentivano pel bosco gli urli dei lupi affamati...

- *Questa volta è finita. I lupi mi divoreranno!*

"Well then!" said the young man.

And, reassured, he tore the feathers from the bird's tail and wings, and he put them in his pockets.

The night was long, and he couldn't sleep. He thought about his princess and that ogre. He turned this way and that between the sheets, and he sighed all night.

Into his room came the old woman.

"Why aren't you sleeping, young man? Why do you sigh so?"

"I am thinking about the princess of my heart; I can't sleep."

"Marry my daughter. She is beautiful, very rich, and of royal blood."

"Oh, Grandma, let me be! My fate is sealed."

"Faithful is your heart! Take this hazelnut. When you are in great danger, crack it between your teeth. You will be obeyed."

At dawn, the young man departed.

He walked and walked, day and night, and he found himself in the middle of a forest where the road ended. There were trees, bushes, hedges, and thorns everywhere. He couldn't move ahead, nor could he turn back.

"Ah! This is the land of the ogre!" he said immediately.

He felt very happy, and he pulled out the feather from the tail of the little bird that talked. "Feather, my feather, show me the way!"

The forest opened up. And before him was a wide road that was straight and seemed endless. The more he traveled, the longer it got. The young man had run out of the bread and the water that he had carried with him; and there was no water and nothing to eat anywhere. He was already beginning to feel the pangs of hunger. Meanwhile, darkness fell; it was a night without stars, as dark as a deep cave. And throughout the forest were heard the howls of hungry wolves.

"I'm done for this time. The wolves will devour me!"

Ma ecco laggiù, in fondo, in fondo, un lumicino che si vedeva e non si vedeva.

Il giovinetto si fece coraggio, raccolse le sue forze e tirò innanzi. Il lumicino restava sempre in fondo, che si vedeva e non si vedeva. Finalmente, come Dio volle, il poverino giunse dove quel lume luccicava dalla fessura d'un uscio, e picchiò.
Non rispose nessuno.
Lui tornava a picchiare.
- Aprite, anime cristiane! Ricoveratemi per questa notte!
Ma non riceveva risposta
- Era dunque arrivato in terra di pagani?
E picchiava di nuovo, questa volta più forte.
- Chi sei?
Quella vocina fioca fioca veniva di cima della casa.
- Sono un viandante smarrito. Fate la carità, in nome di Dio! Ricoveratemi per questa notte!
- Zitto, non rifiatare, se ti è cara la vita! Aspetta che io ti cali giù le treccie dei miei capelli e afferrati ad esse.
Il giovinetto s'afferrava a quelle treccie venute giù, e si sentiva tirar in alto come una secchia. Un braccio l'aiutava ad entrare per la finestra, e lui si trovava faccia a faccia con una bella donzella, che lo guardava sorpresa.
- Come sei venuto fin qui? Ci si mette un anno, un mese e un giorno, e chi ci arriva non fa più ritorno!
- Ah! Dunque si trovava nel castello dell'Orco! E quella donzella era la sua amata Reginotta!
Si mise a piangere dalla contentezza.
E quando disse chi era e come e perché venuto, piansero insieme.
Ma già stava per aggiornare. Il castello rintronava degli urli dell'Orco che si preparava ad andar a caccia. La Reginotta fece nascondere il giovinetto in un armadio e finse di ricamare.

However, down the road, far, far ahead, he saw a little light that seemed to blink on and off.

The young man took courage, summoned his strength, and went ahead. The light was far down the road, seeming to blink on and off. Finally, as God willed, he arrived at the place where the light shined through a crack in a door. He knocked.

No one answered, so he knocked again.

"Open the door, dear souls, and give me shelter for the night."

But he got no answer.

"So, have I come to a pagan land?"

And he knocked again, but harder this time.

"Who is it?"

A tiny voice could be heard coming from high in the house.

"I am a lost wayfarer. Please do me some kindness in the name of God! Shelter me for the night!"

"Quiet, don't say a word, if you value your life! Wait, for I will lower the braids of my hair to you so you can grab them."

When the braids were lowered, the young man grabbed them and felt himself being pulled up like a bucket. An arm helped him through the window, and he found himself face to face with a beautiful young lady, who looked upon him in astonishment.

"How were you able to get all the way here? It takes a year, a month, and a day, and whoever arrives can never return."

"Ah! Then I have found the ogre's castle!" And the beautiful young lady was his own beloved princess!

He began to cry for joy.

And when he told her who he was, how and why he had come, they both cried.

But it was already becoming light. The castle thundered with the howls of the ogre who was preparing for the hunt. The princess hid the young man in a wardrobe and pretended to be embroidering.

L'Orco diè un calcio all'uscio. E appena entrato nella camera, cominciava a fiutare intorno intorno.

- Perché fiutate?

- Mucci, mucci, sento odor di cristianucci!

- Andate là! Avete fatto colazione or ora e n'avete piene le narici.

L'Orco s'acchetava e partiva per la sua caccia: - Auhiii! Auhiii!

- Fuggiamo - disse il giovinetto appena l'Orco fu partito.

- Ah, poveri a noi! Di qui non s'esce. Potessimo anche uscirne, non sapremmo ritrovare la strada in mezzo al bosco che per cento miglia circonda il castello.

Allora il giovinetto ricorreva all'altra penna dell'uccellin che parlava.

- Penna mia, penna mia, tutti e due portaci via!

E di botto si sentirono come presi in collo, per aria, e, in men che non si dica, si ritrovarono ben oltre le cento miglia dal bosco.

E di botto si sentirono come presi in collo, per aria, e, in men che non si dica, si ritrovarono ben oltre le cento miglia dal bosco.

Camminarono a piedi per tutta la giornata; e quando furono stanchi, veduto un pagliaio abbandonato, andarono a ricoverarsi lì e s'addormentarono saporitamente.

La mattina di buon'ora, ripresero il cammino.

Ma dopo un pezzetto, ecco da lontano un rumore sordo sordo, che s'avvicinava crescendo:

- Auhiii! Auhiii!

Era l'Orco che li inseguiva!

Affrettarono il passo, anzi si misero a correre; ma l'Orco gli aveva già scoperti da lontano e gli veniva addosso più lesto del vento.

Il giovinetto prese in mano l'ultima penna dell'uccellin che parlava e:

The ogre kicked the door open. And, upon entering, he began to sniff all around.

"Why are you sniffing around?"

"Fee, fi, fo, fum. A Christian soul this way has come."

"Go away! You have just eaten, and the smell of your breakfast is still in your nostrils."

The ogre believed this and went off to hunt.

"Auhiii! Auhiii!"

"Let's escape," said the young man as soon as the ogre had left.

"Oh, woe to us! No one can escape from here. Even if we could get out, we would not know how to find the road again in the forest that surrounds the castle for one hundred miles."

So, the young man took out another feather from the little bird that talked.

"Feather, my feather, take us both away!"

And suddenly, they felt as though they had been grabbed by the neck and tossed into the air. In a flash, they found themselves well beyond the hundred miles of the forest.

They walked for the entire day, and when they got tired, they saw an abandoned barn in which they found shelter and slept soundly.

Early the next morning, they continued their journey.

However, after a little while, there came from afar a very faint sound that got louder the closer it came.

"Auhiii! Auhiii!"

It was the ogre, who was following them!

They speeded up; they even started to run, but the ogre had already spotted them from far away, and he ran after them faster than the wind.

The young man grabbed the last feather of the bird that talked:

- Penna, pennina, lei fontana ed io anguilla!
L'Orco s'arrestò, stupito di non più vederli.
La fontana, limpida come il cristallo, gorgogliava allato della strada, e l'anguilla guizzava nell'acqua dimenando la coda.
L'Orco ebbe il sospetto che si fossero trasmutati l'una in fontana e l'altro in anguilla.
- Fontana, ti berrò! Anguilla, ti prenderò!
Ma, bevi, bevi, quella fontana era sempre allo stesso punto, e quell'anguilla gli sguizzava sempre di mano.
L'Orco s'era già pieno lo stomaco d'acqua, ne avea fino alla gola. Non poteva più articolar la mano, tanto s'era stancato.
Si riposava un momento e poi daccapo:
- Fontana, ti berrò! Anguilla, ti prenderò!
E tornava a bere, sforzandosi.
E cercava di afferrare quella maledetta anguilla che gli sguizzava sempre di mano. Finalmente buttossi per terra, morto dalla fatica, oppresso da quel peso dello stomaco, e subito s'addormentò.
La Reginotta e il suo compagno, visto che l'Orco dormiva, ripresero la strada.
Avevano camminato tutta la notte e metà del giorno appresso, quand'ecco nuovamente:
- Auhiii! Auhiii!
L'Orco gli inseguiva, più furioso di prima.
- Ferma! Ferma!
Pareva che tuonasse.
La povera Reginotta si perdette d'animo e svenne. L'Orco era a pochi passi; già arrotava i dentacci:
- Auhiii! Auhiii!
Allora il giovinetto schiacciò la nocciuola.
- Nocciuola, nocciuola, trasmutaci in roccia e in farfalla che vola!

"Feather, my little feather, turn her into fountain and me into an eel."

The ogre stopped, amazed at no longer seeing them.

The fountain, as clear as crystal, bubbled on the side of the road, and the eel darted around in the water, wriggling its tail.

The ogre suspected that they had been transformed—one into a fountain, the other into an eel.

"Fountain, I will drink you! Eel, I will get you!"

He drank and drank, but the water in the fountain stayed at the same level, and the eel kept slipping out of his hand.

The ogre's stomach was full of water, but he had not attained his goal. He was so tired that he couldn't move his hand anymore.

So, he rested for a moment and then repeated: "Fountain, I will drink you! Eel, I will get you!"

And he began again, forcing himself to drink.

He tried to grab that cursed eel, which kept slipping out of his hand. Finally, he fell to the ground, dead tired and, overwhelmed by the weight of his stomach, he soon fell asleep.

Seeing that the ogre was asleep, the princess and her companion continued their journey.

They had walked the entire night and half of the next day, when again they heard:

"Auhiii! Auhiii!"

The ogre was following them, more maddened than before.

"Stop! Stop!"

It seemed like thunder.

The poor princess lost heart and fainted. The ogre was very near, and he was already grinding his teeth.

"Auhiii! Auhiii!"

So, the young man cracked the hazelnut.

"Hazelnut, hazelnut, turn us into a rock and into a flying butterfly."

E l'Orco si trovò davanti a una roccia scoscesa e brulla, che s'alzava a picco sulla campagna.

Una magnifica farfalla svolazzava qua e là colle sue ali dorate e andava, di tanto in tanto, a posarsi su quella.

L'Orco ebbe il sospetto che si fossero trasmutati l'uno in roccia e l'altra in farfalla.

- Roccia, t'atterrerò! Farfalla, t'acchiapperò!

E si diè a scalzare la roccia, scavando la terra colle ugne; ma non riusciva a spostare nemmeno un sassolino.

Avea le mani tutte scorticate, le ugne tutte rotte; e scavava, scavava. Poi lasciava di scavare e dava la caccia alla farfalla. Ma quella volava in alto e non si lasciava acchiappare.

Morto dalla fatica, sdraiossi per terra, sotto la roccia, e si addormentò.

A un tratto la roccia gli si lasciava cader addosso tutta d'un pezzo.

- Auhiii! Auhiii! - urlava l'Orco, dando gli ultimi tratti.

Così la Reginotta e Il suo compagno poterono rimettersi in viaggio tranquilli, e finalmente arrivarono ai confini del loro paese.

Quando il Re e la Regina ricevettero la notizia del loro prossimo arrivo, bandirono feste per tutto il regno.

Uscirono ad incontrarli fuori le porte della città con tutta la corte e un immenso popolo dietro, e ordinarono subito i preparativi per le nuove nozze della Reginotta col suo liberatore.

Ma lui disse:

- Debbo fare un viaggio. Se fra otto giorni non sarò ritornato, piangetemi per morto.

La Reginotta si disperava:

- Anderai dopo, sposo mio!

- Anderete dopo, figliuolo mio!

Ma la Reginotta, il Re, la Regina non riuscirono a persuaderlo.

The ogre found himself before a steep and menacing rock that rose high above the countryside.

A magnificent butterfly fluttered here and there on gilded wings and, now and then, landed on the rock.

The ogre suspected that they had been transformed—one into a rock and the other into a butterfly. "Rock, I will knock you down! Butterfly, I will catch you."

And he tried to undermine the rock, digging the earth under it with his nails, but he wasn't able to remove even one pebble.

His hands were all cut up, and his nails were broken, but he kept digging and digging. When he stopped, he went after the butterfly. But she flew away and would not allow herself to be caught.

Dead tired, he lay down on the ground under the rock, and he fell asleep.

All of a sudden, the rock let itself fall on him, all in one piece.

"Auhiii! Auhiii!" the ogre howled far and wide.

And so the princes and her companion could resume their journey calmly, and they finally arrived at the boundary of her country.

When the king and the queen received news that they would soon arrive, they declared a celebration throughout the kingdom.

They left the palace to meet them outside the city gates with their entire court and an immense crowd behind them. And they immediately ordered preparations for the new wedding of the princess and her liberator.

However, he said: "I need to make a journey. If I don't return in eight days, you can mourn my death."

The princess despaired.

"Go later, my bridegroom!"

"Go later, my son!"

But the princess, the king, and the queen could not persuade him.

Partì, e si trovò nella pianura deserta dove avea incontrato quella vecchia.

Aspettava un pochino, ed ecco la vecchia, anche questa volta col suo fastello di legna sulle spalle.

- Mi riconoscete, vecchiarella mia?

- Sì, figliuolo, ti riconosco. O che vieni a fare da queste parti?

- Ve lo dirò dopo; datemi intanto il vostro fastello. Faremo strada insieme.

Questa volta il fastello era leggiero leggiero.

- Son venuto per ringraziarvi e per invitarvi alle mie nozze.

- Bravo figliuolo che tu sei!

E, detto questo, la vecchia si trasfigurava. Era diventata una bellissima signora, risplendente più d'una stella, con una verga d'oro nel pugno.

Sorrise e sparì.

Allora lui comprese che quella era una Fata. Ritornò, tutt'allegro, al palazzo reale, e la stessa sera vennero celebrate le nozze.

Così furono marito e moglie:
e lui ebbe il frutto e noi le foglie.

He left, and found himself on the deserted plain where he had met the old woman.

He waited a little, and the old woman appeared, once again carrying her bundle of wood on her shoulders.

"Do you recognize me, my dear old lady?"

"Yes, my boy, I recognize you. What are you doing here?"

"I will tell you later; meanwhile, give me your bundle. Let's travel together."

This time the bundle was very light.

"I have come to thank you and to invite you to my wedding."

"What a wonderful young man you are!"

And having said that, the old woman transformed herself into an very beautiful woman, brighter than a star, and holding a golden scepter in her hand.

She sighed and then disappeared.

With that, the young man realized that she was a fairy. Overjoyed, he returned to the royal palace and, that same night, the princess and he were married.

And so they became husband and wife.

May they enjoy the fruit of their love for the rest of their lives.

For Nina and Ignazio Addamo, *cari zii,*
who introduced me to Sicily.

And

For Matthew and Molly Cornell, my grandchildren, who,
like Capuana's *nipotini,* inspired me to complete this work.

Erice, province of Trapani, Sicily, home of Astro-physics *Ettore Majorana* center (photo by Santi Buscemi).

Cefalù, province of Palermo, on the north side of the Mediterranean, renowned for its tourism (photo by Santi Buscemi).

Typical structure in **Cefalù** (photo by Santi Buscemi).

Another suggested structure in **Cefalù** (photo by Santi Buscemi).

Made in the USA
Middletown, DE
30 January 2015